INCENDIARY

ZORAIDA CÓRDOVA

INCENDIARY

ZORAIDA CÓRDOVA

HYPERION
Los Angeles   New York

First Edition, April 2020
10 9 8 7 6 5 4 3 2 1
FAC-020093-20073
Printed in United States of America

This book is set in Century Gothic, Palatino/Monotype;
Medusa, Sharshock/Fontspring
Designed by Marci Senders

Library of Congress Control Number: 2019957157
ISBN 978-1-368-02380-1
Reinforced binding

Visit www.hyperionteens.com

PARA JEANNET Y DANILO MEDINA

THE KING'S JUSTICE

ORDER #1

By order of King Fernando's Arm of Justice, Guardians to the Temple of the Father of Worlds, Jurors of the Truth, and Warriors of Everlasting Peace, the citizens of Puerto Leones are prohibited from harboring the Moria—fugitives, murderers, and traitors to the crown. Anyone with knowledge of these wielders of unnatural magics must come forward to the patrols. Those who comply will be shown mercy. The king's will is done.

Approved by Justice Méndez

Kingdom of Puerto Leones
Year 28 of His Majesty King Fernando's Reign
305 A.C. of the Third Age of Andalucía

The Grave Robber's Song

I dug up a Moria grave to find
Two silver eyes to peer in your mind.
Three golden fingers, illusions I'll cast!
One copper heart to persuade senses vast
And four platinum veins to lock up the past!
I dug up a Moria grave!

PROLOGUE
3I7 A.C.

CELESTE SAN MARINA DUG A GRAVE THAT NIGHT.

The season's drought had hardened the earth in Esmeraldas, and every strike of her shovel sent pain up her arms, making her muscles twitch and her bones ache. But still she kept digging, dust sticking to rivulets of sweat coursing down her weathered tan skin.

The half-moon hid behind thick clouds that refused to break, and the only light came from the dying oil lamp beside the body loosely wrapped in linens. Thrusting the shovel back into the ground, she didn't stop until her palms were blistered red and there was a hole deep enough for the body. Then she sank to her knees beside him.

"You deserved better, Rodrigue," the spymaster said, a tremble in her voice. Had she more warning, more help, she could have given him the traditional burial, but in times like this, an unmarked grave was all they had.

She reached around his neck and cut the leather cord that held his alman stone—the single remnant of Rodrigue's legacy—and slipped the jagged white crystal into the pocket sewn inside her gray tunic. The stone rested beside a single glass vial carried by every other Moria spy in the kingdom, right over her heart. How many more secrets would she have to collect before she could rest?

Rest was out of the question for that night. With all her strength, Celeste pushed the body into the waiting grave and proceeded to shovel the mountain of earth on top of him.

Another dead Moria. Another dead rebel.

The horse whinnied and kicked at shadows as Celeste packed up her lamp and shovel. She needed to get back to the village before sunrise. She mounted the steed, sinking her heels into the horse's sides. Wind beat against her face, hooves pounded a trail of dust, and stars sparkled above.

With one hand firmly gripping the reins, Celeste kept checking to make sure Rodrigue's alman stone was still in her pocket. All of her hopes and the future of her people were trapped within that bit of rock, mined from veins that ran deep beneath the mountain ranges of the kingdom. Along the Cliffs of Memoria, alman stone once dotted the landscape. Now it was as rare as miracles. Once it had been used to build temples and statues of the goddess herself and cut into dazzling gems and reliquaries by artisans of neighboring lands. But for the Moria, gifted with the powers of the Lady of Shadows, it was always so much more than a stone. Its prisms transformed the surrounding world into living memory. Rodrigue's information was worth dying for. Celeste had to believe that.

She prayed to Our Lady of Whispers that this was the day help would arrive. It had been eight days exactly since she'd sent the messenger to the Whispers, and nine days since Rodrigue arrived at her doorstep half-dead, with news so terrifying that even her hardened heart had stirred. Rodrigue had survived nearly a month under the torture of the Arm of Justice and then the journey from the capital. That alone could make anyone mad—make anyone *see* things.

But if it *were* true . . .

There was no worse fate for the kingdom. The world would be forced to bow to Puerto Leones. She kicked her horse harder, held the reins as tightly as the breath in her chest.

Finally, the horse's hooves hit the main dirt road of Esmeraldas. The village still slumbered, but she bypassed the square, avoiding the cobblestones that would wake her neighbors. Despite the dark, she couldn't shake the feeling of being watched.

Celeste dismounted and locked the horse back in the small stable. She just needed to make it to the door, and then she'd be safe in her hosts' house.

She crept through the rows of thornbushes, hoping Emilia hadn't lost sleep waiting up for her. In her many years as spymaster for the Whispers, Celeste had called several places home, but none had been as welcoming as Emilia Siriano and her family's. They knew her as Celeste Porto, a widow, a midwife, a caretaker. Though they were used to her insomnia, she had never brought trouble to their doorstep. Come daylight she'd have to explain why Rodrigue could not be buried in the cemetery and why there was no family to claim him. Celeste and the Whispers were all the family he had.

Turning her key in the kitchen's side door, Celeste paused, listening. The silence was disturbed by the drying crackle of fire and rustle of her shawl as she slipped inside. Soft light came from the red embers in the hearth. Her bones ached for sleep, but the Sirianos would rise soon. Nights in Esmeraldas weren't usually so cool this time of year, but she loved any excuse to build a fire, busy her hands with simple tasks. That, and the perfect loaf of bread, were the gifts she brought to this household.

A touch of smoke mingled with the sweet, grass-perfumed breeze that pushed through the window as Celeste warmed her wind-ravaged face by the hearth. Flames swallowed the kindling and caught the edges of the dried logs. In moments like this it was easy to let herself believe she was only a housemaid with a simple life. But after decades of hiding in plain sight, her senses wouldn't let her rest. She identified two scents that hadn't been there when she'd left—anointing oils and unwashed bodies. She remembered she'd shut all the windows and doors before dragging Rodrigue out.

Her spine stiffened.

"Celeste San Marina," a clear, cutting voice spoke as the growing fire illuminated the corners of the dark. A man rose from a chair with deadly grace. "I'd hoped our paths would cross again."

Celeste's breath caught. Though he only wore a rumpled white tunic and brown riding trousers, she would have recognized his regal face anywhere. The last surviving son of King Fernando. They called him so many things, but they never uttered his name, as if afraid it would somehow conjure his likeness, no matter the time or place.

Príncipe Dorado.

Bloodied Prince.

The Lion's Fury.

Matahermano.

As he took a step closer in the faint light, she could almost see the ghost of the child he'd been during her time at the palace—a curious golden-haired boy. A boy who would grow up to be worse than his father.

She'd only ever called him Castian.

Before Celeste could run, the prince motioned with his gloved hand, and two soldiers bounded in from the hall. One of them closed a meaty hand around her throat. The second blocked the kitchen door.

"We can make this simple," Castian said, his voice deep and even as he strode over to them. He tugged off his fine leather gloves to reveal hands that did not belong to a prince. Callused and scarred knuckles from years of hard training and fighting. "Tell me where he is, and I will make your death a swift and painless one."

"Life under your family's rule is neither swift nor painless." Celeste spoke slowly, her voice hoarse. She'd waited for the day to come when she would face him once again. "I would not trust the Lion's Fury to honor his word."

"After everything you've done, it is *you* who does not trust me?"

The kitchen seemed to shrink with the prince's presence. She could taste his emotions in the air. His anger was a bitter tincture that would be her undoing. But she'd known that long ago. All she could do for the rebels was stall and take their secrets beyond the veil.

The soldier's fingers dug into her windpipe, and as she struggled to breathe, she kicked out. Every muscle and bone in her body ached from hours of digging and sleepless nights since Rodrigue's arrival. Her eyes flicked toward the Siriano family's closed bedroom door. What had the prince and his men done to them?

Then a terrible thought surfaced.

Had the Sirianos, who'd hired and housed her, who'd believed in peace among all the peoples of Puerto Leones, betrayed her the moment she'd left? A twisting sensation wrenched her already strained heart. She desperately wanted—needed—to breathe.

She pushed thoughts of betrayal aside and concentrated on the alman stone that was still tucked into her pocket. She could not let it be found. She slapped at the guard's hands, scratched at the exposed skin between sleeve and glove, her eyes straining to see beyond bursts of black splotches.

"Enough." The prince held up his hand and the soldier relinquished his hold on her. "The dead can't speak."

"That shows how much you know of the dead," Celeste rasped as she dropped to her knees. Pressing her hands to the cool stone floor for balance, she coughed. She needed time to think, but the prince was not famous for his patience. She stared at the fire in the hearth for focus. Before Rodrigue had succumbed to his injuries she'd promised to do whatever it took to get his alman stone to the Whispers. They should have been there. Unless the reason the prince was here was because they'd already been captured.

For the first time, the spymaster realized that perhaps rest would never come. At least not in this life. Her aging body was no good in a fight. All she had was the glass vial and her magics.

With eyes narrowed on the prince, she twisted the thick copper ring on her middle finger, immediately feeling the strength of her magics pulsing inside her veins as the metal charged her power of persuasion. A primordial buzz surged through every inch of her skin, bleeding into the air, thickening it enough to bring a sweat to the guard's forehead. Her gift was as old as time—old as the trees, old as the minerals and metals that strengthened the power in her veins—and it wanted release. She sifted through the weakest emotions in the room. The guards. Their heightened fear of her was easy to latch on to. Their muscles and tendons seized and left them petrified in place. But the prince was just out of reach. She needed him closer. Close enough to touch.

"Thank the stars your dear mother isn't alive to see what you've become," Celeste said.

Just as she intended, the prince advanced. She pushed her

magics harder. Sweat trickled down the prince's fine cheekbone, where a crescent scar marred his sharp features. Only then did Celeste San Marina stare into Prince Castian's eyes, blue like the sea he was named after, and confront her greatest nightmare.

"Don't you *dare* speak of her." He clamped a hand around Celeste's mouth.

At his touch, Celeste acted quickly. Her magics traveled from her body to his, like a gust of wind cycling between them. Closing her eyes, she searched for an emotion to seize—pity, hate, anger. If only she could grab hold of the thing that made the young prince so cruel, she could draw it out and smother it.

With her Persuári gifts she could take a fraction of any emotion that existed within someone and bring it to life, amplifying it into action. She knew all the colors that made up a person's soul—star-white hope, mud-green envy, pomegranate love. But when she focused on the prince, she could only see a faint, muted gray.

He jerked his hand off her jaw, and she gasped, trying to regain her breath. Her thoughts spun. Everyone's emotions expressed themselves in colors. Gray was for those passing on from the worlds, fading into nothingness. Why was he different? She knew of nothing that could block the powers of the Moria. Her magics drew back, and she was forced to release her hold on the petrified guards. They crumpled to their knees, but with a single wave of their commander's hand, the men pushed themselves back up at attention.

The prince's smile was malevolent in his triumph. "Did you really think I'd face you again without taking precautions against your magics?"

"What have you done to yourself, Castian?" Celeste managed before rough hands grabbed her shoulders and dragged her to the small wooden table in front of the hearth. The soldier slammed her into a chair and held her in place.

"I am what you made me," he said, low and just for her. She breathed in his rage. "I dreamed of finding you for so long."

"You will not find us all. The kingdom of Memoria will rise once more."

"Enough of your tricks and your lies!" He spoke each word like his own personal truth. "I know *everything* you did."

"Surely you can't know everything I've ever done, *princeling*." She wanted to toy with him. To let him know that she did not fear him or death.

"What does a prince want with a lowly runaway? Or are the king's armies so depleted he'd send out his only living child in the dead of the night? I thought you loved an audience for your executions."

"I love nothing," the prince shouted, his temper burning like a lit fuse. "*Where* is he?"

"Dead," Celeste spat. "Rodrigue is dead."

Castian growled his frustration and lowered his face to hers. "Not the spy. Dez. I want Dez."

Celeste ground her teeth. Her magics could not help her anymore. She'd survived the rebellion eight years ago, prison, and decades of hiding and gathering information across Puerto Leones. But she knew she would not survive Prince Castian. So long as the alman stone was safe she could make peace with herself. "If you know everything I've ever done, my prince, you should know that I would never tell you."

There was no room for regret in her heart. There was only the cause—and every terrible thing she'd ever done for the good of her people, she would do again and again.

Prince Castian crossed his arms, a bemused smile playing on his lips as the side door opened. "Perhaps you'll tell *her*."

Celeste's blood ran cold as another soldier entered through the kitchen door, escorting a young woman. The spymaster's mind struggled to place the green pallor of the girl's olive skin. Gaunt in a way that made her look like she'd been drained by leeches. When recognition sparked, tears she thought had long since run dry pooled in her eyes. Celeste knew this girl.

Lucia Zambrano, a mind reader for the Whispers, known for her bright brown eyes and sweet laughter that made it easy to fall in love with her, just as Rodrigue had. Rodrigue, whose grave dirt was still under Celeste's fingernails. Lucia's quick wit was only matched by the speed of her footwork, both of which were useful when she spied for Celeste in Citadela Crescenti. Celeste had heard of Lucia's capture during a raid, and after Rodrigue's tales of what was happening in the dungeons, she'd feared the worst.

That was when she'd believed the worst that could happen to the Moria was a slow, torturous death.

The king has discovered a fate worse than death, Celeste thought now, unable to look away from Lucia. Her eyes were vacant, a house where the lights have been snuffed out. Her lips were cracked and had a white film at the corners. Lucia's bones and veins were hugged by too-tight skin.

"Come closer, Lucia," Castian said.

The girl's movements appeared to be commanded by the prince's voice. She took slow steps, her dead eyes focused on the fire in the hearth behind Celeste.

"What have you done to her?" Celeste asked, her voice small.

"What will be done to all Moria unless you tell me what I want to know."

The realization thundered through every part of her body: Rodrigue was right. Rodrigue was right. *Rodrigue was right.* How would she protect the alman stone now? Castian was somehow immune to her magics, but she could try her best with the guards.

And then what? She wouldn't make it past the bridge checkpoints without travel documents. She had to be there for the Whispers to find—even if she wasn't alive.

"This will be your future unless you tell me where Dez is," Castian said, louder, impatient.

For a moment, Celeste's eyes flicked to the closed door where the Sirianos slept. No, no one could sleep through this disturbance. They were dead. Or they had abandoned her.

Celeste's stomach churned because it didn't matter now. She was out of options, and the knowledge of what she had to do overcame her. She barely had time to turn away before she vomited. The soldier cursed and shook the sickness from his hand, but one look at the Príncipe Dorado and he kept his other hand firmly on Celeste's shoulder.

"I won't ask again," the prince said, his face a vicious mask inches from hers. "I will burn this village to the ground with you in it."

Celeste knew that she had a single moment to get things right. All she needed was to hide the alman stone for another Moria to find. Illan's spies were clever, and if they weren't, then she'd pray to Our Lady of Shadows for a guiding hand. After that, she'd fight until she couldn't fight anymore—but she wouldn't be taken alive.

Despite the pain—despite the bile that pooled across her tongue and threatened to choke her windpipe—Celeste, finally, began to laugh.

One moment, one life.

She wished she had more to give the Whispers.

The prince closed a fist around her hair, pulling her away from the soldier. "You laugh at the fate of your own?"

Blinking her eyes to focus, Celeste stared back at the prince.

"I laugh because you will not win. We are a flame that will never burn out."

Then she slammed her forehead into the prince's face.

He released her, reaching for his bloody nose.

In that moment, she was free, rolling away onto the ground; her quick fingers retrieved the hidden contents over her heart. The guard dove for her. She grabbed the oil lamp on the table and threw it. The glass shattered against the guard's chest, and he screamed as fire caught on his clothes, anointed with oils meant for protection.

It was an ugly way to die, and it would not be her fate. She dug into her tunic pocket and held up the glass vial for the prince to see.

"You're mad," the prince shouted, his heavy steps charging to stop her.

Celeste whispered a prayer to the Lady. *Forgive me. Forgive me for my past. Welcome me at last.*

She swallowed the contents of the vial, slipping the stone that she would protect with her life into her mouth. She gave in to the numbness of the poison rushing through her body, a cold she'd only ever felt when she swam in the mountain lakes near her family home as a girl. When she closed her eyes, she could see that deep blue water, feel the calm of floating for hours, but she could still hear the prince calling her name, the shouting from the guards, the crackle of flames.

Celeste San Marina made a second grave at dawn.

Hers was one of fire.

1

AFTER A WHILE, ALL BURNING VILLAGES SMELL THE SAME.

From a hilltop, I watch as fire consumes the farming village of Esmeraldas. Wooden homes and sienna clay roofs. Bales of rolled hay amid a sea of golden grass. Vegetable gardens of ripening tomatoes, bushels of thyme and laurel. All common to Puerto Leones, but here, in the eastern provincia of the kingdom, the fire burns through something else: manzanilla.

The deceptively bitter flower with a yellow heart and white mane of pointed petals is prized for its healing properties not only in our kingdom, but in the lands across the Castinian Sea, ensuring a steady flow of gold and food into this tiny corner of the country. In Esmeraldas, where the manzanilla grows so wild it takes over entire fields, its sweetness momentarily masks the acrid scent of homespun wool and rag dolls, abandoned in haste as the villagers run along the dirt paths to escape the flames.

But nothing covers the scent of burning flesh.

"Mother of All—" I start to say a blessing. Words the Moria use when someone is moving from this life and onto the next. But I remember flashes of a different fire, of cries and screams and helplessness. A heavy weight settles around my throat. Taking deep breaths, I try to compose myself, but the blessing still won't leave my lips. So I think it instead. *Mother of All, bless this soul into the vast unknown.*

I turn away from the flames just in time to see Dez march up behind me. His honey-brown eyes take in the scene below. There's dirt on his tawny brown skin from that last scramble through the woods bordering the north of Esmeraldas. His fingers rake through thick, tangled black hair, and his broad chest expands with quick shallow breaths as he tries to regain composure. He touches the sword at his hip the way a child might check for a favorite toy, for comfort.

"I don't understand," Dez says. Even after everything we've been through he searches for a reason for why bad things happen.

"What's there to understand?" I say, though my anger isn't directed toward him. "We turned a six-day journey into four by sheer will, and it still wasn't fast enough."

I wish I had something to hit. I settle for kicking a cluster of rocks and regret it when the dust billows around us. The wind shifts, pushing the smoke away. I sink into my boots as if grounding myself to this place will stop my heart from racing, my mind from thinking, *Too late. You're always too late.*

"This has been burning for half a day by the looks of it. We never would have gotten here in time to stop it. But Esmeraldas's exports are worth their weight in gold. Why would the king's justice set it ablaze?"

I retie my forest-green scarf around my neck. "The message from Celeste said Rodrigue's discovery would turn the tide of our war. They didn't want it found."

"Perhaps there is hope yet," Dez says. When he turns to the village at the base of the hill, there's a new fervor in his eyes.

Or perhaps all hope is lost, I think. I am not like Dez. The other Whispers do not come to me for hope or rousing speeches. Perhaps it is best that he is our unit leader and not me. I know two truths: The king's justice will stop at nothing to destroy its enemies, and we're waging a war we cannot win. But I keep fighting, maybe because it is all I've ever known, or maybe because the alternative is dying and I can't do that until I've paid for my sins.

"Do you think Celeste is—"

"Dead," Dez answers. His eyes are fixed on the village, what's left of it. A ripple passes along the fine line of his jaw, his skin darker after our journey in the sun.

"Or captured," I suggest.

He shakes his head once. "Celeste wouldn't allow herself to be taken. Not alive."

"We have to know for certain." I pull a thin spyglass from the inside of my leather vest pocket and turn back to the forest line, twisting the lens until I find what I'm looking for.

A bright light glints between the trees and flashes twice. Though I can't make out her face, I know it's Sayida waiting with the rest of the unit for our signal. I take out a square mirror to signal back. I don't need to communicate that the city is burning, or that we've traveled all this way for nothing. They should see the smoke by now. I signal only that we've made it.

"Go back to the others. The Second Sweep will be here soon,"

Dez says. Then his voice softens. Suddenly, he's no longer my unit leader but something else. The boy who rescued me nearly a decade ago. My only true friend. "You shouldn't have to see this."

His thumb brushes softly over the top of my hand, and I stop myself from seeking comfort in his arms the way I am always tempted to do. A week ago there was a raid near our safe house, and I was sure we were going to be taken captive. Somehow we squeezed into a crate reserved for sandstone brick shipments, our limbs entwined. The kiss we shared then *would* have been romantic if it hadn't felt like we'd been stuffed into a coffin, sure our luck had run out.

I slam the spyglass between my palms and return it to its hiding place. "No."

"No?" He cocks an eyebrow and tries to twist his features into a fearsome mask. "There are no memories to steal here. I can finish the task."

I cross my arms over my chest and close the distance between us. He's a head taller than me, and as my unit leader he could order me to listen. I hold his stare and dare him to look away first.

He does.

His gaze goes to the side of my neck, to the finger-long scar I got courtesy of a royal guard during our last mission. Dez's hands reach for my shoulders, and a sliver of temptation winds itself around my heart. I would prefer that he give me a command than tell me he's worried for my *safety*.

I step back, though I catch the moment of hurt on his face. "I can't go back to the Whispers a failure. Not again."

"You're not a failure," he says.

On our last mission, Lynx Unit was tasked with finding safe passage on a ship sailing out of the kingdom for a merchant family whose father had been executed by the king. We were nearly to the shipyard when I was caught. I know I did everything right. I had the correct documents and I wore a dress covered in stitched flowers like a chaste farmer's daughter. My job was to rip memories from the guard, enough to confuse him and give us insight into the ships coming in and out of the Salinas harbor. There was something about me that the guard didn't like, and the next thing I knew, I was drawing my sword to defend myself. We won, and the family has spent two months somewhere in the empire of Luzou. It took ten stitches and a week burning off a fever in the infirmary. But we can't show our faces in that town to help other families. In those two months the king's justice has doubled its guards there. Our presence is supposed to be silent. Our units meant to be shadows. We saved one family, but what about the others trapped in the citadela living in fear of their magics being discovered? Even if Dez is right, and I'm not a failure, I'm still a risk.

"*I* have to be the one to find the alman stone, and *I* have to be the one to return it to your father."

A smirk plays on his lips. "And here I thought I was the glory seeker among us."

"I don't want glory," I say, and manage a bitter laugh. "I don't even want praise."

The wind changes again, smoke encircling us. When I look at him, he could be one of my stolen memories, coated in a layer of gray, somehow distant and close all at once as he asks, "Then what do you want?"

My heart twists painfully, because the answer is complicated. He of all people ought to know this. But how could he, when even in the moments I'm the surest of the answer, a new kind of want overpowers the next? I settle on the simplest and truest words I can.

"Forgiveness. I want the Whispers to know I'm not a traitor. The only way I can do that is by getting as many Moria on the next ship to Luzou as I can."

"No one thinks you're a traitor," Dez says, brushing aside my worry with a careless toss of his hand. That dismissal stings even though I know he believes it. "My father trusts you. *I* trust you, and since Lynx Unit is mine to command, that's what matters."

"How do you walk around with a head that big, Dez?"

"I manage."

I'd still be a scavenger if Dez hadn't petitioned his father and the other elders to train me as a spy. My skill has been useful at saving Moria trapped in the Puerto Leones borders, but no one among our kind wants a memory thief like me in their midst. Robári are the reason we lost the war, even if our side has been on the losing end for decades. Robári can't be trusted. *I* can't be trusted.

Dez believes in me despite everything I've done. I would put my life in his hands—have done it before and will do it again. But for Dez, everything comes so easy. He doesn't see that. Among the Whispers, Dez is the cleverest and bravest. The most reckless, too, but it's accepted as part of what makes him Dez. And yet, I know, even if I were *just* as clever, *just* as brave, I'd still be the girl that sparked a thousand deaths.

I will never stop trying to prove to them that I am more. Seeing destruction like this in Esmeraldas makes it so hard to hold on to what little hope I have.

"We're going in together," I say. "I can handle myself."

He makes a low grumble at the back of his throat and turns from me. I fight the impulse to reach out for him. We both know he won't send me away. He can't. Dez runs his fingers through his hair and reties the knot at the base of his neck. His dark eyebrows knit together, and that's the moment he relents.

"Sometimes, Ren, I wonder who the Persuári is—you or me. We'll rendezvous in the Forest of Lynxes or—"

"Or you'll leave me at the mercy of the Second Sweep for being too slow." I try to put humor into my voice, but nothing will stop the flutter of my heart, the memories pulsing to be freed. "I know the plan, Dez."

I begin to turn, new purpose coursing through my veins. But he grips my wrist and tugs me back to him.

"No. Or I'll come looking for you and kill anyone who tries to stop me." Dez presses a hard, quick kiss on my lips. He doesn't care if the others are watching us through their spyglasses, but I do. Wrenching myself from him leaves me with a dull ache between my ribs. When he smiles I feel a heady want that has no place here.

"Find the alman stone," he says. He's Dez again. My unit leader. Soldier. Rebel. "Celeste was to meet us in the village square. I'll search for survivors."

I squeeze his hand, then let go and say, "By the light of Our Lady, we carry on."

"We carry on," he echoes.

I drum all the nervous energy in my body down into my legs. Pulling my scarf over the bottom half of my face, I take one last breath of fresh air, then run alongside him, down the hill from our lookout point, and into the blazing streets below. For someone built so tall and broad, Dez is fast on his feet. But I'm faster, and I make it to the square first. I tell myself not to look back at him, to keep going. I do it anyway and find he's watching me, too.

We split up.

I plunge deeper into the ruins of Esmeraldas. Flames as large as houses don't crackle—they roar. The heat on the smoldering cobblestones is oppressive, and the snap of roof beams caving in sets my teeth on edge as houses crumble along the road. I say a silent prayer that their inhabitants have already made it out alive. Smoke stings tears from my eyes.

In the square, fire has eaten through every building it has touched, leaving nothing but black ruins behind. Hundreds of footsteps mark the ground, all of them leading east toward the town of Agata. By now there is almost no one left in Esmeraldas. I can tell by the sickening silence.

The only thing untouched is the cathedral and whipping post in front of it. God and torture: the two things the king of Puerto Leones holds dearest to his heart.

There's something familiar about the bone-white stone of the cathedral, nearby flames glinting off the stained-glass windows. Though I've never been to Esmeraldas, I can't shake the impression of having walked this very street before.

I brush away the feeling and make my way toward the whipping post. Occasionally, if there is time, doomed Moria hide messages or small parcels in the last place the king's men would think to look— and what better place than where the accused are taken to die?

Alman stone isn't conspicuous on its own, though when it captures memories, it glows like it's been filled with starlight. Before King Fernando's reign, it was common, but now, with temples desecrated and mines run dry, Moria are lucky to find it at all. If Spymaster Celeste had enough warning, she would've hidden Rodrigue's alman stone for the Whispers to retrieve.

"What happened to you, Celeste?" I ask aloud, but only the crackle of fire answers, and I continue my search.

The executioner's block has dozens of long grooves from where a killing blade struck. The wood is dark, stained with dried blood. As I run my hands along the base, I am thankful I always wear gloves. The thought of heads rolling—of bodies hanging, of people locked into the paddocks and beaten senseless—makes my stomach turn and my legs tremble. My body reacts the same way to blood as it does fire. And that is precisely why I force myself to be here.

I move to the hangman's noose. Esmeraldas is such a small village. I wonder when they find the time to practice so many forms of execution. Kneeling, I run my hands along the wooden boards beneath the noose for a break or a loose slat. Nothing. I walk around the whipping post, but all I find is a thin leather cord with a long strip of skin dried to it. Bile rises to my throat. I drop the whip, and when I do, the strangest sense of remembrance moves through me, and a vivid memory—one that does not belong to me, but is mine anyway—bursts into my mind.

I squeeze my eyes shut and palm my temples. It's been months since I've lost control of the memories living in my head. Silent smoke gathers in my mind's eye, then clears to reveal a scene drained of all color, and I'm forced to relive a stolen past as the Gray cracks open. I see the same street, the same square, but as it was once before the fire—

> *A man adjusts his grip around a freshly cut tree and drags it down this street. His shoulders ache, but his thin gloves protect against splinters. His mud-covered boots stomp blue-and-gray cobblestones into the heart of the village. A crowd gathers in front of the cathedral. It is the sixth day of Almanar, and his neighbors carry branches, broken furniture, cut trees. They stack and stack the pyre until no one can reach the top. Music spills from open cantina doors. The drummers have come around, slapping leather skins in time with the festive songs. Couples dance as torches are lit. He sees the faces he's been waiting for—his wife and child run to him. They help him drag the tree*

onto the pyre—their offering for the festival of Almanar.
Together, they sing and dance and watch the pyre burn.

Now I know why Esmeraldas felt familiar. Every memory I've ever stolen is a part of me. It's taken years of training to push them back, keep them in locked compartments. But sometimes, they find a way out. I should thank the stars that the memory that has spilled from the vault of my mind is a joyous one. A rural harvest where everyone comes together to burn the old year away. And yet, my hands tremble and sweat drips down my back. I don't want to look at it anymore. I force myself out of the Gray, shoving the memory back into the dark where it belongs. I've heard it called the curse of the Robári. Curse or not, I can't let it get in the way of finding the alman stone.

My eyes sting from smoke and the piercing pain that stabs my temples. I push my weary bones to stand. There is no alman stone here. If I were Celeste, where would I have run?

Then I hear it. A single sound pierces the air.

At first, I think it's from another unwanted memory slipping out of the Gray, but it grows clear as cathedral bells on Holy Day. A voice crying out for help.

Someone in Esmeraldas is trapped.

2

They say it didn't use to be like this. That there was a time when the kingdoms of Puerto Leones and Memoria were at peace. Were prosperous. Even when Memoria fell, conquered by the family of lions, there was a treaty. Order. My kind didn't hide our magics, our bodies, our everything, in fear of a king. This is what we tell our children. Stories. The elders of the Whispers say a lot of things to make the days and nights pass by more quickly, but for many of us the world has never stopped burning.

It was a fire just like this one that changed me from the inside out. Even now, eight years later, that fire lives within my bones and blood and muscle. It's brighter than this, brighter than the colorless Gray of my stolen memories. What I told Dez about forgiveness was the truth, but deep inside I know that I'll always be trying to outrun flames that will never be extinguished.

I swallow the ash that forces its way into my nose and mouth, and race down a narrow street, following the desperate voice. I hurl myself over the debris that blocks my way. My scarf keeps sliding off. Smoke obscures my sight, and I nearly collide with a horse charging down the road. I skid into a muddy bank to avoid it.

A door swings from a nearby empty stable—it is here in front of a small house where the cry is loudest. The flames have burned through everything, and I have a feeling this is the origin of the destruction.

The door hangs slightly ajar, and footsteps large and small go in both directions. Who would return to a burned house? I toe the door open and wait a breath. The roof has already caved in over the living space. The white walls left standing are striped with black.

"Hello?" I call out.

No answer.

Behind the rubble is a hall that still holds. For how long, I can't be sure.

"Where are you?" I shout again, forcing my way down the hall and into a small kitchen.

The room is hazy with lingering smoke and smoldering embers. I chance another step, my eyes sweeping the room. An upturned wooden table and roughly carved chairs, one of them broken into splinters. My next step crunches on broken glass and I make out various sets of footprints, dark with mud and something wet—oil? Blood? I crouch down and touch the substances. When I bring them to the tip of my tongue, I taste both. I spit on the floor.

There must have been a terrible fight here.

"Hello," I say again, but my courage slips from me.

My attention snaps to the kitchen door swinging open and closed in the breeze. A chill passes over my skin, prickling with warning when I turn to the fireplace. A large bundle lies on the ground, bits of glass strewn all around it.

I stumble backward so quickly I fall.

It's not a bundle.

It's a person.

When I close my eyes, my own memories are bright flashes that suffocate me. *The blazing orange and red of fire, like the great mouth of a dragon, devours everything in sight.* I slam my fist into the floor and the shock of pain snaps me back to the here and now.

My morning meal comes up until there is nothing but bile on my tongue. I wipe my face on the sleeve of my tunic. This can't have been the sound I heard. I tug at my hair, fearing I've followed one of my vivid memories by accident, like the time I swore a woman was drowning in the lake and I dove in and found nothing, or the time I didn't sleep for a week because I was certain there were children playing in my bedroom, singing a lullaby that kept me up all night. I live a life with the ghosts I've created, and as this house groans against the wind I swear my power will one day lead me to my death.

I brace myself on my hands and knees to stand. I have to get out of here. I have to reach the rendezvous point before Dez comes searching for me. A ray of sun beams through the kitchen window and illuminates the glittering glass along with something else, something clutched in the corpse's hand.

A copper ring.

Inching toward the body, I breathe through my mouth. But that only makes it worse, because I can taste the death in the air. I flip the body over, knowing I'll find a woman. My heart already knows what my eyes take time to see. Half of her body is charred. I brush away the smoldering rubble from her unburned brown skin. Her hair is silver with age, bright red blood is caked around her mouth, and a single brown eye is open and lifeless. If I walked past her in the village square, I would have seen just any older woman in the kingdom with gray-and-black homespun clothes.

But what marks her as one of us, one of the Moria, is the thick copper ring. The intricate etchings reflect her ranking among the elders of the Whispers, and the copper tells me she's a Persuári. A refrain from the cruel rhyme sung in schools and taverns throughout the kingdom pops into mind—*one copper heart persuades senses vast.* On closer inspection I notice the green saliva dried on her chin. Poison.

"Oh, Celeste," I whisper, an ache in my chest as I pocket the copper ring to bring back to the elders. Purple-and-blue bruises mar her wrists like bracelets. She must have fought hard. In her hand I find a small glass vial drained of the poison we all carry with us.

It was Celeste who'd insisted that Robári not be turned away from the Whispers. Most of the elders refused to train us, but Celeste was different. I hoped that I could be different with her help, too. Over the last decade the king has forced the Moria living peacefully in Puerto Leones to flee the kingdom. Celeste has helped families stay and trained young ones to use their powers without hurting others.

I draw the symbol of Our Lady over her torso, marking the V pattern of the constellations of the goddess. "Rest in Her Everlasting Shadow."

Then I whisper, "I'm sorry."

I have to search her body for the alman stone. Dez would do it in a heartbeat, I know. Perhaps Sayida would hesitate the way I do, but we came here for the mission. So, holding my breath, I pull back her ash-covered cloak.

"Mamá!" a voice warbles from somewhere deeper in the house. "Mamá?"

A child's voice. I *wasn't* hearing things. There's a survivor in here. I know I should focus on my task—find the alman stone—but the weakness in that cry cuts into me, urging me away from Celeste and to the back of the house, where I discover another door. It's unlocked, but when I try to push it, there's a weight blocking the way.

"Don't move!" I shout, my voice muffled by the scarf. "I'm here to help you!"

"I'm trapped!" the child sobs. "The man tried to pull me out but I ran back in and then everything fell—"

"Just stay there," I say, eyeing the door. I take a few deep breaths, then charge. I slam into the door with all of my weight, but it gives only a couple of inches. I look around the room for something to help me push. I grab a broomstick leaning against the wall and use it as a staff, wedging it between the opening. With every ounce of strength I can muster, I push.

Inch by inch the door widens enough so that I can squeeze into the room.

At the sight of me, a boy whimpers. "Who are you?"

He can't be older than five—six, at most—with large brown eyes, skin made darker by smoke, and a mop of auburn curls. A heavy wood crossbeam has pinned him to the floor and there's a stitched doll clutched in his fist. Is this what he ran back in here for? He should have run away and never stopped. There was a time when I could have been this child, parents taken by the king's justice. Thank the Mother at least he doesn't have any external injuries.

"I've got you," I say, making sure my scarf is tight over my face. He might be a child, but it's best he doesn't get too good a look at me. After all, I'm still a Whisper.

The boy starts screaming. "Mamá! Mamá!"

I didn't realize what I might look like to a child trapped in a house about to collapse—my face and hands covered in soot, my dark eyes rimmed with kohl. Daggers at my hips and black leather gloves reaching for him. I was about his age when I was taken, though the palace guards wore decidedly finer armor.

"Please," I beg. "Please don't be scared. I'm not going to hurt you."

He doesn't stop screaming. His panic makes him choke and cough even worse until, for a moment, he pauses to gasp for air. And in that pause, I can hear a sharp metallic whistle pierce the sky. Esteban's signal—the Second Sweep has arrived.

Over the pop of fire, the terror of the boy's whimpers, and the thunder of my own heart, there's a rumble of hooves pounding the parched earth.

I pull down my scarf, breathing in short, shallow gulps of air. We need to get out—now. Holding out my hand, I show the child that I want to help.

"Don't be afraid," I tell him.

The words don't mean anything to him. I know that. But I also know that I can't leave this boy behind to die—and I can't wait for him to calm down before the Second Sweep finds us.

The gallop of horses is getting closer.

I grab the boy by the wrist. The elders have warned me against using my power unless it's on people they choose. They don't trust that I can control my magics. But its side effect is one sure way I know to put him into a painless stupor long enough that I can carry him out to safety.

The boy's screaming louder, unable to do anything other than call out for his mother. Keeping hold of his wrist with one hand, I bite the tip of my glove and pull, my hand now exposed and clammy. The glove falls to the ground as the cry for a mother who won't answer pierces my eardrum.

So I do what I must. What I am feared for. Why the Whispers distrust me and why the king's justice used me.

I steal a memory.

The raised scars whorled on the pads of my fingers heat up, stinging like a match on bare flesh as a bright glow begins to emanate from my fingertips. When I make skin-on-skin contact, my power burns its way through the mind until it finds what it's looking for. The magics sear fresh scars onto my hands as I grapple with something as slippery and transmutable as a memory. When I was a girl, I screamed and cried every time I used my power.

But now the heat and pain focus me. Entering someone's mind requires complete control and balance. Once the connection is made, a number of things can go wrong. If I let go too soon, if we're interrupted, if I steal too many memories, I could leave his mind hollow.

As my power latches on to his most recent memory, I brace for the shock of seeing into the child's mind.

He can't sleep. Papá and Mamá sent him to bed, but Francis wants to wait for Aunt Celeste to return from one of her adventures. Then he hears footsteps.

Clang.

The noise comes from the kitchen. Maybe Aunt Celeste is back! Francis pulls off his covers. Cold toes touch the stone-tiled floor. Maybe she'll keep him company, tell him one of her stories of ancient princesses from the long-gone kingdoms of Memoria and Zahara. Or of the old glowing temples of the magical Moria. Last time she put her finger to her lips and made him promise to never repeat those stories.

He tiptoes to the door and twists the doorknob.

He freezes.

There are strange men in the kitchen. Francis feels his voice creep up, wanting to scream for Mamá and Papá. But a twisting fear in his heart tells him to stay quiet.

There's a crash. Glass breaking.

Then fire.

Men screaming. One of them catches flame, flailing and running across the room.

He sees Aunt Celeste. Wants to call out to her, but then she turns and does something very strange: While the guards try to put out the rising flames, she takes a glowing stone the size of a crab apple from her pocket and swallows it.

The boy's scream gathers in his chest as Aunt Celeste falls like a bundle of wheat. When she doesn't get back up, Francis's cry finds its way out. "No!"

The guards all turn to him. Francis wants to move, but his feet feel like lead.

"Grab the boy," one of the men says, his golden hair obscuring his face as he stands over Celeste's unmoving body. "Arrest the family."

The flames catch on the wall, spreading up and out.

"No one can know I was here," the golden-haired man whispers. "Let it burn."

Francis makes to run out the window, but a large hand grabs the back of his neck—

There's a white light, shouting that's louder than the boy's memory. Something's wrong. A wrenching pain stabs at my temples. The connection is breaking. It's like I'm falling straight over a cliff. I try to hold on to the thread of magics connecting me to the boy's mind, but the thundering gallop of the Second Sweep breaks my concentration. I frantically try to rein back my power, to salvage what I can from the boy's memory, but I've latched on and more memories tumble after, one chasing the other, ripples of color as they're erased from his mind and flood into mine.

I shake from the aftershock of it and let go. I try my hardest to stay upright despite the headache that pounds at my temples. The only good thing is that the boy—Francis—is asleep. He'll never again be able to recall Celeste dying or the soldier trying to grab him. In the years since the Whispers saved me, I've learned to comb through stolen memories. These are the ones that become a part of me. I can see Francis running with the kids across the green hills of Esmeraldas. His father laughing with Celeste while making supper. His mother stitching beans for a rag doll's eyes. Francis running away from the guards to retrieve it.

I don't have time to pick up my gloves. I heave the plank off his body, grunting as I lift, and let it slam to the ground. Tucking the doll in his pocket, I scoop Francis into my arms and glance around the room. What fate did his parents face if he ran back here on his own? Who will he have in the world? We'll take him with us until we get to the next town. Sayida will be able to keep him calm, while Margo can search for allies to take him in. I carry him out the door and into the kitchen, where Celeste lies dead with the alman stone. And this time, I know exactly where it is.

But before I can take another step, the side door slams open. I stumble back and hold Francis closer to my chest.

"Put the boy down," the Second Sweep guard commands, leveling his sword at my face.

3

I'VE DONE TWO OF THE THINGS THE WHISPERS HAVE TRAINED ME NOT TO DO—
used my power on a civilian and gotten caught.

Panic and fear course through me as I consider my options. I'm
fast enough to outrun the guard if I make for the front of the house,
but I can't leave Francis or the alman stone behind. Either I abandon both, or I stay and fight. Before I can lower him to the ground,
the boy snaps awake from his daze. He kicks out of my grasp and
screams when he sees me.

"You're safe now," the guard tells the boy, softening his voice.
His uniform is pristine, clean, and his youthful face welcoming.
"No one is going to hurt you."

My blood boils. I know exactly how this works, how easy it is
to fall for. The Second Sweep is the caress after the king's brutal
slap. The weapon to show his mercy—putting out fires, rescuing

stragglers, offering food and safety. It doesn't seem to matter that the king's men razed the village themselves.

I keep a firm grip on Francis's shoulders. His muscles tense, but he doesn't try to bolt. The guard terrifies him just as much as I do, apparently.

"Let go of him," the guard demands, but fear makes him stammer. He shifts his weight from side to side, sweat dripping down the sides of his face. "You're surrounded. There is no way out for you, *bestae*."

I scoff at the insult, but I know he's right. What would Dez do if he were here? Shove the kid aside and fight. The dagger at my hip is no match for his sword. My real weapons are my hands, my power as a Robári. This guard would be difficult to grab hold of, and I could do permanent damage to his mind. I swore to myself eight years ago that I would never make another Hollow. Dez's voice rings clear through my mind. He spoke those words during our last failed mission: *It's your life or theirs. Choose the option that brings you back to me.*

I grab the boy by the throat and line up my dagger to his rib cage.

"You're not going to hurt him," the soldier says.

I lift my chin, a dare. "How do you know?"

"You don't have the eyes of a killer."

It's a strange thing for a soldier of the king to tell me. Me, a Whisper. A dissident. A Robári. But it has the desired effect.

I hesitate and the soldier lunges.

He's right. I wouldn't kill the kid—but I would hurt him, if it means saving us both. I give Francis a hard shove as I swipe my dagger in a wide arc. The guard just dodges the tip of the blade.

"Run!" the soldier yells to Francis.

Francis, whom *I* saved. Francis, who now looks at me as if I were the one who set the fires in the first place. He kicks open the kitchen door and runs out into the streets. This is what the king and his justice do. They twist the truth to make us out to be villains—the force behind all the raids and the scorched towns, the reason the kingdom is suffering. I've played into their hands.

"In the name of the king and the justice!" the soldier shouts, and I feel the pressure of a blade in the nook between my neck and shoulder.

Stupid, Ren. I can practically hear Dez growl the words at me.

"You are under arrest!" He presses the edge of his sword a bit harder, and I move instinctively toward the door, but I know he has no plans of letting me go. The blade slices into my skin, stinging cold against a warm trickle of blood. I grind my teeth, not wanting to give him the satisfaction of hearing me cry out.

"There are more of us," I hiss. "There will always be more of us."

He may be behind me, but I sense the rigidity in his body, like an extension of his sword against my neck. "Not for long."

Choose the option that brings you back to me.

My hand is close enough to my pocket that I can reach for the vial of poison. A brief moment of pain instead of capture. I think of Celeste's body a few feet away. She had the strength to drink it rather than be a prisoner again. Maybe I'm not as hopeless as I think I am. I want to live. I do. *I'm out of options, Dez,* I think.

As if I've conjured him, Dez appears through the smoke like one of my memories coming to life. He is covered in soot and ash from head to toe. A gust of wind tousles his dark hair, and there's a wildness to the melted gold of his eyes. When he sees the blade at my neck and the blood running down my chest, a calm deadliness overtakes him. He draws his sword.

"Let her go," Dez orders.

But the sword stays where it is. I stomp on the relief blooming in my heart because he shouldn't have come for me, and I know when this is all over, I will have to answer for my mistakes. Blood drips from my cut, hot and sticky, down onto the floor, sweat stinging the open wound.

I see the commander in Dez take over as he must realize two things: First, I cannot help him. A single move from me, and the soldier will push his blade fully into my throat, cleave me in half. Second, Dez is too far away to stop him.

But Dez is no ordinary soldier. His thick black brows knit together as he works his magics. He palms the copper coin I know is hidden beneath his tunic, drawing on it to strengthen his gift of persuasion.

Robári are to be feared because we can leave a mind hollow. But Persuári can sense emotion and twist it into action, making you live out your most hidden impulses.

Dez's power bends the very air around us. It intoxicates the senses. He can tap into your desire to do good and make you hand over your coins to a stranger. Proclaim your heart's desire. Jump off a cliff—but only if the impulse already exists.

The soldier grunts as he's overwhelmed by Dez's magics, frozen in place. His trembling hand causes the tip of the blade to waver against my skin, digging into my wound. I cry out despite myself, a stinging sensation spreading along my neck and arms.

Dez comes within inches of the soldier. His magics prickle along my skin, like invisible beetles crawling all over me.

"Let. Her. Go," Dez says again. When he uses his power, his words are accompanied by a hypnotic chime, like a spirit calling out from another realm. Effortless, as Dez's magics always are.

He must be amplifying the soldier's obedience and using that to twist his body. Except now he's taking orders from a Moria, and the soldier screams against the movements he can't control. The soldier trembles, fighting with all his might. But he isn't stronger than Dez, and finally he does as he's told.

Free of the blade's edge, I stumble away from Dez and the soldier, crawling back toward Celeste's corpse. *I still have to get the alman stone.* Blood runs down my skin, but the pain of the cut is nothing compared to the heat that scorched new scars on my hands.

"Drop your sword," Dez says.

The soldier's face turns red. I've seen others bend easily, but this one strains against the force of it, his body locked in place like a statue coming to life.

This is why they fear us. This power that alchemy and clerics can't explain. A power that is a gift and a curse.

"You don't need another soldier's sword," I mutter to Dez as I crouch next to Celeste's body.

"Perhaps not, but I want it." Dez holds his hand out, and the air undulates around the guard like heat on the desert.

The soldier twitches, his hand shaking until he relinquishes his hold. The metal clangs on the stone floor. Dez is swift to pick it up and turns the bloody blade on the soldier.

"Kill me, bestae," the soldier spits at Dez. "Do it!"

Dez moves gracefully around the soldier and presses the sword's point onto the Fajardo family's crest stitched on the front of the guard's tunic—a winged lion with a spear in its mandible and flames roaring around it.

"Killing you is easy," Dez says, punctuating his words with a grin. "I want you to return to your men. I want you to tell them that it was a Moria bestae who spared your life. That the Whispers will take back their lands and you'll never be able to hurt our people again."

"The king and the justice will destroy you," the soldier says, his body overcome with tremors. "All of you!"

While he's distracted by Dez, I take this moment to turn Celeste's face toward me. I press my fingers along her throat. I don't feel anything, but I saw her in Francis's memory. I watched her swallow the alman stone.

As I pry her jaw open, a soft white light emits from the back of her throat. The acrid stench of vomit and charred skin makes my stomach roil. I shut my eyes and reach in, feeling along the swollen slick of her tongue. *May the Mother of All forgive me.*

Letting go of an anxious breath, I get my fingers around the alman stone, then pocket it.

"Let's go, Ren. Provincia Carolina is a day's ride."

I nod, even though I know we have no outpost in the Carolina region. The soldier doesn't seem gullible enough to take this misdirect, even under Dez's persuasion, but he'll have to report his encounter in excruciating detail to his superiors. It'll send the king's men on a fool's errand and split their forces, perhaps even give us time to reach our base undisturbed.

"Wait outside and don't move until we're long gone," Dez commands. But the minute Dez is out of reach, the spell will break. We have to move quickly. I chance a look at the soldier. His face is red, spit bubbling at the twisted snarl of his lips. I know today will only fuel his hatred of us. For now, we have to save ourselves.

Dez drapes my arm around his shoulder, and together we hobble out the door and vanish into the smoky streets.

4

WHEN DEZ AND I REUNITE WITH THE REST OF OUR UNIT—SAYIDA, MARGO, and Esteban—the five of us head north for half a day, following a winding path through the Verdina Forest. Even the king's guard can't be everywhere at once, and the dense trees and gnarly roots jutting from the ground make it a hard enough journey by foot. It would be nearly impossible for the Second Sweep's horses.

We move with purpose, cutting through dew-covered brush, following the rays of light that filter through the thick canopy of verdina trees. We keep walking until it's safe to stop, until the insides of our boots wear the skin of our feet raw, until we reach the bank of the Rio Aguadulce. The rapid white river is such a welcome sight. The five of us discard our packs and weapons and kneel at the water's edge. I tug off my spare gloves and drink until my belly hurts and my fingers are numb from the cold. I remove the makeshift bandage Sayida made for me when Dez and I first returned to the rendezvous point.

Sayida is a Persuári, like Dez, though she is also skilled in medicine and healing. For centuries, when the kingdom of Memoria was free and thriving, those like Sayida and Dez were often medicuras by trade because they can tend to ailments while keeping their patients calm and serene.

I grind my teeth to muffle the cry that scrapes my throat. Splashing ice-cold water onto the wound helps a bit, but now that we've got a place to stop for the night, I'm going to have to let Sayida take a needle to it.

"We'll set up camp here between these boulders," Dez says, surveying the area by the riverbank, where the roots are so high above the earth, it's as though they're trying to get up to take a stroll. It's a good enough location with plenty of shade and a fallen tree trunk that will be of help when we have to wade across the river. He wastes no time in cleaning his stolen sword.

Esteban frowns at me, which I'm used to. "I worry about the king's men," he says, scratching at the uneven tufts of facial hair he's attempting to grow. With his smooth brown skin and full lips, he'd be quite handsome if he shaved it, though that wouldn't do anything for his personality. "The Second Sweep will alert the toll men on the route out of the provincia. The inspections will be more thorough or they'll increase the travel tax—we can barely—"

"Let's get through this night first," Dez says, trying to keep his voice light. "It wouldn't be a complete mission without a good deal of worry to keep us sharp."

Esteban's thick black lashes rest on high cheekbones as he takes a moment to compose himself. It's a hard thing to do, standing up to Dez. One year younger than me, Esteban came to the Whispers from Citadela Crescenti, with its tall palmetto trees, scorching sun, and never-ending festivities. He clears his throat. "But—"

"Not now," Dez says, voice strong but with a hint of weariness. He examines his polished sword as he stands, and for the briefest moment, Esteban flinches. Sayida keeps her head down, her dainty fingers busy with a suture kit.

"When?" Margo comes up behind Dez, hands on narrow hips. She's four fingers shorter than him, but her anger elongates her somehow. Margo's blue eyes are heavy with dark circles, her freckled face red from the wind and sun. She doesn't try to cover up the burned splotches, like many other Illusionári would do. The only vanity Margo allows herself is her set of pebble-size solid-gold earrings. And even those are only worn as metal conduits to enhance her magics.

"Peace, Margo," Sayida says softly, sensing a fight like a seabird might a distant storm.

Esteban scoffs. "There's none of that to go around."

"Are we going to talk about what happened in the village?" Margo demands. "Or does the little incendiary get to do whatever she wants, even if it means putting us all in danger?"

I wince at her words, but Sayida remains beside me. She places a calming hand on my uninjured shoulder. Anger simmers beneath my skin, but I won't try to pick a fight with Margo. Not while I'm wounded, at least.

Dez's nostrils flare. "What do you want me to say, Margo? We did everything to get to Celeste as fast as we could. We were too late, but not all is lost."

Her blue eyes fall on me, cold and loveless. Wide pink lips curl into a scoff. "Not all is lost? We couldn't be sure the pair of you got out alive. Then you show up, *this one* half-dead and you with a new toy. You're the one always saying not to bring attention to ourselves! Why didn't you show the Second Sweep the hidden passage through the mountain while you were at it?"

I hate the way she says *this one*, but I swallow the names I'd call her because I will make things worse.

"Enough," Dez says. The echo of his deep voice lingers.

Sayida unspools a long black thread and cuts it with a flick of a pocket blade. Margo's frustration turns her lips into an ugly scowl. Esteban twists the cap of his flask. I listen to the sound of a woman singing, Francis's mother. My tear ducts sting, so I close my eyes and usher that stolen memory into the dark with the others.

"I know you're tired," Dez says, dragging his fingers through his hair. "But we recovered the alman stone and we're not far from the mountain borders. We'll be safe when we're back in Ángeles."

"And then what?" Margo says, the last word coming out strangled. "It's been ten months since we lost our hold of Citadela Riomar."

Dez goes completely still. We all do. But Margo keeps throwing his biggest defeat in his face.

"If we lose more ground, if we're pushed back any more, we'll be going right off the cliffs and into the sea. We can send as many refugees as we want across the sea and into foreign lands, but there is no such thing as safe anymore."

"I know exactly how long it's been since I lost Riomar," he says with more patience than I've ever summoned on my own. "I think of it every day. Every day."

"I didn't mean—" Margo starts.

"I know what you meant. Hear this. I will do everything I can to win this war, but I can't do it alone. I need all of you. A unit." His golden eyes cut to Margo, who straightens up, not at attention, but like a challenge. "And if you didn't believe there was any hope at all, you would have left us long ago, Margo."

She tilts her chin up and points a finger at me. "I stay to make sure she doesn't betray us again. You're careless with your life when she's on missions."

I'm used to Margo, more than Esteban, getting her digs in when I make a mistake. Across all the miles we've traveled, my insides have been knotted against their disdain, but this feels different. When Dez pulled me from the scavenger unit and onto his, Margo was the first to claim that I was too slow, too loud on my feet, too weak to carry a sword. I trained every day and night to prove her wrong, but it hasn't been enough. It's like she's waiting for me to go running back to the justice. I hate that everything I am can be summed up in few words. *Scavenger. Thief. Traitor.*

Will they allow me to be more? Today I stuck my hand in a dead woman's throat to retrieve a magic stone. I don't have the energy to fight with Margo. But Dez does, and I wish he wouldn't.

"Come now, Margo," Dez says, his face set as if daring the others to contradict him. "Are you angry because I went back for her or because Ren saved a boy's life? It wasn't you who ran into the burning village alongside me."

"You *told* us to stay behind," Esteban bursts out. "We had to retrieve the packs."

Dez bares teeth in a humorless smile. "You see? We all played our parts. We're alive. Ren retrieved Celeste's alman stone."

"And got caught," Margo mutters.

"When we get caught, because it *does* happen to the best of us, we figure out a way to keep fighting. Keep the mission alive. Destroy the Arm of Justice. Restore our kingdom and the lands of our ancestors. Or have you changed your mind?"

"I haven't," Esteban says.

"Good. We are all alive, and we are together. That's more than I can say for Celeste San Marina." We all nod, and he lets a tight moment pass before he says, "Sayida, can you stitch Ren up, please?"

"I'll do what I can," Sayida says. The needle and thread are on a swatch of clean cloth, and she washes her hands with a square of soap in the river.

"The rest of us will make camp," Dez says, trying to catch my eye.

I refuse to look at him. He doesn't understand. He can't. I don't want him speaking on my behalf. It only makes things worse with the others.

Above us, dark clouds move quickly across the sky, leaving a cool breeze. Perhaps the goddess is still looking after us, and perhaps this is her mercy on rebels always running from a mad king—a reprieve from sweltering heat.

I sit on a patch of dry grass while the others finish building a ring of stones for a fire. Sayida cuts another swatch of relatively clean cloth with her pocketknife and uses it as a rag to blot as much of the blood around my wound as she can.

I try to stare at her face and ignore the burning sensation that spreads across my shoulders and chest. Sayida's eyes and hair are dark as midnight, and the gentle outward slope of her nose is accentuated by a tiny diamond stud on the left nostril. Her skin is the light brown of the sand dunes in the Zahara Canyons with a smatter of black beauty marks across her chest. She always has a slightly red tint to her lips, a habit left over from her time as a singer four years ago. Now, nearly nineteen, she's still the nightingale of the Whispers, singing as she mends our cuts and sews up our wounds. It's almost enough that you don't think about the pain. *Almost.*

I grimace, tensing my shoulder as she puts pressure on the wound.

"Sorry! Mother of All, this is a long cut, Ren," she says, never taking her eyes off her own swift fingers. A nervous chuckle leaves her lips. "But, of course, you knew that."

"Now I've got matching scars on either side of my neck," I say, maudlin. "The world simply insists on attempting to behead me."

"Or Our Lady of Shadows has sent her guardians to watch over you." Sayida strikes a match and runs a long needle through the small flame.

I make to laugh, but something about the fire makes me gasp and nearly fall backward. It's silly, utterly pathetic how I can build a flame at camp and run through a razed village and watch a boy's memory of a guard set on fire, but then this small drop of flame causes me to lose my breath.

"Ren?"

It's happening again. *Why* is it happening now? Sayida squeezes my arms to try to snap me out of it. My body feels paralyzed as my vision splinters with pain. A memory I keep locked in the Gray breaks out.

Small hands grip the windowsill of the palace. Diamond glass panes reflect my face back to me. The stark black night sky explodes with the bleeding orange and red of sunrise. My rooms fill with smoke. It sifts through the seams around the door.

Fire! Not sunrise, I realize. Fire.

My head spins and I crouch down, grabbing hold of my knees for support as I struggle to breathe. Someone calls my name, but it's like they're a hundred meters away, and the brilliant colors of my memories still swirl dizzyingly through my vision.

Then something soft brushes against my cheek.

Dez. The callused pad of his thumb rough on my skin. *Be calm.* The word chimes around me, *through* me. My body relaxes, muscles unraveling like string pulled from a tapestry, and as my heart slows, Dez's warm magics fill my senses. I'm overcome with the need to be calm, still. And suddenly, my mind feels clear. The Gray retreats and I slam the door shut. Sayida and Dez have moved me away from the camp and to a soft patch of grass. How was I so out of it that I didn't even feel it?

I curse and slam my hand into Dez's hard chest, regretting the shock of pain it brings me. "I told you I don't want you to—"

"I'm sorry," Dez says, his voice low but steady. He's not sorry at all. "Sayida can't sew up that wound if you're shaking."

"Are you done yet?" Margo asks, her sharp blue eyes on Dez. "We need help with the bedrolls." Then her eyes flick toward me, and her upper lip curls into that familiar sneer. I can't be certain if she's upset because Dez used his magics on a fellow Whisper, or because he touched me so intimately. Perhaps both. Perhaps it's just because no matter how much I bleed or run or fight in the name of the Whispers, my existence is a reminder of everything that has been lost.

Dez grunts an apology and silently withdraws to add a log to the fire.

"Come now," Sayida says to me, returning to her suture kit. "Esteban, would you be so kind as to share your drink?"

Esteban, who has begun preparing our meal, scowls. "It's probably already infected. You'd be wasting good drink."

Dez stares at Esteban with the kind of steel that has made better men soil themselves.

"Just a splash," Esteban grumbles to Sayida, but narrows his eyes at me when he tosses the flask to her hands.

"Ignore him," Sayida whispers in my ear. "It won't hurt too badly, but you can bite down on your belt if you'd like."

"I think we have different definitions of 'won't hurt too badly,'" I say. "But I'll be all right."

She giggles when I glower at the slim flask of aguadulce. The drink might be made from the sugar cane stalks plentiful in the southern provincia, but there is nothing sweet about the clear liquor. Once Dez poured it over an open cut on my leg before digging out a thick shard of glass that was lodged in there. I couldn't walk for weeks, and I couldn't stomach the smell of aguadulce for even longer.

Sayida gives me a warm smile. "What happened? I've never seen you react to a flame that way."

Sayida never has to use her Persuári gifts to influence my mood. There's something about her that makes me want to spill my secrets, even the things I can't always voice to Dez.

"It's nothing," I say. "I remembered something from when I was a child."

Her thick eyebrows arch with surprise. "That's good, isn't it? You haven't been able to access the Gray since you were rescued from the palace, right?"

I hold my hair back and stare at the grass while she cleans and dries the wound. "I've been working with Illan to try and recall more from my time with the king's justice to use to our advantage, but nothing has worked. He thinks that I compartmentalized my memories so my mind wouldn't crumble. That I created the Gray to hold all my memories from that time. The other elders believe that the Gray is a side effect. A punishment, really, for the Robári who create Hollows. It's what I deserve, I suppose."

"Don't say that, Ren." Sayida frowns and presses a dry cloth to the flask of aguadulce. I brace for the burn of alcohol. "We all have darkness in our pasts. The goddess says we all deserve forgiveness."

"I shouldn't be forgiven just because I hardly remember the first nine years of my life."

"And look at all you've done since," she whispers, then covers my wound.

My vision flares red and I swallow my scream, if only because I don't want Margo and Esteban to think me weak.

"Hold still now." Sayida waits for me to stop wincing, then threads the needle. I shut my eyes and hold my breath as the metal pierces skin. The silk string follows through and tugs.

I breathe hard and fast. My temples pulse with a dull ache. I have to keep the Gray under control. The elders believe that perhaps there's something there that could help turn the tide of the Moria rebellion against the king. But deep down, I wonder if the reason I couldn't access the memories with Illan's training is because I didn't want anything resurfacing.

Unlike the Whispers, I spent part of my childhood in the palace, not as a captive—as a guest of the king and the justice. A kind of pet, really. Ten years ago, the justice began to seek out Robári children all throughout the kingdom to be used as weapons. And though there must have been a few others like me—Robári are rare, not extinct—I don't remember them. Maybe they were old enough to refuse the work the justice demanded, and were executed for their belligerence. But I didn't refuse.

I did as I was told.

Justice Méndez had singled me out. He would sit me in one of the palace's many parlor rooms and bring trays of delicacies for me to choose from. He told me that my ability to pull memories from people was the most powerful he'd ever seen. I didn't know then that I couldn't give the memories back. That I could steal one too many. That when I was finished—when I emptied people of *all* their memories—I was leaving behind only a shadow of a person. A Hollow.

I didn't know I was the justice's greatest asset in the beginnings of the King's Wrath, when thousands of my kind—including my parents, I later found out—were massacred. The crime was using our magics against the king and people of Puerto Leones.

"There," Sayida says when she's finished, applying an herb salve that cools my burning skin. Admiring her work, she smiles. "That should hold you over until we get back to Ángeles."

"*If* we make it back," Esteban says, snatching the flask from Sayida's hand before she can put it away.

"Always the optimist. Have you so little confidence in my ability to get you home?" Dez calls good-naturedly, but I hear the challenge running beneath the question.

"I trust you with my life, Dez, but I worry that scavenger's mistake will follow us." Esteban runs a hand over his coarse, curly hair.

"This *scavenger* also happens to be the only person in Ángeles who can read an alman stone," Dez says, an edge to his words. "Unless you've acquired talents I wasn't aware of."

"If you call that curse a talent," Esteban says.

I stand abruptly and leave—but not because of Esteban, whose insults are as familiar to me as the whorls on my palms. I glance at Dez once because I know that he is going to follow.

Treading away from our camp, I keep along the river until we're out of earshot. Dez's presence looms behind me, his steps matching mine.

"Esteban was out of line," Dez says when I finally stop to face him. "I'll speak to him."

"Esteban is always out of line," I say sharply. "And I don't *want* you to have to speak to him. I want you to let me deal with him myself."

Dez glances skyward, confused. "Let me help."

"Don't you see what you do?" I take a breath because between running in and out of Esmeraldas and my memories trying to break out of the Gray, I feel stretched too thin. "They'll never respect me if you come to my defense at every turn."

"You're still the most valuable person in this unit. In all of Ángeles. Without you we'd be in the dark."

"You don't see it," I say, shaking my head slowly. "I'm not talking about my value."

He smiles. Now, of all times, he *smiles* at me—with that look that makes me want to do senseless things.

"Then tell me," he says. "I can't read your mind, not for lack of trying."

"Can you change the past?"

He takes my hand, and I imagine that I can feel him through the soft leather of my gloves. "Ren—"

"I'm serious."

His smile falters but only for a moment. "You're always serious, Renata. I'm sure you were born serious."

"Being responsible for thousands of deaths will do that to a girl."

"You're not a girl," he says, caressing my shoulders. "You're a shadow. You're steel. You're vengeance in the night. You're a Whisper of the rebel Moria."

I know he means to compliment me. Among our units, we are as good as our skills. But when he tells me I'm the whisper of death, and not a girl, it's like an arrow in my chest. I stare back into his eyes, wishing he were a little less reckless. And yet, then he wouldn't be Dez.

"You didn't answer my question."

"No, Renata." He sighs. "I can't change the past. If my father's bedtime stories serve me, there's only one way to change the past, and that's with the Knife of Memory."

I laugh because if I was born serious, then Dez was born brazen. The Knife of Memory. A blade so sharp it can cut away whole swaths of memory at a time—whole years, whole histories. A classic Moria children's tale.

"You can't make this right, Dez. Only I can."

He wags a finger at me. "As Margo so lovingly reminded us, we lost our last stronghold because of me. I couldn't defeat the Bloodied Prince. If she's going to turn her rage on someone, it should be me."

"That wasn't your fault. We had no allies and were outnumbered ten to one, Dez."

He looks away but agrees with a nod. Something inside me twinges at the hurt on his face. Under the shade of verdina trees, I allow myself to finally relax into the strength of him. His tunic is loose and unbelted. I brush the wild black waves of his hair that never want to stay tied down. It hurts to move my neck, so I stand on a thick tree root.

"Why do you get to comfort me, but you won't allow me to do the same?" He chuckles and rests his hands on my waist. We're eye to eye, and I surprise him with a kiss. The fear that's dug its claws in me all day lets go. I can let go when it's just the two of us. He wraps an arm around my lower back and presses me against him. Everything about him is sturdy, dependable as the great trees that surround us. He draws back to catch his breath. When I rest a hand over his heart, I can feel it race. His crooked smile brings a tight sensation in my belly. "Not that I'm complaining, but what was that for?"

"I've wanted to do that since we left Ángeles," I whisper. "Thank you for today. For coming back for me."

"I will always come back for you."

Those are bold words, an impossible promise that he can't actually keep. We don't live in a world that allows for those kinds of vows. But I choose to believe them. I want to.

He reaches around his neck and unties a black leather cord with a copper coin strung from it. On one side it has the profile of a nameless woman with a laurel crown, and on the other side three stars around the inscribed year, 299. As long as I've known him he's never taken it off. It takes me a moment to realize he's offering it to me.

I shake my head. "I can't take that."

"Can't?" he asks. "Or won't?"

"Illan gave you that pendant."

Dez holds the coin along its edge. "And he got it from my grandfather, who was a blacksmith for the crown. There were exactly ten of them minted before the capital fell under siege by a rebel group from the former queendom of Tresoros and all production stopped. My father says King Fernando keeps a gallery with his trophies, and the other nine coins are there as a reminder that Puerto Leones was once surrounded by enemy lands—Memoria, Tresoros, Sól Abene, Zahara. Their fate was to be conquered by the lions of the coast."

"How come I've never heard that story?" I ask. To be fair, there are dozens of versions that tell of how the Fajardo family of Puerto Leones conquered or "united" the continent. But the queendom of Tresoros was an ally. I didn't know there were still rebel groups over a century after its fall. I wonder, will we still be in this fight in another few decades?

Dez brings me back to the present by gently tucking my hair behind my ear. His smile is so beautiful it hurts to look at him for too long.

"Consider yourself lucky to miss many of my father's ramblings of ancient times. That doesn't change the fact that I want you to have it."

I shrug my good shoulder. "I can't wear anything around my neck."

"Keep it in your pocket. In your boot. Just keep it with you." He presses it onto my open palm and closes my fingers around it. "It's worthless if you try to buy anything with it, but it's the only family heirloom I have."

"All the more reason I shouldn't have it."

He licks his lips and sighs. "When I realized today that you hadn't gotten out of the village, I knew there was a possibility that I wouldn't see you again. That I'd never hear you yell at me or correct me when I'm wrong. I'd never hold you or see you in the courtyard back home. I couldn't bear it, Ren. Everything is going to change soon, and I don't know who's going to make it out alive, but I want you to have a part of me."

"I have nothing to give you, Dez." Emotions swell in my chest. I lean into him with my eyes closed, because if I look into his eyes I will be weak. I will take his trinket. I will soften when I should be sharp edges and steel. He kisses the mound of my cheekbone, and then I can't help it. I look.

"You give me your trust, and I know how hard that is for you."

I've known him for too long, and I don't think he's ever spoken so honestly. Dez never hides his feelings, but I wonder if there's something he isn't telling me. Something about the mission and in the alman stone that is more dangerous than we thought. When he looks at me, I see a flash of fear in his eyes. The Dez I know is not afraid of anything. But maybe I imagine it. Maybe it's the excitement of the day and the shadows of the setting sun.

"I will cherish it." I hold the copper coin close to my chest and kiss him once more, too briefly.

From our camp in the distance comes Dez's name. It's time to read the alman stone and discover what Celeste San Marina died to protect.

As the sun sets, we gather closer around the fire. I've never transcribed an alman stone outside our fortress in Ángeles. It has to be done in the presence of at least two elders and a Ventári. Because of our pasts, they don't trust Robári to tell the truth.

Ventári like Esteban can see if I'm lying. He'll look into my mind as if peering through a window and write everything down. The day I don't need one of the mind-reading Ventári to *prove* I'm telling the truth is the day I know the Whispers trust me.

Margo and Sayida watch quietly from the other side of the fire pit while Dez paces around us in that slow, predatory way of his. I take the alman stone from my pocket and set it on the makeshift tabletop. I have the passing thought that this is what a fallen star might look like—a white crystal with light trapped inside.

I pull off my glove, then rest one hand on top of his. The pearlescent whorls and scars are a bright contrast to the rest of my olive skin.

Esteban's onyx eyes roam my face. "Ready?"

He wears a silver bracelet, the metal conductor for a Ventári's powers. Esteban once described the bracelet as a torch, helping him illuminate the deepest thoughts in the human mind. The Moria are said to have metals in their blood, that they're the key to strengthening our powers. I always remember the stories Illan would tell us as children about Our Lady of Shadows plucking the veins of metal beneath the earth and imbuing them with her power. She gave that magic to the Moria to protect the world she created. That's one story, at least. It is difficult to protect anything when all you can do is hide.

"Ready," I say.

I shudder as the chill of his magics seeps into my skin. Esteban is the only Ventári I've let read me. If you didn't know what was happening, the tension behind your eyes might be confused with the start of a headache. For me it's close to having someone step into my skin. The intrusion brings a shock of panic because when I look at Dez, all I can think of is the kisses we traded not too far from here. Breathing deeply, I try to keep my mind as blank as a lake on a windless day. No need for Esteban to know—

"Know what, little incendiary?" Esteban smirks.

"That you're an ass. But I suppose we already know that." I concentrate on the time Esteban accidentally fell into the compost pile back in Ángeles, and Esteban's eyes flash dark.

"I've told you," Esteban says. "You can always fight against my power. Show me what you want me to see. If you'd only bother to practice."

If I did that, it would only incur suspicion and he knows that. "Get on with it."

54

Holding the alman stone at eye level, I concentrate on the core of light pulsing in the stone like a still-beating heart. No one, not even the elders, knows why only Robári like me can read the images an alman stone captures. The stone itself was once so sacred it was only used to build the temples and statues of Our Lady of Shadows, divine mother to the Moria. When the kingdom of Memoria was conquered by Puerto Leones, many of the histories and texts were destroyed. Though elders tried to pass down stories, we don't always know what is myth and what truly happened. Ten years ago, during the King's Wrath, all remaining statues and temples were crushed to dust. The pieces of alman stone we've been lucky enough to find are used to communicate across the network of Whispers in the provincias.

This stone means everything to me.

The lines on my palms light up the same way they do when I'm about to take a memory. Unlike when I enter people's minds, the images in an alman stone have bright white edges. Everything about them is too bright, as if the sun were right above the scene no matter where or when it took place. The sound is like trying to communicate from behind a wall of glass. As the forest fades away and the warmth of Esteban's magics snake up my arm, the last thing I hear is the scratch of his quill.

"Hurry, Rodrigue," a hushed voice, hidden beneath a black cloak, says. "Get her and get out. The guards change posts at midnight. You have but moments."

The hooded figure heaves open the heavy wooden door with rippled glass panes. Rodrigue watches his reflection in the warped surface. His dark brown skin glistens with nervous sweat. He can't recognize himself in the stolen palace guard uniform — too violet, too tight on his broad *shoulders. He nods once more to the cloaked figure and hurries into the dungeon.*

A dimly lit, narrow corridor. Torchlight burns long shadows into worn stone walls. Water drips into puddles from the porous ceiling. Rodrigue breathes heavily as he turns first one corner and then another. Voices and jingling metal echo nearby, and he flattens himself against a depression in the wall. A guard saunters past.

When the guard is long gone, Rodrigue keeps running. He passes cells full of people. Some hold ten souls. Some three. Some contain only mice scavenging through piles of hay.

Dozens of eyes watch him stride through the corridor. Rodrigue tries not to make eye contact, but he catches a woman's gaze. She frowns. Does she know he stole this uniform?

He clears his throat, grips the hilt of his stolen sword. He counts seconds in his head, knowing he is running out of time.

"Lucia?" he calls out.

At the end of the corridor, there is no torchlight. Rodrigue grabs one and illuminates his path through the empty darkness. He holds the flame up to the cells, searching the grimy faces that slink away. Their eyes narrow at the light. Their cracked lips hiss at the intrusion. Then he sees her.

Alone in a cell so large she looks like a child sitting at its center.

"What did they do to you?" he whispers. He fumbles for the lock, but the tumblers are so rusted they won't turn. "Lucia, come to me."

Her head snaps up at the sound of her name. But she sees right past Rodrigue and lowers her gaze once more. She is thin, so thin he is afraid to touch her when she reaches him. Her fingers, skinny as twigs, wrap around the iron bars. There is a sickly gray pallor to her skin. Her hair long and brushed back, as if someone tended to her recently.

"The Magpie couldn't give me more time," he says.

He can feel midnight approaching. Voices echo from the direction Rodrigue has come. Using the sword, he swipes at the lock until his muscles burn. But it isn't strong enough to break through the justice's metalwork.

Rodrigue grabs hold of Lucia's arm. His sobs reverberate off the walls. He is out of time. He touches his finger to her temple. "Lucia, Lucia, please, say something. I can't read your thoughts. They're—"

She looks up vacantly, silver veins spread across the skin around her eyes and the base of her neck, like snakes across the sand.

Rodrigue jumps back. Those veins pulse, glowing beneath her skin.

He drops his sword and it clatters to the ground. He can't hear her thoughts, can't see anything inside the mind he loved so deeply. More than that, he can't find any trace of her power. It is as if her essence—her soul, her spark—is gone.

"This is a surprise." A deep, even voice speaks behind him. Rodrigue whirls around. Two guards shove him into the wall. Their fists strike his face, chest, groin until he falls. The ground is wet and cold.

A third man looms over him. Shadows cut across his

*angular face. His trim graying hair is brushed back. He
pushes aside dark robes and kneels beside Rodrigue.*

*"What did you do to her?" Rodrigue spits blood on
the man's face. He doesn't wipe it away and it speckles his
sharp cheekbones.*

*"The same thing I will do to you. Rid you of your unnat-
ural magics. You will never harm another soul again."*

*Rodrigue raises a fist to fight, but the guards pull him
back down. He turns to Lucia—his life, his love—who
shows no reaction. No fear. No concern. No empathy.*

*"Do what you want to me," Rodrigue said. "The
Whispers will never be silenced."*

*The man stands, his face turning slowly to Lucia.
He holds up a finger decorated with a jeweled gold band.
"That was before. It is a new dawn for Puerto Leones. I
want you to know exactly what is in store for your upris-
ing. You are quite wrong, you see. Run to the ends of the
world if you'd like, but with our new weapon, we will
find you." The man seizes Rodrigue's chin. "Tell me who
the spy in the palace is and I will allow you to spend one
more day with your Lucia."*

"Lucia!" I gasp, my voice ragged, disbelieving. I yank my hand
away from Esteban, whose face is twisted in fear. He doesn't even
reach for the flask of aguadulce he always keeps close to chase away
the migraines that accompany his magics.

"What is it?" I'm suddenly aware that Dez is by my side, hands
soothing, brushing my hair from my clammy temples. Just his
hands. The susurration of his voice in my ear. "Ren. What did you
see? Is Lucia still alive?"

"Dez, the king—the justice— Somehow— They took it—" I don't know what I've seen. I don't know how to put words to what Rodrigue went through. The justice was there, and his is a face I was not prepared to see.

"Esteban—Ren—I need you both to speak."

Margo snatches the paper Esteban was writing on, his letters sloppy, as if he couldn't keep up with the speed of the memory. Her blue eyes flash wide, moving faster across the words pulled from my mind.

"They've figured out how to win this war," Margo says, and crunches the paper in her fist before smoothing it out again. The notes are meant to be presented to the elders.

"What do you mean?" Sayida asks, taking the parchment from Margo's shaking hand.

I still hold the alman stone. The light has been snuffed out, turning it into another bit of translucent crystal. Ordinary. Empty. I think of Lucia's face, so strange, covered with silver veins, so much like the magic whorls that burn across my hands. Then there was the justice himself. It's been years since I saw him or heard his voice. I want to scream. I want to jump into the river and be carried away. I don't know if I'm strong enough for what is supposed to come next.

"They can rip out our power," Sayida says breathlessly. "But how?"

We look to Dez. Each of us sits around the fire, the way we might have when we were children telling stories. Now our monsters are real and we don't know if we can defeat them. Dez takes the parchment last and reads, then looks to the canopy of trees, the white light of the moon just visible between gaps. He's worried, yes, but he doesn't share the surprise the rest of us feel.

"You knew," I say.

Dez meets my stare. "Yes."

Margo and Esteban curse under their breath. Sayida presses her lips together, nose flaring. I feel something cold settle into my heart.

"I couldn't tell you," he says. "The order came from the elders themselves."

Margo stands and kicks at the closest pack. Mine, naturally. "You owe us an explanation, Dez. I believed Celeste and Rodrigue had information that could *help* us. Instead all we know is that our enemies have figured out a way to *end* us."

"Yes, the Arm of Justice has created a weapon to rip out our power," Dez says. "My father learned this four months ago."

"Four *months*?" I repeat.

Dez stands and stomps around the fire, unable to keep his nerves hidden. "He heard it from a spy called the Magpie. I don't know who they are, or if they're Moria at all. My father never reveals his spies to anyone, not even other elders, for fear of endangering them."

"How did this Magpie learn of the weapon?" I ask.

"That's what Lucia was sent to discover," Dez says, rubbing his hands over his face. His golden stare is distant, and he pulls away from us in a way he's never done before. "She was caught. Rodrigue left on his own to find her, but we now know what happened. We had hoped to uncover what the weapon was and destroy it. But the fact that it can do more than steal magics . . ." He trails off, almost breathless. "We couldn't dream up such a cruelty."

"Where did it come from?" Margo demands, as I ask, "What else can it do?"

"We don't know how they forged it." Dez stops pacing, arms crossed over his chest. "That man told Rodrigue that they can find us anywhere we go. It can detect our power. It won't be safe to travel in numbers."

"What about the rest of the families we're to help smuggle across Luzou?" Sayida asks.

"We have to get them there sooner," he says, slowly regaining his resolve. He meets our eyes again. "We've always had to be one step ahead of the justice. That can't change now."

Margo faces the fire, flames dancing in her blue stare. "They can rip out our powers. The way you rip out memories."

We're all silent. I didn't want to make the connection, but Margo has done it for me. It's not enough that she already sees me as a danger; she wants to align me with something so monstrous? My hands ball into fists. "You didn't see what became of Lucia. She was standing. She was lucid. But her eyes held no life. When I made a Hollow—"

"Ren, you don't have to—"

"I do," I say. "When I made a Hollow, it emptied the mind of all memories. The body was left alive, but the damage done to the mind was permanent. They fell into a deep sleep. I never saw them again. So no, it's not the same thing, Margo."

"But you live with those memories," Sayida says. "Where did Lucia's power go after it was taken? What does the king do with it?"

"Forget the ship to Luzou," Margo says. "I say we go to the palace at first light. Let's end this. Break in. Kill the king. Kill the Príncipe Dorado. The palace burned once—we can do it again. I'm sure you remember, Renata."

I think of my room in the palace filling with smoke, watching from the window as the capital burned. Sayida reaches for my knee and squeezes. Everything in my body wants to run away, to scream, to leave this place and never come back. But I made a promise to myself that I would do everything in my power to right the wrongs I committed. I shut my eyes and see the man who threatened Rodrigue. I knew him well once. I knew the palace.

Rodrigue escaped the bowels of that place and got a message to us. He died for it. Celeste died for it. An entire village burned. I remember what the guard said in the boy's memory.

"Margo is right," I say, surprising everyone, but especially Margo. She frowns, as if I'm playing a trick on her. "We should go as soon as possible. When I took the memory from the boy, Francis, one of the guards said that no one could know they were there. Why not parade Celeste in front of everyone in Esmeraldas? Why not use the weapon on her?"

"They're protecting it," Sayida says. "The Bloodied Prince likes a spectacle. I say they're waiting for the right time."

"All the more reason to head them off at the pass," Margo says.

"We're outnumbered," Dez says.

"We're always outnumbered!" Esteban throws up his hands. "You once charged the Matahermano himself in Riomar with no one behind you."

"And I lost," Dez snaps. "We all lost that day. I won't make that mistake again. The mission was to get the alman stone and discover what was so urgent Celeste was willing to risk exposing herself. Now we know this weapon can detect Moria magics. Destroying this weapon *is* our first priority, but we have to be smarter than the king and the justice. We won't get a second chance. Believe me—going back to Ángeles is difficult for me, too, but we can't afford to fail. This is too important. Do you trust me?"

"Yes," Margo says without hesitation. And the rest of us follow.

Dez's brow is set with a tense frown. I don't foresee any one of us sleeping tonight.

"It's settled, then. We keep making for Ángeles at first light."

For every league we travel, we sink into a different kind of denial.

Denial that we've lost the war to King Fernando and his justice. Denial that each and every one of us is going to end up like Lucia. For most of us, the worst the king could do was lock us up and torture our bodies. But that was before. The idea that our very magics are at stake—the core of who we are? It's unthinkable. And yet there's no other explanation for the memory I witnessed. Are they out there now using this weapon to find us? Justice Méndez's face floats in my vision as we move. His sharp cheekbones, his meticulously groomed black hair shot through with streaks of silver, and gray eyes that noticed everything. I have countless blank spots in my memory, but I could never forget him. The man who was both a captor and a father to me.

I fall back behind the group to compose myself. My heart races too quickly, my breath too sharp. Dez is far up ahead of me, but he hasn't spoken a full sentence since last night anyway. He still strides with the confidence of a general. Sometimes when I see him, his build, his posture, the way he walks, from this far off, I am reminded all over again of why we are all so willing to follow him, to listen to what he says. Even if we don't agree with him.

My heart would follow him anywhere. Especially in times as bleak as these.

"Perhaps it's a trick," Margo says to me as we make our way across dusty Via de Santos. "A way to draw us out of the Memoria Mountains. The king keeps Moria at his disposal as weapons, doesn't he? *Hypocrite bestae.*"

She's talking about the Hand of Moria. The way he keeps one of each of us, like a collection, for his own purposes, even while killing off or torturing the rest in droves. Four Moria stand behind his throne as a symbol of his conquest over us.

"I saw all the little incendiary saw," Esteban interjects, keeping his head low, hands gripping the straps of his pack. "Rodrigue's alman stone was well hidden. The justice did not expect him to escape."

I slow my pace, spirit as heavy as my boots. This morning's river crossing has left us with trench foot, but there's no stopping until we clear the last tollhouse that marks the end of Puerto Leones and beginnings of the Memoria Mountains—all that's left of what once was the great kingdom of Memoria. The army of Puerto Leones could never navigate the terrain on foot or horseback, but we know the hidden pass. Besides, the mountains are too arid and rocky to sustain our entire population, so they hold no value to the king. I would never tell the others, but I believe that is why the crown has not tried harder to break through the mountains. They've already taken everything they think has value.

Walking along these empty roads feels like trekking across the ghost of a country. I have lived in Ángeles for eight years. Ever since the Whispers' Rebellion failed to assassinate King Fernando. But where they succeeded was in rescuing their stolen children.

I wonder, how long have they been working on this weapon? Was the final straw Riomar? What if it started even before that, when I was a child at the palace? If I try to access the Gray, perhaps I could find out—

But what if I can't control all those memories? Innumerable sights, sounds, and emotions layered on top of my own. I don't know if I could bear it.

"Illan will know what to do," Sayida says after a long silence. She tries to stay close to me, but even she gets lost in thought. There's an emptiness to her words, like she hasn't yet convinced herself.

The way home feels still too far, and the two safe houses we know of on this route have shut their doors, leaving us in the sweltering heat.

The only way to quickly travel in broad daylight is to disguise ourselves as devout pilgrims, stowing our weapons out of sight of the tax farmers who collect from anyone traveling across the kingdom. We wear itchy black clothes and drape alder-wood prayer beads around our necks that symbolize the Father of Worlds.

The Memoria Mountains are a jagged dark promise on the horizon and the Via de Santos a winding dry road that will lead us there. Pilgrims and citizens of the kingdom stop before the mountain, at the Blessed Springs, whose baths and waterfalls are said to originate at the very body of water where the Father of Worlds emerged into being. We wait until nightfall and sneak past the tax farmers, who are drunk with coin and wine.

No matter how many steps we've taken, the mountains never feel closer. Hours later, under the naked sun, sweat drips down my neck and stings my stitched wound. Shouldering the weight of my pack is nearly unbearable, even with Dez emptying half the contents into his, but the only thing stronger than my pain is the fear of what I witnessed. Justice Méndez's threat: *We will find you.*

We come upon a hill crest where we're not the only others on the Via de Santos. A group of shepherds leers as our paths cross, their heads covered with white scarves to protect from the worst of the sun and dust. My heartbeat drums in my ears, louder than our boots crunching on the gravel path. Sayida quickly calls out a blessing to the Father of All, her musical voice and smile disarming them. They mumble a reply and turn their attention back to their sheep while our unit lapses into tense silence.

When the sun hovers over the mountains and the beginnings of sunset bleed into the sky, we come to a stop. There's nothing around but arid earth, yellow grass, and the via.

"Can you hear Illan?" Margo asks Esteban. Her beautiful, throaty voice sounds strange in the eerie stillness of the countryside, the soft whistling of dry grass along the edge of the road.

"I'm trying, but we're still too far," Esteban replies.

Illan's been training Esteban to hone his Ventári ability, how to use silver to heighten his power and stretch the range for communications so that the two of them can speak into each other's minds even from afar. Esteban twists his silver bracelet cuff and scrapes the back of his ear.

"Try again," Dez urges him, shouldering out of his pack. "He needs to know what Ren saw."

Esteban pinches the wide bridge of his nose and puts a hand up to silence us. He pulls back the hood of his cloak and undoes the clasp at his throat as though it chokes him. Then he stiffens.

I recognize the magics Esteban is working in the Ventári's stillness, his closed eyes and the tilt of his head, as if he's trying better to listen to the whisper coming from the faraway mountain.

"It's him," he says, his brown eyes drifting into the distance. "It's your father."

Esteban separates himself from the rest of us, seeking quiet so he can concentrate on Illan's thoughts moving through his own. I wonder what it's like to hear voices, *see* inside someone's mind, and then simply walk away, free.

"Are you sure?" Esteban asks, his dark eyes focused past us, on the horizon. Sometimes, when he's in a trance like this, he starts responding to his thoughts and it's like he's speaking to a ghost. "But— Yes, yes, of course."

By the way his brow furrows, Illan's instruction must not be what Esteban wants to hear. He sighs deeply and presses his palms against his face to shake himself from the headache that comes with such a use of his magics.

"Well, speak," Dez commands.

Esteban's eyes scan our faces—the life has drained from his. "We aren't going home."

"What?" I blurt out.

"Illan has ordered us not to return. To set up camp in the Forest of Lynxes," Esteban says, though he winces from what must be a terrible headache. "Hawk and Fox Units, and the elder council themselves, will rendezvous with us there in two days' time."

"The elders?" Sayida gasps.

Any doubt that the weapon was a trick is gone. The elders never leave the safety of the ruins. They preserve the history and traditions of the kingdom of Memoria. Why risk it now?

"Wouldn't it be best if we meet at the capital?" Margo asks.

Esteban shakes his head, his mouth set in a taut line. "The elders have word that the king's justice is raiding citadelas and villages near the mountain pass. Word of rebels setting fires in Esmeraldas has spread."

"Lies," Sayida spits.

"This is your doing, little incendiary," Margo mutters so only I can hear her.

"West is the safest option. I know the Forest of Lynxes," Dez says. "I named our unit for it. The goddess smiles down on us."

While Margo looks alight with our orders, Dez carries a new stiffness around his shoulders. I grip the coin he gave me and look at it, unable to shake the feeling that Dez is holding back. He snatches up his pack.

Marching away from the Via de Santos and into the field of dried grass to the west, Dez glances back, his familiar smile flashing across his face. "Come on, you rebel bestaes. You wanted a fight. Now we have one."

6

IN THE DEAD OF NIGHT, AND UNDER THE COVER OF TREES, THE WIND CHILLS down to the bones. A nervous quiet settles over our camp. We spread out our bedrolls around the fire pit for warmth and share what's left of the bread and salted dried meat in our packs. Sayida makes irvena tea and we sip it. Two days. We'll have *two* days to hide out in the Forest of Lynxes until the others come. So much could go wrong before then. Margo scouted ahead and returned with news that the neighboring towns of Sagradaterra and Aleja are also being raided. The Second Sweep has plastered my and Dez's likeness across markets with a reward.

Two days to not get caught.

Two days to replay everything that went wrong in Esmeraldas.

If only I'd been faster in finding the stone. If only I'd gotten the boy out before the soldier arrived. If only I had controlled my power better. If only I hadn't been distracted enough to let myself get wounded.

If only, if only, if only.

Sometimes I wonder if a person can have so much regret they'll drown in it.

At the memory of Celeste, of me reaching into her mouth for the alman stone, my food feels like coal going down my throat. I don't dare waste any, though, because who knows if we'll catch any game tomorrow. I swallow more water to help keep it down.

"How's your headache?" Sayida asks Esteban.

"Better. Instead of feeling like I took a mace to my skull, it feels like one of Dez's right hooks." He takes a swig from his flask. Dark eyes roam the canopy above, the trees that conceal the stars and give nest to all sorts of critters. He offers it to Sayida, who declines.

"You'll be able to see across far distances yet," Margo says, ripping bread with her fingers. She washes it down with her water-skin, giving him a broad smile. "Your duties as a postmate will be complete."

"I am *not* a glorified messenger," Esteban says, trying for dignified.

Sayida and Dez chuckle. I break off a piece of the hard goat's milk cheese and nibble at it. I'd like to tell Esteban that when he uses his power to contact Illan across leagues he appears to be talking to a ghost, but I wonder if he'd take that with the same humor as this. It's hard for me to insert myself in their conversations, so I remain quiet. I drink. I eat. It's so hot out we go through our water too soon, tapping the last drops onto parched tongues.

"We should rest early and refill our water reserves," Dez says, undoing his leather vest and tunic ties. Even though we've all seen each other in various stages of undress while out on missions, I look away from him. "I'll lay some traps."

"For the guards or for our breakfast?" Margo asks.

He flashes a cocky smile. "Both."

"I don't care for the taste of guards," Sayida says, wrinkling her nose.

"I hope the Hawk Unit brings a jar of pickled peppers," Esteban says dreamily.

"Not if Costas eats them before he gets here," I say. When we're back home, one of the youngest Whispers, Costas, is known for eating everything in sight. Only Sayida chuckles, and Dez gives me a pitying smile.

"Esteban, Margo, will you refill the waterskins?" Dez asks.

"I can do that," I say. I get up, dust crumbs from my hands.

"You're wounded, Ren. Let us help you," Dez says, and I wish he wouldn't look at me the way he does—as if I'm fragile and breakable. I should remind him that I'm supposed to be a shadow in the night and all of those things he called me in Esmeraldas.

Margo lets out a tiny grumble for my benefit, but she and Esteban gather the empty waterskins. He lights an oil lamp, and they head off into the dark. The rush of the river is loud enough to find, and the ground of this forest is easier to traverse than yesterday.

While Dez takes his ropes and iron traps into the forests, Sayida and I wipe mud and dust from our packs. Even when something doesn't belong to us, we help each other this way. Living with the Whispers was different than my time in the palace. I learned to share, even when I didn't want to. I learned that if we all spent the same amount of time cleaning our rooms and our training weapons, we'd get everything done faster. It was supposed to teach us how to be a family, regardless of blood. But part of me can't connect. As I dump out the dirty water, I wonder why I keep trying.

I wash my face and clean my teeth with the gritty paste that staves off gum rot and bad breath. The water is ice cold, but I rub the towel along my bare arms until my skin is red. Sometimes it's like I'll never feel clean. Unraveling my hair from the tight braid releases some of the tension at my temples.

"You could join me if you feel restless," Sayida offers.

She sits close to the fire and meditates to keep her emotions balanced. The elders encourage all Moria to do this, but I hate having so much time with my thoughts. Her hands are loose at her sides, fingertips dug just into the earth like she's drawing power from it.

I shake my head, but realize she can't see me. "Another time."

A low whistle coming from the trees signals Dez's approach. Relief unwinds the muscles of my shoulders, and I let go of a small anxious breath when he comes into full view. He's undone the laces of his tunic down to his sternum. He grins when he catches me staring, then nods, eyes sweeping over our camp.

"Are Esteban and Margo still gone?" he asks suggestively.

Sayida lifts one eye at him, her smile lazy like a cat's. "Let them be."

"On the contrary," Dez says, shooting a wink in my direction. "I only worry one of them might make the other smile."

He takes his position at the edge of our campsite, leaning against a roblino tree like a sentry, his stolen sword staked in the ground at his feet. He told me once that the Forest of Lynxes was his favorite place for how green the leaves always were, the trees with bark so thick they retained water and could be drained of sweet sap. Long ago, lynxes roamed this forest, but they were hunted so much that the creatures haven't been seen in a decade. It's why Dez chose to name us Lynx Unit.

The campfire crackles and sparks, warming my skin as the sun sets, bringing out a chill in the air. I think of the brush of Dez's thumb on my cheek, the easy curve of his lips, the gold flecks in his eyes. When I realize Dez is staring at me, something in me wants to leap forward. I wrench my gaze away and busy my hands with wrapping the rest of the cured meat in waxed paper and stoppering a bottle of olive oil and throwing another log in the roaring fire. I look at anything but him because I know a person can never really belong to another—I should know it better than anyone. And yet, when Dez looks at me the way he just did, I want to believe he could be mine.

Suddenly, Sayida is leaning into my ear, her meditation over. "We should change our unit name to Squirrel Unit. Instead of walnuts, our commander collects swords and daggers."

Despite my best efforts, I laugh. "I don't believe our commander would appreciate being compared to a furry rodent."

"That boy would let you call him anything, and you know it." Her voice is low and conspiratorial among the chitter of night birds and insects. "Should we find out?"

I gently shove her away, but the movement still sends pinpricks of pain up my stiff arms. "Be serious, Sayida."

She laughs in reply, the music of it is a beautiful thing.

"What's so funny?" Margo asks.

She and Esteban drop the swollen waterskins in a heap, then settle in for the night. Margo's lips appear puffy, and Esteban's tunic is inside out.

"I was just reminiscing about Ángeles," Sayida says, fighting back a grin.

"Soon we'll take back the lands of Memoria and you won't have to reminisce," Margo says. The fervor of her words brings an end to our silly gossip.

"If we survive at all," Esteban says.

"Always the optimist," Dez says. "Tell us, Margo, does he at least smile when he kisses you?"

Esteban grabs a flat stone and throws it at Dez, who doesn't move at all as the rock misses. I draw my knees closer to my chest, but unless I walk off into the forest, I can't escape this conversation.

Margo leans forward across her bedroll to me. "Tell us, *Ren*, does Dez ever stay quiet long enough to kiss *you*?"

A hot sensation starts at my sternum and spreads across my chest. I glance at Dez. He does delight in being the center of attention. Maybe it's the impending attack we have ahead of us, or Margo is in a particularly good mood, but I don't feel on the fringe of their teasing this time.

"Dez has never been quiet in his life," I say, matching her playful tone.

He winks at me, and everyone falls into an easy laughter. It's better than thinking about what's happening at the palace or what this weapon is or what would happen if the king and justice use it everywhere from the populated citadelas to the tiniest hamlet. What if they already have? What if that's the real reason the justice set fire to Esmeraldas? What if we're too late?

I snap out of it when Margo lays claim to all the sugar bread the moment we're back at the Ángeles ruins. This time, Esteban doesn't suggest our demise. Instead, he offers his flask to me. I hate the smell of it but take a swig of the aguadulce anyway. It's so cold it tastes like ice water at first. Then it burns going down, leaving behind the slightest taste of flowers. I pass it around, and even Sayida takes the barest sips.

The chatter turns to things everyone misses from their childhood, and the drink burns even worse when it comes back around. Dez fishes in his pack for a set of his favorite ivory dice. He and Margo take turns rolling them, using their pocketknives, bootstraps, and pesitos as wagers. Esteban doesn't play, because he doesn't like to lose. But we watch and take sides and share this brief moment of joy.

I think about how we are joined by the magics we were born with. It is the one thing that unifies us and makes us Moria in a world where our ancestral lands have been swallowed whole. When Memoria was first annexed, Moria families settled all over Puerto Leones. We were meant to become Leonesse, but our magics would always set us apart. Illan says that there was peace for a time. Esteban's family settled in the tropical south of Crescenti. Sayida's family never left their roots in Zahara. Margo's people were fishermen in Riomar. Dez and I were both born near the capital. I can't miss a place that I betrayed, can I?

"Are you ever afraid of who you'll be when this war is over?" Esteban asks, lying on his back. His long fingers drum on his abdomen. "What if we win, but this weapon gets into the wrong hands? Worse than King Fernando. What if we cut the head off the lion but it doesn't change anything?"

Margo rolls her eyes while Sayida replies, "Can you let us dream a little, Esteban?"

A sad smile tugs at his mouth, but he quiets. I wish I could admit that I share his worries, but I decide it best to keep them to myself.

"Tell me more about your dreams, Sayida," Dez says, punctuating his words with a wink. "Am I in them?"

Esteban frowns and Margo nearly chokes on her aguadulce while Sayida throws her head back to laugh. "Of *course* you are. I've composed many songs about you."

Dez perks up at that, though none of us believe it. "Sing us a song, Sayida."

We beg her enough that she relents. There is one thing Sayida would never part with, and that's her small guitar. It's red wood with golden paint that's chipped away over time. She strums and twists ivory knobs to tune the strings. When Sayida sings about a love lost, we all fall silent. It could be anyone. Friends, parents, siblings, partners. Her soft alto voice wraps around my heart and squeezes. Tears gleam on Esteban's face, and eventually, he closes his eyes and falls asleep. Margo follows.

"That was beautiful—thank you, Sayida," I say.

She wraps her guitar in its red cloth, then slips it into a leather pouch. She curls onto her side and whispers, "Buonanocte."

I echo it, but I'm keenly aware of Dez watching me from across the fire as I settle into my bedroll, too. Like most nights, sleep doesn't come. When the campfire is nothing but red burning coal and snores join the serenade of night animals, I tug on my boots. With the oil lamp in my hand, I walk away from the campsite and down to the river.

"Are you deserting, Ren?" Dez's voice, teasing, comes from behind.

I turn, seeing nothing but trees. The silhouettes of moss hanging from crooked tree branches move like the ghosts in my mind. No Dez. And yet—I can feel him. I don't know how, but I can. Even if we were in a crowded city, I could pick him out from thousands.

"You know me better than that," I say. Straining my senses, I think I detect a small shift of dark against dark. My oil lamp is a tiny flicker, no better than a firefly here. The metal handle squeaks. The next step I take crunches on dead leaves and rocks.

"I thought I taught you to be stealthier." His voice floats to me from somewhere behind a thicket of alder trees. "You'll wake the dead with that heavy tread of yours."

"A heavy tread for a heavy heart." I wait a beat, then I lunge, ready to grab him. Instead, I grab a fistful of air.

"Share your burden with me, Ren."

"I can't."

I feel him move in the dark, the slightest breeze in my hair. There's leather and the bitter scent of smoke that has seeped into our clothes. He's right behind me, but I don't turn. He wraps his arms around me. My heart jolts like a stroke of lightning, right down to my belly button, as Dez's warmth is at my back. Every time, it's always the same—a spark that singes straight through me.

"Maybe you're not as good a teacher as you think considering you fell asleep during your own watch."

"I was thinking with my eyes closed." His chuckle is muffled as he lets go, and a chill tickles my skin where his hands just were. "Besides, I set traps, remember?"

For the first time I realize there's a blanket rolled under his arm. "What's this?"

"I thought you might get cold." He threads his fingers through mine. My desire to be alone with my thoughts wars with my need to be with Dez.

In the flickering shadows of my oil lamp, I can make out his sharp jaw and a week's worth of stubble that makes him look older than he is. The worry mark on his forehead is prominent, and for a moment, I have a tiny bit of insight into the man he could be one day. A great man. A beloved leader. Mine.

Then his smile is gone, and the weight of what's to come hangs heavy between us.

"Why are you out here?" he whispers, stepping so close I feel his warmth radiating.

I keep walking along the river, knowing if we're approaching one of his traps, he'll warn me. "You know I can't sleep. I thought you'd be used to it by now."

"You always surprise me, Ren," he says, and manages to look boyish when he smiles. "Like today. It was the first time this trip I didn't think you, Margo, and Esteban would rip one another's throats out."

I laugh, and a bird answers. "They're afraid. Fear makes people do things they normally wouldn't. Like share a drink with someone they despise."

"Things like take long walks in the dark?" he offers.

We stop near the riverbank on a flat stretch of grass. The half-moon above makes the rushing river look like a shot of silver cleaving a path across the rocky forest. I set the oil lamp on a small boulder, and he smooths out the blanket. We sit side by side facing the running water.

"I know these woods better than any of the king's guard," I say. "Better than you, even."

He takes my gloved hand in his. "You've never told me that."

"I was born just outside of here. It's been so long, but I think I could find my way home. If there was a home to return to."

He sighs, eyes full of sympathy. "I'm sorry. It can't be easy for you when we reminisce about our parents."

What do I remember of them? I know my father used to hunt in the Forest of Lynxes. I can't picture his face, but sometimes when I look in the mirror, I remember a voice that says, *You look like him, you know.* But I'm not always sure if it's my mother's voice or someone else's.

"Can I tell you something terrible?" I say.

He sits up to face me, his eyes searching and waiting for me to speak. Part of me wants to take back the question, because I don't want to say it aloud.

"When I hear others talk about their parents, the first person that comes to mind is Justice Méndez."

Dez averts his eyes, a deep frown in his brow, but his words are soft. "That man took you from your home. He used you—"

"As a weapon," I say, taking his face in my hands. "I know. I thank the goddess every day that the Whispers came for me. Who would I be if I had never left? A monster. A killer."

"You would still be Renata Convida." He presses a kiss on my jaw, then pulls back to watch me blush, even in the dark. "You would still be my Ren."

"I don't know that. All I know is that he's connected to this weapon. And I can't *ever* see him again, or I don't know what I'd do."

My heart is racing as Dez pulls me close. Everything about him is warm. "You won't ever have to do that. I promise. I'll kill him myself. For you. For everything he's done. I will end the Arm of Justice."

I don't want to turn Dez into a vengeful thing. Besides, if Justice Méndez was gone, one of his underling judges would be waiting to take the title.

"That isn't what I want for you." I brush his hair from his eyes. Maybe it's because we've grown up together and fought side by side that I know him better than I know myself, but there's something there. I've had this feeling wedged beneath my skin since we received our orders to hide in this forest. His promise to kill Méndez has a certainty none of our other missions have. It's like he knows something we don't. "You've been holding something back since we recovered the alman stone."

"I have," he says. "What you saw in the alman stone—" He starts, then stops, raking his fingers through his hair before trying again. "This weapon has the potential to expose all Moria. My father couldn't believe the king was capable of that kind of alchemy. Hells,

I didn't want to believe it either. How long have they been developing it? How many have they tested it on? Every time I let myself think about it I want to set the capital ablaze once again."

Our silence spins like a spider's web between us. There's the rush of the river nearby, the cry of night birds, and the thud of my heart, all competing to be heard.

"How much do you really know about it?" I ask.

Dez makes a guttural sound of frustration, and for the first time I see the true fear in his eyes. "They say it started as a 'cure.' Or that's what *they* called it. A way to control us by removing our power."

A "cure." For our magics. Our souls.

"How will we know what to look for when we're in the palace?" I ask.

He turns to face the pitch-dark path that leads back to our camp. He's avoiding my stare, and I know that when his mind is set, even I can't change it. But that won't stop me from trying. "I have a plan. The king and the Bloodied Prince will never suspect us."

There's always venom in his voice at the mention of the prince. The cruelty of the royal family knows no bounds, not even from one another. King Fernando usurped the crown from his own father. Prince Castian is said to have drowned his younger brother in the river that cuts behind the palace. His mother, Queen Penelope, was so inconsolable that she died of heartsickness. Over time, the stories have been changed, twisted, exaggerated, excused. But one story remains the same: For the centuries the Fajardos have ruled, Puerto Leones has grown bigger, stronger, richer, but it has never known peace.

I rest my hands on Dez's arms. I want to tell him that I feel just as helpless as he does, that we'll find a way to fight back against these evil men, but I can't seem to get the words out. A memory lifts from my troubled mind. *Delicate hands trace the length of a man's naked chest. His eyes stare back with a look I can't quite name.* I take a sharp breath and push away the stolen image and Dez at the same time.

"What is it?" he asks.

I crawl to my feet and move a few paces toward the river. My heart rattles in my chest. I should have my mind under control by now. Why won't the memories stay back? If this keeps happening, it'll be Esmeraldas all over again. This is too important.

"I'm a liability, Dez. I can't go on the mission."

He looks back as if I've slapped him. "Ren—"

"It's one thing if I could fight, but I'm injured. I'll put you in danger."

"You won't have to fight." He grips my shoulders. His eyes skim past me to the dark water. Why won't he look at me when he says this? "But your Robári gift is useful."

"There's something *wrong* with my power, Dez."

"You can't keep blaming yourself for what happened to that boy," he says. "Any of us would have gone into that house to save him."

I shake my head and scoff. The words tear through me, angry and bright. "Can you honestly tell me that any of the others would be sorry to see such a weapon turned on me?"

"Is that what's had you so upset?"

"*Yes.*" I couldn't quite parse my feelings until now, but now that I've said it I can't unthink it.

"Don't ever say that," he says, anger sharpening his voice. "Don't ever think that."

But how can Dez understand? How can he begin to know what it's like to have curses follow you everywhere, a sibilant kind of guilt? To watch horror dawn on people's faces when they realize that standing before them is the reason that their father is gone, their sister is dead, their child was taken?

Dez is beloved by the Whispers. The son of Illan, leader of the rebellion against King Fernando. Dez is the one who dared fight Prince Castian in Riomar. We lost the citadela, but Dez and Margo blew up their reserves and allowed for the Moria of the citadela to escape with their lives on stolen ships. Dez is the one who protects his people with his every act.

I shake out of his grip. I have to go—somewhere, anywhere.

"Stay," he says quickly, softly. "Stay with me, Ren."

My body betrays me and I stop. My eyes burn with unshed tears. Fear digs into my bones at the uncertainty, the cruelty, of the mission that's to come. But the anguish in my chest is because of Dez, because I want to stay. Dez wouldn't use his Persuári magics to compel me. It's a crime among our people. I'd be able to sense it. That kind of magic is warm against the skin and makes his voice metallic like bells.

This need to be near him and forget everything else is simply *us*. He's too free with his heart and I shut down because deep down I know I don't deserve to have this kind of happiness. The sight of him warps my thoughts; his voice is like an anchor weighing me down. Sometimes, when I'm alone, I wonder if I've stayed with the Whispers for the rebellion, to restore the kingdom of Memoria, to find peace. Or if I've stayed for him.

Perhaps they are the same thing in the end.

"I know you have your doubts about your power," he continues in a low voice, as though he's afraid he'll startle me away into the forest, "but I have never doubted you. I know we will win this war, Ren."

"I don't know if I'm built to keep fighting like you," I say, and speaking the words feels like pulling a cord out of my heart. "Sometimes I think I was built to be used and nothing more."

He takes two steps forward, and his hands rest on my shoulders, careful not to disturb the bandage over my wound. The touch shocks me into stillness. His hands trail down my arms, and there is nowhere to look but the endless gold of his eyes.

"Renata." There is no emotion in the word—no hint of pleading or passion or fury. It's just my name, like a final wish. "You're the strongest person I know. I'll prove it to you."

His hands slide down to my wrists, to the very edge of my gloves, and suddenly my heart is wilder than the rush of the river as he waits for me to say yes.

Slowly, I nod.

He tugs off my gloves one by one.

Instinctively, I curl my fingers into a ball, trying to hide my scars, the scars I've gained from every memory I've stolen, the evidence of my thievery. He unfurls my hands, presses our palms together. His hands are almost twice as big as mine and marked not by magics, but by the kiss of steel. I shut my eyes and memorize the calluses of his palms. He closes the distance between us, until all I have to do is tilt my head up to feel his lips against mine. He leans down, his mouth grazing my ear. He leads one of my hands to his face.

His temple. "Take a memory."

My eyes fly open. "I knew you were reckless—"

"I've never claimed to be anything but," he says playfully.

My words are a staccato, breathless whisper. "Something is wrong with my power, I told you. I've been away from Illan's training for too long."

"Let me help you, then." Suddenly, the play is gone, replaced with a vulnerable thing that feels breakable. "I trust you. I know you."

"Dez."

"You're not the only one whose nightmares won't let them sleep." He brushes a thumb over my cheekbone. "Please."

I wonder if he can feel my heart racing. That's the thing, isn't it? I want him so much I stay away, out of fear of hurting him. If I touched him, and my power got ahold of me. If I injure him. If I break the connection too soon. If I drain every memory. If I make him forget me. There are so many *ifs* that flood my mind. But I don't move away from him. I sink into his hold around my waist, trace my fingertips along his forehead.

"It'll hurt," I warn. "During and after."

He shivers against me. "I know."

The raised scars that trace the pads of my fingers heat up, as if there's a fire ignited from within. He's never seen me use my power this way, just the aftermath of it when it goes wrong. Dez's eyes widen at the sight of my hands, at the light that races along my palms. What startles me most of all is that look on his face. Not fear but wonder.

No one has ever looked at me this way.

"How does this work?" he asks. "Do they all go into the Gray?"

I shake my head. "The Gray is my own creation, I think. I've never known another Robári long enough to compare. But most of my memories up until I was nine are locked in there."

"Why nine?"

"That's when the Whispers burned down the old palace. That's when I met you." I press my hand over his heart and smile when I feel how fast his pulse is. "This memory wouldn't be locked away. It would just be mine."

The wrinkle on his forehead deepens, but he holds on to me tighter. His voice is nearly pleading. "Do it."

And I do.

I reach for his temples and take hold. He gasps through the pain, hissing when his skin burns under my glowing touch. I'm an intruder, breaking down the walls of his past. But Dez is all too willing to let me in now, and I dive into the vivid memory he offers.

Even the sea is on fire.

Ships break apart and sink beneath dark waves.

Bells ring from the cathedrals.

Bodies are draped across gray stone streets, their blood running between the cobblestones like rivers searching for a way back to the ocean.

He knows he shouldn't be there. The Whispers have retreated. Riomar has been lost. But he has one last thing to do.

Dez stumbles over the dead. He can't tell the broken bodies apart. He's searching for familiar faces. He hears his name, a strangled cry from a man trying to keep his insides from spilling out. General Almonte. The man who taught him how to wield a sword. Now Almonte's gray beard is streaked with blood. He shuts his eyes, and then he's gone.

Dez looks up at the darkening sky, but he cannot scream. Everything within him is numb. The purple-and-gold flag with the Fajardo crest of Puerto Leones is being raised in front of the palace. Up on the balcony is a sight that splinters his vision. Prince Castian watches Riomar descend into chaos. People ravage the dead like vultures, seizing the Moria's jewelry, weapons, armor. Desecrating bodies. The prince just stands there taking in his victory. Hate and anger surge through Dez, propelling his body into a run. He climbs the carved walls of the palace, his hands caked in dirt and blood and sweat. There is still one thing he can do to end this.

Kill the prince. Kill the prince. Kill the prince.

Dez lands on the balcony with heavy boots.

Prince Castian's long golden hair is matted to his face. A tender bruise blooms on his high cheekbone like spoiled fruit, his full lips split open and bloody. He's still in his chain mail, though it's been hours since the Moria forces, what's left of them, retreated from the citadela.

His blue eyes light up with fury as he realizes he's not alone. But he does not call for his guards or for help. He unsheathes his sword and walks across the balcony.

"Run home, boy," he spits to the side. He levels those cold eyes of his at Dez's still-approaching figure. He's tired and injured. It must be why he gives Dez a chance to leave. "Do you have a death wish?"

"I do," Dez says, rage strangling his words. "Yours."

Prince Castian swings his sword first, and Dez raises his to meet it, the clash of metal drowned by the ringing of the bells. The crackle of fire. The cries of the dying down below. The revelers.

Each blow strikes Dez, rattles him down to the bone. The prince is stronger than he looks when parading on campaigns. His footwork fast, like he can predict each and every move Dez makes. Dez's arms are growing tired, but he pushes through the fire in his muscles, the sting of sweat and blood in his eyes. He draws the prince's blood, slicing across his cheek. Castian hisses. For a prince, he seems too accustomed to bleeding.

There's a loud **boom** *as one of the ships blows up in the water. It draws the princeling's attention long enough for Dez to ram into him with every ounce of strength he has left. They hit the ledge of the balcony. Castian's*

85

sword goes over and down into the pit below. Fighting. Fire. Screams. Singing. Somewhere, on a night like this, someone is singing. Dez inhales the scorched air. Blood is like rusted iron filling his mouth when he breathes. He cannot let go of the prince, and he cannot throw him over without killing them both. But isn't that why he walked all the way back there?

Castian slams his face into Dez's. Pain flares through his nose. He shakes his head, but the night stars and fire of the city spin in front of him. He's too weak to call on his magics, and in his hesitation, the prince recovers. Using his fists, punching and smashing Dez's face like a common river rat. He drives his knee into Dez's chest. Dez's hands are too slick, and his sword slips through his fingers. Pitch-black flashes. Dez falls. Can't breathe. The balcony tiles are slippery. It's begun to rain. The air is thick with it. He tries to turn around.

"You should have gone home," Castian says, his voice distant.

I am home, Dez thinks, but he cannot get his body to breathe.

Air scrapes through his throat. He crawls on hands and knees to the glint of his sword. His hand is around the hilt, and he staggers to his feet. Castian lets out a growl. Dez lunges and strikes true. Castian's eyes flare with surprise. Dez's blade pierces the weak break in the prince's armor just beneath the breastplate, while a sharp sensation stabs him at his side.

They are a mirror image, falling to their knees. Dez grabs the prince's throat and the prince does the same.

*They will bleed and choke together and be the ruin of one
another, but he will end this.*

"Ren," Dez gasps.

*Castian's hold on Dez slips, but he grabs hold of the
copper pendant around Dez's neck, so tight the leather
cord breaks. His eyes are confused and full of rage, then
they move past Dez. Whatever the prince sees makes him
falter. For the first time, Dez sees fear on his face.*

"Andrés!" comes a strained, familiar voice.

"Father?" Dez cries.

I gasp for air, pulling my hands from Dez's temples as the
memory fades into black. I crawl on top of the blanket, breathing
hard. Dez rolls onto his back, and both of us stare, breathless, up at
the sky. The wound on my neck pulses with a sharp ache.

"You were right," he groans. "It hurts."

I turn my face toward him, and I press my hand on his chest to
feel the seed of his heartbeat. "I didn't know you went back. You
almost died!"

"But I didn't. No one knows." He presses his hand over mine.
The brush of his thumb across my new scars helps the dull pain
to fade. "Except my father and his apprentice Javi. When they saw
I left the caravan, they doubled back for me. The Príncipe Dorado
finally called his guards and we barely got out of there."

"Thank Our Lady." The strain of his injuries from that fight
settles into me. I can still feel his helplessness, the fear that he would
die and the last person he would see was someone he hated.

"That was the day we lost the last stronghold of the kingdom of
Memoria."

"Memoria was lost half a century ago, Dez."

"I know," he says softly, regret in his voice. "Some part of me hoped our allies would come to our aid, to stop Puerto Leones from seizing total control of the continent. But no one came. We fight alone."

"Why give me that memory now?"

"You're afraid that you might have to face Justice Méndez again. I'm terrified that I won't be strong enough to do what needs to be done. That I'll fail like I did that day. I wanted you to know that."

"You said my name."

"I wanted to come back to you."

Instead of letting go, I curl my fingers around the front of his tunic and give a light tug. Nothing can stop the smile creeping across my lips as he pushes off the ground and slides on top of me, bracing his weight on his forearms, his knees resting between my legs. There's a nervous flutter along my skin. As his fingers frame my face, gently brushing my tangle of hair away from my neck, I wonder if I feel the need for him more now because I possess a part of him I can never give back. When I close my eyes I can hear Dez speak my name, and then Illan coming to rescue his son. The horror on Castian's face when he realizes he's outnumbered.

"Andrés?" I say. I love the weight of his true name on my lips.

"Only my father calls me that." He chuckles and lowers his nose into the crook of my neck. My skin sings as he stops his lips before they touch. "Don't tell anyone."

"Why?"

He draws back to meet my gaze. "It never suited me."

I brush the stubble along his jaw. I remember a few years ago, when he could barely grow it out. His soft lips brush my knuckles. His mouth is like warm, wet dew on my skin. My left hand trembles, and Dez takes hold of it. My fingers open up for him like rose petals for the sun. He kisses the inside of my wrist. The center of my palm. The whorls and pads of my fingers. The tingle—the ache of it—is almost too much.

He kisses my lips once, then draws back. I remember the first time I stole a kiss from him in the grove behind our ruins two years ago. We've traded kisses in secret, during moments we thought we were going to die and because we didn't. He's kissed me in the rain when I ran away. I kissed him when I stayed. Our lives were forged together by fire. Sometimes I'm afraid that fire has never left me.

My back arches as I return Dez's kiss with a fury I've kept locked inside. I hardly know where to put my hands. All I know is that I want to touch every part of him. I push up the hem of his tunic and let my fingers trace a jagged scar along his ribs where the Bloodied Prince's blade nearly killed him. He hisses from surprise, his muscles tightening at my touch, but doesn't stop kissing me and instead the pressure of his body on mine tells me how much he wants me. I undo the button of his pants and even though he whispers my name, he pulls away.

The absence of him, even for this moment, hurts. There's that smile of his, crooked as the summer day is long. I push his tunic halfway up, but he pulls it off and discards it to the side. The cool breeze rustles the dark waves of his hair.

"We should go back," he says breathlessly.

"We should stay," I say. I unbutton my shirt down the center.

His finger hovers over the injured curve of my neck. "I don't want to hurt you."

"Then don't. Just once I would like to kiss you when we're not waiting for imminent death."

"Is that not what we do every day?"

"You know what I mean."

"We will have that. I want to make a better world for you. For all of us."

"In the meantime," I say, and continue undoing the brass buttons of my trousers and then his. "We have this forest and each other."

He shuts his eyes and makes a sound I've never heard him make before. Under the half-moon I can count the muscles on his back as he positions himself in front of me. He kisses the bare skin of my stomach. The crosshatch of scars from fighting side by side. I used to hate the marks on my skin, but it is the one thing that makes me feel like I am part of the Whispers, part of Dez. His fingers hook around the waistband of my trousers and tug them down. Hands squeeze my thighs and I gasp from how good it feels to be touched this way by him.

"I love you, Renata," he says, haloed by the moon. "I need you to know that."

I know it. I think I've known it for a while. I wanted to blame it on the stress of facing our enemies, of not knowing whether or not we'd live to see each other again. People consume each other when they're afraid, don't they? But I know this is real.

I love you, too, I want to say, but I can't. A cord in my heart snaps. I pull on his arms to come back up to me, so I can return his reverent kisses, run my fingers through the dark waves of his hair. His grin is wicked as he kisses the inside of my knee.

"Andrés," I whisper.

I may know little else, in the chaos of this world. But I know this for sure, something I couldn't put into words until now. I love this boy and I would do anything to keep him safe. I'll face my past if I have to. When Dez pushes one of my knees aside, I am sure we are bonded together by more than blood and loss. We are as inevitable as the dawn.

7

Dez falls asleep nestled against my chest, his tunic and pants rolled under my head as a pillow. I thread my fingers around his soft black curls. He mutters and moans in his sleep. I wonder what he's dreaming about. My body is wide-awake even though I'm perfectly at ease. Were we reckless? No, because we both drink the tea all spies in our rank take if they want to prevent pregnancy. But now I'm left wondering what comes next. Sharing your fears with someone else changes things. At some point today the other units will arrive and we will have to be soldiers. That's the only way we can get through it all and make a better world together.

I trust you, he said. Since leaving Esmeraldas he's been different in a way I can't explain. Is it my own nerves that I'm projecting? I dig for the token he gave me. Affection. Presents. Dez has always given me these things. But tonight, it almost feels like he was trying to fit a lifetime of love into a few moments. Maybe in his heart he doesn't believe we're going to survive the attack on the capital.

The thought needles at me as I turn the copper coin in my fingers. I think of the moment the prince ripped it from Dez's chest. A terrible shiver puckers the skin of my arms when I remember the cold edge of the prince's blade. Dez almost died, but he didn't leave that balcony without his family heirloom. I trace my thumb over the stamp. Who was the woman minted on one side? Only the Fajardo men grace the kingdom's currency. I don't wear it. That feels like the kind of promise we shouldn't make until after. . . . I pocket the coin and try to let sleep take me.

Despite the calm of the forest just before dawn, the running river, and the steady beat of his heart, Dez's sleep is fitful. He moans again, turning away from me and onto his back. His features are softened by the pale early morning light, but when I press my palm to his chest, I feel the thrum of his heart, the way his muscles jerk as if he's trapped in a nightmare.

Back in Ángeles, the nights are often filled with recruits' sobs as they relive memories of sorrow and death in their dreams. The cloisters we use as a stronghold are drafty, and the sounds carry through their long halls. Sometimes, I'd listen to those sounds all night, and in the morning I'd know to expect poor souls asking me to take away the moment that haunts them. Often, I'd do it out of a sense of duty or a desire to be liked. Perhaps if I steal the memories I helped create, I'll be absolved of my past. Perhaps if I crowd my thoughts with so many strangers, I'll forget my own damage. But it doesn't help, so I've started to say no, and they leave cursing my name.

I give Dez a shake to wake him from whatever has him so fitful, but he chokes on air. He mutters words I can't make out and then whimpers. I know that terrible feeling of being trapped in your own mind, as if you're being suffocated from within.

I know you, Dez told me. *I trust you.*

I brush my fingers along his face, so familiar that I don't need the sun to break over us to see where I'm going. I want to soothe him the way being around him makes me feel more at ease. I press my fingertips to his temple.

The connection is instant, the way it always is when a person is unconscious. A rush of emotion hits my chest that comes with being in a different mind, the blinding light and sting that spreads from my fingertips to my skull.

But what I find isn't a single memory, but a cluster of them. A sequence of thoughts that replay over and over:

> *Dez, five years old, plays with a great black hound that licks his face. He collapses into the grass, and they both howl like wild things.*

> *Dez in the kitchens of San Cristóbal steals an orange behind Cook Helena's back. The sweet, tangy juice drips down his chin.*

> *An older Dez watches the port city of Riomar, his eyes focus on the purple-and-gold flag of Puerto Leones that waves above a ship's sail.*

> *Dez strides toward a girl polishing her daggers in a clearing. She holds one up to the light, then sees his reflection in it. She turns around, and his heart quickens as she smiles. Her brown eyes alight with something warm and familiar.*

Gently, I break the connection between us, and I lie back on the scratchy blanket beside him, giving my magics a rest, and my mind a moment to catch up with all the memories as they are absorbed into it. Giving myself a second to realize—Dez is dreaming of me.

I am the girl with the warm brown eyes. The girl smiling when she looks back at him. I brush a lock away from his shut eyes. He's dreaming of *me*. In a clearing somewhere, my hair short from when I cut it two years ago. I search for the memory of polishing my blades, but I can't find it. Why would he choose that one out of all our time together? My own memories are always the hardest, and most painful, to uncover.

Who am I supposed to be if I can easily recall the past life of a stranger but not my own?

Feeling the steady rise and fall of his chest beside me, I allow myself to drift off to sleep. My eyes flutter shut for a blissful moment, until a shrill scream pierces the dawn.

Dez rockets awake, and we are both up. He takes in his surroundings, as if he's forgotten where he was. I throw his clothes at him and fumble with the laces of my boots. The shouting is coming from our campsite. I make to speak, but he presses a finger to his lips.

My hand goes to my hip. My dagger. Dez shakes his head because I'm sure he's thinking the same thing. All of our weapons are around the fire.

Then we're running, my blood pumping in my veins like the roar of the river. We weave through the forest until we're near our camp, dodging between the thick trees, though it's hard to remain quiet when the ground is littered with branches. We come to a stop behind a mossy mound where the thick, fallen trunk next to our campsite provides a barrier.

A young man is slumped against the dirt, nursing a bloodied foot. Dez's metal trap is beside him. He must've been left behind. He looks up at us with narrow eyes and opens up his mouth to scream, but Dez knocks him out with a punch to the face. The boy slumps to the side, unconscious.

Dez signals to me to stay hidden with a squeeze of my forearm. We keep low and listen. The voices are unfamiliar, barking orders I can't quite make out. Was it Sayida who screamed? I don't hear them fighting back. If they're screaming, they're still alive. If they're not—

I raise myself just over the tree trunk, digging my fingers into the soft earth for support.

We should've been alert.

We should've been there.

From my vantage point, I make out three royal soldiers who have Margo, Sayida, and Esteban on their knees, their wrists bound behind them. Sayida's eyes are closed. Esteban's lips move as if in prayer. Margo spits on the set of leather boots in front of her.

A ripple of anticipation circles the guards as a fourth man walks into camp. With all the stolen memories in my head, strangers' faces often blur and bleed into my thoughts, as if everyone I meet is somehow familiar.

But I immediately know *this* man.

I have Dez's fresh memory of him swimming in the forefront of my mind.

I shoot back down and lean into Dez's ear, uttering one word. "Castian." Then return to my position.

While I've only seen the prince's face through stolen memories, there's no mistaking his young bright eyes, that taunting smile and hard jawline. His long golden hair falls like a lion's mane against his shoulders. He wears less armor than his men, the leather dyed a red so deep he looks like a bleeding wound. He dons leather gloves with a ring of gold spikes around the knuckles. The spikes glint in the morning light as he points toward the river.

"Find them," he orders. "He can't have gone far."

Two of the soldiers bow their heads to him before sprinting toward the water.

Dez tugs the hem of my tunic and pulls me down. With our backs against the dirt mound, he squeezes my hand in his.

"I'll cause a distraction," he whispers. "Free the others."

I grab him by the wrist. "No. You're unarmed."

He turns back to me with a grin, and for a moment I have a fool's hope that he'll stay. We'll make a plan together. But I know him better than that.

"Not for long."

His grin disappears as he threads his fingers through my hair and pulls me against him. His lips find mine, pressing urgently, parting them slightly. I kiss him back, but it's over so swiftly I can hardly breathe.

"Dez—"

"Trust *me*," he whispers, voice ragged. He takes the sword from the unconscious soldier. And then he's gone, melting into the forest like one of its shadows.

I chance one last glance over the fallen trunk and watch Dez prowl through the forest, silent as a lynx.

Castian stands in front of Sayida, his lips obscured by his hair, but even from here I can hear him shout, "Where is Dez?"

The remaining guard's mistake is standing too close to a tree. He's young. Probably recently drafted. Dez slips out of the shadow behind him. I brace myself, swallowing deep breaths to ready myself to jump over this mound and scramble to the camp where our weapons lie in a pile. *Free the others.*

I hear the sickening, wet sound of a sword slitting the guard's throat. The soldier tries to talk despite the rivulets of blood running down his neck and mouth. He swings his sword once, then hits the ground hard.

Castian spins around to find Dez, and I know this is it. Now is the only chance I'll have to free our unit. I scramble over the mound, sliding down the dirt slope and landing with the barest of thuds. I force myself not to look at Castian and Dez fight, not to think that the last time they were together, Dez barely got out alive. They're both bigger now, with another year of battle scars and practice.

I grab my dagger and tuck another under my belt.

Sayida spots me first, relief in her midnight eyes. This close, I can see a new bruise darkening her cheek. I bring my sword to her binding, but a low, arrogant voice draws my attention.

"There he is," the prince taunts. "The savior of Riomar."

Dez doesn't have a chance to respond before Castian swings his sword, a showy thing with emeralds and rubies glinting off its golden hilt, just past Dez's ear. He turns, sidestepping Castian while leading him away from us at the same time.

A muffled cry comes from beside me. Margo, her bright eyes desperate for my attention. I let go of a shaky breath and finish cutting through the ropes around Sayida's hands and feet. As soon as she's free, she pulls a quill-thin blade from her black hair and gets to work on Margo's bindings while I help Esteban.

"Hurry!" Esteban hisses.

My fingers are clumsy, like my mind hasn't caught up to the reality that this is all happening. That Dez is fighting Castian. Their swords clang together like bells at high noon, and Dez's memory of their last encounter washes over me. He fights without the fear of that day, without the memory of Castian's dagger slicing into his side. While it's made Dez all the more confident, it makes me desperate.

Esteban's ropes snap. I haul him to his feet. Sayida finally has Margo free, and they're running for our stash of weapons when the pounding of boots draws near.

"Lord Commander! They're getting away!" a guard shouts.

I raise my dagger at the soldiers returning from their failed search for Dez. The pair of them register the young guard's slit throat and charge us.

I leap aside as the soldier lunges for me, protecting my face with my arm. The tip of his sword drags across my forearm. Searing pain scorches my flesh. I cry out, losing my balance as I wrench back to stop the blade from severing my whole arm. Esteban throws a punch at my assailant, breaking the skin of the man's ear.

I roll off the ground and push to my feet. The cut is shallower than it feels, but I swallow the pain and breathe in the putrid scent of wilting flowers around us. I have to help Esteban, but my eyes are drawn to Dez. The blood seeping from cuts on his arms.

Trust me.

"Ren!" Esteban shouts. He's holding two daggers in front of his face, bracing against the pressure of the guard's sword.

My vision spins as I race forward and slash my blades across the guard's ankles. He buckles, and part of me feels hungry with victory. My body is hot, surging with a violent energy I've never felt before.

Sayida and Margo have their opponent pinned to the ground, binding him with ropes. He doesn't fight, and there's a dreamy glaze to his eyes. Sayida must have compelled him to surrender, perhaps playing on some kindness in his heart. I remind myself that the king and the justice show no kindness, and force myself to look away. I'm brave enough to smile. To take the hand Esteban extends so we can make our way to Dez. For a moment, I think we can win.

But Castian knocks Dez's stolen sword to the ground, and moves in before I can blink, threatening to puncture his throat.

Dez looks from the sword point to where I stand, then his gaze glides past me.

It's that look that tells me we're surrounded before I can see them.

Men dressed in the king's dark purple and gold flank us from all sides. Where were they hiding? How did we not see them? Did they watch Dez and me hide behind the mound, toying with us before revealing themselves? Did they use the justice's weapon to find us?

There is one guard for each of us. I recognize the boy we left unconscious—he's sporting a bruised eye and a limp. Sayida reaches for my hand, as if to remind me that I can't act without thinking.

"Drop your weapons," Castian says calmly. He winks at Dez and says, "Stay," before striding in our direction, the four of us standing in a helpless line. My memory—Dez's memory—is so fresh in my mind that it is like I'm seeing two of Castian. There's the Bloodied Prince clutching Dez's throat, so full of rage. Then there's this Castian, flashing a victorious smile.

A third vision of him sparks like lightning in the dark of my thoughts: Esmeraldas. Celeste. A child's memory of strangers setting fire to his house. The same voice that's telling Dez to *stay* like a dog. *No one can know I was here*, he'd said. But Prince Castian is known for his pageantry, riding from village to citadela *protecting* them from the threat of the Whispers.

This Castian looks and sounds like the glimpses I have of him, but there's something different. An overconfidence that reeks of someone who knows they've already won.

"Thank the Father you're consistent," Castian tells Dez, tracing the crescent moon scar on his cheekbone. "Nearly a year since we last met and you've still got a death wish."

The casual nature of his voice doesn't belong in this forest, among our unit, while our lives hang in the balance. I hate everything about him. I want to rip every memory out of his head. The Matahermano's strange blue eyes settle on me, frowning like I've spat in his food, before moving down the line.

"Let them go," Dez growls. His hands are balled into fists, blood blooming like petals on the sleeves of his tunic. My body lurches forward, but Esteban wrenches my wrist.

"Dez!" Margo shouts, and the soldier behind her yanks her back by her hair.

Sayida throws that slender knife of hers and Margo catches it in the crook of her arm, driving it upward into the soldier's eye. The man's screams send birds flying from the canopies. Only one of the soldiers helps him stand.

Dez is still watching Margo and whirls around too slowly as a fresh-faced soldier—the one who nearly severed my neck in Esmeraldas—surprises him with two daggers, one at the neck and one over his heart. Dez's eyes widen, a new stream of blood running down his neck where the knife-happy soldier has cut him.

"You took my sword," the boy says.

"Stop!" Castian tries to keep the steel of victory on the smooth plane of his brow, but those eerie blue eyes spark with worry. The prince squeezes a hand into a fist, the spikes across his knuckles poised as a threat to the young boy. "I need him alive."

We shift ranks, the soldiers protecting their prince while the four of us keep our weapons drawn in wait.

"They're nothing but scavengers," Dez says, and spits a mouthful of blood at the ground. He keeps his arms out wide. "It's me you want. Take me."

Castian's face is bloody from a red cut on the fine slope of his regal nose. I hope it hurts. He flashes a smile from us to Dez. "Why would I do that?"

Dez takes this moment to slam the back of his head directly into the soldier behind him. The young man falls, cradling his face, but doesn't get up. Dez reaches into his pocket before anyone can advance and draws out a glass vial. Poison made from the olaneda blossom that grows in the highest peaks of the Memoria Mountains. One of our alchemists created it, trying to develop a cure for the plague that swept the continent years ago. Instead he discovered a quick death.

"Dez," I say.

He doesn't look at me.

Castian raises a hand to signal his men to stand back. He bites down so hard his jaw tenses. Is that fear in the prince's eyes? Dez might not be able to remember the way Castian nearly killed him, but I do. I feel it so deeply that it takes everything in me not to scream.

Castian's upper lip is a snarl. "You wouldn't."

"They are worth my life," Dez says, his words so even and strong no one could doubt it. "I'm the son of an elder. I'm the leader of the Whispers. It's me you want."

"You overestimate your value."

"Then why'd you come looking for me?" Dez asks. "Because the spy is dead. Celeste is dead. But you must know that already. You want me alive to get your revenge for that pretty scar I gave you."

What Dez said last night before thrums in my mind. *Trust me.*

Is this what he meant?

I want to believe Dez would never die by poison. There is no shame in it. But if this is the path he chooses, it means that there is no hope and no chance for the rest of us. And yet, he sets the vial between his teeth. He could bite down and break the glass. The poison would work before he even swallowed any glass shards.

Castian's hands become fists at his sides. I imagine those pointed knuckles driving through Dez's skull.

"Ren," Esteban whispers beside me. "What do we do?"

The only thing I can do. I yank off my gloves and hurl myself at the prince. I just need to lay one finger on him and tear out every memory he has ever had until he's as good as dead. Hollow, through and through.

"Don't!" Esteban yells, and I pause, confused.

Suddenly, it feels like roots have sprouted from the earth and wrapped themselves around my ankles. My bones heavy as mortar. My mouth numb, my tongue so thick, I can't utter a word. Useless. And all around me, the air ripples with Dez's power. He is holding us back.

It takes a second to register that Esteban's *Don't* wasn't for me at all. It was for what Dez was about to do. He must have skimmed Dez's thoughts too late.

"That won't work on me," the prince says, but he still steps back from my outstretched fingertips.

"Stop it!" Margo protests just as Sayida's face grows red with the effort to move.

They are being held in place by the force of Dez's magics, too. Tears sting at my eyes, blurring the image of the guards waiting for their orders. Castian. He's a ripple of red and gold, but when I blink, I see the fear in his eyes that his prize might expire before he has the opportunity to torture him. Dez with poison between his lips. I shut my eyes and remember those same lips on my skin, smiling, grinning, laughing, living.

How can he do this?

It is the prince himself who steps between us, his predatory gaze flipping between me and Dez. "I accept."

"Swear it," Dez says, holding the vial to his lips. "Swear my unit will walk freely out of this forest and not be harmed by you or your guards."

"I don't make promises to Moria scum," the Bloodied Prince says. He assesses each of us, lingering on my scarred hands. "Will there be others?"

Dez sets his teeth together and hisses, "*Yes.*"

We say nothing, frozen in different stages of outrage. I try once more to break free of Dez's magics, but it is as if my body is not my own.

I will never forgive you. The words come unbidden. Are they mine or from my memories coming undone?

"There's always more, isn't there?" Castian steps closer to me. His dark brow is furrowed, his golden skin flecked with dirt and bruises and scars. The blue of his eyes fades to a green at the center. I want to claw them out. Perhaps he sees my hate, because he can't hold my stare and moves on to Margo. "You four will tell the Whispers to stand down. This rebellion is over or your *prince of rebels* dies without a trial. I will expect your complete and total surrender in three nights, or he will be executed on the fourth day. Do we have an accord?"

"They can't answer you," Dez says.

Irritation flashes across the prince's face. "Then answer for them."

Without taking his golden eyes, hard and glassy, away from Castian, Dez nods once. The defeat I hear is so foreign I fear I'm staring at an impostor. "They'll do as you command. Remember everything I've said."

One of the soldiers comes up quickly and knocks the vial out of Dez's hand. He grabs Dez by the wrists while another kicks the backs of his knees. They tie his arms. And all the while, Dez doesn't struggle. He breathes fast and hard, and I can't look away from him. I can't even lift a finger as they bring out a brown sack to put over his head. His eyes are locked on mine. I hate the brightness of the day. I hate that he won't let me go to him.

"Remember everything I've said. Remember—"

The last of his words is muffled as the guards tug the filthy grain sack over his head.

It's one of the guards who speaks. His sienna-brown skin is covered in sweat, and he looks like he might get sick on his prince's boots. "But . . . But, my lord, King Fernando and Justice Méndez—they had their orders. No survivors."

For a moment, it's as though Castian didn't hear the man standing mere paces from him. Then there's only the sharp metal of his fist flying through the air, spikes ripping into a fleshy cheek.

"Are you on my guard or Justice Méndez's?" Castian asks, but doesn't wait for an answer. "I will keep my word to spare these rebels. Is the word of your prince not good enough for you?"

The guard nurses his mangled face, then utters a single cry of understanding.

I want to scream. I want to fight. I want to die.

But I can't move. How can Dez do this? How can he twist my feelings this way? I refuse to believe there's even a part of me that doesn't want to save him. Tears spill silently down my cheeks. All I can do is watch Castian and his guards drag Dez away, leaving the four of us—Sayida, Esteban, Margo, and myself—as living statues, as the forest slowly comes awake with the dawn. Inevitable.

Finally, when Dez is far enough away, his magics release us. Without their support, I stumble. My head spins.

Dez is gone.

A burning sensation like a corrosive liquid runs through my veins. I felt that fire before when I was fighting.

Dez is gone.

I smell rot. Decaying flowers. But it's not time for the foliage to wilt. I realize it wasn't only the fight that raged through my skin.

Sayida catches me before I hit the ground. Despite everything that's happened, it's my arm that's heavy, a deadweight pulling me to the earth. My eyelids flutter, and before I sink into total blackness, I hear her say, "Poison."

8

When I open my eyes, it is dark once more. I register a tent. A low-burning lamp on the floor beside me. My lashes brush against soft fabric, not the dusty blanket I've been carrying for a week. The skin at the base of my neck is tender, the stitches like cords strung too tight. I let out a pained wail as the last thing I remember crashes over me. Dez's voice rings in my thoughts.

Remember, Dez said.

"Dez." I sit up and blink to adjust to the light.

Sayida presses her hands on my chest, and immediately my breaths slow as her Persuári magics move through me in a warm pulse. She's always described her power as seeing the colors that make up human emotion. I wonder what color mine is right now.

"Stop," I say, and she does.

I try to stand. Instantly, a wave of dizziness makes me sway.

Sayida puts her hands on my shoulders, gently guiding me back down to the cot. "Please, Ren, you have to stay still."

"Where's Dez?"

She pauses, sighing slowly, as if to hold back tears. "You know he isn't here."

"I don't need magics right now," I say. I need Dez but I can't say that, even to my own friend. "What happened?"

Sayida hesitates. "You were cut with a poisoned blade. Alacran venom mixed with blood roses, judging from the scent. Illan says you need to lie down."

"Illan is here?" I ignore Sayida and remain sitting. "And the units? Are they ready to counterattack?"

Shadows of trees playing against the tent's canvas walls. The same creatures I heard last night when Dez and I . . . We're still in the Forest of Lynxes.

Over Sayida's shoulder, Esteban comes into focus. He isn't looking at me with his usual contempt, but his arms are crossed over his chest to keep his distance. He's shaved the scraggly beard, leaving smooth brown skin. Softly, he says, "The entire council is here, Renata."

Renata. Esteban never says my whole name. *Incendiary. Scavenger.* Hells, even *You.*

"Am I dying?" I ask Sayida.

She shakes her head and smiles despite the sadness that weighs her down. "Illan got most of it out. But he couldn't do anything about the nightmares."

I close my eyes again and I can smell it, like someone holding a poultice under my nose. My stomach lurches. I'm ravenously hungry and nauseous at the same time. I don't remember nightmares. That's the thing about the Gray and the more recent memories I've taken.

They're always there when I'm awake or sleeping. On the rare occasion I do "dream," I'm recalling stolen pasts.

"I feel like I was trampled by a bull," I say. I run my tongue over the inside of my mouth where there's a touch of numbness. "How long have I been asleep?"

"The better part of two days."

The Príncipe Dorado's voice rings in my ear. *This rebellion is over or your* prince of rebels *dies without a trial. I'll expect your complete and utter surrender in three nights, or he will be executed on the fourth day.*

"Two days?" My chest hurts. Blood pounds in my ears, making it hard to think. I press my fists on the cot to try again to stand, stretch my aching leg muscles. "Have they sent a rescue mission to the palace? We can't surrender, but we can't let Dez face trial. No one is ever found innocent."

Esteban's frown deepens while Sayida looks down at her lap, twisting her copper ring.

"We've been ordered to wait," she says quietly.

"Wait for *what?*" I shout. She flinches, but she won't yell back, I know she won't. Sayida is all softness and warm light, and I am hard edges and shadow. What did Dez call me? *Vengeance in the night.* "We have to save him. Dez would do it for us."

Someone pushes back the tent flap, a hand gripping the silver handle of a cane.

"There will be no surrender." Illan's voice cuts like the sharpest blade. The elder strides inside, his thick powder-white hair nearly grazing the top of my tent. Eyebrows the same stark black as Dez's knit together at the sight of us. His cane digs into the forest ground, and he grips the silver fox head even tighter. The mark of the Mother of All, a crescent moon surrounded by an arc of stars, dances across his right shoulder, exposed by the drape of his tunic. All the elders bear this mark.

Illan de Martín, elder and leader of the Whisper rebellion, and the most powerful Ventári alive. He inhales deeply, as if he's taking the strength out of the tent. "And there will be no rescue mission."

"But—"

Illan throws up a hand, and the sleeve of his tunic slides back. "If anyone disobeys me, they can take leave of their unit and the Whispers' safe houses and never return."

I fight a surge of rage that bubbles in my veins. "He's your *son*."

The silence in the tent is resounding. Sayida and Esteban keep their gazes pointedly away from mine while I glare at Illan. The elder isn't known for being gentle, but he is known to be just. It doesn't make sense. He's staged far more dangerous missions. Like when we snuck into Citadela Crescenti to find the descendants of an old Memoria high-born family. Or when Dez and I attended a masquerade ball at a lord's estate while two units robbed his stores.

"I need a moment alone with Renata," Illan says, never taking his eyes from mine. I scowl back at him as Sayida and Esteban scurry out, clearly grateful to be dismissed.

"I don't understand," I say as soon as the tent's flap falls back down.

"What is there for you to understand?" Illan asks. "My parents watched their kingdom stolen by a wretched king. I saw the vestiges of those lands ripped apart by his son. Cut apart. We cannot surrender."

"It's Dez," I choke out.

"We are in the middle of the greatest fight of our rebellion," Illan replies. "Not fighting just for land but for our survival. I'm not here to discuss Dez. My order stands. None of our fighters go after him or I will see them permanently discharged from our ranks, is that understood?"

I want to disobey him. I want to push back. But I have nowhere else to go, so I turn my face to the side and he keeps speaking.

"What I need from you, Renata, is information about the palace."

My mouth goes dry. I knew that my value to the Whispers was because of the memories trapped in the Gray. It's why Illan has trained me all these years to try to unlock it, but nothing works. What value would I have now if I refused to remember a place I have not seen since I was a child?

"No. I will not try to access the Gray until you send a mission out for Dez," I say, not caring that I'm being belligerent. "Nothing else matters."

"Need I remind you who saved you from that place?" Illan's voice is cold, not angry, though he has every right to be—I've never spoken to him like this before. It's likely no one has.

I can't meet his eyes, but the seeds of my anger sprout like vines, twisting around my throat until I can hardly breathe. "I never need reminding. I see it every day."

I speak the truth, though not how Illan interprets it. He led the raid on the palace that freed me, the Whispers' Rebellion. They failed to kill the king, but they stole their children back. Illan even gave me a safe place to call home, but he's not the person I see. When I think of that night, when I close my eyes, all I see is a dark-haired boy, his hand reaching out from a hidden door in the palace walls, leading me through the smoky stairwell and into a safe embrace. I think of Dez.

Illan nods, satisfied. "King Fernando's reign must come to an end before there is nowhere left for us to run. I expected your cooperation above everyone. Remember the mission, Renata."

"End the Fajardo family's rule. Restore the Moria temples. Reclaim our stolen lands."

"This weapon stands in the way."

I know the mission. But all I can hear is the echo of Dez shouting as he was dragged through the forest by our enemy. *Remember.*

Illan exhales hard. "Who will live on these lands? Who will visit these temples? If we do not keep the Moria safe, who are we? You know what Celeste discovered. There is nothing more important than destroying the weapon the justice has created."

"All the more reason to go to the capital!" I shout. Frustration slices at my patience. "While we're there we can rescue Dez. We can—"

"Dez doesn't need to be rescued," Illan says, impatient. He glances at the tent opening, then lowers his voice. "I tell you this so you do not let your feelings get in the way of the mission. Dez is exactly where he needs to be."

I stare at him. A chill returns to my skin. "What?"

Illan sits beside me and lays his cane against across his lap. "When we heard rumors that the king's justice developed a weapon able to rip out our magics, Celeste and I sent our best spy to meet with my informant."

"Lucia?" I ask.

He nods gravely. "She sent word that they called this weapon *the cure.*"

Even thinking the word sours my mouth. The cure to us. The cure to our existence. "What is it?"

"That's what we don't know. A tonic? A trinket? Lucia would know best, rest her soul. We were going to wait until my informant could gather more information within the palace. But Rodrigue went after Lucia. And, well, you know his fate."

"What does this have to do with Dez getting captured?" I ask.

I think of Dez and me near the riverbank. He was scared of going to the palace, but not for the reasons I thought. Because he wasn't telling us the whole truth.

"My informant feared someone was getting close to discovering them as my spy. Without them, we have no way of knowing where the weapon is kept within the palace. We needed someone else inside. My spy made sure a patrol would find Dez. He was supposed to leave camp that morning, but the prince must have intercepted the message. Either way, he is where he needs to be."

Dez was going to leave me in the morning. Would he have said good-bye? It's a petty, terrible thing to wonder at the moment, but I can't stop it. I hate that I don't get to be angry with him because he is risking his life.

"How will Dez do that from the dungeons?" I ask.

"How would *we* break through the palace walls? We've done this before. Dez is our best chance. I gave my son the code to break free after his capture. The prince gave us three nights, I believe? When they go to execute him at dawn, Dez won't be in his cell. He will find this so-called *cure* and destroy it. And that, my dear, is why there is no rescue mission necessary."

Remember. Trust me. Dez had planned this all along. The anger that coiled in my gut is gone, unwinds into worry. So much could go wrong.

"Why are you telling me this?" I ask. "You didn't trust me before, so why now?"

"I know the"—Illan's face is impassive, searching for the right word— "*bond* you and Dez have always shared. I tell you now simply because I do not want you doing anything reckless to compromise this. No one but my son and the elders know of our plan. Dez will use the code to break out, steal away into the palace, and retrieve the weapon."

For a moment, I allow myself to remember the cells beneath the palace of Andalucía, though my memory of them is hazy with the murk of childhood fear. I never liked it when Justice Méndez brought me down there to see the prisoners. Still, I recall that outside each was a metallic cylinder as thick as a scroll. Standard code locks have four keys that turn like gears inside a clock. Méndez had a custom-made lock of ten keys, and changed it often, just in case I was able to memorize it. But I wasn't concerned with escaping. Not then.

"What's the code?" I squint my eyes as if it'll make all of this come together.

"Rest, Renata. I expect Dez back at camp by nightfall tomorrow while the executioner is still sharpening his sword. For now, we need everyone assisting in the safe passage of those leaving for Luzou." Illan's eyes are faraway and he absentmindedly rubs the silver head of the fox on his cane with his thumb. "And with the weapon destroyed, we buy ourselves another day to live and keep fighting."

It's a dangerous game Illan and Dez are playing, but if anyone can pull this off, it's Dez. When we were twelve, he was caught by a tax farmer near the mountains. I ran to get help, but by the time we came back to him he'd already picked his way out of the locks. I recall the fervor with which he fought Prince Castian at Riomar. I know he'll return to me. Dez can get out of anything.

"You don't need me to give you information on the palace, then?"

Illan's face darkens with what I recognize as a fleeting memory. Regret. "Once Dez has carried out his mission, we will need to get back inside the palace walls to rescue the prisoners in the dungeons."

Slowly, I nod. "I'll do what I can."

After Illan leaves, my stomach still hurts, but when Sayida returns, she assures me the feeling is just the dregs of the poison leaving me. Yet, as I watch the sky darken from the blue of the

Castinian Sea to that of a bruised plum, I'm not so sure she's right. I can't shake the terrible feeling that twists in my gut.

Andrés. I say his name in my mind. Then his voice: *Don't tell anyone.*

Again, I face another sleepless night, my mind a flurry of thoughts fighting for dominance: Dez. Illan's plan. The twisting dials of a cylinder lock. Four letters that click into place. Four letters that get scrambled every night by a new guard.

A strange feeling tightens in my belly.

Nerves, I tell myself.

In the darkness, I search my mind for signs of hope—in Sayida's comfort, in the promise in Dez's kisses. In the way Esteban saved my life. After a while, hope finally ignites, tiny and distant, but alive and buzzing like a firefly within my heart. I hold on to that tiny light. It comes and goes, but it's something.

Four letters. Dez knew them. He would have had to memorize them.

I push and pull my covers, too hot, then too cold in the unsettling night.

The Gray gathers in my mind like storm clouds. My temples ache. I struggle to push them back. To think of anything else. The most recent memories of Dez help. His full mouth trailing kisses along my neck. His eyes like fire in the moonlight. A promise made in the dark. How I watched him sleep and struggle until I took Dez's nightmares, with the grazing of my fingertips on his temple.

But they weren't nightmares, only a string of memories, a tumble of images that didn't make sense together. And yet, perhaps they do.

Four words.

Dez chasing the hound.

Dez eating the orange.

Dez watching the flag.

Dez searching for me.

My mind turns like metallic gears. Like the keys of a cylinder lock. Four letters.

Hound. Orange. Flag. Ren.

A mnemonic device for remembering a code: H. O. F. R.

I bolt upright, my head throbbing, my vision spinning. . . .

A mnemonic device that *I* now know, but that Dez no longer does. Because I took the memory as he slept.

Because I allowed myself to touch him. Because I truly thought in that moment that if I loved him, it meant I couldn't hurt him.

Dez doesn't have the code to set himself free.

I do.

I should have known better. My power only destroys, nothing else. I will always hurt those I love the most. *Never love a Robári. You will lose yourself.* That's what they say, and they might be right.

I push aside the blankets, frantic. Around me, the camp is quiet with sleep.

Panic floods my veins—never have I felt like this. My muscles tremble so hard I have to stand still, so very still, in order not to shake. I temper my breaths. In. Out. Inoutinoutinout. I fight with my mind to rationalize what could be happening. Perhaps I'm wrong. Perhaps the memories I pulled were meant for something else.

But another voice whispers inside me, curling its truth around my chest and squeezing so hard I can't breathe.

If I ripped away Dez's memory of the code, he won't be able to break free. If Dez can't break free from his cell, he won't be able to find the weapon. And then? He'll be in his cell the morning of the execution. In two days. We are a full day from the capital. That leaves so little time. I remember again the prince's white grin as he sparred with Dez. The feline grace of his movements. His preference for blood and spectacle. The way he struck his own soldier when questioned. *I don't make promises to Moria.*

I have to tell Illan what I've done. But as I scramble out of my bed, wincing at the lingering pain in my shoulder, I realize that if I tell Illan, he'll have to call a meeting of elders to make a decision. There'll be a debate, voting, procedures that take time. That's time Dez doesn't have.

I have to be the one to go to Dez—no matter what Illan or the elders decide.

No matter that I will never be welcomed back to the Whispers, because once again I've betrayed them. What have I done?

My hands shake as I strap my sword back onto my belt and hurry into my boots. The air already feels thinner, the night giving way to the coming day, as I sneak out to the horses, whispering softly to calm them. Dez will die the day after tomorrow, and it will be my fault. The thought is choking, blinding. I have to steady myself. I have to make it to him. I breathe in, breathe out, and mount.

I trust you, Ren. That was his mistake, wasn't it?

Never trust a Robári.

I can't think as the horse picks up speed. I can't feel anything but a dark, pulsing shudder of truth. He will die, and I am the one who sentenced him.

Unless I get there first.

9

THE FIRST TIME I TRIED TO RUN AWAY FROM A WHISPERS' SAFE HOUSE IN
Citadela Salinas, I was thirteen. Much like now, I stole a horse. The
beasts are precious to the Whispers, but I didn't care. During training the other kids lobbed cruel names when they thought Dez and
Illan weren't nearby. My teachers saw right through me. My parents
were dead. I simply couldn't stay there. So I saddled a horse as best
I could and ran. I got far and lost along the Cliffs of Jura, but Dez
found me.

Now it's my turn to return the favor.

I ride.

I ride until my thighs revolt with agony. Until my fingers cramp
around the reins. My face burning from the wind. The thunder of
hooves against a road I shouldn't be on because it leads right to

Andalucía, the capital of Puerto Leones. My eyes play tricks on me, my skull throbs. People appear like ghosts on the sides of the road and then vanish into sails of the Gray. The land tugs the memories to the front of my mind, forcing me to recall the lives that walked this very same road. The last few days have put so much strain on me that the vault in my head is cracking open. I want to laugh because Illan thought it would be meditation, patience that would help me break through. I should have told him sooner that I needed something inside me to break so thoroughly I could never be put back together. That's what will happen if I don't get to Dez.

I hear his voice as I ride. *I know you're afraid. So am I.*

Over the years, Illan has never sent me on a mission to Andalucía. I prepare for seeing the towering buildings, the palace that glitters when the sun is out. The jewel of Puerto Leones. I hate the girl I was. I've wanted to believe she died in the fire, but a part of me wonders if the reason I stayed away was because I'm afraid she's still there waiting for me, wretched and destructive.

I know you're afraid. So am I.

"I'm terrified, Dez," I say to the wind.

Sounds play tricks on me, too. A great drumming rhythm coming from the east as the sky bleeds with the beginning of morning light. I look behind me, and for the first time in hours, my heart swells like a great wave breaking over me, through me. Because they've come.

I'm not alone.

When I crest the hilltop, I pull on the reins to bring my horse to a stop. He moves to the side, kicking up dust on the road that snakes down toward the small town before the capital.

Two horses line up on either side of me. Esteban and Margo on one and Sayida on the other.

"What are you doing here?" I manage to ask.

Margo wears a wide-brimmed wool hat, creating a shadow over her pale blue eyes. Esteban holds the reins around her, a red scarf covering the lower half of his face.

"Same as you," Margo says, voice hoarse. She must've been crying. I can see it in the streaks of dirt on her white skin. "You should have come to us."

"There was no time." I breathe hard to stop the swell of emotion. I am not alone. "I didn't think you'd follow me."

"That's my fault," Margo says. Is it difficult to admit this to me? "The elders are wrong. This is the right thing to do."

"He'd never leave us behind," Sayida says, pulling down her indigo-blue scarf.

Except he did leave us. Back in that forest. They don't know of Illan's plan. They don't know that I've stolen Dez's memory, that I'm the reason he won't be able to get free. My tongue feels swollen with the fear of revealing this truth, so I say nothing.

Instead, we stare at the grim warning laid out before us.

Both sides of the main road that snakes to Andalucía are lined with spikes. Dozens, hundreds of spikes, each one a yard apart. Decapitated heads of captured Moria and other innocents doomed to be displayed beside thieves, traitors, and murderers alike. All of them distorted, with rot and decaying flesh punctuating each stalk. The head closest to us is half-eaten by bugs the size of libra coins, eight legs climbing into an eye socket.

The stench hits my nose when the breeze shifts, and my horse rears on his hind legs, as if trying to retrace his steps. I grab the reins and pull. He is my courage, and I will ride him through that walk of death.

The four of us make the symbol of Our Lady over our torsos at the same time, then I click my tongue and lead us onto the wide road. We're forced to slow down so as not to draw attention to ourselves.

We've ridden for hours, pushing our stolen horses onward without rest as the landscape changed from the Forest of Lynxes to the lush greens that border the Rio Aguadulce, but Andalucía is an oasis in a dry valley. I rub the flank of my horse. The capital is filthy, so we won't stand out in our travel-worn clothes. Margo tucks her necklace into her brassiere. She never speaks of where the golden starfish pendant came from, but no matter where we are she doesn't take it off. The others put away any visible metal. I have no jewelry to heighten my power. Robári are matched with platinum, a metal so rare, I've never even seen it, not even so much as a button. Though I can't help but wonder, if I did procure a piece, would the Whispers even allow me to keep it?

We can't pass as pious pilgrims, so we'll be young farmhands trying our luck in the bustling, boisterous, rat-infested city everyone talks about.

The palace is at the very center of it all, the heart surrounded by streets that course like arteries and alleys like veins. The justice's cathedral and the executioner's square are beside the palace, connected beneath the city by a maze of tunnels that lead to sewers.

I remember Dez standing at the bottom of a hidden stairwell while the city burned around us. I trusted him the minute I saw him, but when he led me to Illan and the Whispers, waiting with the other children they were able to rescue, I screamed and fought. I remember closing my fist around one of the iron gates. Was it Illan or Celeste who yanked me free? My heart races and a sick feeling floods my gut. I turn over the side and throw up what little is in my stomach.

"I don't suppose you ran away with a plan?" Esteban asks. When I sit back in my saddle, I realize he's offering a handkerchief to me. It is the smallest gesture, but my eyes sting as I clean myself.

"Dez is in the cells," I say. "I can retrieve the code, but I have to get down there."

"How can you get the code?" Sayida asks me.

"I'll steal the memory from the guard," I lie.

Slowly, we canter up the final hill. My muscles are sore from riding and the poisoned cut throbs, a dull memory of pain that feels near and far. The Ren who lived in this city was rosy-cheeked and had a taste for sweets. She was spoiled, naive. Even at this distance, my nerves twist and warn me to go back, because perhaps I'm still naive to think I can save him, to think I've changed at all.

"I've never seen the capital before," Esteban says nervously. He reaches into his jacket and pulls out a narrow spyglass.

"Get a good look," Margo says dryly. "It might be your last."

I expect Esteban to respond with a teasing remark or, at the very least, a smile. But instead, he kicks his horse and rides ahead of us.

The traffic into town is heavier than I'd expect for so early in the morning. There are vendors lugging wagons brimming with fruits and vegetables. There's a round woman who has four small children sitting on her rickety carriage and a fifth one who waves at me from atop a mountain of potatoes. But there are also young country girls in simple blush-colored dresses walking arm in arm, likely to spend the day at the market stalls. A group of boys in their Holy Day best riding in a carriage with their parents. Of course. It's Holy Day. The justice doesn't hold executions on Holy Day because it belongs to celebrating the Father of Worlds.

I kick at my steed and ride faster. Andalucía looms ahead. The shimmering palace juts above the other buildings like a gem encircled by rocks. Even its surrounding hedges are tall, taller than the iron gates that twist like ivy and create a perimeter.

To get there, we'll have to go through the market square, where stone buildings with elaborate spires reach toward the sky. The wealthier rows of houses will be on the other side of the city, with their colored glass rippling in neat lines, and though I'm too far away to see, I know they depict scenes of the Father of Worlds and his creations.

As we approach, I imagine the best route for us to take once we cross the pillars that mark the entrance to the city. Here, buildings on the fringe of the bustling market and courthouse are mostly five or six stories and boxed around the cathedral. The closer the buildings are to the cathedral the tighter and taller they are, packed like crooked teeth leaning into a gap.

The fringe has a line of posts for horses, as the cobblestone streets are labyrinthine and crowded. The right of way is for pedestrians like those farm girls with small brass libbies in their pockets. Esteban is already tying his horse to a post, the creature lapping up water from a trough. He pretends like he doesn't know me, which is no different than when we're in Ángeles.

"Take your gloves off," Margo murmurs as she comes to a stop beside me. "They're a dead giveaway in the height of summer."

I do as she says and ball my bare hands into fists, feeling naked in the morning light.

"Stay close to me," Margo whispers. She links her arm with mine, and my entire body tenses. Warmth radiates off her, the pull of her magics surrounding me, and when I look down, I stare at my hands in awe. They're not the flawless, soft hands of a highborn girl, but they aren't the scarred hands of a Robári either.

"Thank you," I say. "For this, and for helping me."

"I'm here for Dez, not for you," she says. "Though I'll admit I was impressed."

"Why?" I'm too tired to laugh, so it comes out as a huff.

"From our lessons, I've always thought of you as Illan's pet. I never thought you'd defy him."

"Not my fault I'm his most clever pupil."

"Obedient is not the same as clever," she says with a smirk. I realize it's not for my benefit but for the guards changing stations.

In their dark purple-and-brown leather uniforms, they remind me of the men in the forest. The one Margo blinded and the one Dez killed.

We enter the open city gates in silence. Esteban and Sayida keep their distance so as not to draw attention to our group, but we try to remain in one another's sight.

The capital has a way of making you feel like you're adrift at sea. There are commotions everywhere. Loud voices shout out the price specials for bright green tomatillos, and dairy farmers offer samplings of salty, stinky cheeses. Vintners from the southwest of the kingdom sell their products by the barrel while wealthy merchant women stroll in high-heeled boots so as not to dirty their fine silk dresses with the sludge that dots every street corner and fills the empty spaces between the cobblestones.

At one point, a child as tall as my knee brushes against me, and I look down in time to see a hand dip into my pocket.

"Hey!" I say, but before I can do anything, the girl darts away, disappearing immediately into the crowd.

"She must be training," Esteban whispers, coming up beside me. "It's clear from our footwear that our pockets are probably empty."

"Training?" I ask.

Esteban shoves his hands in his pockets, flashing an easy smile like we're two friends at a market. "When you're small like that, you usually practice on the people who look just as poor as you. That way if you're caught, you know they're too poor to bribe the citadela guard to help them."

I look at him in surprise. "How do you know this?"

"I was the best pickpocket in Crescenti," he says, his white smile breaking across his brown skin. I can't remember the last time he smiled at me so often. "Folks were so used to looking away from the poor they didn't even notice they'd been robbed blind."

"I didn't know you lived on the streets," I say.

"There's a lot we don't know about each other." Esteban picks up a ripe peach from a vendor and throws a pesito in his direction. The sweetness of the fruit's scent mingles with the smells of the sizzling fried pork belly being readied for the afternoon crowds, the black café beans roasting in a large metal container, and the sewer water that runs in a river along the sidewalks.

"How are we supposed to get to the palace gate?" Margo asks as she sidles up beside me. She pulls out her handkerchief and dabs the sweat on her face.

Sayida and Esteban keep walking to the café vendor. She loops her arm around his to make them look like a couple. She buys two cups, and I don't miss Esteban's frown as he empties his wallet.

I take Margo's hand in mine and point to the cathedral. There are so many bodies gathering for the Holy Day service that they block the paths. Leaflets flutter in the breeze and litter the side-walks, advertising everything from weddings to the justice's orders.

"There's an entrance from within the cathedral that leads to the dungeons."

Behind me, Sayida inspects her reflection at a stand of hand mirrors. She tilts one this way and that while Esteban holds the two paper cups of steaming café. To a casual onlooker, she looks like a vain farm girl, though even with her dust-covered clothes her features are breathtaking. But her black tourmaline eyes don't fall on her reflection. Instead, they watch the alley directly behind her. Lowering the mirror, she leans in to the hairy vendor.

"Where is everyone going?" she asks sweetly, with a flutter of silky black lashes.

"The execution square," the vendor says, leering at Sayida, who tenses just as I do. Margo and I exchange wary glances. "A pretty thing like you don't need to see such a thing. You can wait right here till the crowds settle." He pats his thigh and cocks a lascivious smirk.

Sayida sets down the mirror, hard enough to crack it, then stomps away into the alley while he's too stunned to react. I grab her hand and we fold into the swell of people entering the market. As the vendor searches the rising tide of bodies for a guard, we slip away.

"The execution square," I say, stopping at the mouth of an alley. I press my hands against my stomach to stop them from trembling. Behind me, rodents scavenge through piles of garbage and the hot smell of urine clings to the air.

"I thought—" Margo starts, but doesn't finish what we all believed. The execution is supposed to happen tomorrow at dawn, not today.

Sayida looks grim, her eyes drawn to a rustle of parchment on her boot. A leaflet, the bottom half wet with sewer water.

I snatch the parchment from her hand, stained with oil and dirt, and there's a crude drawing of a man with demon eyes and long fangs. At the top, there is a title: Príncipe Dorado Slays the Moria Bestae.

Skimming down the print, I realize it is an execution rhyme. The words jumble together, refusing to form sentences because all I can see is one name repeated over and over again in the ballad: Dez de Martín.

Andrés de Martín. I think his true name.

I crush the parchment in my hand, but we've all seen it. My

mind is going to break open. I can feel the memories strain against my temples, each one a blade trying to cut its way out. *Trust me. Trust. Me.*

"Executions don't happen on Holy Day," Margo says. "We were supposed to have another day!"

"They knew we'd never surrender. Not even for Dez," Sayida says.

Esteban makes a choking sound. "Think of the crowds. The people who will be present. Everyone from farmhands to lords all attending the same service. What better spectacle than to kill the leader of the Whispers?"

They're going to kill Dez. The reality of it feels like that gut punch on the balcony. I'm desperate and need to breathe, but I can't. Castian's going to kill him because Dez couldn't break out of his cell. Castian's going to kill him because I stole Dez's means of escape.

Trumpets sound in the distance, and this time, the four of us gather in a closed circle, while rivers of people make their way past the narrow alley and toward the cathedral to the execution square. Some carry baskets of rotting food, garbage not good enough for even rats to eat. Others clutch glass bottles of holy water blessed by the royal priest himself. Anything and everything they can throw, they bring with them.

"This changes nothing," I say breathlessly. "I don't care if I have to rip Dez off that platform and kill the executioner myself."

Esteban balls his hands into fists. "Look around. We'll never break through the crowds."

"We don't have to get through," Sayida says, running to the dead end of the alley. I see what she sees. A metal drainpipe. "If we can't walk the streets we will race across rooftops."

In the dark shadow of the alley, we grab the rungs on the side of the pipe that empties out the eaves trough on the roof of the building, and climb up. Everyone is so preoccupied with the idea of a Moria Whisper's death that they don't bother to look up.

When I get to the top, I balance on the lip of the roof, and a wave of vertigo hits me as I take in the scene. At first, the dark mass in front of the cathedral looks like a hive. There are so many of them that they can hardly move. Vendors put away their wares as people fill every single space of the market square. It's as if they taste the blood in the air, the wrath that comes from a crowd this large.

From where we are, we can see everything. There's a row of nooses that dangle in the breeze. But what my eye goes to is the thick wooden block at the center of it all, where a judge sharpens a blunt executioner's sword.

The shock of it leaves me cold and struggling to breathe.

They're going to behead him.

"We have to get closer!" My voice strains as I fight to be heard through the noise of the capital. I sprint and jump across the foot-long space between this roof and the next. My boots splash through murky puddles, stick to the grimy black surface. The blazing sun radiates against it, making steam rise. On the next roof, the surface is so slick, I can't catch my footing. As I fumble, Sayida is suddenly there, holding my hand and pulling me forward. From here, we have a better view of the block.

"Wait," Margo says, pointing to the wooden watchtower beside us. Guards have climbed it to survey the crowds. "We can't go farther yet."

A loud cheer goes up as the prince is announced by dozens of trumpeting horns. Common doves take flight from the streets and search for higher places to roost. It has been three days since I laid eyes on the Bloodied Prince. He's not dressed in the sullied armor he wore in the forest.

The prince rides out on his horse. Brilliant rubies drip from

his circlet and the sun catches his gold crown, creating a halo—
an angel of death. He's decked in deep red finery tailored to his
large frame.

People make a path for him around the block. His steed trots
back and forth, and then the Príncipe Dorado gives them a devastating smile. A smile that says he knows something the rest of us
don't. That he lied. He broke his word. What good is the word of a
royal? When he rejects the executioner's weapon for his own bejeweled broadsword, the crowd goes wild with adoration.

The disgust at the display makes my stomach roil. I taste the
wretched market air and bile, but I can't break apart yet.

"We have to go," I say, my voice rising. I whirl on Margo. "Can
you cloak me and create a diversion for us to make a run for it?"

Her eyes are glassy with tears, and a deep line cuts across her
forehead. "Renata Convida, I am not that powerful."

"You have to be," I whimper.

There's a loud ripple of voices down below, and automatically,
we all look back to the crowd. The people below move back and
forth like a tumultuous sea, churning and churning, until a hush
falls over them as Dez is brought out.

Even from this distance, I can tell he's hurt. He can barely stand
on his own. Despite all of that, my body relaxes at the sight of him
alive. While he's alive, there's still hope.

The guard who holds him is an ogre of a man, with a bald head
and brown skin covered in scars and tattoos. He grips Dez around
the neck with one beefy hand and parades him up and down the
platform.

I want to look away. Dez would want me to look away. He
wouldn't want me seeing him like this, brought to his knees by the
thing he hates the most. But I let the sight fuel my fury.

He's pushed forward, and then the royal priest hobbles onto

the platform. He holds a golden chalice and begins the blessing ceremony of the prince, his sword, and the hungry onlookers who gather at the platform edge like vultures.

I have as much time as I'll ever get—but I have to do it. Now.

I break away from my unit, leaving them behind in a flurry of shouts. By the time I hop onto the next roof, their pleading is nothing but a distant echo. This is my mission, not theirs.

I run from one end of the roof and jump across to the next. The closer to the center of the capital, the more the houses are pressed against one another. My fear of falling threatens to grip my heart and render me useless. But my fear of losing Dez overpowers my senses, my reason, my everything.

A volley of cheers goes up as the blessing's end is announced by trumpeting horns and the royal priest's handheld bell. The sound chases pigeons from the streets, where they've been dive-bombing the rotten food in baskets. The crowd brandishes tiny purple-and-gold flags bearing the lion crest—the flag of Puerto Leones, as if Dez's blood and bones weren't born from this very earth, too.

I need to jump six more roofs to be close enough to make a run for the executioner's dais. I take my wrist knife and throw it at the nearest guard across the street. It hits him right in his shoulder, and he goes down to his knees.

Suddenly, there's a shout, and the crowd below seems to change slightly. But I can't afford to stop and watch what's happening. The trumpets that blast a call for quiet only make the crowd grow louder still.

I leap over the next roof and the landing rattles my spine. And that's when I hear it, a cry of "Fire!"

Stumbling a second, I look back.

From the rooftop where I left my unit comes a billowing cloud of smoke, black snakes twisting around each other. And as I watch, the smoke begins to unfurl from other rooftops nearby, until it looks like the whole city is on fire.

I smile. The smoke simply hangs there, endlessly twisting, and as the dark cloud rolls toward my current rooftop, I feel no scorching heat. Smell no ash and hear no crackle of flames.

It's an illusion. I can feel it in the seesaw feeling in my gut that comes with it. Illusionári magics. Margo's work.

The commotion below grows louder and louder. "Fire! The city is on fire!"

I resume my sprint across the rooftops, rage fueling my legs. How many times has the justice set fire to villages across the kingdom? How many people have they burned to ignite fear among others? These people know nothing of fire. Know nothing of how it actually feels.

Cathedral bells begin to clang, tolling out a warning. I take loose bricks and iron tubes and anything I find on top of the roofs and fling them off into the crowd, adding to the chaos.

Then I run, and hop over to the next roof, keeping out of sight.

I trust you. His voice rings in my ears.

You shouldn't have, I think as I reach the sixth house and look at the dais. Prince Castian is shouting at the crowd, pointing his finger at the guards nearest to him.

Then there's Dez, smirking—recognizing the smoke for what it is.

My heart soars for a moment, and then I realize, even if I get to the street, I'll have to barrel to get across the throng of people between us.

I open the rooftop access of the building and scramble down two flights of steps. There are women screaming in the bedchambers. Others standing outside rooms with long cigars between plump red lips, wearing nothing but undergarments and heels.

I kick open a door, and the morning light is blinding compared to the dark brothel. I run across the plaza, holding my arms up to protect my face, weaving through people hurrying away from the executioner's platform. Dozens of Leonesse flags litter the cobblestones along with spoiled food meant to be thrown at Dez's lifeless body. I slip occasionally, skidding on peels and pungent juices as I batter my way through a sea of legs and elbows.

I can see him clearly now.

Dez is chained to the platform, but he pulls against his restraints. He's always been a fighter, and he'll never stop fighting. The guard next to him kicks his back, forcing Dez to stay kneeling over the wooden block.

Don't look away, I tell myself.

A large man barrels into me, nearly knocking me over, but I grab hold of a woman's hair and pull myself up. She screams and lashes out with her nails. They draw blood on my cheek. I throw my weight at her and slam her to the ground.

A purple blur reaches for me—a guard, his dirty hands grabbing my sleeve and pulling me down. There's something wrong with his face. His mouth is wide open as he falls to his knees, and then forward. A slender knife juts from his back; the rose carved on its hilt glints. Sayida's knife. *I am not alone.*

There's another bell, and I spin around.

Dez sees me. I know he sees me. He blinks. Then he opens his eyes again, a look on his face as if he's seeing a mirage. I need him to know it's me.

"Andrés!" I shout.

One of his eyes is nearly swollen shut, but the other is trained on my face. His dry, bleeding lips move. *Ren*, they say.

Ducking and dodging, I climb over falling bodies. Prince Castian raises his sword, and I draw the dagger at my hip and bite down on the flat blade. I hurl my entire body forward. The tips of my fingers grip the edge of the dais. Lift my left leg to get up and over.

Dez shuts his eyes.

Hands, brutal and rough, grab hold of my neck. My dagger falls when I throw my elbow back, rivulets of pain spreading from the stitches at my neck.

Too late. You're always too late.

I scream until my throat is hoarse, until Prince Castian raises his bloodied sword back in the air, until something hard rolls across the dais, and until the final bell stops ringing.

10

Prince Castian tightens his grip on his sword. His sweat runs in rivers down his face, tilted toward the body slumped at his feet.

Dez's body.

I shut my eyes for a moment because I can't look. Can't move. Can't breathe. The ground beneath me seems to be moving, but when I force myself to see, I'm the one off-kilter. My hand breaks my fall, and I start at the pain that stabs up my arm as sharp gravel breaks the skin. It helps me focus on Castian.

Slowly, the prince—the Lion's Fury—turns his attention to the fire that appears to be spreading toward the square. Citizens scream, fighting one another as the royal guard descends on the marketplace and around the executioner's block. Yet despite the commotion, Castian's shadowed gaze cuts to me. It's impossible that he's spotted me of all people in the throng of bodies that run like a disturbed ant colony, but he takes a step forward into a puddle of blood.

Hands clamp on my shoulders. No, he isn't looking at me. He must be observing the guard trying to slip my hands behind my back. For a moment, I let the guard start to arrest me.

I wonder if Castian recognizes me from the forest. The prince tilts his chin up. The day's light bathes him so he appears to be glowing from within. *The prince slays the Moria bestae.* His eyes are brighter than when I saw him last, like crystal blue pools. For a moment, he looks serene.

Pain splinters under my eyelids, a memory trying to push its way forward from the Gray. *Not now,* I plead. Hatred snakes through me at the sight of him—his golden circlet bejeweled with fat rubies, dark as the blood splattered on his face.

I want to ruin his serenity. I want to ruin him.

"I will kill you," I tell him, my voice as calm as the eye of a storm. I'm close enough to the dais that if I can break free, I could tackle him. The guard at my back squeezes my wrists in his rough hands.

But before I can try anything, there's a blast on the other side of the square. A wave of terror resounds from everywhere at once, and I know I have to take this moment. I throw my elbow back into the guard's gut, his grunt hot in my ear as he tries to pull me against him. His nervous sweat is slick against my rough palm, and I push my weight forward, slipping free like river trout. Holding out my hands, I steady myself on the ground, then kick back with all of my strength.

I don't see where I hit him, but I feel my boot landing its mark. I throw my weight and cartwheel into a standing position at the edge of the executioner's dais, the stained wooden boards at eye level.

Prince Castian is gone.

"No." My breath hitches. "NO!"

At the bottom of my vision, there's a dark tangle of hair.

I know I should look. I know I have to look. He deserves for me to look.

But I can't.

My ears ring amid the screams and cathedral bells. Something sharp in my mind breaks open. The ghost of a voice whispers as my heart pounds in my chest and colors go bright, then fade into gray.

Hands, small and chubby, press against a window. The city is burning.

I wrench myself out of the Gray and train my eyes on Dez.

The strongest man I know, cut down. Blood drips from a severed neck. There's the white of bone, blood vessels, a mass of tender insides that makes us mortal. Breakable. No matter who we are we are breakable.

I reach. I reach for the tangle of wet black curls.

Something inside me snaps in two, like I've been splintered down the center. My fingers graze a single errant thread in the air, and then I drop my hands. I grab hold of the wooden platform because I can't stand on my own anymore. My hands come away wet and sticky. My screams scrape across my throat like jagged nails.

Strong arms wrap around me, but this time, they don't belong to the guard.

"I've got you," Sayida says, breathless. "We need to leave, *now.*"

"No," I say, helplessly. Lost. Adrift. "I have to kill Castian. I have to—"

"Shhh," Sayida says urgently. "You're going to get us killed instead."

She tugs on me, and I struggle against her, but she's stronger than she looks. Or perhaps I'm tired of fighting. I can't do it anymore. My screams dry up, but my throat burns.

We move quickly, hiding in alleys and turning onto narrow streets. She half carries me, half drags me into a building that smells of firewood and fish.

The Gray blurs my sight, billowing like storm clouds.

A little girl points at the sky. There is a shower of stars.
Someone picks her up and brings a kiss to her cheek.

The image is sucked back into the Gray and replaced with another.

Small fingers pick at a tray of chocolates decorated with
sugar pearls.

"Ren! You have to snap out of it. I can't—I can't carry you the whole way." Sayida's dark-lined eyes run with her sweat and tears.

I slam my fist into the nearest wall, and the pain that splinters across my knuckles helps me focus. Helps me out of the Gray.

Sayida directs me down a flight of stairs into a small window-less room and locks the door behind her.

Crates of potatoes and jars of olives and pickled fish line the walls. Sayida pushes a rack containing nothing but sacks of flour to reveal another door. A hidden room.

"Where are we?" I ask, and realize I'm shaking.

Margo's lying on a pile of rice bags, a cloth over her eyes. Esteban sits on the stone floor, his head resting against a brick wall, turning only when he realizes we have returned.

"Ren?" He hurries over to me. "Are you all right?"

At least, that's what I think he's saying. His lips move and his voice is an echo that's already fading.

Fingers snap in front of my eyes.

Suddenly, Sayida wraps her hands around my shoulders, gentle as a caress. Her fingers spread out around the curves of my sweat-drenched back. Her magics flood my body, like a cooling balm on a sunburn.

> *Dez sits under a tree in San Cristóbal. He cuts the skin of a bright red apple with a pocketknife. There is something about the way he smiles at me—*
>
> *Dez returns from a solo mission. Before he goes to report back to his father, he finds me in my small chamber. "I brought you something." He pulls out a box of sweets—*
>
> *Dez searches for me in the dark and pulls me close. Closer still. "Stay a little longer, Ren."*

"No more," I beg Sayida. The emotion she's pulling gathers at the base of my throat. I want to name it, but I can't. With her power she's found *my* memories. I don't want them. "Please."

Sayida sits back, rubbing her hands against her trousers. "I'm sorry. I wanted you to find your happiness."

I turn my face toward her. She's blurry, as though I'm staring at her through the thin veil of a funeral shroud.

I slowly sink down onto a rolled-out cot on the floor. It hurts to swallow the metallic taste on my tongue. "Even I didn't know that's what you'd find."

When I wake, I snap up and reach for my sword.

"What do you think you're doing?" Margo asks, standing with her hands on her hips. I can't meet her red-ringed, swollen eyes for long because they mirror my own.

All three of them are in similar borrowed clothes. Plain loose trousers and white tunics like cantina servers. There's a bundle at my feet.

"Where are we?"

"My nan's boardinghouse," Esteban says.

"You have a grandmother?" He'd said he had family, but I thought that meant a distant cousin. So many of us have lost everyone that the word *grandmother* sounds strange to say. I never even met mine. I try to picture Esteban having someone to care for him, and a want springs forth that I didn't even know I had. "I thought you were from Crescenti."

"My family left after the King's Wrath," Esteban says, biting at his already raw cuticles. "I went to the Whispers and Nan came here to help the elders. She's one of the Olvidados," he says. There's the shadow of bruises on his brown skin. One on his cheek and a couple on his forearm, as if someone grabbed him and wouldn't let go.

"The forgotten ones?" I remember stories about the Olvidados. They were people born to Moria families, but their magics never surfaced. Centuries ago, in the kingdom of Memoria, the old priests and priestesses named them Olvidados—forgotten by the Lady of Shadows.

"My nan's family didn't shun her for not having magics," Esteban explained. "In Citadela Crescenti, Moria born is Moria no matter what, as long as we keep the Lady of Shadows in our hearts. We were separated after the King's Wrath, but she found Illan and offered to be his eyes and ears in the capital. One of them, at least."

Margo nods solemnly. "We do not betray the identity of our spies. But—"

Her voice quivers, and she doesn't have to finish, to say, *But under the circumstances.* But Dez is dead.

"We shouldn't be here," I say.

"She brought us fresh clothes and food for the night. There's water to clean up," Sayida says carefully, like she's trying to keep a wild animal calm.

The ceiling creaks beneath the feet of boarders, but the silence in the streets carries its own weight. I need to get out of these moss-covered walls. I need to find him.

"Eat," Esteban says roughly. He won't look into my eyes. "Nan was kind enough to bring us dinner. Don't let it go to waste."

"I am grateful for that," I say, sounding like I gargled with sand.

"You aren't acting that way," he says.

"I just watched our leader get *beheaded*," I snap. "Forgive me if I can't stomach food just yet, Esteban."

Margo kicks a sack of rice beside her. "Stop acting like you're the only one who cared for Dez."

Sayida steps to the center of the musty room. Her soft black waves are loose, and out of all of us she's the most calm. What must it be like to be in control of your emotions that way? Can her Persuári magics drown out her sorrow? Could she do that for me? Take my emotions the way I take memories?

"We are all hurting," she says. "We will all deal with this in different ways. Shouting at each other isn't going to be one of them. He wouldn't want that."

I stare at the cold ground between my feet. I let my heart slow down, the vines tighten around it. I know that I'm the only one who can move forward from here. I know that none of them understand, not even Sayida. Dez was all I had, and I killed him.

"We can't stay here," I say as I lace up my boots. I ache from my fingertips to my toes. I ache so much that if I stop moving I might not get back up.

"We can't return to Ángeles yet. There are sweeps all over the city," Margo says, anger shrouding her words.

"I'm not going back there. I'm going to the palace. I'm going to kill the prince."

"We barely got out of there alive." Margo steps to me like a challenge. "They're looking for us, even now. They know Whispers were there for Dez."

I laugh, a cruel sound. "We weren't *there* for Dez. We— I failed. Dez is dead."

The three of them trade glances seeped with the same guilt I feel.

"You're hurting," Sayida says softly. "But now is not the time to act without thinking. We give it some time. Head back to Ángeles."

"Illan told us not to come back."

"He will forgive us," Sayida says. "I'm sure of it. We can make it to the ship heading to Empirio Luzou. It'll be safer on the coast with the guards concentrated in the capital. We'll endure Illan's punishment."

"And let *Dez's* death go unpunished?" I demand. Standing, I wince as a dozen new bruises make themselves known.

"The Whispers need us."

"For what? It's over."

"Do you hear yourself?" Margo asks. "Is this what Dez would want? This version of Renata Convida? The rebellion doesn't die with him."

"All the more reason to stay," I practically shout. I do know what he wanted. Dez always walked around with his heart for the world to see. "To complete his mission."

"It was Illan's decision." Sayida tries to comfort me. "He gave the order."

But her words are far, far from comforting. Dez didn't die because I wasn't fast enough. He died because I stole the key to his freedom.

I cannot return to the Moria. I don't belong with them. As a child, I wanted to please my palace captors. I caused the deaths of hundreds, thousands, and turned hundreds more into Hollows. But I didn't belong in the palace either. I don't belong anywhere.

Deep in my heart I know there's one thing I can do to make things right. I can make sure that Dez's murder was not in vain. Somehow, I have to get into the palace and finish what he started.

"We can't even bury him," I say. The end of my words gets caught in my chest and I take deep breaths to steady myself. Behind my closed eyelids I can see my fingers reach for a strand of black hair. The hesitation. I couldn't even bring myself to touch him because I'm a coward.

The other three don't say anything. They just stare back at me, pity in their eyes. Except for Margo, who seems to look at me with disdain.

"We're mourning him, too," she says, her eyes sharp as sapphires in this light.

Trying to ignore them, I pour myself a glass of water from a metal pitcher in the corner. My body craves food, but I can't bring myself to take a piece of bread.

"Two days' time," Esteban says. His eyes sweep the small hidden room. "That's how long Nan can give us. Then we head back to Ángeles."

We're supposed to be a unit, but we aren't. We're a bunch of broken pieces trying to fit with one another because we don't belong anywhere else. That isn't a reason to stay together.

"Be safe on your journey," I say, finally. "Trust no one, not even our allies. Make straight for Ángeles."

Sayida frowns. "You're really not coming with us?"

I shake my head. This is my burden, and I can only carry it alone. If we go in a group, Justice Méndez will suspect something is wrong. A plan moves in my head, stacking and restacking what needs to happen in order to be in the right place at the right time. Justice Méndez is my way to the weapon and to Castian. But Sayida won't give up on me, so I must give her a reason to.

"You can't think I'd be welcomed back with open arms? After all I've done? You've said it yourself, Margo, Esteban—I should never have been on this mission. I should have stayed rummaging through the garbage where I belong."

Margo makes an ugly scowl I didn't think was possible. "I shouldn't have said those words to you. I'm sorry."

"It's done." I practically spit out the words. "Even you three can barely stand me on a good day. And now this is all my fault—"

"It's not—" Sayida tries to protest again.

"Don't say things you don't know," I respond shortly, ignoring the wounded expression that flashes across her face. I look deep into her eyes, daring her not to look away. "Without Dez, there's no reason for me to stay with you."

"You don't mean that," Sayida says.

Margo crosses her arms over her chest, long wheat curls tumbling down her back. "Of course she does."

"Very well," Esteban says. "You'd be a burden to shoulder with your weak, simpering whining."

I clench the sword hilt in my hand and take a hard step in his direction, when there's a knock on the door.

The four of us jump, tensing into fighting stances. A tall, broad-shouldered woman peeks her head through the crack. Her hair is covered with a scarf, flour dusted on her black skin.

"Nan?" Esteban steps forward, his face slack with relief.

"There's a patrol making their rounds up the alley." She speaks quickly, wringing her hands. "They're arresting everyone and anyone who has so much as a hair out of place."

"You have to go," I tell the others. "Now before it's too late. You can't risk being taken."

Sayida grips my shoulders. "Please don't do this, Ren."

I feel a cold shock in my mind, the sensation of being watched. "Get out of my head, Esteban!"

"I'm sorry, I can't help it," he mutters. "Everyone is thinking so loudly."

"What are you planning, Ren?"

"She's going to get herself killed," Esteban answers. "You can't seriously think of returning to the palace alone. They'll be waiting for a counterattack."

"If I don't, they will move the weapon," I say.

"You don't know that," Margo snaps. "We have to *think*. We have to plan."

"By all means," I say. "Make your own plans. I know how Méndez's mind works. After all, I was one of them."

They avert their eyes. Are they embarrassed that I've said what they must be thinking?

"Very well. Imagine you find the weapon," Margo says, exasperated. "How will you get out?"

"She doesn't plan to," Sayida says.

I hate putting that hurt in her voice, but it's easier this way. If I go back, Illan will read the truth of what I did. He'll see that I destroyed Dez's only escape. They'd be right in blaming me. To try me for a crime against our own. This way, if I stay, my death will have a purpose. "Esteban is right. I'd be a burden. This is the only way I can help the Whispers. Go, now."

"The girl is right," Nan says, anxiously twisting her apron into a rope. "The Second Sweep will be here in moments. My boy—" She reaches for Esteban's cheek, the gesture so tender that I have to look away. Did my mother ever hold me that way? Surely she did, but—

"Ren," Sayida says.

"This is your best chance," I say. "Take it."

There's silence, except for the faint trickle of water from a leak in the corner. Then finally, Sayida nods. Without speaking, they shuffle toward the hidden door, their weapons clinking gently as they stoop to exit. I stare at the low beams of the ceiling, holding back my tears.

There's a small thud as the door closes behind them, then quiet again. It's a silence so long that my chest tightens. I feel their absence in ways I will never admit aloud.

"They're gone," Nan says upon her return, her voice like a splash of cold water. Sayida and Margo called her Lydia.

"We must move quickly," I say, and I walk out of the hidden room and into the storage area. There's a coil of rope hanging on the wall, and I grab it. "You must tie me up. Tell the guards that you found me stealing from your stores."

Lydia sets her brown eyes on me, the deep lines of someone who once loved to laugh crinkling her face even without a smile. Now her features are like stone as her gaze moves to the rope in my hand.

"My boy told me about Dez," she says softly. "There's another way for you. I know what it's like to lose your love, but you don't have to lose yourself along the way."

I want to tell her that I didn't *lose* him, that she knows nothing about me, but even in my grief, I won't talk back. She's sheltered and fed us and showed me kindness even though she didn't have to. For a moment, when I watch her, I think of the grandparents I never met. Would they risk everything for me like this, knowing the powers I wield? Are they still alive somewhere?

Lydia doesn't seem to understand, and so I hold my bare hands out to her. With Margo's illusion gone, my scars are visible again.

"I was lost long before Andrés," I say.

"Robári." She doesn't sound fearful or angry but full of pity. She says it as if it is just a word and I am just a girl and there is nothing outside of this storage room except for us. "My mother used to tell me that some were gifted with too much power and others with not enough."

Our magics don't feel like a gift right now, but I don't tell her that. "Why do this? You could have a normal life."

"I'll have a normal life when I can live with my grandson again. Maybe even live to see great-grandchildren." She reaches out a hand to my cheek. "Borrow some of my hope, child."

Part of me wants to recoil from her touch. For what comes next, I cannot afford a soft heart. Her eyes scan my face, perhaps searching for weakness. Something that will make me stay. But there is none. It's been carved out of me. There is nothing she can do to change my mind, and she knows that.

Finally, Lydia takes the rope, and I sit in the corner of her storage room, letting her bind my hands and ankles together.

"May the Mother of All bless the path you walk," she says before she returns to her kitchens, "for you do not know what you'll encounter along the way."

I wait, listening to every sound that filters through the crack beneath the door—the people in the boardinghouse who are blissfully unaware of what's transpired here and the cooks and their dinner chaos, an entire world so removed from me that I can't even begin to imagine being a part of it.

Then there's a pounding fist on the door. Muffled voices. Lydia's terrified cry. Hurried footsteps getting closer and closer.

The door slamming open.

"There she is," Lydia says, a tremble in her voice. "I caught her stealing food. She's one of them. Look at her hands."

The guards eye me warily before turning back to Lydia. "You've done your kingdom a great service."

"Are you sure she's one of them?" the second guard whispers to the other.

"Don't matter." He pulls a velvet pouch from his breast pocket, takes two fat libra coins out, and pockets them before throwing the rest on the floor. "Toss her in with the others. Our night is made."

I wish Lydia wouldn't look at me, but I feel her kind gaze as the guards twist my arms around my back and shackle them before dragging me out of the house. Their armor clinks in the narrow alley like a set of keys.

I don't struggle as they take me to the chained wagon at the end of the street. My body moves as if I'm floating, and I half feel as though I'm watching myself from above. When the guard opens the wagon doors, the putrid stench of bodily fluids and too many people sharing a single space assaults my nostrils. Unable to hold my nose, I duck my head into my shoulder, but it's useless. The odors are too strong.

There are two benches on either side of the wagon. It would fit perhaps eight people comfortably. Somehow, though, they've crammed fifteen bodies in here. I slip on the greasy floor as the guard pushes me in, and when he locks the doors, everything is dark.

"I'm not one of them!" a young man's voice shouts from inside the wagon's belly. There's a series of thumps that I imagine are his fists against the walls. "My father's a merchant! Let me send a post-mate to the Duque Sól Abene. He'll sort this out right away."

"Which unit were you in?" a disembodied voice asks me. "Is it true there are Whispers here to rise up against the justice once again?"

"No one is rising up against anyone," a hard, angry voice answers.

"I heard they're curing us," the someone says, thin as a ghost. "Finally, a cure for all of this."

Cure? My stomach drops. *The weapon.* More people know. I want to ask him where he's heard such a thing, but the smell is overwhelming, and I don't dare open my mouth to speak.

As the horse pulls the wagon across cobblestone streets, I feel every bump, and I begin to tremble. I wonder if maybe I acted too rashly. Terror flows through my veins. I dread going back to the place where everything started. The palace of Andalucía, and the cathedral beside it, headquarters of the king's justice. Prince Castian's home and capital of the kingdom.

But as we roll closer and closer to our destination, and I again hear the familiar sound of the wrought-iron gates opening to let us in, I sink so deeply into my fear it becomes part of me. Fueling me instead of hindering.

After all, I'm no longer the seven-year-old they stole from a forest clearing. I've spent eight years training beside the strongest Moria in the world. Training beside Dez. I've spent eight years learning to find a cause to fight for.

I know you. I trust you.

That was his last mistake.

I am ready now.

And I will be ready tomorrow. And the day after that. And the day after that. I have a plan, and this time, I can't fail.

I think of Justice Méndez. He won't be able to resist coming to see me once I tell the guards I'm a Robári. . . . I can already feel his skull in my grasp. But first, I will find the weapon.

Dez's death will be avenged. After all, I made Castian a promise I intend to keep.

11

SILENCE FALLS IN THE DARKNESS OF THE WAGON AS IT JOSTLES FROM OUR EXCESS weight, a ship in a storm. I keep my eyes down and try to become aware of the capital's deep night sounds. Hooves on cobblestone. Cheering from a tavern. Guards laughing from the wagon's seat. From somewhere, a cry for help that won't be answered.

An older woman who was crying earlier has sobbed herself out and is now nothing but a tremor beside me. Crammed as we are, I can feel the shake of her shoulders as they brush against mine. The smoothness of her skin makes me think of luxury. What could she have done to get captured by the Second Sweep?

Trying to make more space for myself, I grab the chains that link my manacles together and tug them, doing my best not to think about the sticky substance they leave on my skin. My elbow hits something soft.

"Watch it," a deep male voice growls inches from me. There's a sliver of light filtering in from the gas lamps in the palace court-yard. A face that's all angles and covered in bruises, and his breath stinks of liquor gone sour.

I pull my arms tight to my body and try not to breathe through my nose. Waste and urine mingle in the midsummer humidity, which eventually bleeds into the smell of rotting food as we pass by the kitchens. And beneath all that is something sweet. Something that doesn't quite belong. We must be near the narrow alleys that link the cathedral and the palace.

My lungs long for the clean air; my heart craves light. For a moment, I try to imagine that I'm back in Ángeles, in my drafty, small chamber in the San Cristóbal cloisters with creaky wooden floors, a window narrow but tall that lets in the sun to wake me up. I'm never going to see that room again. I'm never going to walk through the wide halls or sit in the library with a stack of parchments the elders encourage us to read. *Learn our histories before they are rewritten by the Bloodied King*, they said. I'll never sneak down the turret to meet Dez at the waterfall, or skin my knees falling during sparring drills. I will never.

I made that decision, but a shudder rips through my lungs because also I never thought I'd be back at the palace. I picture a younger version of myself walking hand in hand with Justice Méndez. A rag doll in Dauphinique lace and satin gloves.

The wagon halts, and there's the rattle of a cylinder lock's keys turning until they sigh with release and reveal the guards in the flickering light. The first guard, the one with a gap-toothed sneer, gives his torso a bit of a stretch. He's dramatic in all of his move-ments, like he's taunting us with his ability to move freely. I can tell he likes to cause pain. I've seen that look before. Castian had it in his eyes when he fought Dez in Riomar and when he drove his spiked gloves into his own guard's face.

I'm dragged out of the cart with the rest of the prisoners, and that's when I finally place the smell: incense. The stench of it does little to cover up the filth of the capital and the dungeon. For a moment I see nothing, only feel the steady beating of my heart concentrated in my ears.

I promised myself I wouldn't come back here. If my old mentor could see me now—what would he say? Méndez is not a man with remorse. But he was never cruel to me. Would he order me killed on sight or chain my hands and use me for my power once again? If I managed to sneak into the palace, he'd never believe that I was there of my own free will. No, this deception has to start in the belly of the palace.

My palms itch with the anticipation of magics. Castian's face takes up most of my waking thoughts. He clouds everything. Worse than the other memories and the Gray. The promise of emptying the prince's mind and leaving him in a comatose state thrills and horrifies me. I will be the monster I've feared. The kingdom will mourn their prince, and I will live with the memories of Dez's killer. At least I won't have to live with them for long. But the walls in my mind darken. There is a shadow around my vision. I do not, cannot, see another way out.

You are not a girl. You are vengeance in the night.

That's what I have to be for Dez.

The dungeon's gate nestles in a depression that links the palace and cathedral as the kingdom's reigning power structures. The Second Sweep hands us over to the two guards posted at the entrance, though I know there are more waiting inside. There's a metallic moan as one of them turns the keys in the lock and opens the gates up, like a sea monster's mouth ready to swallow us whole.

It's time.

I watch the guards. The second one averts his eyes as more bodies stumble out of the wagon. My instinct tells me that he's the one I need to go to. When I take a step closer to him, I can see he's young, with the dark brown complexion of Tresorian ancestry, like Esteban. This soldier's face is too soft, delicate. He probably couldn't buy himself out of the draft like the wealthy merchants and lords of his provincia, and now he's here, leading us into our cells. Or perhaps I want to imagine that there's an innocence in his large brown eyes that isn't there.

He seizes the chain of my manacles and yanks me forward to the open gate leading into the dark tunnel, but I grab hold of his hands. His dark eyes flick to the whorls that cover my hands, and he stiffens, eyes wide as if I've already started to drain him of his memories.

"Let go! Let *go* of me," he says, a scared boy who dwindles in stature at my barest touch.

"I must see Justice Méndez," I say, digging my thumb into the inside of his wrist. My nearness sends him into a stuttering frenzy because he knows exactly what I can do to him if I want. I've always hated that reaction, but now I'm counting on it. "I don't belong here."

Behind me a commotion erupts. I whirl around as an older guard with sweat-matted brown hair and a long scar across his chapped lips pushes the other prisoners aside to get to me. He snatches a fistful of my hair and tugs. His olive skin is covered in dozens of tiny scars, and I'm surprised they'd let a survivor of the plague enlist.

"What's the delay, Gabo?"

Gabo yanks his hands from my grasp. "She says she wants to see the justice, Sergeant."

The sergeant arches a thick brow, studying me. "In a hurry to have your trial?"

Raising my chin so that it's out of his grasp, I gather all the strength I can into my voice. "Tell Justice Méndez that Renata Convida has returned to the fold."

There's a moment of silence between the guards, as they consider my words. Gabo seems truly terrified. No one—not even the magic-less Leonesse—would willingly seek out Justice Méndez. I note that his name still inspires the same fear, perhaps worse than before.

"Maybe we *should* get the justice, no?" Gabo whispers to the sergeant. "Look at her hands. Her scars. Méndez said to send all possible Robári to him as soon as—"

"I know what he *said*," the officer snaps, "but I take my commands from the prince, not Méndez. She goes in with the others."

Something in his words gives me pause. Does that mean that he's going to call the prince instead? Could my fate be this simple—to meet Castian in these cells? What if . . . My thoughts speed too quickly, trying to make a contingency plan in the event I come face-to-face with Castian instead. Would I be able to prevent myself from draining his memories? I grin at the thought.

"Why're you smiling?" the officer demands.

I know the justice has all kinds of ways to know every word that is uttered about him, ears and eyes all over this kingdom. I know what happens when his orders aren't carried out. Gabo trembles, averting his eyes. No. I decide he's still my best chance.

"Because Justice Méndez is going to kill you for this."

The torches are few and far between, spotting the muddy stone walls of the dungeons. Water trickles from gaps and crevices, creating puddles. I lose count of the steps we take. The tunnel thins out the farther we go; the walls are closing in. If I held out my arms, my elbows would bend. If I kept running into the labyrinthine passages, the way would become so thin that only a child could slip through. The justice who designed these paths a decade ago used to let prisoners go free. He wanted to play a game. See how far someone could get before they were caught, before they got so lost in the winding dark that they realized it was easier to stay put. There's no better way to crush someone's spirit than to give them the false hope of freedom.

The deeper into the bowels of the dungeons we get, the more I begin to realize that if I lost myself to my stolen memories, my mind would be as desolate and gray as this.

Someone down the line retches, and then there's a series of cries as the guards divide us into cells. They're little more than cages. They were never meant for long-term prisoners, but now they're used that way, with humiliating buckets brimming with bodily waste in each corner and hay-stuffed cots ripped at the seams. They fill cell after cell but keep me behind. Anticipation coils in my gut, hoping that I will be brought to Méndez after all.

But when we get to a heavy wooden door studded with iron and a single slat to shove though meal trays, I realize where I am. Solitary.

I sit on the ground, cold and wetness seeping through the back of my tunic. When I look at the ceiling, there's a dark stain that seems to keep spreading. But everything is dark in here, except for the rectangular window on the door. The door hinges groan as the lock tumbles into place.

I wonder how long someone has to be down here before they're forgotten and discovered dead. A bead of water drips onto my fore-head. At least, I hope it's water. Footsteps echo in the distance. I wonder if Gabo will defy his officer. The thought brings a bitter laugh, because now I'm the naive one.

I wrap my arms around my knees, thankful I wasn't stripped of my clothes. The stench conjures a memory of when I was a girl. When I lived in the palace as Justice Méndez's ward, my rooms were draped with blue chiffon and white ruffled lace imported from the kingdom of Dauphinique east of the Castinian Sea, always an ally to Puerto Leones. Two dozen dolls with real hair on their heads lined my shelves, and wide doors led out onto my own private balcony. Porcelain bowls throughout my rooms were always filled with dried rose petals to mask the smell on the days when there were public executions, though the king has outlawed burnings in the last year. I vaguely remember the small forest cottage I lived in with my parents before that, but they're only the shadowy impressions of a seven-year-old, so faded that they might never have existed at all.

Back then I didn't know that I was the first of the Hand of Moria. Moria power, enslaved to the crown, used to do its bidding, used as symbols of the king's dominance and control, threats to the parts of the known world he had failed to conquer.

I shudder as I push my way out of the Gray. I can't relive that. But I know that if I'm going to survive long enough to carry out my plan, I may have to eventually. For now I allow myself to recall a moment of the good in my life—Sayida singing folk songs. Dez's grin before a fight. I fish in my pocket for the token he gave me. I turn the coin across my knuckles, a trick Dez taught me when we were kids. He was always so good at sleight of hand.

A strange noise rattles my solitary cell, and I drop the coin.

I snap up. There's nothing but my own frantic breath. My hands slapping cold stone until I find the coin and pocket it.

It happens again. And this time, I recognize it as a breath that strains to be taken. My eyes, now adjusted to the dark, see the shadows in the corner move toward the weak light at the center of the cell.

I am not alone.

12

"Who's there?" a man asks, his fingertips tapping the space around him.

Moisture drips from the ceiling, every drop sounds like a hand smacking a tub of water. A draft escapes from a thin crack in the door and whistles.

I sit just out of reach.

The man's breath is ragged. Understandable, as there are more shadows than air. The cell is musty with the stench of rot and bodily waste. Less understandable, however, is the way the man's bones jut from beneath his skin. Though the weak torchlight reveals a metal flap in the door wide enough to slide food through, it's clear no one has in a long time. How could they have *left* him in here? It seems more cruel than the public displays and executions the justice is known for. The Fajardo reign must end.

"I mean you no harm," I say. It's a small relief that the rage has ebbed from my voice, leaving a weary rasp.

His eyes look in my direction, but there's a thick film over the left one, like the membrane of an egg. With crooked fingers, he reaches out to me. "May I? It's easier this way."

I don't know why I'm so surprised, but I am. He's a Ventári. It's common for them to go blind in old age. All of our powers eventually wear on the body in different ways. The magic overpowers the parts of us that make us mortal. Permanent bruises on Illusionári, heart sickness and seizures in Persuári. Robári—I have the Gray and scars, but I am the only one I've ever met. Perhaps we lose our memories in old age. Perhaps we become Hollows in the end, too. I doubt I'll ever find out.

I creep forward and let him touch my temples. His magics burn along my skin, a pressure that builds all the way to the front of my mind. Like someone walking in your skin. Then he lets go with a start.

"You're a Whisper," he says, fingers trembling. "We all end up here. All of us."

"I'm not a Whisper," I say. "Not anymore."

He rubs his hands together, trying to keep warm. The tunic he wears is more dirt than cloth, torn at the seams and thin as old parchment. Sun spots mark his pale slender arms. I wonder who he was before he was relegated to this prison.

I take off my jacket and place it over his shoulders. A strange numbness travels across the inside of my mind.

"Renata," he says, turning his face to the sound of my voice. "I've heard of you. Even before I saw your thoughts."

A cold current runs down my body. I've been gone from the palace for eight years. Surely he hasn't been down here as long as that?

"Who are you?" I ask. "How do you know of me?"

"I worked in the palace before the plague," he says. A coughing fit racks his frame. He rests a hand on his chest. I watch it rise and fall with what seems like great effort before he can speak again.

"I didn't know there were Moria in the king's employ," I say. This place has a way of twisting minds.

He smiles with black-and-green–stained teeth. "We were on his council once. Before the creation of the Arm of Justice. Back then, Puerto Leones was at war with Empirio Luzou. It was not a war supported by the people. Even those closest to the king could not intervene."

I have a vague memory of one of the elders saying Luzou has always been the Moria's greatest ally. But where were they when Riomar fell? I think back to my lessons on Leonesse history.

"The only thing that stopped the fighting was the outbreak of the plague," I say.

"At least they've taught you that." He sucks in a breath that sounds painful.

"You didn't leave?"

He shakes his head. "I could not. King Fernando kept me as the Memoria ambassador. I sent the Whispers messages. Up until I was discovered and captured two years ago." The old man gives a wheezing cough.

"Are you the Magpie?" I ask, thinking of the person who alerted Illan that there was a weapon in existence.

"No." His voice is gruff. "Illan's informant is unknown even to me."

"What did they do to you?"

"I was in Soledad prison for a time." His bony fingers hover over his shoulder. "When I wouldn't tell Fernando how to find safe passage through the mountains, I was brought back here. A guard ripped my mark for the Mother of All. Sliced off the skin and then kept digging with his dirty fingers."

I think of the crescent moon and arc of ten-pointed stars that create the mark of the Mother of All. Elders carry that symbol on their skin when they achieve the highest rank in the Moria orders. I remember Illan's hopeful face in the tent before he told me Dez's plan. Does he know that this man is still down here?

Gripping his hand, I ask, "What does Our Lady call you?"

A smile breaks across his wrinkled face and when he blinks, tears fall. "Our Lady hasn't called me anything for quite some time. But once—I was known as Lozar."

He turns his face to the side and coughs up mucus and blood.

I'm angry. I am angry at Illan and the Whispers for never telling us of this man. I'm angry at Dez for scheming behind my back while asking me to trust him. I'm angry at the skies, the earth, the sun. I'm angry at existence and this tide for swelling beyond my control.

"It's all right, Renata." Lozar's voice interrupts my rage. I recognize that sensation inside my head. He's seeing into my thoughts— even in this state his power is strong. I wonder—is that what's keeping him alive despite the cruelty he's experienced?

"Was it worth it?" I don't know what makes me ask this. "You've been left here by the Whispers, by Illan—"

"I knew what it would mean to be a spy and remain at court," Lozar says calmly. "And I'd give my next life to the cause just as readily. As I told the other boy, that time is soon. Now."

He pulls down the tattered collar of his shirt and reveals a terrible gash. I've never seen a cut like that. Even for the justice, this kind of torture is vicious.

"You're in solitary. What other boy?" I ask.

"They don't see me when they open the doors. They've forgotten

I'm here a month now. It is solitary to them." A buzzing sensation blankets the inside of my head. "The boy you've come to avenge. He was here. And then he was taken. Andrés."

I let go of Lozar and clutch my stomach. I press my hands to the floor and let a cold wave of dread fill me. Dez was here. *Of course.* They would have shoved him in one of the high-security cells. *Of course,* I am where he was, but too late.

I get up and run to the door. If I slip my hands through the rectangular slot, I could reach the lock. Would they have had time to change the code in all the commotion? "I can get you out of here."

Lozar wheezes out a laugh. How can he laugh at a time like this? "I couldn't find my way through the tunnels, let alone make it to a safe house."

I breathe hard. I can't let him die. He's lived through too much and suffered for too long to let this be it. But if I leave, I'll lose my best chance at reinstating myself with Justice Méndez. I'll lose my revenge. My eyes burn, and I blink back the hot tears that threaten to spill.

"I can get you out of here and take you to the Whispers."

"I am slipping away, Renata." Lozar coughs for a long time. "He wanted to help me, too."

I would do anything to hear Dez's voice again.

Without speaking, Lozar squeezes my left hand, free of cuts and blood, and presses it to his temple, the glow from my scarred fingertips illuminating his pale, weathered face. When someone gives a memory willingly, the magics buzz through my veins, images are easy to find, like low-hanging fruit, ripe and waiting to be plucked.

Black as the longest night.
　　The click of the locks reverberate in the damp cell. Feet

shuffle in the corridor. They are bringing another prisoner. Lozar searches for the far end of the wall and makes himself small. He's lived his adult life invisible to others.

The door creaks open, the wrenching of metal drowned out by guttural cries and fists hitting flesh. Bodies slap against stone walls. From his corner he has full view of the door, his vision cloudy as warped glass. Two men, one a prisoner in chains, one a guard obscured in shadow.

"You don't have the right!" the prisoner shouts. His voice is hoarse, as if he's been screaming all day.

The prisoner grabs the soldier by the collar. Lozar wonders if anyone knows he is still down here.

He flinches as the prisoner is knocked to the ground with a knee to his stomach.

"I have every right," his captor spits back. Faint flickers of torchlight illuminate a small wooden box in his hands. "I have to do what no one else will."

Lozar stares at the wooden box, transfixed by the gold etchings across the surface. He knows what's in there. Knows how valuable it is.

"Liar." The prisoner rises to his knees, his mouth pulled back to show his teeth. "You're a monster. Get that away from me."

"You'll see the light soon enough," the other man says, then slams the door shut.

The boy rushes it, pounding his fists as if he imagines it is his captor instead. His exhaustion renders him weak and weary near Lozar's feet. His body shudders with every breath. A copper cuff around his wrist. He mutters his rage.

"What does Our Lady call you?" Lozar asks.

The boy's face snaps up at the sound of a voice. But his surprise disappears when Lozar comes closer.

"Andrés," the boy says. "Don't worry. We're going to get out of here."

I wrench my fingers from his temples, breaking the connection that's burning new lines of magic across the top of my hands. This is the hardest memory to break free from. Being able to hear Dez once more leaves me shaking. *We're going to get out of here.*

"Dez," I say, sinking back into the sorrow I felt when I first came to, after the execution.

"Dez?" A momentary confusion crosses Lozar's face as he reaches for his memory where Dez's name used to be and is now empty. "Is that the boy's name?"

"Was," I say softly.

You'll see the light soon enough, the prince told Dez. That was Castian shoving Dez into the cell in Lozar's memory. That was him holding the small wooden box that made even Dez flinch, and that was *his* voice, leaving Dez to his death. Even if I couldn't see his face well, I know it like I know the hate carved into my own heart. I heard his voice in Esmeraldas. In Dez's memory of Riomar. Castian was in Celeste's home. *No one can know I was here*, he said then. I didn't understand why Castian would care if he was seen. Then I think of what I saw in the alman stone: Lucia with her blank eyes and strange glowing veins, her lifeless husk of a body, still moving even though her magics had been carved out. Castian wanted to break Dez. He taunted Dez with the weapon before the execution. When will he use it next?

I gave the prince everything he wanted.

I slam my fist into the door.

I feel the pain like nails driving into my arm. Blood runs down my fingers. I stare out the window on the door and watch the flame of the torch crackle. I have to get out of here.

Days ago, I wanted to climb my way up the ranks of the Whispers. I wanted to help get Moria to safe lands while we fought a silent war here. Today, I want to kill Prince Castian, *need* to kill Prince Castian. I want to see my face reflected in those sadistic blue eyes. Catch him by surprise. Match his violence with my own.

"You can't do that. Not yet," Lozar wheezes.

"What?" That sensation is back—one of a buzzing gliding along the inside of my head. I've been so consumed in my thoughts, I didn't realize Lozar was observing them, too.

"You cannot kill the prince—not—" He struggles to speak over my protest, holds a finger in the air. "Not until you uncover where the weapon is kept."

I pace around the cramped cell. Castian would never tell me willingly. I'd have to rip every memory from his mind until I uncovered his secrets.

"How often do the guards check on you?"

"Before they forgot I was in here?" Lozar asks weakly. "Once every week, maybe longer."

I don't have a week. If I break out now, I'll be outnumbered by the guards before I find Castian. If I stay here until my so-called trial, he could move the weapon before I get to it.

"You know what you must do," Lozar says. "Stay for more than your vengeance."

I think of Esteban and Margo. They never trusted me. They never wanted me in their unit. They didn't believe I was part of the cause. When you're alone for so long you forget how to depend on others, how to have others depend on you. I don't know how to be more than myself. The moment I found Celeste dead, I knew things would be different, but I didn't think it'd be so soon. Dez was my hope. The Whispers'. His father's, too.

Stay for more.

How can I do more with a power that is only meant to take? Perhaps for the first time, my power is the only thing I can count on to see me through.

We're silent for a long time, Lozar's breath so labored I fear he's going to die before he can get the words out. He says with a small gasp of realization, "You are one of the stolen Moria children."

"I was."

"With this weapon—what's to stop the king and the justice from repeating their sins?"

"That's why I came here," I say.

"But your resolve is weakening because of your thirst for vengeance."

He coughs, blood dribbling down his chin from the corner of his mouth. "He named you, Renata. When he could not escape, he still remembered your name. You must stay for more."

I shut my eyes against the sting of tears, swallow my guilt. I take a deep breath to steady myself. His words anchor me, and it's like wading out of the thick fog of my anger.

"I can help you," Lozar tells me.

When I close my eyes, I visualize my fingers pressed against Prince Castian's temples. I can see the light of his life extinguished. I see myself retrieving the wooden box and destroying the wretched cure within. I will savor that moment, my last, and give the Whispers a way to keep fighting.

"How?"

Lozar doubles over, nearly coughing up his lung. He's going to die in this cell, and no one is going to notice. A desperate swell of tears rushes to my eyes. I wipe them away and grab hold of the bars in the narrow window.

"Mercy."

Slowly, I turn at the word. Watch as he hacks up more fluid. His eyes turn to the sound of my breathing. His extended hand trembles, shaking the rest of him. I force myself not to look away.

Mercy.

"You can't ask me to do that." I do not know this man well, but I am sure as the sky is blue that I cannot take his life.

"They have forgotten me. What if they take me when they come for you? The justice loves the sound of screams. They'll use the weapon. Mercy, Renata."

My skin feels like thousands of spiders are hatching beneath it. My lungs are tight, straining to breathe through the smell of rot and disease spreading on his chest.

Mercy.

It is a lovely thing to call murder.

As much as I want to turn away, to call for guards, I know that if they come they won't lift a finger to help Lozar. The justice has dozens of ways to keep a body alive in order to inflict pain. I cannot save this man. But I can't deny him this.

Mercy for Lozar. I'll use up whatever mercy I have so that I won't have any left for the prince or myself. My arms shake, my legs give beneath me.

"You must do something for me first," I say.

The cell feels darker somehow. He touches my hand, and I feel him in my thoughts again. "You need the justice to trust you. This is a start."

"I must prevent Justice Méndez from being able to use my power. I will show you mercy, if you will do this for me."

Lozar nods. "I have no strength left. But Dez. He dropped a weapon here. He couldn't find it before they took him."

I crawl to the corner where Lozar was when I first noticed him. When I pat the ground for what feels like forever, something pricks me. I wrap my hand around a small dagger. Even before I bring it to the center of the room where there is the faintest light, I know it is the knife Dez carried in his boot. The handle is a rough wood, nothing ornate. But it's the first knife he ever made. Even if he'd found it, what could it have done against all those guards?

"There might be another way," I say.

"There is nothing left of me, Renata. Do not suffer my fate."

I wrap my arms around his body.

His heartbeat murmurs against my skin. He lets go of a sigh, relaxing into my hold. When I first got to the Whispers stronghold in Ángeles, I was too angry to be around the other children, and so I worked in the kitchen. It was Dez who taught me to hunt wild game—rabbits, turkeys, deer. It was the cook who taught me how to snap their necks. At the end of the day, we are as frail as our prey.

I hear a rattle down the corridor, another sharp breeze, and I know the guards would rather leave this man to wither away than to show mercy.

Mercy.

It was Dez who taught me the Whispers' songs. He and Sayida and I would hum as we returned from a hunt after days, shoulder to shoulder in the tall grass hills of the Memoria Mountains.

And so I hum to Lozar, whose fate is forever linked to mine in a way that I didn't expect to find down here. He sings along, a hoarse sound, a rebel's final yell.

"Mercy," I whisper.

There's the crunch of his bones. I remember the first time I snapped a hare's neck in my hands.

A dull pain seizes my heart and holds on until I'm singing alone, and the only heartbeat I hear is my own.

I don't notice the people that have gathered at the cell door until I hear the sharp clicks of the cylinder keys falling into place. A voice I have not heard in a long time calls my name.

I drop the man in my arms, and Lozar's body slumps into a corner. I make a silent promise. *No one will bury you, but I will remember you as long as my memories are my own.*

"What in the Father's name?" The sergeant stomps in, splashing through the filthy puddles. Torchlight floods the dark cell. His bewildered stare takes in the dead man in the center of the room.

I must be a sight to behold. My left hand is a bloodied mess. Moments after Lozar passed, I grabbed the boot knife and stabbed it through my hand. One of the elders, a medicura who once taught in the university, showed us where in the human body to strike to kill swiftly. Where to make it bleed the most. Where to injure but not cause permanent damage. After all, we were not the monsters.

The guard picks up Lozar's limp hand. The dagger I placed there falls with a light *ping*. It is the same older guard with the pox scars on his face who walked me down here. He snatches me up by my shirt and shakes me. Pain splinters from my palm and from the sudden jolt of my neck. Blood trickles down my chest where one of the stitches must have come undone.

"Stand down, you fool!" the familiar voice says.

Justice Méndez sweeps into the cell with Gabo at his heels. The justice's fine leather shoes slosh through the muck covering the ground. He was never afraid to get dirty. At the sight of him my heart revolts against itself. His gray eyes take in Lozar's body, the knife, then the mess of me. His hand is extended, as if he can create a wall between me and the officer. Then he seems to remember himself, his elegant features turning to stone.

"Uncle," I whimper.

I can see his age in the silver weaving through his short beard and thick black hair. He's thinner than the young medic that I remember, but not sickly. It's like he's been carved out and tapered to show his strength. His face sharp as diamond edges. There is a war in my heart over the man I despise. The one who traded candies for my power. The man who read me stories before bed and then later signed away the lives of my family and others. How can I have no memories of my own parents, but now that he is in front of me, something inside me unhinges? Memories of him drift from the Gray. Form and re-form like ink in water.

I catch the moment when he softens. He sees me, as if for the first time, like the day I was presented in front of him by the guards who'd plucked me from the woods outside my home. A little Moria girl with crude hand-stitched gloves.

"Renata." His voice weighs me down, like my feet are encased in mortar. It takes all of me not to look away from the intensity of his stare. "Can this be you?"

"Yes," I say, my voice strangled. "I'm sorry—he was trying to kill me."

"Renata." The way he says my name has an edge. I shouldn't have sought him out. It was a mistake to think he'd be happy to see me. He knows where I've been these past years. He knows that I can't be trusted. He takes my bloody hand, and I use all my strength not to withdraw. His thumb traces the freckle at the base of my thumb. Dez kissed me there once. "Do you remember what I said to you when we last saw each other?"

The day the Whispers stormed the palace and set the capital on fire. The day I first met Dez and he saved me from this gilded cage. The day I last laid eyes on Méndez and swore I never would again.

"You said—" I swallow the choking cry swelling to the surface. "You said you wouldn't let anyone take me away."

I stiffen as his hands rise in the air, not to strike me, but to wrap around me.

"You have come back to me," Justice Méndez says. He takes my face into his hands and examines me this way and that, as if I'm a horse he plans on purchasing. But then I see his eyes land on a distinct cluster of freckles along my jaw. He's trying to find a way I could be an impostor, a look-alike. His thumbs trace the scars on my palms, over and over like he's trying to memorize their pattern. Is it that dark in here or are there tears in his eyes? "I do not believe it."

My throat aches as I find the courage to lie and lie well. "The Whispers are in upheaval. I was able to break free from the safe house. I made it to the capital, but I had nowhere to go. I had to steal—I haven't eaten in days—I was captured and brought here."

I wince when he holds my injured hand tighter. He keeps his finger pressed over one of the cuts. His gray eyes snap to the guards waiting in the shadows.

"My justice—she killed the prisoner—" the older guard says.

"He was a Ventári," I say, and wince again at the burning pain in my palm. "He saw that I had run away from the Whispers and tried to kill me."

"You let this man have a weapon?" Méndez's voice is colder than the draft squeezing through the crack of the door.

"We didn't know he was here," the older guard stutters. "The cell was empty before—"

But Méndez silences the guard with a pointed finger, then returns his attention to me. The hard edges of his face soften.

"My Renata." Is that satisfaction in his voice? He wraps his arm firmly around my shoulder. I let myself soften in his hold. Relieved. Grateful. Pliant. I let out a real sob. I'm betraying everything I love because a fissure in my being remembers how safe I once was with this man.

Méndez guides me through the dark. We step over Lozar's body. I killed him, and we are walking over him as if he's a puddle in the market square.

"Clean this up." Justice Méndez waves a dismissive hand at the guards and they scramble to lock the cell.

"Yes, my justice," Gabo says, and bows.

"You did well in telling me, Gabo. She should've been brought to me as soon as possible." Justice Méndez's eyes cut to the officer. "You, on the other hand, Sergeant Ibez—I am disappointed in you. I understand you chose to not follow my instructions."

"Your Royal Justice, please!" The words are said in a frenzy. "I believed her to be a liar. As you preach, they are charlatans. Deceivers—" His dark eyes widen with shock.

Deceivers.

That's the last word he manages before Gabo slashes the dagger across his exposed throat.

I swallow my scream as Méndez's hand grips my shoulder even more firmly.

"Come, my sweet," he says. "You are safe now, with me."

13

I SHOULD NEVER HAVE GOTTEN LOST IN THE WOODS. WITH JUSTICE MÉNDEZ'S arm around me, it takes all of my willpower to remain calm. It's the Gray that won't keep still, releasing a memory like dust from an unearthed tomb. It is so clear, swirling with the color that normally bleeds out of my memories from the Gray. For the first time, I'm not swallowed into the memory, but it is simply there for me to grasp.

When I was a little girl, our home always had an altar dedicated to Our Lady of Whispers with her crown of stars and the moon at her feet. Back then, I knew nothing of the goddess or the people she gifted with magics that vein the earth. I knew that I had a power I couldn't always control, and I'd wonder at the strange glow that traveled under my fingertips. I didn't have the burn marks that come with taking a memory because my parents never let me take my gloves off outside the house. My mother was a Persuári and my father an Illusionári. I remember my mother channeling her warmth into me when I was afraid of the dark. I remember my father casting shadows on the wall to take the shapes of the stories he told me. Those are the magics the king and the justice claimed were responsible for the most devastating plague in our history.

The day I got lost, I tugged on my wool gloves and followed my father into the woods. The flowers on our altar had withered, and so I was to help pick new ones.

"You must be very careful, Nati," my father would warn. I've never seen kindness in anyone else's eyes the way it lived in his, even when he was serious. When I let myself remember him, I realize he was scared, too. "Stay close."

But I didn't stay close. I found a patch of wild gazenias in full bloom. I followed their orange hearts and yellow petals through the dry woods until I came across an open field. I'd never been so far from home before and I'd never left the woods. I tried to turn back, calling for my father and mother until I came across soldiers in the king's dark purple-and-gold uniforms.

"Are you lost, little one?" a woman asked, coming close. I wasn't supposed to talk to strangers, but I can still remember the fear that overpowered me then. I nodded and told the soldiers exactly where I lived and what my house looked like.

They didn't take me home. They brought me to the palace, with promises of seeing my parents there.

I was taken to a nursemaid who washed my hair and changed my clothes before bringing me to Justice Méndez's study. I was made to sit in the same chair I sit in now. It has a leather groove and a high back that stretched far above my head.

Méndez always had a smile for me. His patience was remarkable with a girl who did nothing but cry for her parents at first. He sent up cherry cakes with fresh cream and oranges encrusted in burned sugar and drizzled in clover honey. He said I could see my parents if I followed instructions.

Nameless guards brought a blindfolded man into the room. His mouth was gagged and his hands were tied. I cried again, but now Méndez knew he could calm me down with more delicacies. At home my mother fried potatoes with rosemary and cooked squash we grew ourselves. We ate meat once a month if there were enough rabbits to hunt. I'd never seen or tasted such wonders as I did my first time in the palace.

"This man," Méndez said, "has a secret. Have you ever seen snow, Ren?"

I wanted to correct him. My father called me Nati. It was comforting, familiar, my name. Anything else made me feel uneasy, out of sorts, like an entirely different person. But I wouldn't correct this man. There was something in the justice's gray eyes that made me stop. So instead I answered his question with a nod.

"All you have to do is find this man's secret. He's keeping something very dear to me hidden in a place with snow."

"I don't know how," I said, and it was true. I'd never used my power before. My mother explained it once. She said I was blessed with the magics of memory. Only the Lady of Whispers knew everyone's secrets and it was a gift I had to keep to myself.

I can't remember how, but I did it. I pressed my unmarred fingers to the bound man's temples and pulled out a memory of Citadela Nevadas up in the mountain range of the same name. I described the small wooden houses with chimneys puffing out black smoke. Men hauling wood through a snowbank and into a cabin full of swords and other weapons.

Before I could even finish, Méndez shouted, "Citadela Nevadas. Send an infantry right away."

Now, as I lean back in the chair that I've grown into, my eyes flick to the wall behind Méndez. There's a map of the kingdom of Puerto Leones hanging there. It changes bit by bit every year, erasing provincias. There's a mountain range west of the capital, the only place in the country where it ever snows. Three years ago, I was sent on a mission to scout Citadela Nevadas.

It was nothing but ruins and I couldn't remember why, but I knew it was because of a memory I had stolen. I didn't know it was once a holdout from the queendom of Tresoros, which never recognized the treaty between their former country and Puerto Leones.

I can't find Nevadas on the map, either, but the mountain range is clearly drawn and capped by white snow.

The justice's study hasn't changed in a decade, except perhaps for a different guard standing at the door, and the smattering of gray in Justice Méndez's dark hair. His sharp cheekbones have a touch of red, as if he's been somewhere sunny recently. Though he must be in his early forties, he has the wrinkleless face of someone who seldom smiles or laughs.

Méndez takes a white cloth, dips it into a brown jar on the right side of his desk, and rubs the table down with it. The liquid is pungent with lemons and orange rinds. Once the wood gleams, he pats the surface, on which stand neat rows of metal instruments, small knives, vials in clear bottles the shade of pond water, a porcelain bowl full of balls of cotton, long, slender needles, and black thread.

Before Méndez became the head of the king's justice, in charge of overseeing peace and order, he had been a medic in the king's army. It's part of the reason why he knows what is most harmful to the body and how to craft the best instruments of pain. From the drawer, he takes out a clean pair of calfskin gloves and tugs them on.

This would be so much easier if I were a Persuári to guide his emotions or a Ventári to see what he's thinking.

"Come, Renata." His storm-gray eyes focus on my face, silently interrogating my features for any signs of deceit. "Your hand, please."

Dez's boot knife is in front of me. I consider grabbing it and stabbing it through the thick veins on the top of his hand. It is a wild, sudden impulse that vanishes as quickly as it appeared. Extending my bare hand to the most powerful man in the kingdom, save for the king and prince, I lower my head with shame that is far too real.

My knuckles are a bloodied mess of torn skin, and the gash on my palm has clotted. I can't help but wince and bite my tongue as he pulls my fingers open to assess the damage.

"Are you afraid?" he asks. Those gray eyes never miss a thing. He did not become this man by believing every story that was brought to him. His body is rigid, but the anger he showed to the guard—the dead guard—has been replaced with careful suspicion. I would be a fool not to be afraid.

Some part of me doesn't believe that he would hurt me. Not when I am more useful to him alive.

"Yes," I say.

His cheek twitches. "I must assume the rebels have poisoned you against me."

"They tried." My voice grates in my throat, these recollections taking the shape of daggers. "The Whispers kept me among them. I was too valuable to kill. Too dangerous to trust. They—" I cut myself off, letting my rage fill the silence. None of these words are lies and perhaps that is the spark of the anger that makes me tremble. I have not forgiven Méndez for using me as a weapon, and I have not forgiven the Whispers for doing the same.

"Hold still," he warns. "This will kill any infection you might've contracted in that muck. Though I'll have to keep an eye on it. The skin is too red for my liking. He missed your tendons, thank the Father of Worlds."

"Thank the Father of Worlds," I echo.

Then all my thoughts evaporate as he pours a solution over my raw and bloody hand, and it stings so much that I fear I'll faint.

"Don't tell me the rebels have taken your courage," he says.

I frown, shaken by his words. "What do you mean?"

His dark lashes cast long shadows over his cheeks. Of all things, a smile breaks across a face otherwise carved from marble. "When you were eight, I wouldn't let you go with the other court children to visit Tresoros Manor. You packed a bag and decided to climb out of your window. You got halfway down before you slipped. Broke your arm." He selects a set of sharp tweezers and points to the pale scars on my right forearm. "You had ten stitches and couldn't use your magics for weeks. But when I patched you up, even when I set your shoulder back in place, you didn't flinch. You didn't cry. There were no tears in your eyes. Not like you have now."

I try to swallow, wet my tongue, but everything is dry. I don't have this memory, but as he gently, meticulously plucks splinters from my knuckles, I believe him.

"Pain takes a toll on everyone," I say.

He makes a noncommittal sound. I take the moment to study him.

Gray eyes. Graying hair. Graying beard. It's like he's been coated in salt from the middle valleys. His touch is soft, holding my hand as if he's putting together pieces of fine Andalucían glass. When he at last sets the tweezers down, he washes my wound once again with the burning solution and turns my palm faceup. The cut extends from the base of my fingers to just above my wrist, red at the sides but no white or green of infection. He takes a breath, as if relieved, before threading the needle. Kisses the tip in the candle burning on his desk.

"Tell me, my sweet Ren," Méndez asks, "how did you escape?"

Without warning, he pushes the threaded needle into my skin. The thread follows through. My heart spikes. I bite down on my molars. Does he want me to be that fearless little girl once again? I don't want to remember her. But if this is the way to get closer to the weapon and to Castian, then so be it.

"Illan's son," I manage to say. I feel a hitch in my throat and take a moment to smooth out the wrinkles in my lies. "His capture had the rebels distracted."

"I was surprised to hear Illan wouldn't surrender for his own son," Méndez says. "But the bestaes do not value life the way we do."

Can he really forget that I am Moria, too? Was I such a good traitor that he counts me in his terrible *we*?

The tendons of my throat hurt. For a moment, I think of Dez's caress along my jaw, down to my clavicle. Embarrassed, I focus on the map behind Méndez. There is an empty space in the north of the kingdom where I know the Memoria Mountains to be. Is it that easy to wipe out the memory of a place? Simply redraw lines and leave gaps in the world?

The next stitch is followed by a cold numbness. I wonder if Dez would be proud of me. I didn't even flinch that time.

"They're unraveling," I say. "I saw a chance. I knew I wouldn't get another. They don't allow me in meetings, but I listen when I can. No one was afraid of me going anywhere."

There's a green fleck in one of his gray eyes. Was that always there? "Why was that?"

"I suppose," I say, "because I had nowhere to go."

It isn't wholly a lie. All truth changes depending on who tells the story.

He holds my hand hard in his. I stare into his eagle eyes, probing into mine to find the betrayal. "You could have returned to me."

"If I could have, I would have been at your side. As long as I can remember, one of the Whispers has been with me." Dez rarely left my side when we were children. Even when I wandered around the San Cristóbal ruins, there was always someone there, watching. I look at my hand, where his fingers leave imprints. "You're hurting me."

He lets go, breathing hard, like he's shocked at his own display of emotion. It's hard to look at him this way. It's worse to think that he actually cares for me.

"A few more," he says. As he adds stitch after stitch, I remember a time I walked with Justice Méndez in the palace gardens, forbidden to all but the justice of the crown, and he let me read under great gnarly trees draped with Leonesse moss and pale cosecha flowers. When the wind sailed through them, pink petals rained on me, so at night I had to untangle them from my braids. I would soak my hands in rosewater and powdered gold like the other girls at court to get rid of blemishes and impurities on their skin. It never worked on me. I am a network of scars, and I fear I'll never be much more than that.

Finally, Méndez lowers the needle, and wipes away the excess blood that bubbles up. "It'll scar."

"It'll blend in. Thank you, Uncle." I let my voice soften even more. "I'm sorry, I meant *my justice*."

"You must understand, Ren," he says, holding my hand the way one might cup the severed head of a rose, afraid the petals will come loose and spill. "Now that you're here, you will face an audience with the king. You will be under my protection, but you must prove yourself."

I nod quickly. "It's why I came back. You don't know how lonely I've been."

He doesn't respond, but I see his brow set with resolve. I remember the way his silence meant he was planning, always planning. What will it take to gain his trust?

Then his eyes snap to the door. Loud footsteps march in, the ragged breathing of someone who just finished sprinting. I whirl around to find a young man in the deep black-and-red robes of a judge, the rank that makes up all in the Arm of Justice who are waiting to take Méndez's place upon his death. He's got thinning brown hair the color of sparrow wings and a ruddy complexion. His brown eyes flare wide when he takes me in. Nearly tripping on robes too long for his average height, he makes a beeline for us.

"Is this it?" he asks. I've heard bleating goats with less grating voices. "A real Robári for the Hand of Moria. King Fernando will *finally* be pleased with our efforts."

Does he not know I can understand him? My every muscle is tense. I want to smack him for referring to me as *it*.

"Alessandro!" Justice Méndez snaps. There's a crack in his calm exterior. And I realize, perhaps the real reason he's so happy to see me, so ready to present me to the king, is because he needs me. "I do not remember summoning you."

The young judge takes a step back, stuttering through an apology. He genuflects over and over. The way he grovels makes my skin crawl. But isn't that what I'm doing? Trying to get back into the good graces of the man who destroyed my life?

"My sincerest apologies," Alessandro says, speaking lightning fast. Méndez's face is aghast that this boy is still talking, even though he holds his hand up in a way a king would silence a subject. "I am at your service. I am simply overjoyed that our mission will move forward. I only want—"

"The best for the kingdom," I say, interrupting him.

"How dare it speak for me." Alessandro practically recoils from where I sit.

Méndez's gray eyes slide in my direction, a pleased smile curling his lips.

I want to say, *It does more than that. It can rip your memories from your head until there is nothing left of you but a fumbling shell.* But that is not the girl I have returned to be. I bite my response and wait for Justice Méndez to speak.

"This is Renata Convida," he says.

"The girl stolen by the Whispers?" When he grimaces, his neck practically disappears. His eyes dart from Méndez to me, as if only now realizing he shouldn't have spoken so freely. If there is a rift between the king and the justice, perhaps I can use that to my advantage.

"She has returned to us, Alessandro," Méndez says, regaining his steely calm. "I would like to speak to her alone."

"My justice—you shouldn't be alone with such a creature."

I breathe deep to stomp on the violent impulses coursing through my bones.

"As you can see," the justice says, "she cannot hurt me in her state."

"I would never," I say.

The disdain in Alessandro's eyes tells me he does not believe me. When he smooths his hair back, I notice the marriage band on his finger—simple polished wood. No one in the Arm of Justice would want to wear metals associated with the Moria.

He bows once more. "I will return with updates."

"Shut the door when you leave," Méndez says.

"The young justices can marry now?" I ask, the moment Alessandro is gone.

Justice Méndez sits back down, returning to the items on his desk. He selects a bandage.

"The king, in his infinite wisdom, has decreed that the next generation of Leonesse must be loyal to the crown. What better place to start than among those sworn to protect the kingdom from its enemies?"

Who will protect the king from me?

Unrolling the strip of cloth, he wraps it around my palm and wrist. When he guides my fingers open again, I have the vague notion that I make quite the marionette girl. Margo's voice rings in my head. *Obedient is not the same as clever.* While I'm here, I have to be both.

"There we are," he says. "All better, for the moment."

He pulls off his blood-splattered calfskin gloves and bundles them in a piece of cloth to be dealt with by a servant who cleans the justice's office. He pulls out a sweet from his desk and hands it to me: a stellita. He used to always give me them.

I suck in a short gasp, cradling the candy in my hand. My mouth twitches with the need to smile. I decide that it would be an appropriate reaction.

"I haven't had one of these in—"

"Eight years."

"Thank you," I say as I take and chew the sticky candy. My jaw aches from not having had anything to eat in so long. The sugar melts quickly. A rush comes over me when I consider my rashness. What if it had been poisoned? I chew to buy myself a moment to think. Méndez needs me to present to the king, who has been displeased with Justice Méndez. He wouldn't dare. I decide I've done the right thing. This is the way I show him that I trust him, rushing to consume the treasures he's giving me, no matter how small. Still, I need to be more careful.

Méndez waits until I swallow before he snaps open another drawer to pull out a piece of dark fabric with something metallic attached. It isn't until he holds it by the metal cuff that I see it is a single locked glove.

It's been years since I've worn the design of his own making, but I hold out my good hand to him. It's like my muscles remember his every command, and I feel like my body has betrayed me. The gloves, the candy, the story he told me about when I was injured. We are stepping into the past, into a time when he trusted me. I need that trust to find my way around the palace.

He places the glove on my hand, the leather soft but snug over the calluses along my knuckles and palm. Then he clicks the iron bracelet into place. It's a pretty thing, for a manacle.

"This will have to do until your other hand heals and you can wear them both." He rings his bell, and a moment later, a boy scurries in, dressed in the sunflower-yellow uniform of a justice's page.

"Take her to Lady Nuria's former apartments," Méndez orders. "The attendants should have arrived by now. When you've delivered her, let Leonardo know he will have his work cut out for him before the royal presentation."

My stomach turns into knots at the thought of being brought before the king and prince. Perhaps if I start now, I will be able to control myself when I see him. *Stay for more*, Lozar had asked of me. I owe too many promises to the dead, it seems.

The page nods and begins to head to the door, and I stand, ready to follow him. Dazed not just from the day's events or the wound that throbs slightly, but from hope.

A heavy weight descends on my shoulder. Méndez's hand squeezes once, and his voice takes on a familial tone. "I'm glad you're back, Renata. It'll be as if you never left."

And as I follow the servant down the cavernous hall, that's exactly what I fear.

But I am wrong. Some things—like the sprawling mosaic of griffins on the floor—are the same, but not everything. The halls appear smaller. When you spend nearly a decade sleeping under the sky, or in the wide-open spaces of the Moria stronghold in Ángeles, a place like this is bound to stifle. It's like wearing an old article of clothing and finding it no longer fits. The gold-painted molding and halls filled with sculptures, panels of glass from the best artisans in the town of Jaspe. King Fernando takes pride in surrounding himself with the riches of Puerto Leones. All he allows to be imported are silks and a violet dye only found in the kingdom of Dauphinique, and the bananas that flourish best in Empirio Luzou across the sea.

I'm led through halls decorated with vases, tapestries in vivid greens and blues. We ascend stone stairs that smell strongly of incense, and step into a sky bridge with arched columns glittering with tiles in the old Zaharian style. When the boy turns down a long corridor, I get the dizzying sensation of remembrance. I'm most struck by a simple wooden door. The skin of my arms turns to gooseflesh as I slow down. Rusted hinges and a keyhole filled with dust speak of a forgotten place.

But *I* could never forget this door.

I know exactly what's behind it.

I remember it so well I can almost taste the dust of its books, feel the softness of the plush velvet chairs that line the small library. I grab for the doorknob, but it's locked.

"We have to keep going, miss," the page boy says, his voice climbing an octave, and I realize I've been staring at the closed library door for who knows how long. Releasing a pent-up breath, I keep walking.

As soon as we get to the end of the hall the boy bows a fraction, then scurries back the way we came. I step inside. The stone walls keep the room cool. The apartments I'm to stay in give me the sensation of walking in someone else's skin, like I'm not even here. I wonder if this is what people feel when I take a memory.

Lamps decorate the dressers and table. Everything is the color of summer blush wine with powder-white accents. The silk brocade drapes hide the night sky, and sheer white cloth hangs around a four-poster bed bigger than any I've ever slept in.

I find the three attendants Justice Méndez spoke of already waiting for me in the washroom, standing next to a full porcelain bathtub with rose petals drifting on the water's steaming surface. My bandaged hand is practically useless. I allow the attendants to undress me before I dismiss them.

"Our orders are to clean you up," one of them says.

"Or *try*," another mutters.

No one wants to be near a naked Robári, even one wearing a glove on one hand and a bandage around the other. Too dangerous. How long has it been since they've seen one? And what happened to the one I'm now meant to replace?

"Get out," I snap, narrowing my eyes at them.

One of them squeals as if I've advanced on her, but they leave all the same, and even though it's what I wanted, I can't say it doesn't hurt.

When they're gone, I sink into the water until it reaches the top of my breasts, and warmth hugs my body. A moment of sheer bliss. And then I hear the click of a lock from the outside of the apartments. Locked in. Did I expect anything else?

My arms tremble, and I sink deeper into the tub. It's been so long since I've had a proper bath. The last time was in one of the hot springs in Tresoros five months ago. Hot water is a luxury. Everything is a luxury when you're on the run. And yet, I sink into it, allowing the warm water to envelop me the same way vengeance hugs my heart. Words and images jumble in my mind.

Castian's cold blue eyes. Lucia's magics, carved out of her. The cure. Castian. Dez. Lozar's brittle bones snapping. A little boy standing amid smoke. A set of dice and children laughing. Fire.
Fire.
Fire.
Always fire.

I sit up so quickly that water sloshes out of the tub and onto the floor. The fire in my mind burns bright, in full vivid color.

I try a technique Illan taught me to clear my thoughts. It's easy for a Ventári to be able to think of nothing when they possess the gift to peer into the minds of others. Less easy for one haunted by a thousand stolen pasts. No matter how many herbs he gave me, how many solitary walks, even a quest for a magical spring, nothing could completely crack open the Gray inside my head.

But truth be told, I never wanted those memories to come out. Every Hollow I created felt like a living voice inside me. If I multiplied that innumerable times—I wouldn't be able to think. Terrible headaches plagued me until I could barely wake. For memory thieves, the past demands to be seen, even if it means swallowing memories of your own. That's what Illan believes created the Gray. My own mind constructed such a thing and my own life got swept up with it, leaving gaps in my story. Being in this place is rattling something loose. My temples stab with pain, giving in to the pressure of these wretched days and nights.

"*Please*, go away," I cry out. "Leave me alone."

I plunge my head beneath the water's surface. It doesn't stop the memory of flames from coming:

> *I am nine years old, and after two years in the palace, I am a proper little lady. I warm my back by the small pine-cone fire in the library, sitting on a long settee in front of a window as tall as the ceiling. If I look out, I will be able to see all of Citadela Andalucía. The capital with lights along twisty streets that turn at strange angles and wrap themselves around alleys like the mazes in the palace. The justice and the king love mazes, and so I decide I love them, too.*
>
> *It's late, and the other Moria children were sent to bed ages ago with their attendants, but Méndez said I could stay awake until the next bell chimes.*
>
> *I pop a stellita in my mouth and sigh with content-ment as its sweetness covers my tongue. They're my favorite, specially made by the king's candy maker, crafted from honey caramels that look like marbles flecked with bits of edible gold. The shimmer matches the paintings in my book. There's Queen Penelope, sitting in her garden. I try to flip the page of the storybook, but the parchment sticks to my sugar-stained gloves. The page rips slightly as I move to the next picture—the Lord of Worlds stand-ing on the horizon of his creation. The orange inks are so vivid, it's almost as if they glow, filling the library with light.*

I look up, squinting. The light's not coming from the storybook. Setting it down, I turn my head over my shoulder and peer out the window.

An incandescence has settled over the capital, like an illustration of the Lord of Worlds come to life. Like the glow of angels. At first, the fire is just a line against ultimate darkness, consuming the small forest that borders the capital.

My hands begin to prickle.

Today, during memory lessons with Justice Méndez, I saw a picture of that forest in my mind. He brought a man to me whom I recognized—an old neighbor from my village, named Edgar. I liked the picture I pulled out of Edgar's mind, the one of Mamá and Papá outside our wooden house, Mamá culling weeds from the garden and Papá chopping wood. Mamá's hair is less black than I remember, more gray. And Papá's shoulders, always broad, seem to slope. It's the first time I've seen them since I got lost. I pulled away from Edgar, and excitedly told Méndez that I knew where my house was! I knew where my parents were, and if I could please bring them to the palace to see me? Mamá would love a stellita, and I knew Papá would love one of the little chocolates crafted to look like a roaring lion.

Méndez promised he'd send them a message.

Now, not only are my hands prickling, but my heart feels itchy, as if it were about to explode. Why is the forest on fire?

As I watch, the fire spreads from the forest and toward the city. I can't look away. I press my hands, small and chubby against the window, leaving sweet smudges on the glass panes. The fire is even closer now, racing through the narrow streets, as if trying to finish the maze as fast as it can.

I start to scream. People cluster in the streets set aflame. They dash away from the fire, some holding torches and others becoming them.

Their screams find their way to the palace, and then within the walls.

There are shouts in the hallway.

"Watch out, Illan!" a woman's voice cries. "The king's men are behind you!"

There's a clang of sword against sword, but the pounding of my heart is even louder as I run away from the door. I don't know what's happening, but I know I need to hide! I stuff myself behind a plush armchair, its feet carved into lion paws.

The door opens, and I hear someone enter. At first, I think it's Méndez, but the footsteps are too light. Then I see a pair of boots standing in front of the armchair.

"You!" A young boy's voice is a whispered rush. "What are you doing here?"

The sound of water slapping onto the tiles is suddenly louder than the clatter of swords in my memory. Opening my eyes, I realize the faucet is still running, and the water spills over the tub and pours onto the floor. I quickly turn off the tap.

The entrance of Dez into my life has come and gone in segments, never continuous like that. Renata Convida, the Robári of the Hand of Moria vanished that night in the flames. But here I am, back in a similar room decked in finery. What if she's not gone from me, after all? Perhaps I've made a mistake in coming to this place where my mind can never know peace.

That night the Whispers' Rebellion was able to rescue me along with a handful of others. The rest, sleeping in their rooms, were killed by the justice before they could fall back into enemy hands, knowing too much about the interior workings of the justice and the palace.

It was also the night that María and Ronáldo Convida died in their little wooden house, set ablaze by a raging fire.

And all of it started because I wanted more sweet things.

I submerge myself beneath the surface of the water again and hold my breath, knowing no matter where I am or what I do, I will never escape the heat of flames and the taste of ash. But I no longer want to escape. I want to wield that fire and watch this place burn.

14

THE NEXT MORNING, I STRUGGLE TO BLINK OPEN MY EYES, RUBBING AWAY A layer of crust. This bed is too large, too soft, too—beautiful. At the San Cristóbal ruins in Ángeles, everything we own is modest, and when I was old enough to start training as a Whisper, we slept out in the woods. Where are Sayida and the others sleeping now?

I push away the feather-soft blanket and examine my injured hand. The stitches are swollen and red. It hurts to stretch them, and blood still trickles from the stem of the cut. My other hand is itchy inside the tight leather glove. I've never felt as useless as I do now. I'm only glad no one can witness this humiliation. With a damaged hand, I could only manage to wiggle myself into a thin silk robe last night, which I now regret as a draft sends shivers racing across my skin.

I swing my feet over the edge of the bed. The vast room is dark, and I pad to the floor-length curtains, but hesitate upon a closer look at the material. They said this room used to belong to Lady Nuria. I do not remember her from my time at the palace, but she had expensive taste. Feather silk is the lightest fabric ever made, imported from Dauphinique. I wonder if there's so much of it because the newest queen of Puerto Leones is from there. Just a swatch of it is worth more than anything I've ever owned, and Lady Nuria used it for something as mundane as drapes. I'm afraid to even touch them, but I don't fancy sitting in shadow.

When I pull back the curtains, golden morning light filters through in thick stripes. The immense windows are barred on the outside with black iron, and a cylinder lock on the latch keeps the glass panes closed. My throat tightens. I shouldn't be this surprised, but I am. As a child, I had free rein of the grounds. Méndez doesn't think of me as that naive seven-year-old anymore. I will have to regain his trust and find where the weapon is being kept in the palace. I have dozens of old safe houses I can give them. It would thin the justice's forces and allow the Whispers to smuggle out more refugees. I can stay for more, like Lozar said.

From up here, we're so high that I can see the entire city center, the familiar maze that seems to have only grown more complicated since I last saw it. Just beyond, there are the green treetops of a forest beginning to grow anew.

Foolishly, I let my eyes drop, falling onto the square below. The memory of the Whispers' Rebellion rears again, everything crashing back at once: the sticky streets, smoke in my nose, ash on my skin. Bodies shoving and crushing and burning.

"Awake, O Scarlet of the Sands!" an alto voice singsongs cheerfully behind me.

I let out a startled cry and reach for my knife—only for my fingertips to graze silk. Of course. These aren't my clothes. This isn't my room. This isn't where I belong.

"Who in the Six Heavens are you?" I pull my flimsy robe tighter as I take in the man now standing in my room. He's young, maybe older than me but not by much. Tall with a gleaming head of brown curls that frame a handsome oval face and light brown skin. The king's jeweled seal catches the morning light on his right jacket pocket.

"Me? I am the royal sun who comes to shine his light on you," the boy continues to sing, his voice a pleasantly surprising ring. For the first time, I notice a bundle of scarlet in his fine hands, the hands of someone who's never done manual labor.

I frown. "I don't know that play."

He holds the dress out for me to see. I don't look at it. I already know it's ridiculous.

"Then we must educate you about the theater if you are to be the lady in my care."

"Not a lady." I take the dress from him and, remembering the way the other attendants acted toward me, am surprised when he doesn't flinch away. The dress is in a choke hold in my leather-clad fist. "I can dress myself. There's no need for you to be here."

"I only just took an iron to that, Lady Renata," the boy tells me, gently removing the dress from my hands.

"I'm not a lady," I say again.

"That may be so, but I must still treat you as one."

"Because Justice Méndez asked you to."

The boy gives a little shake of his head. One of his curls falls out of place and lands over his forehead like a tendril of smoke, or a very tiny snake. "You must know more than anyone that Justice

Méndez doesn't *ask* for anything. Now, please, let us dress before we feast. You must look your best for the king."

He takes long, sure strides away from me and through a door leading to the dressing room where he's already set out perfumes, combs, and brooches. Did I really sleep through the rattle of keys and the heavy tread of his boots? Margo might've been right. I have no business being a spy.

"What are you doing?" I say, impatiently following him.

"You see, Lady Renata," he starts. "There is most certainly a *need* for me to be here. Your injured hands leave you practically indisposed. The justice has entrusted me, Leonardo Almarada, with your care. You wouldn't want him to be upset with me, would you?"

"Actually, I'm wondering what you did wrong that you'd be sent to attend someone like me."

His mouth twitches and his jaw muscles tighten. His sharp green eyes hone in on me. "I'll have you know I am quite good at my job. I have an incredible amount of patience. When I was a stage actor, I trained a dozen larks to sing to accompany my musical number. Pity there's not much work these days."

"I don't sing," I say, and do my best to frown. To put him off and scare him away like the girls last night.

"I'm sure that is best for us all," he says. "Now, let's get to it."

He holds the dress by the shoulders, a ridiculous smile playing on his lips because he knows I can't do this on my own. There are at least two dozen unnecessary buttons on the back, and my wretched hand is still swollen and red. A voice that sounds remarkably like Dez's whispers in my head. *Think of the advantage.* If Méndez chose him to attend me, then that means he trusts him. The justice might not know he's given me a gift. Even if he does sing this early in the morning.

"Fine, Leonardo."

He gives me a small bow. A warm, devastating smile. "You can call me Leo."

I keep my eye on the sun traveling across the sky while Leo works to ready me for an audience with King Fernando. There are pots of powders and glistening liquids that make my cheeks rouged and lips blushed. He finishes it all by spraying a pungent perfume that reminds me of bitter oranges. The nobles pay a high price for these scents, imitations of a world they experience at a distance, but one I know all too well. It makes me miss the fields behind the cloisters. The smell of earth in the hot springs. Dirt under my fingernails. The forest before and after the rain. Grass on sweet, sweaty skin.

"There we are," he says, most pleased with himself.

Who are you? I want to ask the reflection looking back at me. She's cleaner, more polished than I've been in years. The silk skirt ripples on the ground like the ruby lake in the middle of Citadela Tresoros. The red corset makes me look longer and digs into my ribs. The black velvet cloak feels like wings at my back.

"Do you like it?" Leo asks from behind me, smoothing out a wrinkle.

I meet his eyes in the mirror. Leo's thick lashes seem impossibly long and dark, and there's a slight flutter there. Why would he care if I like it or not?

When I don't say anything, Leo continues, "I've highlighted your best features to please the king and the justice."

He is very good at filling the air with his words. I bet he can make anyone feel at ease. He and Dez would have been fast friends. I panic at the thought of Dez, fearing it'll make me spiral again.

And for that reason, I ask, "And what, pray tell, are my best features?"

"It's hard to choose," Leo says, without a trace of irony. "You're tall but too bony to be in fashion at court. Justice Méndez says the wretches who kidnapped you starved you. If I were writing you for a play—"

"Are you a scribe, then?"

"I *was* a stage actor. But don't interrupt me while I'm being brilliant. I've turned you into the Maiden Cuerva, who flew on black wings over Mountain Andalucía to guard the kingdom."

I know this story a little differently. For the Moria, the Maiden Cuerva was a guardian of the underworld. She carried the souls of the dead to rest. A troubled feeling stirs in my stomach. He's too friendly to someone like me. He keeps talking about birds. Could he be Illan's Magpie?

"I thought that myth was not allowed to be performed?" I say, and meet his eyes in the mirror.

He gives me an easy smile. "What could be harmful about an opera? It was performed in front of the king himself. As I was saying. You'd be the Maiden Cuerva. The thing about you—well, really everything about you is so dark. The way you stare at people, your eyes, your hair. Someone else would have put you in something bright and garish to hide the very thing that makes you *you*."

It's a good answer. Almost too prepared. I make a mental note to be aware around Leo. "I'm not sure if you're insulting me or complimenting me."

"You'd know if I were insulting you. Now, for your hair."

Sitting in front of a vanity mirror in the dressing room is

strange. Everything here seems designed to be pleasant to look at, delicate. I only see it as breakable. Glass boxes filled with oils and lotions and soaps rendered to pearlescent liquid forms. He brushes my tangled black mane and I frown every time he hits a snag. He braids a crown around my head and dabs oils in my hair to smooth the waves into curls over my shoulders.

When he's finished, Leo sifts through the drawers until he finally pulls out a tray of sparkling baubles.

My fingers reach for a bright hairpin. The flowers are wide and red, made of a thick silk meant to imitate the real things, with yellow beads woven at the center. It's eye-catching, but I'm more focused on the steel clip it's sewn to. I press the end of it on my leather glove, feel the metal end, sharp enough that it could rip through the fabric and follow through into my finger.

"This one?" I ask.

Leo looks away from the tray of jeweled combs. "You don't want to wear that. Those are last season. This season, it's all crystal gems and pearls."

"I don't care about court fashions. I haven't worn a dress since I was nine. Are you sure I can't wear trousers? I thought they were becoming more fashionable."

In the mirror, I see Leo duck his head. "The king *prefers* his ladies to wear dresses befitting their stations."

"And did the king outlaw flower hairpins?"

Leo stares at me and then bursts into laughter. I'm oddly proud that I've made this boy of light and song laugh. A terrible pang hits me when I think about how much he resembles Sayida.

"Fair enough, Miss Renata," he says, and fastens the flower clasp on the right side of my hair, nestling into the intricate braid of loops and curls. His smile broadens in the mirror, and he pushes my hair over my shoulders.

"Perhaps there's hope for you yet."

I let myself smile back, but it feels empty. I don't need hope. When the time is right, I need true aim, and the strength to drive this pin through Prince Castian's heart.

The palace in Andalucía is said to have been King Fernando's greatest creation. Four towers that glimmer in the distance like jewels. Each one ends in a point, as if to show how close to the Six Heavens the king is. The palace can be seen from miles away. The four towers connected by sky bridges. Eight years ago, half of it was burned to the ground during the siege of the Moria and the days following the Whispers' Rebellion. They failed to defeat King Fernando, swinging for a deathblow but only putting a nick in the man's armor. Still, they managed to free prisoners in the dungeons and rescue me along with a couple of others.

The memories gather at the edges of my mind. The Gray is always there, a winding dark that, today, looks more and more like the tunnels beneath the palace. I can't repeat what happened in the bathtub last night. Today, I push back with everything I have. I touch the flower clasp in my hair again, the pointed edge sharp enough to keep my mind focused.

Leo locks the door as we leave, standing in front of it to hide the combination, a sobering reminder that he is no friend of mine. I swallow a strange swell of hurt and hurry down the hallway. Once again we pass the plain wooden door, and once again it gives me pause—this time it's slightly ajar.

The smell of old books and dust wafts from the opening, more powerful than any memory. I remember reading books on a long chaise against the tallest window. The only friend I had in the palace, a young boy, would sneak in and pass the time by rolling dice across the floor. I take in a sharp breath and place my hand on the open door. My heart races in my chest. I need to remember, need to see, and yet the memory of this room is suffocating.

But before I can peer inside, Leo is with me.

"My, you are in a hurry now, Lady Renata." His green eyes glide toward the door but he doesn't appear fazed at the idea that someone is in there. "Shall we?"

A headache threatens at my temples, and so I give a quiet nod.

We take the sky bridge that leads to the new northeast tower. Here, the design is different. The colors vibrant and blue, as if dedicated to the nautical and river towns and villages of Puerto Leones. Real shells and pearls embedded in the stone.

I stop for a moment in front of the pillars that mark the entrance of the northeast tower. I have a sweeping sense that I've been here before. Unlike the adjacent pillar covered in deep blue mosaic tiles, this one has muted, softer blues, as if it once belonged elsewhere. Perhaps I'm wrong. Perhaps it's part of the design. The feeling prickles my skin.

"A word of advice, Lady Renata. Always address King Fernando before anyone else, even the prince," Leo rattles off. "Prince Castian likes to be addressed as Lord Commander, not Your Highness or even Your Grace. Don't look at him directly in the eye unless you're ready for the longest staring contest of your life. Understood?"

Without waiting for my response, Leo tugs my gloved hand around the pillar and back on course. It's strange to have someone I don't know holding my hand like this, but I force myself to not pull away.

I see the massive doors at the end of the corridor and my heart flutters at my throat because I can see myself in their mirrored surface.

"That's a new design," Leo says as I stare ahead. He leans into my ear as if to fix a tendril. "He can see you from the other side."

I keep one hand on Leo's arm and the injured one rests over my stomach, where everyone can see. I wonder, who is behind those doors other than the king and the justice? There are no guards posted. No need—not when they can see you coming.

"Ready?" Leo whispers. He reaches for the door handles, a set of lions with open mouths, bodies midpounce.

I shut my eyes for a moment and see Dez instead, clear as glass, backlit by hundreds of stars. My heart thrums in my chest. I'm back here for him. I'm back here so his death matters. I can feel the pin against my scalp like a branding iron. Opening my eyes, I nod.

Leo yanks the door open.

The small court that's gathered ceases its chatter. Whispers are traded from across the room. The sound of it is like wasps gathering around my head, ready to sting.

I keep my eyes on the ground because I'm afraid my feet are going to give out beneath me. There's something equally unnerving about the sound of my heels, *clack clack clack*, echoing in the deadly silence of the room. The sound of a sword hacking away at bone. The sound of a mallet crushing a skull open. I think of terrible things to keep my mind sharp because when I stare into Prince Castian's eyes, it'll take all of my willpower not to immediately slit his throat. First, find the box.

I do as Leo instructed and keep my hands clenched in front of me. He stops a few paces ahead. My cue to look up.

I feel myself sway, but Leo subtly steps close, using his body to keep me upright. It gives me the split second needed to compose myself.

There, surrounded by Justice Méndez, other judges, and a gaggle of young courtiers, is King Fernando. He sits so straight it's like he's tied to the back of his throne. To his right sits Queen Josephine, the king's young third wife and princess of Dauphinique. Her elegant features and polished black skin make her youth stand out against her husband. To the king's left is an empty seat. Prince Castian is nowhere to be found.

I breathe to steady my heartbeat. He should be here. Where is he? Did he take the wooden box with him or leave it with Méndez? Dread runs cold through me. What would my unit do if they were in my shoes? They wouldn't have come here alone, clearly. Margo would find out everything she could about where the prince went. Sayida would be patient and stay close to Méndez. Esteban would befriend the palace guards and find secrets that way. He learned that from Dez.

My heart sinks with disappointment, but the feeling is quickly replaced with uneasy wonder as I take in the display before me. The throne room is narrow, as if streamlined to get a look at whoever is approaching on the other side of the mirrored doors. Arched windows depict the history of the Fajardo conquest of Puerto Leones, each a splash of color that filters prisms of light into the room and leads right to where the king sits on a throne made of alman stone.

Pure, solid, carved alman stone.

Before this palace was destroyed, I remember flashes of a different room. The walls were a gray granite and there were no windows. The king's throne then was an intricate weaving of gold. The armrests each had the head of a lion. This is less ostentatious but a statement nonetheless. This is cruel in a way only I can feel.

Where did they find so much alman stone in a single form? *Stolen*, my mind answers. My fingers twitch to put my hands on it. It glows faintly as if there's a small light coming from the center. I know I should be doing something—speaking, pledging my allegiance, asking for forgiveness. I know I should be doing more. But I'm mesmerized because I've never seen the stone in such quantity or so whole. It was only used to build statues of Our Lady of Whispers, which means the king must've found some untapped source or a temple that was left intact. What secrets could be trapped within?

I must tell Illan, I think instinctively. But I can't do anything to compromise the reason I'm here.

The sound of wasps gets louder. I look to Leo, who is on the floor, kneeling. He turns his head only to give me a stare that screams incredulity.

I drop into my curtsy so quickly I fall to my knee. The sound of it is a hard smack on the floor. The men look embarrassed for me, and the courtiers snap their colorful fans open to hide chuckles and smirks.

"Your Majesty," I say, hardening my voice to silence those who are laughing. "I am Renata Convida, and I have returned to the service of the king and the justice if Your Grace will allow it."

"Forgive her," Justice Méndez says, stepping forward. Why do I feel a traitorous relief when his gray eyes settle on me? When he's at my side, I breathe a little easier. "The girl is unrefined in the ways of her superiors."

"Rise," King Fernando says, and I look up in time to see the flourish of his hand.

Keeping my face emotionless is the hardest thing I've ever done. King Fernando inspires a different fear than his son. Where Prince Castian has a patient arrogance and a calm as deceptive as a serpent lying in wait, King Fernando is brusque, his hatred for me—perhaps for all things—radiating like a torch. He doesn't react to the titters from the court or Méndez's apology. He simply stares at me with infinitely black eyes. He doesn't dress extravagantly like Castian. His clothes are black from head to toe like someone in mourning.

My lips are so dry that they burn, but I bite my tongue to keep from licking them.

Don't look away, I tell myself. *Let him know you can be useful.*

King Fernando does something curious.

He gets up from his throne and crosses the distance between us. This close, I can't stop comparing the king to his son. His only living son. Castian stalks his prisoners like a mountain lion playing with its food. The king watches me as if I'm something to be torn open and later inspected. Where Castian laughed at his victory, Fernando is liberal with scowls of disgust. I physically offend him by standing here. How he tolerates the presence of his Hand, I do not know. This is the same man who allowed Lozar to live until he was caught? I can't believe it.

"I've found you a new Robári, Your Highness," Justice Méndez says, keeping his head bowed. "As promised."

"If I'm to understand, you did not *find* anything," the king says. Even I feel the cold sting of his words. Méndez only remains as he is.

King Fernando's a bit shorter than me, but he stands as straight as an elm. I don't have many memories of him, mine or stolen. I remember seeing him once when he barged into Justice Méndez's library. He was more muscular then, with ink-black hair and a full beard that made him look older than he was. Now he's thinner, hair thick and gray as ash with crinkles across his forehead and the angry corners of his mouth. His eyes are the most youthful thing about him. This is the same man who took the throne from his father at seventeen and expanded the borders of Puerto Leones. Who secured himself an ally across the sea and a brand-new kingdom through marriage. His skin is like warm milk, pale against his dark beard and brows.

"Let me see your hands," King Fernando commands. A voice that's used to having orders followed.

Méndez hurries over with the small key and removes my one glove.

To my surprise, King Fernando grips my unblemished left palm, confident I won't suck the memories right out of his flesh.

Do it. Do it and spare the world more of this.

"Tell me," says the king, flipping it palm-side-up like a common market square fortune-teller. "Why did you not escape the rebel bestaes sooner?"

I flick my eyes to Justice Méndez. He gives me a nod of encouragement because I'm taking a beat too long to answer.

"I tried, Your Highness." I don't let my voice tremble because I'm not lying.

"You tried for the eight years you were gone?" His voice dripping with skepticism. The court answers with haughty little coughs.

My mouth is so dry, the corners stick together when I part them to speak. "Every day it became more and more difficult. I lost everything. I lost hope."

The best lies are like bends of light. They play tricks on you.

"Would you like to see the scars they left on me every time I tried to escape?" I reach for the straps at the back of my corset. It is a bluff, but I have to follow through because any pause might be suspect.

It's a bluff that the king of Puerto Leones is happy to meet. He raises his hand, and I stop short of pulling on the string. He might be a murderer, a bigot, a tyrant, but the thing he prides himself on is a twisted sense of chivalry.

"Leonardo?" King Fernando calls the attendant forward, and Leo is beside us in a few of his long steps. His head is bent, eyes toward the floor, so his curls flop over. "You have dressed this creature. What did you observe?"

I swallow and revisit the memory of this morning. Leo's tiny gasp when he buttoned me up, and how I stiffened. He didn't ask how my back came to be a maze of scars, just continued singing his upbeat song.

"I believe the scars on her back were left there by those who held no love for the girl."

I've underestimated Leo. Not only is he trusted by Justice Méndez, but his words are truth in the king's eyes. He couldn't be the Magpie. I wonder how a stage actor came to be so entrusted in the palace. Leo's catlike green eyes flick to my hands but betray nothing else.

On the contrary. He would make the best kind of spy, I think.

"The Whispers do not trust Robári," I say, holding my hands in front of me. "Even now they keep us in the ranks only as thieves and scavengers. Among my company I was one of two, though we were separated. The other Robári died five years ago during a raid."

It's a lie, but I want to see his reaction. This seems to bother the king, and I wonder if it's because he sees a missed opportunity.

"Constantino," the king says.

In my focus on the king I somehow missed the two men hovering quietly behind the throne, like pets at the king's feet waiting for a treat. They're young, midtwenties perhaps, and dressed in tailored uniforms. At first glance they could be any of the king's guard, except these uniforms are a stark black instead of the imperial purple and gold. They each wear a medallion over their breast pocket bearing King Fernando's family crest—a winged lion of legend with a spear in its jaws and flames roaring around it.

The shorter of the two steps forward, and I notice the intricate embroidery is actually made of copper. I look to the other and realize his embroidery is silver. These are Moria, a Ventári and a Persuári—what is left of the Hand of Moria.

While the king has ruled magics illegal, he has always kept his own private collection of Moria, one for each of the four strands of power. After all, what better way to defeat his enemies, fighting fire with fire? What could he do if he controlled all Moria this way?

I don't recognize either of them from my time here. Then again, Méndez did his best to keep me isolated from the rest. To keep me safe.

"You won't mind if our Ventári verifies your claims?" King Fernando asks, the challenge clear. "My Ventári has caught every traitor among my ranks."

Fans flutter and lips whisper and my heart drums like a warning. I extend my left hand. "Of course not, Your Highness."

"See," King Fernando comments into the young man's ear.

Constantino isn't like Lucia. They haven't removed his magics, but there's something not right about him—or the other man who stands to the side of the throne like a living statue. I wonder how they came to be here. Were they snatched from their homes like I was? This would have been my fate had I not been saved. Had Dez not saved me.

I swallow my grief and remind myself why I'm here. I grip the Ventári's hand before he can grab mine. Esteban taught me how to control my mind when someone tries to skim it. Like all magics, it requires practice, and every Ventári has different strengths. To my relief, Constantino is not as strong as Esteban. I never did learn how to fully close my mind against him. But a weaker Ventári—I can.

I let Constantino see the day I got the scars on my back. It was a young Moria who dragged me into the thorn reeds in the river and I fell, tangled and thrashing so much I nearly bled out. I allow him to see the fights I've had with Margo. Illan shouting at me. The time I had to be put in chains because I was trying to hurt myself. Nameless Moria spitting in my path whenever I walked in the cloisters.

I let him see the worst.

He lets go first, breaking the connection so it leaves me with a dizzying feeling. Leo holds out a hand to steady me.

Constantino's face is blank as a new day. His voice is flat when he says, "She tells the truth, Your Highness."

King Fernando stares at me in uncertain judgment. Constantino's youth hasn't given him the knowledge both the king and I have—that all truths are subject to circumstance. But Fernando does not question his pet mind reader. In the moment he flashes an arrogant smile, I'm hit with how familiar it is. Finally, I can see his wretched son in his features.

With a booming clap of his hands, he signals his palace guards, and I prepare for them to slap manacles around my hands again. Justice Méndez takes a single step between King Fernando and me, as if shielding me with his body.

"At last"—the king slaps the justice's arm in a gesture that sets the court abuzz again—"you've brought me a Robári I can use. My set is nearly complete. You've done well, my old friend."

Beside me, Méndez shuts his eyes and lets go of a sigh, as if he's been spared from a hangman's noose. "It is my life's work to serve you, Your Highness." He places a hand on my shoulder. Old memories sink claws down my back. Méndez reading to me before bed. Méndez teaching me how to write. I swallow the knot in my throat and stop my body from recoiling.

Constantino slips away, back to the stage behind the throne.

"First my son's victory, and now this." He snaps his fingers in the air. The two guards who had vanished return. A man in chains is dragged out. People crane their necks to have a better look. "The Father of Worlds has continued to bless this kingdom."

The prisoner wears a fine silk blouse and an embroidered doublet covered in muck. I don't recognize the house sigil on his breast pocket—a briar rose whose stem crosses with a sword. When he looks at me, his face pales with fear.

Don't you know what people see when they look at you? Margo shouted at me once when she was angry because Dez chose me instead of her for a mission.

I shake off the start of that memory the Ventári shook loose. I concentrate on this man because I know what he sees.

He's dragged before my feet. Pushed to submission, his lips inches away from the heeled shoes pinching my feet.

"Put yourself to use, Robári." The king stands tall and addresses his court. "This man has broken faith with his crown and country. This man has betrayed me."

I watch the courtiers react. Fans flap like dragonfly wings.

"His betrayal was discovered last night on one of his vessels. Instead of casks of aguadulce and the fine wine Lord Las Rosas has built his family name on, there were Moria scum. The vandals who set fire to the village of Esmeraldas and attacked our capital were among them."

This isn't right. He's putting the blame on Lynx Unit because he has no one else to blame. But I can't speak out. I focus on Leo. I stare at the seal on his jacket. Looking at this is the only thing keeping me from screaming. It would be too far for Lynx Unit to have made it to the coast in time. But what about Illan and the others? The worst part about King Fernando is that he makes me doubt myself. What if he's telling the truth? What if Sayida and the others caught up to the ship and snuck on board?

"The vessel was on its way to Empirio Luzou," King Fernando says gravely. He towers over Lord Rosas, eyes black as tar. "I can't think of a better punishment than to have a taste of the Moria power you thought was worth betraying your country for."

The nobleman weeps through the gag in his mouth. He shakes

his head, and I'd bet my life that if he were free to speak, he'd claim innocence. I know the king is lying, but I don't feel anything for Lord Las Rosas weeping at my feet. Should I? Nobles like this were the first to turn out the Moria from their homes and lands and onto the streets—their friends, attendants, soldiers, their own sons and sisters and fathers if they were suspected of having magics, even if it was false.

Justice Méndez places a hand on my back, gently pushing me forward. This is what I was brought here to do, once again. A piece to complete a set. Power only the king is allowed to wield. It is the cost for being at the palace. But I made a promise long ago never to create another Hollow. I will keep that promise.

"Of course, my justice," I say breathlessly. I hold my hand out and flex my fingers. My face is practiced discipline.

Lord Las Rosas tries to move his head back, and I know that I can't do this. His wheat-gold hair is dark with sweat. I summon my magics, and the light of power moves through the burn marks on my palm. The court watches, a single breath held as I reach for the man's mind.

Then I let out a cry and throw myself on my knees in front of Justice Méndez. He grips me by my elbows, careful not to injure my right hand any more than it is. I hate that his grasp on me is gentle, careful. I am like the glass ornaments on my vanity—fragile, delicate, breakable. I cradle my hands to my chest.

"Renata, what is it?" Justice Méndez asks.

"What happened?" King Fernando says impatiently.

I contort my face into a wince and hold my hands out. "My justice, I can't."

I hold them out so he can see the damage once again. I move the lines of light and power and let them flicker. Méndez doesn't know the tricks I've learned without him.

"She's *broken*," the king spits at Justice Méndez. "What good is a weapon I can't use?"

Weapon. The word rings in my ears.

"She's hurt," the justice counters. He is perhaps the only man in the kingdom who can. He wraps an arm around me. "Lozar did this to her when he discovered who she was. She killed him for it."

"Lozar," King Fernando says. After hearing the old Ventári's story of being on the king's council, I wonder if he'll show remorse. But what comes out is anything but. "I thought he'd perished long ago."

I bite down on my tongue to stop from spewing obscenities. Instead, I let out a muffled moan.

"Her hands are the key to her magics," Justice Méndez says. With both of them crowding me, my mouth fills with both of their scents. My blood races through me and I freeze because if I don't, I know my body will overtake me and I will run. "She is the only Robári we've found since—"

"I am well aware," King Fernando cuts him off.

I wonder who they're referring to. I wonder what they did to them. I wonder what they will do to me if I cannot get out of here. If I fail. "Forgive me, Your Highness. Leonardo and I will see to her wounds, and she will recuperate quickly."

King Fernando walks away toward his throne. Queen Josephine twists her pale blue dress in her hands. She looks like she's holding her breath as he approaches her. The entire court is. He is the sun in the room, and everyone else is a weed leaning toward him every way he turns. The alman stone is a white shock against his dark clothes. I find myself wanting to reach for it. Though it isn't pulsing with the light of memories, I wonder if there is something buried inside.

When the king whirls around, his dark eyes are on me. My heart skips, and a dread I haven't known in a long time carves its way down my spine.

"The Sun Festival is coming up," says King Fernando. "That should be time enough for your hand to heal. The empress of Luzou and her court are attending. It's time our neighbors south of the Castinian sea understand what they are getting in the middle of."

"You have my word, Your Highness." Justice Méndez and a cluster of other judges bow in acknowledgment of the order.

The Sun Festival is less than two weeks away. I have twelve days. Twelve days to find the weapon in the palace, and destroy it. After that I get to kill the prince. I cannot be here when the festival arrives.

I bite down on my teeth to freeze my features into submission. In this moment, I've carved my own small victory by fooling them.

King Fernando takes a breath, and it seems as if the whole room does, too. His dark eyes bore into me, prying me apart.

"Get Las Rosas out of my sight," King Fernando finally commands with a flick of his many-ringed fingers, and the whole court lets go of their held breath.

A long moment slithers past while Lord Las Rosas is taken away and back to the dungeons. I wonder if nobles are put somewhere else, a cell with a bed and food because even if they are criminals, they're still not commoners—or Moria. I wonder if the court can see themselves in this display, that it could be any one of them taken away.

The two prisoners who form the Hand of Moria stand united in silence. Glassy eyes stare at the wall behind me. I know if I heal and do not complete my mission, I will become one of them. With me in their grasp, the Hand of Moria only needs one more—an

Illusionári, almost as rare as myself. I think of Margo's ferocious eyes, her stubborn determination—just snuffed out. No matter what was between us, I cannot allow even the possibility of that fate.

"Very well, Renata Convida." When King Fernando says my name, I feel a great weight press on my chest. He draws a dagger from his hip. It is a small, pretty thing with sapphires encrusted along the hilt. Now, I realize, I know what the dark stain at my feet is from. "Until you can perform your duties as my Robári, will you swear your fealty to my court?"

I should be relieved that my deception worked and my injury can buy me enough time. But my thigh muscles strain as if rejecting my actions as I lower myself to the cold, marble ground.

"I swear it," I say, squeezing my hand so hard I feel a stitch rip and blood trickle.

"Will you give your life in my name, should the time come, and fight for the survival and traditions of Puerto Leones?"

"I will."

"Her hands can stand no further injury, Your Grace," Justice Méndez interjects. Challenging the king once again in front of the court can't be good for him. And yet, I can see the splinter in the king's eye, the vein that throbs in his neck.

"You said her hands," King Fernando replies, words as cold as the dagger he uses to slice a long cut across my chest. I suck in a breath, then bite down on the cold sting. "Break the skin and it will bleed well enough."

The courtiers gasp, their voices buzz louder and louder, their fans move so quickly they could summon a hurricane. I don't look to Leo or Justice Méndez.

"With this blood, are you the servant of the king, the justice, and the Father of Worlds?"

To spill my blood in the name of this man goes against everything I fought for.

I will never be as good as Margo or Dez.

But I am Renata Convida. And as I lean forward and let the cut over my left breast bleed at the king's feet, I make an oath to myself, a silent vow between me and all who witness. I will find this cure. I will destroy it. Even if it takes every bit of my soul, I will destroy the king and justice.

My blood pools between us, and I answer, "I am."

15

Leo and I walk in silence down the corridor, through the two-way mirrored doors, and across the sky bridge. My nose is assaulted by the scents of the palace—warm bread wafting from the kitchens, wood burning in fireplaces, soap from sheets drying in a court-yard. How can such a dangerous place feel so comforting? To my right I hear tinkling laughter of what could be attendants having a moment of peace from their daily work or court ladies who spent the days taking sun in the labyrinthine gardens below. The day is too bright, and in this light the citadela to my left can't hide the dirt that permeates its seams. Not even the rain can wash it away.

"Here," Leo says, not breaking his stride.

I don't want to look at him just yet, but I can see the handkerchief he holds out to me from the corner of my eye. It's a useless gesture, as if a small square of fabric could mop up my blood-covered dress, but the kindness behind it is hard to dismiss.

A part of me so wants to like him, but the way the king asked for his advice was too familiar. I know that whatever I say to Leo is being reported back.

We take the grand winding stairs, and he fishes inside his pocket for the key. His body isn't simply straight, it's rigid, like he's hiding something. He hasn't looked at me since we left the throne room, and he hasn't spoken a word other than *here* until now.

"Lady Renata," Leo says. I'm in the center of this cavernous room filled with hand-carved tables, imported rugs and lace, crystal chandeliers, and fine silk sheets from worms in the Sól Abene *provincia*, and I'm dripping blood on the carpet.

"I told you not to call me that." I hate how soft my voice sounds, like dust drifting across a beam of sunlight.

"I didn't know—"

"Let's not speak of this. I know the way back to my cage. You may go."

"You don't want to be called a lady, but you certainly command like one," he says, attempting a crooked smile. *Crooked smiles for crooked hearts,* Sayida liked to say. "Now, please, we must get you bathed and dressed."

"I took a bath yesterday," I say, the thought of wasting more water absurd. I haven't even run in muck or broken a sweat, and blood comes off easily enough.

"Justice Méndez has given me orders. You are to report to him for supper and training."

I feel myself sinking. It's like I'm not in control of my body. The weariness has seeped into my bones. For the second time today, Leo catches me.

"You don't let people take care of you, do you?" he says sweetly.

Suddenly, I am that same child in the palace, that stupid, greedy girl, ignorant of what was happening around her. I don't want to be that girl. I don't want to be anything. How long am I supposed to keep up the ruse of not being able to use my power? Maybe I wasn't made for this. Maybe I should give up or give in, because all roads I take will lead to my ruin.

Leo helps me undress carefully. I don't even feel him touch my skin, only my clothes, and he holds out a robe for me to step into. I'm too tired to object. I sit in front of the vanity while he runs the water to fill the tub. I wonder what Margo or Esteban would say if they saw this water system. In the cloisters there are only cold baths in the ponds and lakes, and the hot springs are half a day's walk north.

I rip the flower from my hair and shove it in my robe pocket while Leo selects bottles of soaps and oils and a sponge instead of a stable brush. He empties out two of the bottles, and the tub fills with bright blue-and-yellow foam that turns the water a shimmering peacock green.

Enough of this. A stranger's voice pops out of a memory.

I take a deep breath and push away the melancholy that is stitching itself in my skin like the thread on my hand. I step into the tub, the heat a comfort to my tired muscles.

"That went better than I expected, all things considered," Leo says.

"Yes, splendid," I say dryly. "For a man who conquered the entire continent, he's a generous soul."

Leo's eyes widen, and I know I've spoken too freely. He lathers a white foam into my hair. "Don't ever repeat that, Renata."

I scramble to take it back. "I'm sorry, I forget myself," I say. What is it about Leo that makes me lower my guard? Is it the loneliness that clings to me like a shroud? Did the king send him to me for this very reason?

Leo shrugs one shoulder and dabs an oil on his hands. He holds his palms up. "Have you ever had your shoulders massaged? There's a Zaharian bathhouse in the lower district. Your body is a rock."

I shake my head. "I doubt Justice Méndez would approve."

"You're right. But it is divine." He nods and hands me a sponge. "Here."

Most of the blood has washed away in the bath, but some dried spots remain on my clavicle. I don't want to enjoy this. The easy friendship Leo offers, even if I can't trust him, or the access to things I haven't had in a long time.

I wash under my arms and my stomach as Leo busies himself putting away the glass bottles. He talks about this lord and that lady. How Lord Las Rosas was a shock to the entire court, especially because the ports are monitored by the king's men. No one knows how he possibly could have managed it.

His voice becomes pleasant background noise.

I touch my hand to the knobs that release the water into the tub. A memory slams into me. It slips out from the Gray without warning: my father's face. The way he worked with metals and how his hands were always covered in ash.

I push it away. It hurts too much to remember love. I choose rage. Sea-blue eyes. My heart speeds up when I think of the prince who was missing from court.

"Why wasn't Prince—the Lord Commander—beside his father?" I ask, punctuating the question with my attempt at doe eyes. Sayida was always so much better at this.

Leo hums thoughtfully. "If you want my unsolicited advice,

Lady Renata, it's best to not wonder about the prince too often or speak his name in public."

I gather bubbles into my injured hand to buy myself time to answer. The bubbles dissipate, collapsing into one another. "We're in private now, aren't we?"

Leo gives a dismissive laugh, but his eyes betray something like fear. "Within these walls, just between us, Prince Castian comes and goes at his leisure. When he's here, he only attends court to select which lady might, well, *accompany* him on any given night. I suspect he does it because it infuriates the king. But the Sun Festival is soon. Even the prince won't risk his father's anger by not attending, especially after missing it the year past."

I sink into the tub once more before I'm ready to come out. Leo is there waiting with the robe for me to step into.

"Careful, Miss Renata. You almost look as disappointed as the courtiers."

I twist my face into an ugly frown. My reaction is visceral. "I am *not*."

"Let's speak no more of this. Forgive me for saying, but you look a bit green. I will bring you a tea tray, and you are not to move until tomorrow."

"But Justice Méndez is expecting me."

"I will go to him. He, most of all, needs you well." Leo ushers me out of the washroom and into the bedchamber to dress me. I catch my reflection in the mirror, and I don't see the green pallor he's referring to, but I feel the ache in every muscle, the stiffness in my right hand, and the burning from the slash on my chest. I know that if he weren't here, I'd sink into a puddle of my own misery and weakness.

I dry my hair on a towel and get into bed. I realize, with the prince absent, his chambers will be empty. He wouldn't leave the weapon somewhere anyone could find, but there could be clues. Now, to get there alone without Leo or an escort will be my challenge.

As Leo adjusts the bedding, I take hold of his hand, and he seems almost surprised when I say, "Thank you."

He pats my gloved hand, wet despite how hard I tried to keep it out of the bathwater.

As I drift off to sleep, I don't know if the voice comes from Leo or from the tunnels of the Gray, but it is as clear as cathedral bells. "Don't thank me just yet."

I jerk awake at the sound of heavy footsteps. The sky is still dark.

I slip out of bed and listen at the door of my room. There's a lock barring me from getting out. I kneel in front of the doorknob to see if there's a way to pick it open. Cylinder locks are only for prisoners, and that's what I am. Then I see a shadow. And another. Footsteps. Two sets of them pacing back and forth in front of my door.

Guards.

Now, are they to stop me from getting out or someone else from getting in? Perhaps both. I hold my breath, try to be as silent as I can, and get back into bed, reminding myself that no matter how comfortable and decadent everything in here is, it is still a cage.

16

A DIFFERENT ATTENDANT COLLECTS ME IN THE MORNING AFTER LEO GETS ME ready for the day. He calls the girl Sula. Her brown hair is neatly parted with braids pinned at her nape. She walks as if her clothes are made of wood, her arms tight against her sides. I can practically smell her fear. For a moment, I consider asking her about Prince Castian, but I notice her grip a circular wooden pendant that is sold in market stalls everywhere. It is nothing but a bit of verdina wood carved and polished with holy oils. It couldn't ward off a mosquito bite, but ever since a merchant claimed it would protect the Leonesse from Moria magics, they've come into fashion.

I'll have to find another way to get to the prince's rooms, with her hovering close by.

We cross the sky bridge toward the southwest tower on the way to Justice Méndez's office. In the early sunlight, the green-and-gold mosaics glitter like sunshine on dewy petals. The archway is etched with vines and heart-shaped leaves. No doubt this tower is meant to resemble the green forests that cut across the center of Puerto Leones.

A cluster of five courtiers turns the corner and halts when they notice me. They gather behind their lace fans. Their snickers travel even across the bridge. I think of what Leo said last night. Does the prince truly only attend his father's court to pick lovers? How can anyone want to be touched by him?

"We must wait for our betters to pass," the attendant says in a small, high-pitched voice. She folds her hands over her stomach and lowers her head.

I don't want to do it. I don't want to bow. *Obedient is not the same as clever.* But Margo has never been in the palace. She doesn't know that sometimes it is in the long run.

The girls glide across the bridge. I already know what they're going to do before the first one reaches me. Sula is invisible to them and, as much as I wish, I am not. When they reach me, the first girl shoves me aside, like she's clearing a path in a crowd. Her round hips knock me off-balance, and I grab for her with my right hand. Stitches pull against my tender skin, but when I make contact, my magics rise from deep within me. Anger bubbles up and I lash out, plucking a memory from her.

He would never notice her. But she has to try.

The orange-and-gold ballroom is lit by torches and fat white candles that illuminate the floor-to-ceiling mosaics. It isn't the best lighting for her face, or so her mother reminded her before she was sent to Queen Josephine's court.

A troupe of musicians plays in the center of the room,

where the crowned prince watches with a bored pout. The prince hasn't danced a single time, no matter who approaches to congratulate him on his capture of the rebel leader. He gestures and his majordomo runs over with a covered wine goblet that he places in the prince's capable hand.

She takes a breath, gathers her skirts, and strides across the ballroom. If she wants to stand out among the others, she has to be bold. Future kings want bold queens, don't they?

Prince Castian looks at her with blue eyes that seem to glisten. When he blinks they're a bit green. Her tongue is thick as she loses courage. He's so beautiful. So beautiful her heart gives a painful squeeze.

"Lovely night, isn't it, Lady Garza?" His voice is smooth, like thick crème cake. It skims against her body.

"Yes, Your Grace. Much safer now, thanks to you."

His brow furrows, and she dips low into a curtsy. So low that she can't hold her balance and she falls, her hands smacking the cold mosaic floor.

Prince Castian takes a drink from his goblet and hands it back to his majordomo. He does not speak. Does not acknowledge her fall. He steps over her dress and walks away and into the twisting gardens outside the great hall doors.

She stands, and keeps her teary eyes on the brass of her shoes as she runs away from the cruel smiles and crueler gossip.

I slink out of the memory, but the courtier's delicate hurt clings to me like wet cloth. I breathe to shake it off, but all I can think is that Prince Castian held a ball to celebrate capturing Dez. Coppery blood stings my tongue where I bite down to stop myself from screaming.

"You clumsy imbecile!" one of the other girls shouts.

"She scratched me!" Lady Garza hisses as they scurry across the sky bridge. "Look! Look! I'll get rabies. I'll get the plague!"

"I'll see to it she's declawed like the feral bestae she is," her friend says. But they keep moving, their fans fluttering like petals in the breeze.

I rush over to the side of the bridge and take long, deep breaths. I shouldn't have done that. The memory was short, but there were so many girls around us. What if they'd noticed?

"You're late," says a familiar voice.

I snap up to see Judge Alessandro marching across the bridge. He snatches up my hand, and I yank away because he doesn't get to touch me this way. "You're hurting me."

I hate the weakness in my voice, the way my heartbeat is erratic with his cold, clammy hands splaying my fingers open. That's when I realize that he saw. He must have seen because his dark eyes are searching my hands for something. Magics. Anything.

A red welt appears on my bandage and blood runs freely from a fresh tear. I cradle my hand against my chest and force him to meet my eyes. "Look what you've done. I'll need new stitches."

The young judge stutters and flaps his hands like a lost fowl. "Wretched Lady Garza. I'll be sure to tell the justice. Follow me."

Even Sula starts at Alessandro's lie. But she keeps her head down, rubbing her warding pendant the entire way to where the justice is waiting.

Méndez has a weakness for beautiful things.

His apartments within the southwest tower of the palace are as large as any of the ones belonging to the royal family. I still remember the first time I was here. I was given an attendant who was younger than I am now, fifteen perhaps. I don't remember her name, but I liked her because she reminded me of my mother with her peachy skin and ruddy cheeks, her hair dark and plaited in braids to keep it out of her face. My attendant brought me to these same chambers, where Justice Méndez and his council sorted through our powers and gave us shiny new clothes and stellitas by the fistful.

For two years, I reported to this same place. A thick wooden door with the special cylinder locks Méndez had designed during his creation of the Arm of Justice. A study with leather couches and floor-to-ceiling bookshelves. Cloth- and leather-bound volumes that date back to the first age of Puerto Leones, when the peoples migrated there from the seas that surround the great island. Maps with faded edges, lines of a continent drawn and redrawn to suit the victors. Globes with tiny swords plunged into the lands where the king and crown have made a conquest. I push it, watching it spin before I make my way through an archway that leads to his prayer room.

It's been updated to fit the palace's change of taste to a Dauphinique aesthetic of lace and shimmering embroidery, but some things remain the same. There's a sword within a circle on the far wall, depicting the symbol for the Father of Worlds. An altar surrounded by candles and incense that was just lit. He was praying. I wonder what a man like Méndez can pray for, but there he is, with his head bent toward the altar, his hands holding open a slender book.

"Wait here," Alessandro says.

"But the justice is waiting for me."

"How dare you question me. I said wait here. You, attendant. You may go." He doesn't even glance at Sula before dismissing her. When she runs out, I remember Margo and Dez instructing me on my footwork. I wish I could tell them how much easier it is to be silent when I'm not wearing heavy leather boots.

That wish is gone as I press myself against the door, where I can hear their voices. I can picture Alessandro's dark fluttering robes as he talks.

"Alessandro," Justice Méndez says, genuine surprise in his voice. Was he not expecting the young judge? Worry pricks at my sides that Alessandro had been following us all along. Was he at my room? How did he know I was late? "I did not expect you back today. Do you have news?"

"Regrettably, no." Alessandro's nasal voice grates on my senses. He's so eager to please. "But we are still searching. We have the forged letters with the royal seal."

Méndez makes a thinking sound, the way he does when he tugs on the silver wisps in his beard. "It's not enough. Lord Las Rosas did not act alone. I wouldn't trust him to find his way out of an open hedge, let alone smuggle a shipful of bestaes."

"The only people with access to royal documents would be in the palace, my justice. Allow me to conduct interviews with all the staff."

"And give the spy time to run?" Méndez nearly snarls at Alessandro's suggestion. "I have other ideas. In the meantime, keep the judges spread out through the palace. Now is not the time to rest."

So Méndez knows about the Magpie, Illan's informant. Would they remain here after the king's display of Lord Las Rosas?

"Yes, my justice," Alessandro says, and bows one more time before leaving. "I will never rest until I find the traitor and see them executed."

Not if I find the spy first, I think.

"Is that all? I'm expecting Renata."

"Yes, of course. That's what I came to tell you. I found the Robári wandering the halls. I brought her here straightaway."

A low grumble leaves my throat, but I dart to the front of the chambers where Alessandro deposited me earlier. He *was* following me to gain better favor. The door to the office swings open and Justice Méndez steps out with Alessandro at his heels. Alessandro gives me a look that says I will see him soon, and then he leaves us alone.

I bow and kiss Méndez's knuckles. The touch sends a terrible crawl over my skin, and I wish I could scrub my face with a scullery brush. But when he rests a gentle hand on my shoulder, when I see how he softens at the sight of me, my insides twist.

"Renata, I trust you're feeling better from yesterday."

This morning, Leo woke me up from a sleep so deep, he had to shake me, as he thought I was dead. I ate a whole bowl of grapes and a loaf of bread drenched in olive oil with poppy seeds and salt.

"Leo works wonders," I say, touching the cut on my chest, already scabbing over. "Though his hand at healing is not as practiced as yours."

He seems to like that, and so he holds out his hand for me to take and presses his fingers over my gloved ones. "He's come a long way. Lady Nuria had him in her employ, but I feel he'll make a great addition to our ranks one day."

Does he mean for Leo to become a judge?

I think of his careful warning last night when I asked about the prince. How he sent me to bed and lied about my pallor. Is the same boy supposed to become a hateful soldier in the king's arsenal?

"Are we going to train, my justice?" I say, realizing that we've walked past the courtyard, where I thought he was taking me to practice, and toward a plain wooden door.

"We are, but it isn't the training you remember." He says no more, and I know not to ask, as he lets me enter the dimly lit stairwell first.

Knots twist in my gut as my eyes adjust to the darkness. When I was a little girl, Méndez used to teach me how to concentrate on the memories he wanted me to find. I didn't know that Robári could create Hollows until the day he forced me to keep taking memories from one man until there were no more. Dead green eyes looked back at me from the floor and I was allowed a week on my own. He called it a reward, but I knew it was because I would start crying every time he tried bringing in a new prisoner. And now they want me to do it again, to turn Lord Las Rosas into a Hollow. That will be the end of me. I must find the weapon before the Sun Festival arrives or I will never leave these halls. I will be just like Constantino. Alessandro will find out my lies, and Justice Méndez will carve them out of me with hundreds of jagged knives.

With every step down the stone-walled stairwells, a part of me becomes more certain he's leading me through a secret passage back to the dungeons or a less glittering cage—that he knows I'm lying.

Finally, five floors down we reach a landing, and I breathe a small sigh of relief at the sight of the alchemy laboratory. A round old man is hunched over vials and blue flames that burn black marks on the bottom of the glass.

Rage fills my throat and strangles my words. I've seen this equipment before, in San Cristóbal, the former capital of Memoria. Now our ruins. The Moria apothecuras' greatest inventions were the distillations of herbs and flowers for medicines. While the people of Puerto Leones were still brewing grass and calling it spiced tea, the people of Memoria were developing alchemy and surgery that would change the way they healed. At least, that's the story Illan taught us. When King Fernando's family conquers a region, they destroy the temples and cathedrals first, the libraries second. They rewrite our histories or erase them completely. Who will we be if King Fernado and Justice Méndez employ their weapon?

"Impressive, isn't it?" Méndez tells me. His gray eyes sweep the large room, the rows of tables and the young and old alchemists who scratch things down on parchment. There's a girl my age who doesn't look up when she hears his voice, she's so focused on pouring liquid from one vial into another and watching the reaction.

I know nothing of alchemy, but I know the pleased expression on her face when she sets the vial down.

"What is all this?" I chance the question, holding my breath. Could this be the source of the weapon?

"Puerto Leones is about to enter the greatest of its ages," he says. "In order to do that, we have to know everything about our neighboring countries. How they make the things they do and how we can replicate them."

That's when I realize what liquid the girl is trying to re-create. The violet color that is too dull in the glass. The dye from Dauphinique, its vibrant purple gathered from the flowers that cannot grow anywhere but their valleys. People have stolen the bulbs and tried to plant them elsewhere, but they will only grow on Dauphinique soil.

King Fernando is trying to cut off trade with his wife's homeland? Where does that leave the Moria? The empire of Luzou?

"That's ingenious," I say, and I feel the daggers I've stabbed in my own heart. "But how is this training for me?"

"Eager to get back into the fold," Justice Méndez says, something like admiration in his deep voice. He continues leading me until we reach a plain back room. My heart has not stopped fluttering, and the hair on the back of my neck bristles as he grips my wrist. I gasp, but only for a moment because I see the key he withdraws from his pocket.

"I won't hurt you, Renata," he assures me softly.

Méndez unlocks the heavy door. There's a narrow empty room. The bricks are stacked at odd angles like it was created to serve as a passage. My stomach tightens and I force myself to keep walking forward instead of running out. At the opposite end of the room is another door secured by a ten-cylinder lock. The justice covers the code as he turns the gears into place.

The strangest thing is that I no longer want to run. My proximity to this door fills me with ease. It settles in my bones and turns to heady excitement. The sensation that glides across my skin is so familiar and somehow new at the same time.

Justice Méndez glances at me once as the lock clicks open and out comes a soft white light.

It can't be.

But I hurry in beside him and take in the sight.

His eyes are bright with the pulsing glow of alman stones. There are dozens of them in different shapes. Some polished into perfect spheres and others jagged pieces ringed with metal wire. Stones as small as pebbles and as large as boulders. There's the bottom half of a statue that must have once graced a temple for Our Lady of Shadows. Pillars split in half and pulsing veins of rock still covered in dirt.

Pure alman stone. More than I've ever seen in my life.

"I always did love your face when you were surprised, Ren. Do you know what these are?"

I let his words slide over me. If he really knew me he'd know it isn't surprise, but horror at seeing these crystals. Smiling hurts, but I do it.

"Illan told us all the alman stones were gone," I say. "Pulverized and thrown into the sea."

Méndez reaches down to pick one up. It's shaped like a cube, but too large for dice. Perhaps it was a weight or a decoration on an altar. "He's not wrong. A few years ago we found one temple that was untouched."

"Where?" I ask, before I realize I shouldn't. I sound too eager.

But Méndez remains fascinated by the pulsing light in the stone. My fingers itch at the concentration of memories in this room. I've been around alman stone before, and it's never been like this. There is so much about my power that I don't know, still. Would this have been the feeling if I'd gotten to go to a temple?

"It no longer matters," Méndez says, but the way he avoids my stare suddenly tells me he's lying. What are they doing with all of this? He gestures to the stone again. "We did manage to carve King Fernando a new throne. Our last Robári found the memories encapsulated within it were gone. Do you know why that is?"

I can't be sure if it's a test or not, so I have to answer with the only truth I know. "The brighter ones have the sharpest memory. The ones that have weak pulses have begun to fade over time. Though it is said to take years, sometimes decades, for a memory to fade. The throne must have been stripped of its memories."

He seems pleased with my knowledge, and I know I've answered correctly. With his free hand, he grips my shoulder. "You were always a clever pupil."

I would laugh at this choice of words if it wouldn't turn into a sob. "Thank you, my justice."

"Now I need you to do something for me."

"Anything."

"You understand that the king was not pleased yesterday." Méndez's eyes flick to my hand.

"I'm sorry I embarrassed you in front of the king."

"As long as you are true to your word, I will protect you." He cups the side of my face, a gesture he once used to calm me as a child. I was always afraid of the dark. He'd say, *There is nothing there, my sweet. There are only shadows.* But he was wrong. There were things there. The start of the Gray.

"What do you need of me?"

"The Moria have turned some citizens into traitors. It is imperative that we know who they might be and what they are planning next."

"A spy?" I am pleased with the surprise in my voice. "Why not use the Hand of Moria? Gather all who live in the palace and have their minds skimmed by a Ventári."

"The spy will know we're aware of them. I expect the Whispers to retaliate, and I will not see this kingdom destroyed by them once again. We cannot accuse anyone of noble birth without proof. The other lords are quite troubled by the fate of Lord Las Rosas."

"But, my justice," I say, carefully, so as to not provoke doubt in my commitment. "My injuries. How will I take memories?"

"You won't. Not yet." He sifts through the collection of alman stone. There's a crystal the size of a cherry strung on a copper chain. It must have been intended for a Persuári. Now Justice Méndez offers it to me. "You are to be my eyes and ears in the palace. Speak to no one. Do you understand? *No one* can know of what you're doing."

I realize I'm frowning because he asks, "Is this out of your abilities?"

"On the contrary," I say. I *need* the freedom to roam the palace. "It's just—the courtiers and the maids. They're repulsed by me."

"You must understand, Renata. Your powers are a sickness. But your guards are there for your protection."

How can he call my magics a sickness and still use them at his will? Am I a sickness or a weapon? Does it matter as long as I can be controlled?

"I'll get to work right away," I say.

Illan's informant may be long gone. But if they're still in the palace, perhaps I'll have at least one ally. I brush back my hair and let Justice Méndez slip the necklace over my head. The alman stone is cold on my skin. I envy the empty bit of rock. It is the only clean slate I will ever get.

He faces me, his sharp features made all the more jagged by the pulsing white light in the room. "I know I can count on you, my sweet."

And despite my dry tongue and racing heart, I say, "I won't disappoint you."

On the way out, he notices my bleeding hand. I have a lie ready if he asks how my stitch reopened, but he doesn't ask. "I shall have Leo add two stitches here. That boy's work is seamless."

Méndez takes my hands in his. I feel a small weight on the center of my gloved palm. A glittering gold stellita. On my way out, I devour it.

When I get back to my room, my thighs ache and my breath is short from ascending the five flights of the tower. Sula returns for me and walks with downcast eyes and folded hands the entire time. I find myself missing Leo's ramblings. His presence offers something like the peace Dez instilled in me. Thinking of him makes my entire body feel heavy as a ton of lead. I want to let that weight drag me down into the earth. It's even worse when I remember that Dez will never have a burial. He will never be anything other than gone.

I press on the wound in my hand and the dark thoughts release me. I remind myself that Leo is not my friend and he is nothing like Dez. Leo is loyal to the crown first. As Sula lights the lamps of my dark room, I sit and massage my hand.

Restlessness digs beneath my skin and makes me scratch. Where could Castian have gone with the weapon? I play out different scenarios in my head. Asking Méndez directly would reveal what he knows through his reaction, but it would give me away completely. With every lamp that ignites, I think of the one clear connection I have to the prince: the courtiers. But how to get close to them?

"What are you doing?" I ask Sula.

"It's laundry day, ma'am," Sula says.

The girl is stripping my bedsheets. Do they think I'm that dirty, or is this customary? That part I can't remember from my time here. It's either in the Gray or I wasn't paying attention to the maids who took care of me. No one notices the maids, despite their backbreaking work. I bet Castian has never looked twice at his staff. *They* will know more about the prince than anyone, even his father and the court.

Sula massages her shoulder for a moment. I sympathize with her pain. "Majordoma Frederica asked me to bring these down earlier, but I was sent to clear out the southwest guest rooms."

I try to cut off her rambling, but there's no gentle way for me to do it. She's afraid of me waving my hands. I shouldn't blame her.

"I'll do it."

She sucks in a breath, like I've punched her. "Oh, no, ma'am. I can't. I mustn't let you do that."

"Why? I am not a highborn lady. I am just like you."

"You're *not*." Her scared face goes mean. Of course the worst thing I could tell her was that we are one and the same. Blood and sinew and bone. Magics or no.

If I keep biting my tongue, I'll snap the tip off completely. "What I meant is, I don't need you fussing over me and changing my sheets. Get out. I can do it myself."

She doesn't move. "Y-you're not allowed to walk the palace alone."

Justice Méndez doesn't want me to reveal myself. Until I see the guards assigned to protect me, I am on my own.

"I won't be alone. I'll be with you."

With a start, Sula relents and lets me help her strip the bed and pillows. Floral. Dainty. Maybe I can ask the laundress not to perfume them. I think of Leo's words. About how easy it is for me to give orders.

In the gray-and-blue stone courtyard behind the kitchens, a dozen lavanderas are preparing the wash. Cauldrons large enough to boil a full-grown man are strung over firepits. Servants of all ages carry logs, pushcarts full of bedsheets and robes. There's a station of wooden vats where girls stir hot lye soapy water and use paddles to beat the stains out. Shady verdina trees sway in the early evening breeze.

The sun is getting low in the sky. My stomach growls, but I don't dare ask for a meal. Sula introduces me to Majordoma Frederica, who is in charge of the palace's cleaning servants. An imposing woman with freckled white skin and ash-brown hair tied back in a winding braid. A beauty mark dots one of her many chins. When she looks me up and down her gaze lands on my injured hand wrapped in gauze. Her grimace is noticeable.

"You'll do yourself lasting injury if you don't take care," she says, her rough accent from the southeast provincias.

I was expecting her to react to me the way Sula did moments before. The girl ducks her head and joins the line of lavanderas and other servants.

"I've had worse," I say, and find myself genuinely smiling. "I'm Renata."

"What's a *miss* like you doing down here?" Frederica asks. Her sharp eyes dart to where Sula adds my not-so-dirty sheets into the vat. "I can't have the justice think I've put you up to this."

There is one way to ingratiate myself with someone like Frederica, and that's to show her I can work.

"I don't belong up there," I say, and that's the truth. "The court-iers aren't going to want me to share their supper table. I'm good with my hands. Despite evidence to the contrary."

The majordoma throws her head back and laughs. This might be the first time at the palace that someone has laughed with this kind of warmth. I'm not a joke to her. I don't know what I am, but perhaps I'm a girl who wants to be useful. Lost in a place she doesn't belong. Trying to complete a mission that seems to slip further from her grasp.

"See the firebush there? That's Claudia. Help her make the lye. Do you know how?"

Lye is awful work, but it's a good thing I'm wearing at least one glove. "I do."

"Then why're you still talking to me? Go on and make yourself useful if that's what you came down here for."

I find the redheaded girl Majordoma Frederica crassly pointed to. Her brown eyes flick from my feet to my face, then to my hands. She wipes her own hands on her apron, and I notice an old burn across her forearm, not that it's hard to come across that in this line of work. Looking around I see many others with similar marks, but the most striking is on a thin older maid.

Everything about her is so drained of color that for a brief moment, my eyes register her as a memory that's escaped from the Gray and come to life. It's the vicious red scar that runs from her mouth across her cheek that reminds me that she's all too real. I can see from her fine bone structure that she was beautiful once. What happened to her? She keeps to herself, the other workers moving around her like a permanent fixture not to be bothered.

The redheaded girl clears her throat, snapping me back to the task at hand.

"Who're you?" she asks, a voice hardened for someone so young.

"Renata," I say, tucking the loose strands of my hair into a low knot. "Have you got a system?"

"Did. Three of my girls are sick to their stomachs with an illness going around. But if you ask me, at least one of them's not drinking their irvena tea and will wind up here again in nine months with a babe strapped to her back."

Another just sidles up beside her and flaps her hands. "Father Dragomar says that tea should be forbidden."

"Of course he'd say that, Jacinta," Claudia says, rolling her eyes. The gesture reminds me of Margo, and I'm surprised that I find myself missing her. It only lasts a moment. "It's hard to fill up a cathedral when near half the population went to the plague heap and the rest to the war against—you know who." Claudia points at me, and it's almost comical the way she does it.

"Claudia, she's *right* here." Jacinta's pretty brown eyes crinkle, and then they laugh. A heart-shaped birthmark covers her clavicle and chest. There was once a time when a mark like that would have gotten her accused of being Moria.

"I can carry the oak," I say.

"We don't use oak ash for the lords and ladies, and, well, you," Jacinta says. "Seaweed. Use these baskets for hauling. Don't forget an apron."

I get to work with the others, sweating through the simple blue dress Leo stuffed me in this morning. I load baskets full of seaweed and bring them to be burned down to ash. The other servants eye me with reservation, but I keep quiet and work. It reminds me of doing chores in Ángeles.

Once my task is done, I fetch water to boil and help them strain the ash without being told to. The soap's finished just in time for the next cart of linens to be rolled into the courtyard. As the sun moves across the sky, the discomfort I sensed from the other servants seems to wane.

I wish I had learned more of Sayida's and Dez's easy charm. They could walk into a room and disarm anyone, even without the use of their powers. How do I find the person who tends to Castian's rooms? Though, at the rate Claudia hands out her opinions, I may just have to stick around her and wait.

While the water is being changed and the fires rebuilt, the scarred older maid steps into the courtyard. Claudia immediately approaches her, helping the woman carry the food out. I watch Claudia say a few words, but am unable to make them out. The older maid only smiles in return.

"Come on and eat," Jacinta says. It takes me a moment to realize she's talking to me.

Under the shade of a spindly tree, Claudia offers me a bowl of vegetable soup, and I wish this gesture didn't make my heart ache the way it does. Not even during my years at Ángeles, among my own people, was kindness offered this easily, and now here, in my enemies' kitchen, I'm handed a bowl of it. I bite back the bitterness that wells up in my heart and breathe in the savory scents of oregano and rosemary.

As I dig in, I notice the older maid sitting far away, by herself. Claudia follows my concerned gaze.

"It's not polite to stare," Claudia teases.

"I'm sorry. I didn't mean—"

Claudia shrugs, unfazed. "Surely you're used to it yourself."

"What happened to her?"

"Davida? Depends on who you ask," Claudia responds, "but all of us here know the truth." She leans in for dramatic effect, clearly excited to be the one to tell the story. "Don't talk back to the prince if you want to keep your tongue."

I gasp in shock. The barbaric punishment for such a small infraction fills me with fresh hate.

"She was about to marry a general and everything," another servant girl says.

"Shut it," Jacinta mutters. "Leave Davida alone."

"Pity about Hector." Claudia sighs, seemingly more from exhaustion than from sympathy. "Lost his hand at Riomar. Never married, neither."

I want to voice my anger, but how can I? I'm the justice's marionette girl. I bled in the stone floor of the throne room. Anything I say, especially down here, would make its way through the palace faster than a flash of lightning.

The other women smile curiously at me. One of them eventually builds up enough courage to ask a question. "How come you're not up in the tower with the other quiet ones?"

"Quiet ones?" I ask.

"The Hand of your lot," Claudia explains.

What she's asking is, why haven't I become an official part of the Hand of Moria. One of Méndez's minions.

"I suppose I must prove myself loyal first," I answer slowly. But I don't want to talk about me. These women are not cruel, not like the courtiers from this morning. But as kind as they're being, I can't let myself fall into a trap. I'm here for information, and I intend to get it.

"Justice Méndez said the Sun Festival will bring foreigners and nobles by the wagons," I say, trying to show the same cheer Dez always used to put strangers at ease. He was more natural than I am. *You were born serious.*

"And we're the lucky ones to change their urine-soaked sheets," one girl mutters. "Drink so much they can't contain themselves."

They chitter, and another adds, "Lucky if a bit of piss is all you find."

"Do you ever notice how Prince Castian's linens never smell foul?" Jacinta says, her brown eyes shining.

"You're dreaming!" Claudia says, smirking crudely. "All men have a stink. Even a prince has to work up a sweat while giving himself a tug or two."

I choke on my soup, my face hot and probably tomato red as the girls laugh at me. I don't want that image of the murderous prince in my head. But Jacinta said something that intrigues me.

"You couldn't possibly know which sheets are his," I say dismissively.

Jacinta's eyes widen, and she juts out her chin. *Pride is a wonderful tool,* Dez used to say. At the thought of him I steel my heart and nearly salivate as I wait for the servant girl to answer.

"*I'm* the one who strips his bed," she says, as if she's been given a position of honor. Which, I suppose, she feels she has. "Though who can say when the prince will return."

"You lot!" A commanding voice rings out across the yard. It's the majordoma in all her ferocity. "Get back to work or five libbies are coming out of your wages."

"Come on, girls," Claudia says. "Someone's got to do the dirty work."

I stay close to Jacinta. This girl has access to Prince Castian. This girl is my way into his apartments.

"Except you," Frederica says, clapping her hand on my shoulder. "Leo's half-mad looking for you."

It's my cue to leave. I unwrap my apron and walk toward Jacinta's station to hang it up. What do I think I'm doing? I can't take a memory from her out in the open. But I need more time with her.

Claudia's red hair obstructs my line of sight. "You're not terrible, Renata. Come back in four nights' time after dark."

I lean in. I suppose "not terrible" is a compliment. "What's after dark?"

She winks. "The lords have their revels, and we have ours."

17

After three days of wandering around the palace, these are the secrets I've discovered: The royal servers spit in their masters' plates during dinner. Two of the courtiers anxiously waiting for Castian's return have taken a guard to their bed. The same guard. He's re-assigned out of the palace overnight. The seamstress is importing spider silk from Luzou, which is technically illegal, but it is said to be sanctioned by the queen herself. The guard posted at my door at night "for my protection" smells of aguadulce and spends most of his time muttering curses while he paces. Surely he has been given the worst duty in the palace.

Three days and no sign of the weapon. No more hidden rooms except the vault full of alman stone. No spy.

If the Magpie was once among the people of the palace, I believe them to be gone.

On the fourth morning, my routine continues. Leo wakes me up to feed and dress me. He takes me to Justice Méndez, who gets worse and worse at containing his disappointment when I have no news. I encourage him. I tell him that all spies make mistakes, because I do not want to lose my privileges of walking around the palace. But when I leave his offices with a stellita in my pocket, I begin to lose hope, too. The palace has too many empty spaces to get lost in. Alessandro is at my heels when Leo is not with me. I purposely walk slowly and turn in his direction. I catch myself wishing I could tell Margo that there is someone worse at sneaking around than I am. When that happens, I remember that she never trusted me, and the only thing that matters now is finishing what Dez could not.

Missing Dez is like living with a ghost limb. Sometimes I reach for him. To remember. Is that what hope is supposed to be?

That morning the castle is a flurry of preparation for the upcoming festival. Ladders are erected to begin the long process of weaving intricate flower arches in every entrance a guest might arrive through in eight days. I file into the throne room like I have every morning since I swore my allegiance to King Fernando. The spot in the marble where I added my blood to countless others' is a bull's-eye. For the others who fill the room—the ladies in their brocaded dresses and polished shoes adorned with sea pearls and noblemen groveling before the king—it is another day.

I am the only one who seems to notice that the Ventári of the Hand of Moria is swaying on his feet. His olive skin is ashen, with sickly green undertones. His hair is wet, dripping sweat.

"Leo," I say, my voice louder and more desperate than I want.

His smiling eyes follow my gaze to the Ventári. He sucks in

a breath. Before either of us can call for help, Constantino falls to the floor facedown and doesn't get back up. I know that he's dead because the blood that runs out of his nose and mouth forms a pool big enough to swallow him whole. No one can lose that much blood and survive. Shrill cries fill the air; a handful of shouts speculate plague.

As Justice Méndez calls for a medic and attendants rush to lead away the screaming courtiers, I am frozen in place. I wish I knew his family name or the provincia he was taken from or what happened to him that he lived out his short life here. Mostly I feel so emptied of feeling that I can't move, even when Leo shakes me. When I look back at the corpse, I see Esteban. Sayida. Margo. I see me.

"My lady, you do not need to see this," he says. Except that I do. I let him guide me away and into the common gardens open to the servants and staff only. He calls for strong café and lets me sit awhile in silence.

The cathedral bells ring, marking the hour. How did he die? The other Moria only stood there, staring straight ahead while his friend fell dead. Were they friends? It burns me up how little I know about them, and yet, a part of me knows it will be easier to leave this place the more I keep to myself.

"Is that what happened to the Robári that came before me?" I ask Leo when the café arrives.

His hand gestures are wilder, and he runs his fingers through his hair so much, he looks like he's just woken up. There's an honesty in the way he peels back his courtly exterior. "Yes. The previous Robári complained about a pain in her eye. Then she was simply not there one morning."

"Was she the first?" I ask, surprised by how small my voice sounds. A dark image bites at my thoughts. I see Lucia after the justice was done using her. The room filled with alman stone. I taste bile on my tongue but breathe through the dizziness that follows. I can't afford to get sick now.

Leo nods solemnly. "I hate to say that I did not notice she was gone until I heard Alessandro speaking to the justice about it. That man is surely—"

I don't know why I stop Leo from finishing that sentence. But I shake my head and tap the alman stone on my chest. He blinks quickly, like he, too, forgot himself.

He clears his throat and finishes in a droll voice, "Surely the best husband Lady Nuria could have acquired."

I feel how wide my eyes go. The woman whose apartments I sleep in is married to *that* judge?

"I've always been curious about how these things work," Leo says, drawing my attention back to him. His errant curl flops over his forehead, and this time he leaves it.

"They capture moments, stories," I answer. "Memories, really. The way you and I are living now."

"No, I know that, but *how*?"

I shake my head. How can I drag memories out of people's minds? How can Margo create illusions that make a city think it's burning again? How can Dez— How *could* Dez. Dez will never . . . I find it hard to breathe until I press my hand on my sternum.

"Unnatural magics," I say, because that is the answer I am supposed to say.

"You're healing nicely," he says, changing the subject.

I watch his features as he smooths the palm of my hand open. Just when I make up my mind about him, he surprises me. Why didn't he agree? It can't be to spare my feelings when he reminds me every morning how much work I have to do before looking like a lady of court. If I say the word *magpie* and wait for his response, it would be strange, but I have proven to be a strange girl. I wouldn't put it past Méndez to see this memory later, though they'll need a new Ventári to transcribe it, and perhaps understand what I'm doing.

I let it go.

The scar down my hand is going to be an ugly thing, but I've grown used to it. The shape begins to look like a mountain range on a map when I stare at it long enough.

"Leo," I say, covering the alman stone with my gloved hand, muffling sight and sound. "There's a party in the courtyard tonight."

He taps his chin, considering it. "And you'd like to attend."

I shrug. A Moria is dead and I'm thinking of parties. But I need to be there.

"I've never been to one before. The Whispers only took me to cantinas where everything ended in fights."

It's not a *whole* lie. It's been four days since I've made any progress about how to get into Castian's apartments. Jacinta is my only lead.

"I don't know," he says, eyes flicking to where my gloved hand is. "Justice Méndez said to watch over you. He detests festivities."

"Please," I say. How can a single word sound so sad? I didn't know Constantino, but he could have easily been me.

"One hour," Leo says, holding up a single finger. "And then I'm marching you up here myself."

Overcome with excitement, I throw my arms around his neck. He chuckles lightly, but the hug he gives me is comforting. I have missed being held this way, even if it's by a friend.

Not your friend, my mind admonishes.

As we continue the routine I've been cultivating, I remind myself that friends don't use each other the way I'm using Leo.

The courtyard is teeming with people. There's music. Bodies pressed so tight they look like the ripples of a wave.

"One hour," Leo reminds me, raking his fingers through his hair. "Don't make me come get you. I'm a dignified attendant, not a nursemaid."

When he leaves to sidle up to a handsome young guard, Claudia appears beside me and rests an elbow on my shoulder. "Aren't attendant and nursemaid the same thing?"

I laugh and take the clay cup of wine she offers me. It's sweeter than the dry vintage Justice Méndez pours from a glass decanter during dinner. I lick my lips and scan the dancing crowd. Everyone from scullery maids to kitchen hands to farm boys bring the court-yard to life. Girls in long white dresses spin, their hems billowing with every twirl. I recognize a surly-faced guard playing guitar beside a man who slaps beefy hands on percussions. Fire pits roar incandescent flames against the surrounding blue stones.

"I don't understand the occasion," I say to Claudia.

"The half-moon is as good a time as any," she says. "This week leading up to the Sun Festival is going to be brutal on us. It was Queen Penelope who began the tradition of letting the staff have their own celebration. She said it would boost *productivity*."

Bringing my clay cup to my lips, I hide what I want to say. We celebrated events in Ángeles. Unions, births, even deaths. But we did it together.

"Thanks for inviting me," I say. "Where are the others? Davida and Jacinta?"

Claudia's cheeks are pink from the heat and wine. "Davida likes to listen to the music from the kitchen. She peels potatoes while she pines for Hector. I tell you what—"

I sense her ramblings beginning. "And Jacinta?"

"Probably asleep in the laundry room," she says. Then adds, "Wrapped in the prince's sheets, I'd wager."

I grimace, hold up my empty cup, and say, "I'm going to get a refill!"

But Claudia is already threading her body into the needle of the crowd. I snag two cups and stop by the kitchens. Davida is there, tapping her foot, working her way through a mound of potatoes. I set a clay cup in front of her. She presses her hand to her chin and pushes it outward. There were some Whispers who couldn't speak and communicated with their hands. We're all taught the basics from a young age. I wish her a good night, then make for the laundry room.

I open three doors and find bags of potatoes, crates of root vegetables, barrels of wheat and grain with the Fajardo seal burned onto the wood. Another room has jars of oils and olives. The last storage I try smells strongly of soap. Towels and sheets are folded neatly in stacks. There, on a pile of half-folded laundry, is Jacinta sleeping in the center like a baby bird.

Her mouth is slightly ajar, a whistling sound coming from her nose. Something twists in the pit of my stomach as I approach her. I pause. How would I feel if I woke to a strange girl, a girl said to possess the murderous power I do, standing over me?

I turn and walk away. But only for a moment. I take off my alman stone completely and pocket it, covering my tracks. I have to get this memory.

I *have* to.

I fix my fingers into stillness and press them to her temple. She doesn't rouse, only wheezes. The whorls of my fingertips come alight with my power, and then I'm wading through her past, searching.

Jacinta gathers her skirts and runs. Her nerves twist as she hurries into Prince Castian's apartments. Everyone knows the prince doesn't like his servants seen, and with her sweaty pink face and slippers dusted in the white clay of the courtyard, she is most certainly visible.

She pulls on the door and weaves through his strange rooms. How can someone as bright as Lady Nuria spend her days in this miserable place? The royal mausoleums have more mirth. Well, now the lady won't have to . . .

Jacinta's eyes adjust to the dimly lit living room. The curtains are shut, and there are two oil lamps on the parlor table. Their hazy yellowed light makes the tapestries hanging on the walls appear to be moving: Stallions saddled by men at war. Ships breaking through waves.

Her cheeks burn at the sight of a lady's glove on the prince's plush couch. Two glasses on the table with a dozen bottles of wine and aguadulce knocked over. The stench of liquor hits her on her next step, and that's when she sees the pile of clothes. Definitely more than one lady was here—though surely no ladies at all. The girls in the laundry will never believe her when she tells them of this.

Jacinta freezes at a flurry of movement. There he stands at the doorway to his bedroom. Prince Castian pulls his robe over nothing at all. His taut muscles flex as he staggers and grabs for another bottle on the parlor table. She can see the moon-shaped scar left behind by that monstrous Moria. Though she'd never admit it makes him even more beautiful.

"Your Highness," Jacinta says, finding the will to bend her body into a curtsy.

He grunts, rubbing sleep from his eyes. His hair is pure gold haloing his face. "Who in the hells are you?"

Alarms play against her eardrums. No, not alarms. Her heart. She can hear her own blood pumping through her, every single beat an answer to the hard blue stare of the royal boy.

"Begging your pardon, Your Grace. Um. Lord Commander. I'm to fetch your—erm—unwanted garbs for my mistress. I'm so sorry about all of this. You don't deserve any heartache, my l-lord."

He is staring at her now, arms crossed like the statue of the angel San Márcos in the center garden. An angel waiting to pronounce judgment. It's like he comes awake. He sees the wreckage of the room. The bottles. The cigars. The clothes.

Those blue eyes dart a path back to his bedchamber. For a moment, his body softens, arms coming down to his sides to rest. He takes a deep breath, as if to brace himself. The kind of breath she'd take if she were plunging into the cold common pools in the capital center. He rubs his lips together, and for the first time she realizes that she has never seen the prince this close-up before. His mouth is the shape of a bow and the pale sort of pink she has never seen on a man before.

Then she realizes she is still standing and still staring and, oh—Father of Worlds—she needs to move. But as ruined and terrible as he is, she's loved Prince Castian since the first day she saw him.

"I don't deserve heartache?" Castian says, tortured, hard. "You don't know what I deserve."

She shakes her head. Has she said the wrong thing? She always says the wrong thing.

He picks up the wine bottle and drinks. Wine spills down his chest. He makes a strangled sound. Is he crying? She hates to see him this way.

"Get out," he says to her, so low she takes a step closer.

She can't leave without his wedding garments. "My lord—"

He throws the bottle across the room and it shatters. "You want my things? Here." He runs into the bedroom. He is a magnet, and she follows despite her fear.

On his bed are two women rousing from sleep. They shrink back in terror at the screaming prince, who tears through his dressing closet. He gathers his groom's clothes and throws them at Jacinta's feet.

"There! Take it. Take all of it."

She gathers up his clothes. They smell like him. Like woodsmoke and salt of the sea. He's worn them. He'd gotten dressed and worn them.

Castian retreats to the farthest corner of the bedroom and turns his back on them all. He is still as marble, the angel at a temple she would always worship.

"Please leave me," he says.

And they leave.

Movement in the halls alerts me to let go. I relinquish my hold on Jacinta's mind and slink back through the laundry room, past the kitchens, my heart racing. No one in the Whispers had heard of this engagement. But one thing is for sure: I have to get inside the prince's chambers. Music spills into the smaller workrooms.

If there were ever a time I could take my chance, it would be tonight.

I quickly retrieve my alman stone from my pocket. Using trembling sweaty fingers to do the clasp, I think of the drunken prince in Jacinta's memory. Memories can't be changed, even when someone wants them to be. She worships the prince, and all of her feelings thread into my skin. I want to tear at it until the sickening longing fades.

The moment I step into the corridor, a body shoves me against the wall. Fragrant holy oils suffocate me. A hand slaps over my mouth to keep me from screaming. I kick out hard and my attacker staggers. It's Alessandro.

"I saw you," he says, grunting as he recovers. "What were you doing to that servant girl, bestae?"

My heart rate spikes. I grab for the closest thing I can get my hands on. A wooden slat used to stir the lye.

"You must be confused, Judge Alessandro," I say. "Her friends asked me to check on her."

He keeps his distance, but I see his mind working, going through each of his options. "You're all deceivers. Your hand works perfectly fine."

I grip the slat tighter. If I hit him, it would be as good as treason. If I let him go to Méndez, all this will be over.

"There you are!" Leo shouts. His flop of black curls is disheveled from dancing and his cheeks are flushed. Has it truly been an hour? I have never been more glad to see anyone in my life. He takes in Alessandro and then me. "What's happening?"

"She's lying about her injury. I saw her preying on a sleeping girl to devour her memories. I'm taking her to Justice Méndez now," he says.

Leo pauses, looking Alessandro up and down. Then his forehead draws together with mild concern.

"I'll accompany you," Leo says gravely as he stands between us. An icy feeling cuts through me. I told myself I shouldn't be surprised, and yet, I am. "Now, just so I can help you back up your story for Justice Méndez, what is your proof? I only want to be certain, Judge Alessandro, so we do not disturb the justice unnecessarily."

What is Leo doing?

"What do you mean, *proof*? I don't have to prove anything. I will tell Justice Méndez, and he will believe me because my word is truth."

Leo nods like he's eating up the other man's claim. "Of course, Judge Alessandro! But"—he glances at my chest as if he's just noticed the stone resting there—"what will the alman stone show?"

Alessandro takes in the stone, then dismisses Leo. "The Ventári expired, no one can verify it until we find another one." I see the moment he understands his mistake. The alman stone will show Alessandro attacking me and Leo stepping in to calm the erratic judge. Anger cuts his features into a terrible scowl. "It won't matter. My word is higher than yours."

"I do not deny that," I say, setting the slat down. I am sure I no longer need it. "There are, of course, hundreds of judges like you in the Arm of Justice, and I am but one Robári."

Leo turns to the side, but I catch the way his mouth twitches.

Alessandro whirls between me and Leo. If he were a stray animal, he'd be frothing at the mouth with anger. He shoves a finger in my chest, on the scab where King Fernando cut me. I bite down so I won't wince. "I will be there when you make a mistake, bestae."

As he sweeps away, Leo and I stand and listen to the music. He saved me from Alessandro. He *has* to be the Magpie. But when I open my mouth, he shakes his head. He covers my alman stone.

"We will not speak of this," he says.

I want to argue, but I can't risk getting Leo in trouble. Especially if he is the spy the justice is searching for. For now, I am content in knowing that I can trust him. I don't protest as we return to my room, and my mind returns to Jacinta's memory.

Castian had been *engaged*. Justice Méndez did say that Leo had started off as Lady Nuria's attendant. Is it a coincidence that I'm in her old apartments? Surely out of every guest room in the palace . . . She's married to Alessandro now but was *engaged* to Castian. My stomach sickens at what they might have done in the same place where I sleep.

The palace at night takes on an eerie stillness. Shadows feel longer, and even the statues along the halls give me the sensation we're being watched. But I memorize every turn we take and every step back to my room because I will have to get myself back there. Leo goes on about how a shipment of wine for the festival met a sorry end in a ditch on the way into the capital, setting the royal vintner into a frenzy. I pocket the alman stone.

"Leo, I heard a rumor tonight," I say, letting my eyes slide conspiratorially from corner to corner. I've seen Sayida do this when she wants to be coy about a subject. I, however, am far from coy and fear he's going to shut me down after what we just went through.

"There are as many rumors as there are citizens in the capital, my dear lady."

"Not a lady," I mumble.

Leo loops his arm around mine and gives the halls a quick glance before stepping onto an open sky bridge. I realize we haven't walked it at night before. It feels like we're walking across a stretch of long black shadow. Each glittering arch and pillar reflects the half-moon's light.

"Pray tell, what is this rumor? Did you spend your hour of party chatting up a scullery maid?"

I laugh, trying to keep my voice light. By the sound of him, the confrontation with Alessandro never happened. "I heard that Prince Castian was engaged once to your former lady."

Leo's face brightens with his usual smile. I wonder how many things he hides with the turn of his lips. "Ah, Lady Nuria Graciella, Duquesa of Citadela Tresoros, was indeed set to wed the prince once upon a time."

Tresoros.

"As in, the family that once *ruled* Tresoros?" I ask.

Over a century ago, the kingdom of Tresoros had the richest earth of the continent before beginning a tenuous alliance with the Fajardo family. Now that Puerto Leones has conquered most of the continent, it's hard to imagine that it was once a fraction of what it is today. When the royals of Tresoros surrendered, they did so under the condition that the royal family be given titles and a place at court. Now those lands are just another provincia where there was once a nation.

"The very same," Leo says. "Lady Nuria is the wealthiest woman in all of Puerto Leones. She owns most of the western provincia, because of the treaty her grandfather negotiated when they abdicated their throne to the Fajardos. I suppose the Whispers wouldn't have known about her scandal with Prince Castian in those mountain hovels you call homes."

And just like that, my doubt about Leo returns. Coming from him, that hurts more than any of the terrible things Alessandro said to me. How could he risk his reputation for me one moment, and then say something like this the next?

"The Whispers are disconnected from the rest of the world," I say. "That is why their rebellion failed." The words feel empty, but the lies now roll off my tongue.

"Perhaps," Leo says. He stops halfway across the bridge. From here we can see the yellow glow of streetlamps that line the

Andalucían streets. It's a pretty sight when the dark can hide the filth and violence of the day.

"Who called it off?" I ask.

"It's a complicated affair," Leo says. "Lady Nuria was betrothed to Prince Castian since before they were born."

"How is that possible?"

"Jústo Fajardo, the king's father, was having a hard time holding the annexed Tresoros territory."

"Tresoros was half the size of Puerto Leones at that time," I say. "How could they hold off the Fajardo attacks?"

"For every man enlisted to the Fajardo army, the Tresoros family could afford to match it with hired soldiers."

"Mercenaries," I say. I bet my life that there is not a single book in the library in this hall, or in the entire country, that details this.

"From Luzou, Dauphinique, even the Icelands in the northern seas," Leo says, his eyes glittering with story. What an enigma he is to have wound up here. Loyal to the crown. Keeper of salacious stories. Tentative friend to someone like me. "The Duquesa's family sits on the largest and most plentiful mines of gems and gold."

"So, what? They sold their descendants off to stop a war?"

"You have no sense of romance." Leo turns on his heel and keeps walking. "I do not know who brought the agreement to the table, but an accord bound the families together. Their children were already promised to others, and so the next best thing was their first grandchildren."

"And how did Nuria feel being betrothed to such a man?" The last word comes out as a curse. I think of all the words the servant girls used to describe the prince the days I helped in the courtyard, even the thoughts from the courtier whose memory I stole. "A devastating man."

"He wasn't so as a child. Lady Nuria and Castian were friends from infancy. They were always together in the palace, or so the stories go. There was a brief period, about a year, when the prince was sent to the Islas del Rey in the south. For his health. That was the only time they were apart."

"No wonder I never saw him during my time here," I say.

Leo racks his brain. "I believe it was before you would have arrived. When he was five or six, perhaps? It was right after the death of . . ." Leo trails off, remembering himself before he finishes the sentence, but I finish it for him.

"The death of the younger prince, his brother," I say, thankful the cover of dark hides the horror I feel. Some say the Matahermano was destined to become as ruthless as his father. A boy who loves pain and death. A man who will die by my hand.

Leo nods. "As for *why* their engagement ended . . . Rumors flew. Some say he couldn't keep Nuria away from other eligible men at court. Vicious lies, of course. Only that could have stopped a union decades in the making. And mere days before the wedding!"

I make a sour face. "Castian might be a prince, but that wouldn't have made him a good husband."

"And what do you know of husbands, young Renata?"

"You are not more than two years my elder, Leo. I might ask what *you* know of husbands."

"Only but the one that I had and lost."

My heart immediately breaks for him, but he won't have it.

"Now, don't make that face, I can't stand any sadness today. Let me finish my story."

We're nearing my apartments and both slow down. "Go on. I suspect you know how to parse the lies from the truth."

"Naturally. Yes, it was Prince Castian who broke off their engagement," Leo says. "They went away on a voyage together and when they returned, it was over."

A year ago? "Was it before or after the Battle of Riomar?"

Leo's dark brow jolts up. "After. It was meant to be a celebration for the prince's victory."

That was the first time he almost killed Dez. I replay fragments of the memory. The Príncipe Dorado and the rebel. My throat constricts with the need to cry, but Leo's voice guides me out of that darkness.

"Until that voyage, they'd loved each other deeply. Everyone envied them for so long. It was a romance for the ages. There are cantina songs about them, you know."

"I don't." I resist the urge to gag. "What could have been so terrible as to break off a century-old arrangement and *true love*?"

"They say that Prince Castian caught Lady Nuria with someone else in her bed. When it came to light, the ladies of court wanted to have her tried for treason. A royal priest wanted to excommunicate her. But the lady is faithful, loyal above anything else. Who would take the prince's word over hers?"

Doubting the prince's word, even in private, is dangerous. But it has been a dangerous night. Perhaps I'm wrong about Leo in many ways. He might not be the Magpie, but now I know his true master. Lady Nuria.

"Doesn't that negate the treaty with their grandparents? Could Tresoros reclaim its independence?"

Leo makes a whistling sound, as if even he can't believe what he's going to say. "That's the thing. She was allowed to keep her family lands and title. The prince fought his own father for her to have them. The compromise was that she was to marry one of the judges of the Arm of Justice."

"But—"

"May I ask why your interest in old royal gossip?" He cuts me off, and I take this as a sign that I've pushed him to his limit. We turn down a dark corridor and for the first time I'm relieved to see the guard posted outside of my room.

I shrug and keep my voice light. Airy. The way I've heard the girls at court speak. "You can't blame me if gossip is all I have for entertainment at the moment. I've been gone too long."

Leo's smile is full of mischief, but if he suspects I have other intentions, he betrays nothing. With a friendly wave, he calls out. "Hector! Where have you been all night? We had to go take a turn around the sky bridge while we waited for you."

The way that Leo lies fascinates me. The name sounds familiar, but after the night's excitement I can't recall why.

The guard leans against the wall directly across my door. His face remains in shadow, but I catch the crop of a dark beard and brown skin.

"Sure you did," Hector mutters. "How was the half-moon revel?"

"Don't answer that," Leo says, walking backward to the door. He draws out a slender skeleton key and unlocks the door. "Good night, Hector."

That's when it hits me. *Hector.* I think of Davida sitting in the kitchen peeling potatoes.

"Parties are for children," he mutters.

Leo makes a face for my benefit, then walks into my room. I'm at his heels when I stop and turn to Hector. If there is a chance, I have to take it.

"Davida's in the kitchens," I say.

Even though his body is cast in shadow, I see it go rigid. "What business is that of yours?"

I shrug and hum the song that was playing when she was working. It's been stuck in my head, familiar in a way I can't explain. "No reason. I thought she was waiting for someone, that's all."

I close the door behind me. As I climb into bed after Leo leaves, the weight of today sinks into my skin. Constantino bleeding out at court and the world moving on without him like he didn't affect it. But he did. Even if he was taken and warped into something unrecognizable, he once belonged to a family.

I get out of bed and rummage through my things until I find the coin Dez gave me. It feels wrong to keep it. I should try to give it back to Illan one day. But for now, it is the only thing I have of Dez to remember that he was real. I close my eyes and think of him haloed by the moon. So beautiful it aches. I press the coin to my lips.

"This would be easier if you were with me," I whisper to a boy who cannot answer.

I tuck the coin under my mattress. All I can do now is hope that my hunch about Hector and Davida is right. It's the only way I will be able to sneak into the prince's quarters.

Hector's heavy boots pacing in circles begin to lull me to sleep. I stare at the canopy over my bed. *Her* bed. It's a strange feeling, living in a room that belonged to someone else, someone who was meant to marry a prince before she was born, before her parents even dreamed her up. A girl whose clothes I wear and bed I sleep in. A girl who was almost charged with treason and might have had dreams of her own. Infidelity among common marriages is bad enough. But she was said to have been unfaithful to the prince. That would have been tantamount to treason. How could she keep her lands and title then? What would be so valuable about their alliance that Castian, ruthless as he is, would have stood for watching her marry another man? Unless . . . Tresoros is known for their rich earth. Minerals and gems.

I think of the prince standing in the Forest of Lynxes. Dez stopped me from using my magics. Castian said it wouldn't work on him. I didn't think of it. So many Leonesse wear their holy wooden wards but they don't truly understand our power. Maybe something discovered beneath Tresoros counteracts Moria powers, just as metals amplify them? Could the weapon have come from Tresoros and therefore the union with Puerto Leones had to be retained?

I lie in the quiet for a moment, and that's when I realize—it's *quiet*. Utter silence outside my door.

I sit up, my blood buzzing and alert. This may be the only chance I get.

I change into a pair of black riding trousers and a black tunic. After rummaging through a drawer, I find the hidden flower pin I wore the day I met King Fernando. I rip off the cloth petals, leaving behind only the sharp metal clip, and secure it into my waistband. Perhaps I'd dreamed of using its sharp steel tip to stab a prince. But it'll pick a lock just as well.

As I move across the sky bridge leading back to Castian's rooms, I feel like the Lady of Shadows herself, in her dress made of night and morning stars. Revelers cry their songs, and the precarious roll of wagon wheels over cobblestones masks my tread.

With Jacinta's memory, I find the Bloodied Prince's doors like true north. The room is unmanned, and my fingers remember the familiar tricks of searching the metal organs of the lock.

When the metal gives and I hear the right click, I hold my breath, look over my shoulder once, and pray the Lady of Shadows is on my side.

I heave open the heavy doors and slip inside the empty apartments. For a moment, I let it sink in that I'm inside the room where Castian lives while he's at the palace. A queasy sensation brings a hot flash across my entire being, because from now until the end of my days I will never be able to think of Dez without thinking of Castian, too.

I let my eyes adjust to the darkness, then cut across the carpeted floor to the window. I part the curtains, letting in waking sky, a strip of pale blue along the horizon. I must hurry. Leo will be appearing at my door soon. He always comes to wake me when the morning bleeds red beneath the lip of the curtains.

There's an oil lamp and matchsticks on the parlor table. My fingers, though steady while I was breaking in, are now betraying me, and it takes me three matches before I can light the damn thing.

I make my way through the blue parlor with its grand tapestries and plush couches, and hurry into his bedchambers. The walls are covered in deep blue velvet, containing waves of sheen and shadow that make them seem to undulate. I pull back the curtains and am startled by the way the light casts an aura on the walls and floor. It is as if the room was designed to give the inhabitant the feeling of being under the sea, of constant sway and motion.

It is a dream, and I hate myself for feeling at peace in here.

I go to the bookshelf filled with leather- and cloth-bound books. I've heard of hidden doors unlocked by pulling a lever disguised as a book. This bookcase is certainly big enough, so I pull nearly every book. Nothing.

I set the lamp on the large dresser in the adjoining closet where Jacinta gathered the prince's marriage clothing. I rummage through the drawers, but there are only clothes and belts and sashes and caps and tassels.

"Where are you?" I whisper to the room, begging it to speak its secrets back.

I continue to a study with a large wooden desk littered with letters, still-rolled scrolls, pots of sepia ink, and a large conch shell, most common in Citadela Salinas. I make to grab it, but my senses fill with leather and salt, and I can picture Castian sitting here and listening to the sound of waves. Anger bubbles in my throat because he doesn't deserve this peace he's engineered.

I move the stacks of parchment to reveal the surface of the painted desk. Solid black with gold lines and stars etched into it— constellations. I can make out the hexagon that marks the Leones constellation, said to have been put there by the Lord of Worlds to mark the new age of the Fajardos' conquest of Puerto Leones.

I always thought it looked more like a cat than a lion.

When I return the parchment stack to its place, I realize that it's a map of Puerto Leones. There are two iron winged lions stamped with ink on Sól y Perla, a coastal town in the east, and home to the most barbaric and dreaded prison in our country. Soledad.

Why would Castian mark a prison he's been to probably dozens of times?

I freeze at the warped creak of a floorboard. The sky is starting to pinken at the edges, and my heart spikes with the distant crow of a rooster. I hold my breath, but no one comes through the doors to discover me. I cut across the room to the wall of painted portraits. There's none of Castian as a child or even him as a grown man, but there are several of seascapes and ships. I never would have guessed the prince was such a nautical admirer, though he is named after the bluest sea in the world. The one painting that strikes me the most is that of a woman.

If I step back, I can see that all the other paintings surround her, as if she is adrift at sea. I pick up the lamp again and hold it closer. She's breathtaking, with long blond hair that curls over her shoulders in perfect rings. There's a golden crown over her head studded with brilliant rubies, fat as blood drops. Something inside me squeezes painfully when I look into the calming blue-green of her eyes, the color of the Castinian Sea. The prince's eyes.

This must have been Castian's mother, King Fernando's second queen of Puerto Leones. Queen Penelope.

I'm mesmerized by the portrait, as much for the beauty as for the questions that now plague my mind. What must she have thought of him? Her oldest son, the heir to the throne, the murderer of her only other child? How far can one mother's love truly stretch?

It is obvious that *he* revered *her*, though, to have given the portrait such prominence in the room. It's so arresting that for a moment, my whole body tingles with something—some longing I cannot name. Perhaps it is the longing of all orphans. There is nothing like the sweet love of a mother, the *safety* of a mother, even if that safety is only an illusion.

And that's when something occurs to me.

Without wasting any more time, I hurriedly dig my fingers along the edges of the frame. At first, I feel foolish, silly, desperate. It's strangely intimate to run my hands along this beautiful portrait.

But then—I find what I'm looking for.

The vulnerable spot.

A hinge.

Moments later, I hear a satisfying click as I lift a latch that releases the portrait's clasp, revealing a hidden vault.

Thank you, Mother of All.

And thank you, Queen Penelope.

I breathe in the dust inside this vault, large enough to fit a crouched body. I set the lamp at the center and go through its contents.

My heart races when I grab the black box in the hidden compartment. I rip open the lid, electricity coursing through my veins, but this is not the box I saw in Lozar's memory. This is ornate and not the right size.

I rummage through the trinkets in the velvet lining—iron toy soldiers with drawn swords, dozens of marbles in all sorts of colored glass, and a small wooden sword a child might have trained with. There're a dozen letters, the wax seals opened and scented with a thick perfume of roses.

I slam the box closed. This is not the weapon!

I rub the sweat from my upper lip and shut the portrait.

Then I can feel the magics before I see the pulse of light. In a decorative bowl full of sea glass, there's a bit of alman stone. It's a jagged rectangle, like it was chipped out of a bigger piece. Justice Méndez keeps the stones under lock and key. Could he have placed this here to spy on the prince? The glow within the crystal is strong, which means the memories are still recent.

I pocket it to read in my rooms. The sky is too bright, but if I run, I can make it back before anyone can see me leave this place.

I quickly whirl around, but I bump into the desk, knocking the conch shell off the table. I dive for it and catch it just before it falls and shatters.

"Careful," a voice says. "Those are quite the collector's items."

Sweat pools between my shoulder blades, and I blink several times to make sure I'm not imagining him.

"Leo." My brain is firing in all directions and it's the only thing I can say. "I—"

"Say nothing." His voice is gruff, angry. He takes the shell from my hand and lets go of a hard sigh as he sets it down. "After everything— No. Let us both say nothing."

How did he know I was here?

Then I realize, this must have been what Méndez wanted. To remove the lock and the guards to see where I'd go. I walked right into a trap.

That is, until I see the item Leo slips from his jacket pocket and sets on the center of the desk. Roses waft from the sealed letter. This isn't correspondence from the king or Justice Méndez. It's clearly something far more personal.

"Follow me," he says, clearing his throat severely.

I do so without question, too stunned to do anything else but walk beside him across the sky bridge we've traversed dozens of times together, and back to my door, where he lets us both in and busies himself with the routine we've created.

I think of the letters in the prince's keepsake box. Whose letters but Lady Nuria's would the prince have kept? Are the prince and Nuria still together after all that happened between them? What message could Nuria be sending him now, through Leo?

As if reading my mind, Leo turns to me with a half smile. Morning light dances across the room. We are bathed in reds and yellows. The illusion of fire follows me wherever I go.

"You're lucky, you know. You're quite the favorite."

"Why is that?" What's he getting at?

"Because you won't have to give up Lady Nuria's lovely chambers, since she will be given apartments suited to the wife of a judge."

"She's here?"

"She arrived not moments ago after three weeks away in Citadela Salinas. But she's returned for the Sun Festival. Hence the missive I just delivered. But that's between you and me, of course. No one's to know I've been helping them stay in touch. Anyway, you get to keep her rooms, and she'll be relegated to guest quarters."

I hardly know what to make of this. Is he telling me so that I will seek her out?

Lady Nuria. The prince's onetime fiancée. Back here.

I must seek an audience with her.

As for Leo—that's the thing about trust. It can also be solidified with mutually assured destruction.

18

FOR THE NEXT TWO DAYS, I AM THE PICTURE OF OBEDIENCE. I GO WHERE LEO and Sula tell me to go. I help in the kitchens and with the lavanderas. The paranoia of getting caught takes over. It's like my body does not belong to me. Even when I'm alone, the sensation that there's someone watching me lingers. It is a feeling that settles ice-cold on my spine, paralyzing me with such fear that it is not until the middle of the second night that I find the courage to read the alman stone I stole from Prince Castian's room.

After I prepare for bed, the fall of footsteps alerts me to the guards outside. I get under the covers and cradle the glowing alman stone in my hands. Each new memory I have of the prince warps the previous one, unraveling different kinds of hatred I didn't know I was capable of. He's a murderer, a madman—power hungry and cruel to the women around him. And yet, everyone still *wants* him.

I hesitate before pulling the memory from the alman stone because I don't know what I will find.

> *Castian takes off his golden circlet. He's covered in blood and dirt. It streaks his face and neck. His clothes are steeped in it. His hands tremble as he undoes the ties of his tunic.*
>
> *An older attendant comes in. Her large brown eyes give her the look of an owl. But when he sees her, he lets go of a long breath. She looks like she wants to go to him, but doesn't. Her rough hands move in the air.*
>
> *Castian nods solemnly. "A bath would be lovely, thank you, Davida."*
>
> *The woman bows and picks up the clothes he's discarded, then leaves. As the sound of water runs, Castian watches the painting of his mother. He stares at her for a long moment, shakes his head, then opens the secret compartment behind the painting. He reaches into the safe and withdraws a long rectangular wooden box etched with gold symbols. His face is stone, resolute. He marches out of the room.*
>
> *When he returns, his hands are empty. Davida reenters and holds out a robe for him.*

I sit in the dark for a long time and process what I've seen.

Castian did have the weapon in his room, but I was too late. I was always going to be too late because that was the day he murdered Dez. I remember the clothes he wore, the pattern of the blood on his face. I remember charging toward him and being stopped.

He came back to his rooms and ran a bath. How could Davida

attend to him? Is that why she's in the kitchens? A place to go when the prince is gone?

When I finally fall asleep, I dream of being swallowed by the sea.

Come morning, Leo and I talk about everything and nothing but finally return to an easy rhythm. He never mentions our run-in at Prince Castian's chambers again, not to ask me why I was there or to explain his own actions, which leads me to believe I'm safe. He clearly doesn't want anyone to know about him being a messenger for his old mistress as much as I don't want anyone to know about me rummaging around Castian's apartments.

With four days left until the Sun Festival, it's difficult to search the palace during the day because Alessandro keeps getting better at trailing me. Sometimes, I'll swear I'm alone, and then I catch him near me. The thing that gives him away is the cloying scent of holy oils. It's like he bathes in them.

I remain with Leo, and I tell myself it is for protection. But really, he's the only friend I have in the world.

Leo fills me in on all the court gossip. Lady Sevilla caught her husband in a compromising position with her own sister and may not attend the queen's garden party. Duque Arias's ship was lost at sea during its voyage back from Islas del Rey, the king's private islands.

We're interrupted by the jostle of the doorknob. Leo's green eyes narrow with confusion. Only Leo has the key.

And Méndez.

The justice lets himself into my room and dread coils in my gut. Dressed in riding trousers and a long tunic with a decorative sword belt strapped around his waist, he looks like he's ready for a long journey. Where would he go less than a week before the festivities?

I hate that he strides in as if he is entitled to be here. I hate that when he looks at me, his gray eyes brighten. I hate that I am relieved to see him, just for a moment.

"Renata," he says, tugging off his gloves. "Leonardo. I thought I might catch you before your duties."

Leo and I rise to our feet at the sound of our names.

"What a surprise," I say, a brightness in my voice I've learned from listening to the courtiers that flitter around the palace. "You've been too busy for me, my justice."

Leo hurries forward. "May I fetch you something—"

Méndez holds up his hand and Leo falls silent. Blood rushes to my face as I wait for him to speak. "I came to see the status of your wound and give you instructions."

"My justice?"

Leo clears the food trays and wipes down the table.

"I am sorry, my sweet. I am called away on matters of the king," Méndez says, but the curt tone of his voice makes me wary to continue to prod.

"I was about to change her bandage," Leo says, returning from the adjoining room with the healing kit. Fresh cloth and tinctures in brown glass bottles. A needle and thread in case my wound has reopened.

"That won't be necessary," Méndez says. "Lady Nuria is here. Please see that she and Judge Alessandro have everything they require."

At the mention of her name, Leo and I look at each other. His dark eyelashes flutter and he tugs on the bottom of his attendant jacket, the only sign that he might be nervous. My heart spikes to my throat, but I break our gaze and begin unwrapping my own bandage.

"Right away, my justice," Leo says, and folds into a low bow before leaving.

"I thank you for coming to see me," I tell Justice Méndez. "I know your time is precious."

He gives a small, weary smile, and takes my bare hand in his. He makes short noises of frustration at the long cut across my palm. My wound is healing quickly, but not as quickly as he seems to need.

"Is something wrong?" I ask carefully.

His thumb drags gently across the scabs on my knuckles. I bite back the revulsion that nearly makes me pull away. This feels like a trap, a snake gliding around my body.

"On the contrary. I have found a new Ventári for the Hand of Moria."

"Where?" A twinge of pain comes alive over my temples. I think of Esteban. I think of the Whispers. I hold my breath to stop myself from shouting.

"Right here in the capital. I will be needing your alman stone for him to read."

I feel sick. There are almost no Moria left in the capital. They must have used the weapon. How else could they have found him?

I yank my hand away, unable to stop myself. My heart races as Méndez looks at me, startled.

"Renata?" He grips me by my shoulders. I can hardly stand. He pulls me against his chest. He smells of incense and sugar. The scents I thought of as home for so long. I am so tired I can hardly push him away. The way he brushes my hair back, like I'm a little girl once again, makes my insides churn. I remind myself that he is not my father and never was. He was the monster who kept me in a birdcage. But when he repeats my name, with more worry than anyone has shown for me, with the exception of Dez, I can't speak.

"I'm well," I manage. "It's nothing."

He sits back down. I take off the necklace and hand it over, wondering if he realizes that only I can read the stone. The new Ventári can only verify what I see. He exchanges it for a new one. This one is smaller, the size of a marble, and rests at my collarbone. I feel the thrum of its magic, like it's calling to my own. "I need you to be more vigilant."

"Yes, Uncle. Can I ask? Has something happened?"

He readies the supplies to dress my wound. "There has been a robbery of sorts. Some of my alman stones have gone missing."

"From the vault?"

Méndez shakes his head once, his gray eyes skimming over my features. At least my surprise is genuine. "Other places around the palace. Two of them are gone."

Justice Méndez is spying on Prince Castian! The realization makes me dizzy. I think of Castian in Esmeraldas. *No one can know I was here.* Did he mean anyone or Méndez specifically? Castian has the connection to Lady Nuria. Castian has the weapon. Could they be rivals for the king's approval?

"Renata?" Méndez's voice booms in my ear.

I haven't been paying attention. I suck in a breath. "I'm sorry. Forgive me, my justice."

"I thought you were going to be honest with me, Renata." Méndez twists off the cap of the tincture and drops the brown liquid over my wound. I know it stings but I can't register it anymore. "If something is wrong, I must know it."

"Sometimes my memories surge back. I can't control them all the time and it becomes painful."

His gray eyes scan my face. He brushes a lock of black hair away from my eyes. "I think about the night you were taken quite often."

As do I, I say to myself. The image of a sweet young Dez pulling me to safety is both a balm and a knife to my heart. I don't want to talk about this anymore.

"I'm better now," I say, and offer a smile that seems to convince him.

"I have brought you something." He fishes out a small blue velvet pouch from his satchel and unfolds it.

I do not want gifts from Méndez. This is how it'll start, and then I'll be right back where I was all those years ago. But the old me would not have refused, so I don't.

The red-jeweled pendant is the official seal of the justice, similar to the one Leo wears. Méndez pins it to the fabric of my dress over my heart.

I take a long, trembling breath. "You honor me, my justice."

He lifts my chin with his finger. His sincerity burns me. "You are more valuable than you know, Renata. Soon, King Fernando will see all the work I have done for our cause."

"The king is pleased?"

"More so since your arrival." His forehead strains. "While I am gone, you must continue being my eyes and ears. Only Judge Alessandro and Leo can reach me."

"Do you have to go?" I ask. "What if you don't return in time?"

"All the more reason my duty calls. The new Ventári must be broken in for the king."

Is that what he's going to do to me? Break me in? A voice that sounds like Margo says, *He already has.*

"When I return, I expect your injury to be healed completely and in time to perform."

Dread pools on my tongue. "To join the Hand of Moria."

"The only Robári for miles must impress our foreign visitors," he says.

The only Robári for miles. The only Whisper in the palace, too.

I watch Méndez's carriage leave from the sky bridge facing the main street. The ruby-and-diamond pin on my chest carries the weight of every person whose life I've touched with my power. Here I am, wearing the justice's seal. I try to tell myself that this is exactly what I wanted when I arrived. To stay here for more than just my vengeance. For the justice to trust me. I am worried that I've played the part all too well.

The Sun Festival is fast approaching. I am far from ready. If the mission isn't complete before then, if I haven't yet been able to secure the weapon and destroy the prince, will I be able to go through with it? To create a Hollow of Lord Las Rosas to keep my cover and continue on for the greater good of the Whispers?

My guilt will kill me one day, but I've decided that's not today. I walk across the length of the sky bridge and rest my gloved hand on one of the pillars for support. From up here, the maze of gardens is a dizzying thing. Glossy tiles form intricate patterns that seem to lead between manicured hedges. The last king had this garden designed as a gift to his wife. Divided into quarters, the hedges and arches covered in blooming roses trick the mind into following a path to the center, where all the royal revelries take place.

In each of the separate garden quarters, there are hidden nooks with stone benches for courtiers to pass the time. The girls dot the gardens like flowers as attendants walk beside them with parasols to block the sun's burn from their skin.

Leo's laughter flits up from one of the gardens. There, under a canopy of sheer fabric and lanterns is a woman surrounded by half a dozen courtiers and attendants as if she were the queen herself.

I move unnoticed past the gardeners preparing for the Sun Festival. They tend to braided trees with white buds ready to flower, and polish armor and statues until they gleam from meters away. A small boy arranges lily pads in the glistening reflective pools that line the queen's gardens. From down here, the tops of the palace towers shine like individual suns. I remember looking at this structure from a greater distance, when my unit and I rode down a road flanked by severed heads. Every time I enjoy the beauty of this place I remember it is equally matched by a hideous heart.

I find Lady Nuria's canopy in one of the quarter gardens. Her face is hidden in the shadow of the canopy, but her long, full body reclines on a plush chaise covered in pillows and white fox-fur throws. She wears her dress cut lower than the other courtiers, in what I know to be the Dauphinique style according to Leo. Her gown is the color of cherry juice, hugging a slender waist and wide hips. Her hair is pinned up, curls arranged to fall delicately around her neck. Her sienna-brown skin gleams like a jewel.

She sits up when she sees me, and when her face comes into the light, she is not what I expected at all. She's younger than I imagined, perhaps seventeen like me. Dark eyes that are somehow both kind and scrutinizing all at once. Her lips are stained as red as her dress, but the rest of her face is left untouched, including thick black eyebrows, naturally arched to give her a look of skepticism. Or perhaps that's merely how she's observing me now. She picks up the porcelain cup with a delicate gold-painted trim and takes a sip with her plump mouth. The half-dozen girls lounging around her do the same.

"Hello, there," Lady Nuria says to me, batting her impossibly long lashes. She sets her teacup back on the saucer and tilts her head to the side, and that gesture reminds me of an owl curiously observing its prey.

"Lady Renata," Leo says in a tone of surprise. He gets up from a cushioned bench and stands at attention. "Do you require me?"

"I lost my way to Justice Méndez's workshop," I say, a little too loudly for the benefit of the courtiers whispering behind their open fans.

One is Lady Garza, whose memory of the prince I stole on the sky bridge. She averts her eyes and sits at an angle that faces away from me.

"*Lady?*" a woman whines to Leo. Her dress is an extravagant thing, not at all suited for tea. There are beads and crystals sewn in patterns across the bust, and her gloves are fine lace. She has a short, haughty laugh as she eyes me up and down. "What is she the lady of exactly? Our Lady of Ruins?"

"Forgive me, Lady Borbónel." Leo swallows hard but keeps his eyes on the ground.

I want to tell him that I was right in insisting he not refer to me with a title. I shouldn't have come here, but I wanted to get a look at Lady Nuria myself. She, however, is the only one of the courtiers not laughing.

Lady Nuria sets her teacup down. Her slender hands rest on her lap. Her smile cuts precious dimples on her face, and in this moment, I want to hate her.

But the moment passes when her smirk lands on the source of my humiliation. "Tell me, Lady Borbónel, before your father was gifted the title of Duque of Salinas by King Fernando, what was he?"

Lady Borbónel's already white skin pales. She flips her fan open in a snap. "A merchant."

"But he was not always a merchant," Lady Nuria says, that smile betraying the sharp edge of her words. "You may correct me if I'm wrong; however, I do believe he was from my citadela, where my father, the Duque of Tresoros, granted his skilled and trusted Majordomo Borbónel a ship to trade under my family's name."

Leo's eyes flick from Lady Nuria to Lady Borbónel, but I'm fascinated by the other girls. They are equally split in horror and delight at their friend being cut down.

"I do not know what you're getting at." Borbónel's face twists into a sour, puckered look.

"I only find it strange that a change of title bothers you when it comes to this young girl, but not when it is advantageous to you."

"My father *earned* his—"

"And who is to say Lady Renata has not earned hers?"

"*That* is not a lady. That is an unnatural creature that shouldn't be walking around the palace as if she owns it."

Everything within me is screaming to turn. To run. To find anywhere but here. But my feet won't move, as if they're sinking into the earth of the garden.

"Tell me, Lady Renata," Lady Nuria says. "Who gave you that seal upon your breast?"

"Justice Méndez," I say, my voice like the crumble of ash.

"The justice deemed you trustworthy enough to wear his seal," Lady Nuria repeats. She picks up her teacup once again and sets challenging eyes on Lady Borbónel. "Do you question the word of the justice?"

"No," the lady says between gritted teeth.

"Please, join me," Lady Nuria says, patting the velvet cushion beside her.

I start to object, to retreat, but Lady Borbónel sucks in a breath. "If she is to join, I will not sit here."

"Then you are free to go," Lady Nuria says with a close-lipped smile. I hate that I'm impressed by her composure. The way everything about her is elegant, even the brown coils escaping from her carefully arranged hair. She holds herself as if she knows how much she's worth, and yet, this fierce, beautiful girl was going to marry my enemy.

Lady Borbónel stands, knocking her chair to the ground. She stomps away and waits. Her two friends rise from their seats and give Lady Nuria a curt nod before taking their leave.

"My mother was right," Lady Borbónel says, exaggerating her loudness for the benefit of everyone within earshot. "We should not associate with the prince's *castoffs*."

If Lady Nuria is bothered by this, her expression does not show it. She simply moves her hand from the seat she offered me. I fear I *have* to stay after all that.

"You did not have to do that on my account," I say.

The two remaining courtiers are a bit older, perhaps midtwenties. Only one of them is already married, by the two rings on her fingers. The other has a crown of golden hair braided in long plaits. She reminds me of Margo.

"Leo, I believe our guest requires a teacup, if you please." When she looks up at Leo, I can see her true smile. He gives me a tiny wink as he steps out of the canopy, leaving me alone with the three ladies.

"Lady Nuria, I have missed your smart mouth in court these past few months." The married woman chuckles—this close I notice the seal of Soria. "The Sun Festival has brought out all the hounds vying for the prince."

"And here, I believed the Sun Festival was about piety," Nuria says, flashing me a smirk.

"I thought we celebrated the Father of Worlds destroying the wicked Lady of Shadows?" Lady Soria asks, completely having missed Nuria's sarcasm.

"Or to make sure Prince Castian finally finds a bride," says the golden-haired lady, and at the realization of what she said, she covers her mouth. "My apologies, Lady Nuria, I didn't mean anything by that."

Lady Nuria doesn't seem bothered at all, and simply keeps drinking her tea. How does she do that? How does she let words roll off her like water over rock?

"No apologies, Lady Roca. Despite the rumors about us, Prince Castian and I remain friends. We've known each other since we were infants. My husband, Judge Alessandro, is quite fond of him."

I can't help but think of the sealed letter Leo left in Castian's chambers. I have a hard time believing Nuria and Castian are only friends. I wouldn't perfume my letters to Sayida. Then again, I don't pretend to understand the ways of royals and nobles—and Nuria's secrecy intrigues me.

Perhaps in it lies a weakness I can exploit. Leo returns, handing me a porcelain teacup, and flashes me a warning eye.

"And where is the good judge?" Lady Soria asks. "He must have missed you terribly while you were taking in the fresh air of the Salinas coast."

There's a pause where everyone drinks their tea. Should I be drinking tea? Leo gestures that I should. But I spill some.

"The air is fresh in the whole of the kingdom," Lady Nuria says amiably. "I was there speaking to an ambassador from Empirio Luzou to strengthen our relations."

"Why ever would we need that?" Lady Roca asks, and I believe she genuinely wants to know.

"Nuria, dear, the first six months *are* the most blissful of a union. You shouldn't take such long trips. Especially when the justice warns the Moria danger is not completely over."

Lady Nuria's beautiful lips become strained. I feel my body heat up at the words *Moria danger,* but I now realize this is why people drink tea during these conversations. To hide their faces in these giant cups. "Alessandro is taking up Justice Méndez's duties while he travels to Soledad prison."

Lady Roca gasps. "So close to the festival?"

I can't control the frown across my forehead, even as Nuria stares at me. Méndez is going to Soledad? I remember Castian's map had the prison circled. Is this where they're training the Ventári? *Not training,* I remind myself. *Breaking.*

How could they risk traveling that far? Then I remember—the justice is free to take the main roads. No hiding in forests. No evading tax farmers. His route will be direct.

I lock eyes with Leo. We've been through enough that I hope, I pray, he will understand how much I hate being here now.

He sweeps into our space and clears his throat. Addressing Lady Nuria only, he folds himself into a bow.

"I'm afraid I must be taking Lady Renata to Justice Méndez's workshop," he says, with genuine regret. I don't actually have to go there, but I will thank him profusely for helping me escape. The ladies make sounds of lament and pet the top of my head as if I'm a domesticated mutt.

"Lady Renata," Lady Nuria says, catching up to us just out of earshot from her guests. When she stands she seems to tower over me. She hands me her fan. I take it in my gloved hand. "It's getting hot these days. And it's a good way to hide that constant frown of yours. You'll have an easier time at court if you can hide what you're truly feeling."

I laugh at that. The fan is delicate black lace with tiny red roses on one side. "Thank you, but I can't accept this."

"Take it. The real reason I wanted to talk to you was to ask a favor."

What could I give a lady like this? When I stare into her brown eyes, I see the sorrow she hides so well. "Yes?"

"I have a memory that plagues me. Would you take it from me?" Lovely brown eyelashes bat at me. It is impossible not to fall in love with her. Why would Castian have called off their engagement, then? "And don't tell me that your hand is injured. I know quite well how Robári magics work."

I was wrong. Lady Nuria isn't just bold. She's reckless. She reminds me a little of Dez. I hesitate for a moment, unsettled by what could plague a lady like Nuria. But I need all the information on Castian I can gather. That and her blackmailing, while subtle, is still laced with a threat. I wonder if her husband told her what he saw me do. But then, why not go to Méndez instead?

I bow my head to her. "Of course."

She looks at Leo. "Please bring Lady Renata to my guest quarters for tea tomorrow afternoon."

Leo raises a curious brow at me. "Yes, my lady."

Before I head back to my room for the night, I stop by the kitchens for my meal and a bit of information. Everyone is talking about Lady Nuria's arrival. Claudia says she's kept away for three months after her wedding, but had to return to be at her husband's side. The king must have been in a hurry to make sure the treaty with the current Duquesa of Tresoros stood. Why else rush her to marry Alessandro? I wouldn't fault her for leaving the palace to avoid the prince.

The young maids fall over themselves to attend her. She is kind and generous with her attention. I can understand why the house staff would prefer to spend the day with her than any of the other nobles at court. I wonder what memory plagues her. My curiosity makes me jittery all through the next day.

Leo is unusually quiet as he leads me to her quarters and deposits me at the door. Lady Nuria's room is in the same tower as mine, but one floor below, a not-so-subtle jab at the change in her social station. But there are no guards posted in front of her rooms.

Lady Nuria is waiting for me wearing nothing but a robe. Her hair tumbles down her back in loose curls. Her feet are bare, but that's hardly the most scandalous thing she's done since I've met her.

I hate that she makes me feel unbalanced. She is not the person I was expecting. This would be so much easier if she were like Lady Borbónel and the others. I could hate her on sight instead of feeling this pull of her kindness the way I felt with Sayida.

"Sit, Renata," Lady Nuria says, dropping the formalities. "May I call you Renata?"

"Yes. I am no lady, after all."

The living room is decorated in simple shades of gray and brown with the occasional green. There is none of the decadent lace or velvet of the rooms I'm staying in. I suppose that's what happens when you marry someone dedicated to an order of hate.

On the center table is a spread of summer fruits, a carafe of blush wine, a glass teapot with jasmine brewing inside it, delicate confectioneries, and pastries.

She plops a grape into her mouth. "Please, eat. I have it on good authority that you are particularly fond of grapes."

I shiver in the strange draft of this room despite the shut glass panes and the heat outside. The words escape my mouth before I can stop them.

"Why are you so—" I pause, realizing how they will sound.

"Don't be shy. I have been called many things."

"Kind," I say, whirling around to see her standing in front of me, holding a goblet of wine and offering me another. Her eyes are black and luminous, like beads made of night sky. "How can you be so kind?"

"I choose it," she says. "But don't confuse it for weakness. Castian never did."

Lady Nuria owes me nothing. She is not my friend, and before learning of her engagement with the prince I didn't think of her as anything more than an heiress. But I can't understand how someone like her could care for Castian so much. Surely she's knows what he's done.

"Why did you return to this palace if you hated Prince Castian?" she asks, stepping around me to return to her table.

"I don't—"

"All I ask is that you be honest with me about this. I told you. Your emotions are practically written on your face."

I'm strangely relieved someone is breaking through my façade. I am tired of walking these halls and eating in these rooms and playing a role that has returned all too easily. To tell this girl that I want to kill the prince would only result in my own defeat. And yet, I can respect her. Everything I've seen her do is a small defiance of the crown.

"I have nowhere else to go," I say. "And I am under the order of Justice Méndez."

"You could have procured forged papers and passage to other kingdoms."

"I had the chance. It's almost hard to determine what I'm more afraid of, dying here or starting over somewhere completely unknown."

"Starting over is never easy. But you chose the most difficult thing anyone can do. Facing your past."

Can she see through me this easily? Méndez doesn't seem to be able to. Or is he playing a part, the way Leo once graced a stage?

"I helped spill a lot of blood here. At the very least, I am rooted to Puerto Leones in more ways than I can understand. Even if it does not want me."

She takes a deep breath. The fireplace crackles with orange flames in the corner of my eye, but somehow I can hear the sharp whistle of wind coming from somewhere. It does not make sense that a girl who is descended from queens would be in this grim and drafty room, but she does not complain. I drink the bitter wine and sniff back the sting in my nose.

"You know you can't get them back," I tell her. "The memories."

She turns her face to the light-filled window opposite the citadela below us and drinks. "I know quite well how your power works. I should tell you, the memory is of Castian."

"I figured as much." I bite my bottom lip. Though she is not like other royals I've come across, I need to tread carefully when I talk about the prince. "It must be difficult to defend him after you were subjected to humiliation when he ended your engagement."

Lament fills her eyes. She looks pretty even when she's sad. "I was impetuous. I was spoiled. I thought I had it all. Others in my position have to choose between an advantageous union for their families or love. I was lucky to have both for a while."

"And then?"

"He broke my heart. People talked as they always do, and I was made a villain. And yet, I know him. I know the boy I grew up with. Together we mourned the deaths of everyone he loved."

I stiffen at the sentiment, trying to picture a murderer in

mourning. When he killed his brother, did he mourn then as well? As if she were a Ventári herself, Lady Nuria nods her head.

"Yes, including his brother, despite what the rumors may say. The prince knew nothing but violence at the hands of his father. It chipped away at him. Changed him. When he came back from the Battle of Riomar, the change was magnified threefold. We tried but it didn't work. Sometimes I wonder if only I had tried harder. Done more. But I don't know how to help him. Didn't know, I should say. Do you have many regrets, Renata?"

And without hesitating, I say, "Every day."

"I can't change what Castian has done. I *can* change the strength of my feelings, but I would need you to take a memory. One that I relive each day, wishing I had listened to his turmoil then. Listened to when he wanted more than this."

Something in me wants to trust her, or at least wants to try. I'm not a good judge of character, I suppose.

"Have you ever been in love, Renata?" Lady Nuria's lashes cast long shadows on her cheeks with the firelight.

I don't answer, but I feel a vein in my neck twitch. I avoid her gaze and think of Dez. I should have told him. . . .

By the curl of her smile she seems to take this as a yes.

"Then you know how terrible I feel. I have to see him at balls and festivals and every time I walk past the statue of him in the middle of my citadela. All I can think, all I can see is the way he's changed. See the boy I love become terrifying, all while I have to pretend to love a man whose presence makes my blood curdle. Consider it a trade. I believe you'd be glad to have me owe you a favor down the line."

I don't want her to owe me anything and yet I know if I want to get inside the prince's head more than I already have, if I want to get the weapon, her memory might lead me there. Perhaps one less memory of him will relinquish the hold he has on her and she will be free.

I nod, and she follows me to the long couch by the fireplace. She pulls a heavy blanket over her legs and faces me. "Does it sting?"

"Yes. Only for a moment." I see the resolve settle over her, eyes focused on me. I flex the fingers of my free hand. The wound at the center of my palm feels stiff, and the fresh bandage doesn't have any blood on it. I realize I will run out of excuses, and soon Méndez will fit me for the second glove.

"I'm ready," she says.

I press my fingertips to the smooth skin of her brow, the soft glow of my magics easing her worry.

"Do you have to leave tomorrow?" she asks, lying on her side to face him.

There's a canopy bed with sheer cream-colored silk around them. She thinks this is what it feels like to be wrapped inside a flower.

"I would stay with you if I could, but General Hector might have some words with my father," Castian says. Nothing but a sheet draped over his hips. His golden coloring makes her feel warm inside. The time away training has been good for him. He's always been tall, but now she can admire more than his sweet-water eyes and coiling gold hair. She can drink in the new muscles of his legs, and when he stretches, the line of dark golden hair at his abdomen.

"What are you looking at, my lady?" Castian asks.

"You," she says, her heart swelling almost painfully because looking at him is too much.

A smirk plays upon his full lips. He kisses her, and they sink into the bed. She traces her fingers along the muscles of his back. Smooth and unblemished. "Why do you have to fight?"

He sighs, and nestles in the crook of her neck. "Because I am the Lord Commander of Puerto Leones. The king wants me to take back Riomar, and I have to do what the king says."

He kisses her shoulder and makes his way down to her wrist. She tries to quell that feeling within her ribs, like she might grow too big for her skin because of how much she loves him. She was warned about this. She was warned by her mother and her father, the Duque and Duquesa of Tresoros, that her body would react this way when she and Castian reached this age. That she could not be weak. Queens had to be stronger to outlive their kings.

Though Queen Penelope's sapphire weighed on her finger, Nuria was not yet queen.

"When you're back, after we're married, will you take me somewhere beautiful?"

He frowns again. If he isn't careful, he'll grow the same notch between his brows as his father. But his fingers are as soft as petals.

"Citadela Crescenti?" he asks.

"Too debauched."

He laughs and nips at the warm brown skin of her belly at the same time. She feels him vibrate against her. "Islas del Rey?"

"You, Castian Fajardo, want to sail?" She threads her fingers in his hair.

He looks up at her and grins. "I spent my whole life trying to not fear the water. I suppose now I need to be around it if I am to be king and keep peace with our allies."

She knows this about him and wishes she could take away his pain as easily as he's dreamed up their future.

He props himself up and watches her. "Do you ever wonder what would happen if we sailed until we were somewhere far away?"

"How far?"

"Until we find what is in the uncharted regions."

She coils his golden hair around her finger. "How will you be king if you're in the uncharted regions?"

"What if I weren't king?"

"Everyone knows your face, my dear Cas. From here to Luzou and in between."

"There's nothing between us and Luzou."

"You know what I mean!"

He laughs, and the vibration makes her body sing. But then he falls too pensive, too sad. "What if I could hide?"

"Like in that secret room of yours?"

His lips tug into a smile. "In another land, maybe."

Her eyes flick down to his mouth set in that way he has when he is serious and thoughtful. The face he reserves for the court and public, but not for her. For her he always has a smile—or worse, that smirk that drives her heart and mind to want to do dangerous things.

"Would you come with me?" His voice is a whisper.

She draws herself to him, brushing her lips against his. "Where? To your secret room or to your uncharted land?"

"We can start in my secret rooms. I'll show you all of them. We can mark each and every room with our love. Starting with the one in your chambers."

"What's gotten into you?" She laughs and they kiss again. He holds her harder than ever, like he's afraid to let her go. Is he scared? Unsure of her? "Promise to return from Riomar whole," she says.

"Would you not have me otherwise?"

She doesn't want to talk of such things. She doesn't want to imagine him not coming back at all. "I would have you, Castian."

There is a flash of sadness in his eyes, but it's replaced with something else when he watches her, like she is made of wonder, a promise yet to keep. She would give anything to have him look at her like this always. Her prince. No, her king.

She tugs at the sheet that covers him.

The memory undulates like light on water.

Castian stands in the garden. He's avoiding her. Their wedding is in ten days, and he hasn't completely healed from Riomar.

"Cas," she says.

She startles him. He grips the branch of a tree for support instead of her. She wants to go to him but can't. He won't look at her. He won't speak to her.

When he turns around, she hardly recognizes him. He doesn't smile the way he used to. His eyes have lost their warmth. He looks at the space between them and neither takes a step to bridge the distance.

"I can't do this," he tells her. "I can't marry you."
"Cas."

Cas, *she says, over and over. Each time she says his*
name her heart breaks.

I stumble back, wrenching my fingers from Lady Nuria's mind. My heart races, just like hers did. Her lingering feelings of desire and heartbreak cling to me like sewage water. I grab a glass of water and drink it in a continuous, long gulp.

Lady Nuria smirks, pouring herself more wine from the carafe. "Are you quite all right, Renata?"

"Yes, my lady," I say, breathless.

"Please, call me Nuria." She reaches for a tiny round cake puff filled with custard and licks her fingers. "It's strange. I thought there would be something left of what I wanted to show you. But it's more as if there's an empty room, cold. Is that what it's like for everyone?"

I shake my head. It shames me that I've never asked. "I'm not sure. Everyone can be different."

"Please stay and eat," she says, her voice soft. "I hate these rooms. I can hear the wind in the middle of the night, and it always feels like there's someone there."

It's a relief to know that it isn't just me that feels this way. We eat in silence at first, but I think Lady Nuria feels she needs to fill space, and so she talks about the queen's reception and the Sun Festival following it. At some point I'm sure she says she'll send me a new dress, but my mind is consumed with her memory, now flashing through my mind as if it were my own.

Nuria was different. More innocent in her love for him. Did she look back on that day and see the misery in his eyes? What did the prince have to run away from when he secured his own rule long ago? Still, I understand her need to feel like she could have changed things.

I can hardly believe that Castian changed his course. He worshiped her. He looked at Nuria the way Dez looked at me. That was real. Then he went to Riomar, nearly died, and returned a different man. Dez did, too, and he still managed to pick himself up. Something else happened. I feel it in the marrow of my stolen memories.

Castian said he spent his whole life trying not to fear the water, but why? Does he see his dead brother every time he's near it? And what did he say about the hiding places in the palace? *I know all of them.*

"I owe you a favor, Ren," Nuria tells me as I leave. "Don't forget it."

That night in my bed, I listen for the arrival of the guards outside my door. They're coming from somewhere. A trapdoor. A hidden stairwell. I'm sure I never hear them walk the corridor.

In my dreams, I see Castian. He's that boy in my memory about to kill Dez on a balcony one moment and the next he's holding flowers in the dark, running from me.

I will find what you're hiding, I promise.

I will uncover everything he's locked away, and there will be nowhere safe for him to hide.

19

THE NEXT DAY, I STEAL MOMENTS ALONE TO TOUCH THE STONE WALLS OF LADY
Nuria's former chambers, searching for hidden doorways. I wonder
if the prince made good on his offer to show them to her. I long to
ask her, but it's too great a risk. I look behind every painting, every
rug, drapery, book. I push against the brick walls and wooden panels. I rummage under the bed. When, at the end of my search, all I
end up with is dirty fingertips and a splinter, I lie down on the floor.
I fish Dez's coin from under the mattress and hold it for strength.

Castian wouldn't have lied to Nuria. Not in that moment. There
has to be something I'm missing.

"What are you doing?" Sula asks.

I scramble off the floor and smooth my deep blue skirts.
"Nothing."

"Looks like you were lying on the floor to me."

One look at my grimace and the servant girl starts. She sets the food tray down and busies herself. Used to her glowering silence, I take my leave and she doesn't question it.

I hunt for Leo, but he is called to Lady Nuria's side to entertain her. After the last encounter with the ladies of court, I keep to the shadows. The more crowded the palace gets, the lonelier I feel. Desperation gnaws my insides raw because I am going in circles. I'm a wraith prowling the halls, admiring gilded paintings of over three hundred years' worth of the Fajardo lineage. I notice there is no portrait of the king's first queen, but Queen Penelope graces an entire wall. I glide my fingers behind each and every one of them, but none turn into a secret compartment or hidden room.

I linger in the sky bridge that leads to my apartments. Bursts of laughter come from the gardens and streets on either side of the bridge. A memory tugs at me, one of my own. If I close my eyes, I can recall running through the woods beside Dez and Sayida. The pair of them teaching me how to be swift and quiet all at once. But everything about me has always been loud, the sound of my heart, the weight in my tread, even the cry I always seem to be holding back.

A washed-out vision of Castian kissing the inside of Nuria's wrist follows. I punch the tiled pillar to snap out of the memory and regret it instantly. One of the scabs on my knuckles cracks and bleeds. I stare at my injured hand. Come tomorrow I will have no choice but to make a Hollow.

Run, I tell myself. There is no justice. No prince. The king and queen are preoccupied with their *sacred* festival that celebrates the defeat of my goddess.

Soft words that hurt like a deep bruise reverberate through me. *Stay for more.*

I have to finish this. I have to.

I turn and run the rest of the way to my rooms. There's one guard on duty, and he's slumped on the floor. I crouch down to better look at his face.

Hector.

There are hundreds of Hectors in the kingdom. But the odds that the General Hector in Nuria's memory is this same one seems plausible. He'd be about the right age. The lavanderas said he fought at Riomar. But how did he go from a general to a patrol guard?

He smells strongly of aguadulce. A black-gloved left hand rests over his lower abdomen. Like me, his other hand is free. But there's something stiff about the way his fingers rest there.

Then his shoulders twitch and the muscles in his thigh spasm. He moans in his sleep, followed by a whimper. So many of the Whispers sleep like this, tormented by horrid memories of the past. Dez did.

"You're dreaming," I whisper. I grip the guard by the shoulder and give him a shake.

He does not wake. He slaps my hand away, then trembles. Shouting words I can't understand. He's crying out for help. Hector's olive skin flushes red as he struggles to breathe. I try to shake him again, but his hand clamps around my wrist. I gasp as he throws me to the side. I land on my shoulder, and Hector lies on his back.

I'm overpowered by the guilt of watching him suffer, knowing firsthand just how painful nightmares can be. Now I wonder if this might be the reason he was demoted to a palace guard, if he is the same General Hector.

Two things occur to me. I need this man's memories of Castian. But the last time I stole a memory from a nightmare, I got Dez killed. Jacinta was fine because as horribly as Castian treated her, it wasn't a nightmare for her, though perhaps her infatuation with the prince would increase. I tell myself that Hector is only a palace guard. That I can help him while getting the information I need. That feels wrong even thinking it, but I can't afford to let this opportunity slip by me.

My hand trembles as I place my fingers on his temple, heart racing because when I touch him, I see Dez. I push my love's face aside and dive rapidly into the guard's mind.

Hector calls her the melancholy queen, Queen Penelope, though he'd truly like to call her the beautiful queen with her hair of gold and sea-bright eyes. It was his first time in the palace, in the great capital city, Andalucía. How a farm boy was recruited into the queen's guard is beyond him. The king and his new justice have made great efforts to help the people of Puerto Leones better their stations in life, and for that he is grateful. The wages will help his parents in Citadela Salinas, where work is nowhere to be found. He is going to be the very best, maybe one day rise to the top of the queen's ranks.

She has the most beautiful voice. Sweet as the ebb and flow of a calm ocean, soft and pleasant. Her words stick in his head, even when she is not around. Golden star, golden star, take the love within my heart.

When she sings to her boys he thinks that is what it feels like to be loved. The melancholy queen doesn't go anywhere without her boys, though the older prince is usually impatient, slapping at the world like a wild thing and shouting at the top of his lungs. But when she sings, he quiets down. He listens. He sleeps.

Even princes listen to the song of their mothers.

A comforting memory at the forefront of a mind often obscures the one causing the nightmares. Curious that he still thinks of the dead queen after all these years. I move my fingers along his sweating skin and brace for the sting of more memories.

> *A bloody battle. Men and women in the king's army raze a village to the ground. Villagers run from their burning homes and into the forests. Whisper rebels fight back. Faces he doesn't recognize. Sharp pain and then black. Screaming, thrashing, agonizing pain in a tent. A wound, bloody and bandaged where his hand used to be.*

Hector hisses, reliving the fresh pain. He thrashes so much it is difficult to hold on, but the images flood like rising water in a sealed room. I must regain control, or I will take too many memories. And he will become a Hollow.

> *The melancholy queen has been dead a year, and the boy's rage grows greater still. His body is different, even for a young man his age. All he does is eat and endure the grueling trials every king's man and guard must pass, like he is carving himself until he is stone, unbreakable. But the boy's heart is impatient. Hector admires the precision of his swordplay. Out of every boy pulled from farms and mills and wharves, he'd be the one to watch even if he wasn't the crowned prince.*
>
> *Hector shouts an order. "Line up! Find your sparring mate and don't show quarter. Don't worry about bruises, fledglings. No one's kissing your ugly mugs as it is."*
>
> *It elicits bitter grumbles from the recruits. Too young. Every season the justice sends them younger to fight and die.*

Hector was like these kids. He watches them spar with each other in sets of two. His small batch of King Fernando's vast army.

A slim figure watches him from afar. Davida, so changed, with a just-healed scar across her face and delicate throat, carries a basket of apples at her hip. Her deep brown eyes always seem to catch when she looks at the prince. He sees them shining with tears and wonders if she remembers the murderous princeling as he was.

She leaves bits of dried bread for the pesky black birds, hoping that will save the apples. He always admired her kindness. She is still as beautiful as the day he fell in love with her. Her touch always soothed him, like she was parting the dark thoughts from his life and making way for the sun. Of course, that was before he lost his hand to a raid. Before the prince had her punished. His rage at the prince resurfaces, blooms like a putrid sprout in his core. Everything he's lost has been because of the Fajardos. And yet, he knows he cannot raise a hand to the boy. His future king.

He can never hold Davida again either. Perhaps one day, they will heal enough to return to each other. One day . . .

"Good day, Davida," he calls out to her.

She starts at the sound of his voice and presses her palm against her chin. Signs her wordless hello followed by his given name. Miguel. Only she calls him that. Only she can.

Hector wishes he were smoother, softer, not a big stumbling oaf with one hand. Even now, the pain of his time in battle is a fresh wound. He'll never outlive it.

Almost like she can sense his anguish, she touches his forearm. Her fingers, though callused, are gentle. It is like being kissed by a cool breeze on a hot day. Is that love he still sees in her eyes? Because there is a swell of turmoil in his heart. It's a hundred cords knotted into one. He wants to forget his station, forget his duty; he only wants to fall at her knees.

And then the knot untangles. Comes undone like a loose spool in his hands. The fog of his anger parts. For the briefest moment, there is only Davida and him.

Just as he is ready to say more to her, the princeling marches toward him, and Davida lets go. She tucks her head between her shoulders and runs away as quick as her feet can carry her. The absence of her is more than he can put into words, and when Castian stands before him, the anger that is a living thing in his heart returns.

"Hector! What is the meaning of this?"

Hector steadies his breath. He might be Castian's general, but Castian is still his liege. Murderer or not.

"The meaning of what, Your Highness?"

The boy throws his helmet on the ground, the blunt sword along with it. "This! You've assigned everyone else a sparring partner but me."

"I fail to see the problem, Your Highness?"

"I am your best fighter." His blue eyes are cold enough to give Hector a terrible shiver as he steps near. The eyes of a monster. Twisted and broken. And yet, Hector can't help but think of his mother's face and hear her soft song and think of how different things were. How different he was. "I'm honorary captain of the forces. Do you expect me to ride into Riomar untested?"

Hector's anger needles at him, and so he says, "Honorary captains do not see battle, Your Highness. How can I allow the king's son to arrive at the council dinner with a black eye?"

He expects the boy to yell. It would be easier to bear. Instead, his blue eyes are calculating as he stares back and says darkly, "When I retake Riomar, I will be the fiercest warrior of Puerto Leones. And when that day arrives, there will be nothing honorary about my title, do you understand?"

Hector nods. He understands many things about the prince, who will always be a prince, and perhaps earn his title of Lord Commander. But to Hector, he will always be the boy who drowned his own brother.

Hector gasps, awakening from his dream. He cradles his wooden hand as he stands, stepping away from me. I have so many questions I want to ask him. Does he know that Davida still attends the prince? I wonder if Hector found her the night of the half-moon celebration.

"Are you all right?" I ask, shaking. "I found you on the floor."

"No," he answers, a stare that sees through me. The guard's fear of the boy, of Castian, lingers in my heart, and so I stay where I am, watching him breathe. "I do not believe I ever will be. I beg your pardon for my impropriety, miss."

He's never spoken to me this softly or this long. Though the anger he felt settles on me like a blanket infested with ants, I want to tell him that I feel the same. That I understand feeling as if you'll never be whole again. But we go back to being strangers, shadows sailing past each other in a dark that will swallow us both whole.

I shut the door and lock it behind me. Hector's memories fill my mind. There is so much hate and anger there. The only time it vanished was when he saw Davida. After all this time, he still loves her. The way she touched Hector tells me that she feels the same. At least she did, in that moment. How much time has to pass before love fades? Will I forget Dez in five years? Ten? Or will I be like Hector and dull my senses with drink and nurture my sorrow?

My eyes feel too big, swollen. My heart seizes as if I'm having an attack. I go to the basin and splash water on my face. I jump into the bed and crawl under the covers with my head pulsing so much it feels like there's a creature in there trying to break out. A memory slips from the Gray. It repeats over and over.

A set of silver dice rolling across a wooden floor.

Dez's voice shouting, "Come on, we have to hurry!"

But I never catch up.

That's not how our escape from the capital was supposed to go. We rode on horses. Does this mean I'm dreaming? I'm not supposed to *dream*, I think. But when I turn into a bird and take flight all the way to the San Cristóbal ruins, I know that something has gone wrong in my mind. Perhaps I'm finally breaking. Perhaps I've taken one memory too many.

Then I realize what kind of bird I have turned into: a magpie. And I'm eating out of Davida's palm.

When I start awake, I know who Illan's spy is.

20

I TELL LEO I'LL BE DOWN IN THE KITCHENS TO MAKE MYSELF USEFUL FOR THE festival preparations. I've seen Davida a few times since the first day in the courtyard, helping the majordomas cook and feed the lavanderas. She's been at the palace for decades. She's watched Castian grow up. She's got access to all the levels of the household, even the prince himself.

In Hector's memory, he and Castian were the only ones who noticed her. But there was something about her touch that was familiar. Hector had a respite from his rage. Not just because he saw Davida. I call the memory forward and sink into the calm he felt. I've felt that way before—when Sayida and Dez used their magics on me. It was like being able to come up for air while drowning.

By the time I get down to the lower level, I am sure of myself. Who else but a Persuári living in the palace might have access to information worth smuggling to Illan? She was feeding black birds while she kept a watchful eye on *Castian*. My heart races like their wings. Wings that had single white feathers. *Magpies.* What better spy could Illan have asked for than someone like Davida?

I find her in the empty kitchen, eating her meal alone in one of the storage closets atop crates of jars.

"Davida?" I knock on the wooden door. The scent of baking bread fills the air.

She glances up with pale brown eyes. Honey eyes. *Dez.* They are nearly the same shade as his, and I have to brace myself against the doorframe for balance. Remind myself of why I need her.

"Do you remember me?" I ask.

Davida nods and pats the seat beside her.

"I've come to ask for your help."

Everything about her is gray. Her washed-out skin, her hair, her clothes. All except the red scar on her lips and the faded one on her throat. But her eyes are still a bit fierce, angry. I can use that. In exchange for her help, perhaps there is something I can do for her, too.

Davida presses her lips together and turns her head. I recognize the sign for *What? I don't understand.*

I cannot deceive this woman, and I cannot wrench a memory from her the way I did with Jacinta and Hector.

"We have an enemy in common," I say. "The person who hurt you also took someone from me. I need your help getting a message out so the others know that I will finish what Dez began. If we work together, we can find the weapon before it's too late."

Her eyes widen at my words. She shakes her head and grabs my shoulder, glaring at the closed door. The others are busy around the palace and it is well past midday meal. I know we're alone, but she must be afraid.

"It's all right," I assure her. "All I need from you is to know where Castian might keep things hidden—secret—where no one but he would find them."

She's flustered, taking my bare hand in hers. She shakes her head.

"I won't hurt you. I came to say that I can take your painful memory of that day. Of the prince's cruelty."

At that her face is overcome with sadness. Her shoulders tremble. A tear runs down her cheek as she guides my fingers to her temples and nods.

"Thank you," I whisper as my glowing fingertips take the memory she offers.

Davida can never say no when the prince asks for a story.

He's getting too old for the same tales, already ten, but he loves them, and while the queen mother is in her sickbed, she knows he needs all the cheer he can find.

"Read me the one about the brother pirates."

"That one again?" She chuckles and settles into the large armchair in front of the fireplace. The first winter winds are beginning to whistle, but at least the queen's library has a fireplace. "Are you certain you don't want me to read the one about the Knife of Memory?"

Castian's cheeks are flushed with cold. His summer-bronzed skin has all but faded as the days grow shorter and darker. "I don't think I believe in that one anymore. It's too fanciful. But pirates, pirates are real."

Davida knows her words are dangerous, but perhaps, if the boy loves stories, then his heart can't be as wretched and closed-off as his father's. "How do you know the Knife of Memory isn't real?"

Castian thinks about it for a bit. He reclines in the chair opposite her, his stockinged feet angled toward the flames. "Because my father says nothing about the Moria is true."

"Have I ever lied to you?" Davida asks.

"No."

"Are you afraid of my magics?"

Castian shakes his head. "No, you help me when my father is angry."

So she starts reading, entertaining the prince with stories to open his mind and his heart. What was done to him was not his fault, and she will use her strength to make him a better man. His face lights up during the Brothers Palacio's sword fights at the helm of their ship. She holds one of the prince's toy wooden swords and wields it high above her head. "How could you have betrayed me, brother? The treasure was meant to bring us together!"

"Treasure only tears people apart," Castian says, finishing the words he knows by heart.

Davida laughs and brushes his tangle of golden curls. "See? You don't even need me to read these to you. You've done quite well on your own."

"Father says I'm to start military training by week's end. I won't have time for stories then," he says.

The anguish in his voice brings tears to her eyes. She is about to comfort him, to tell him that no matter what he does or where he is the stories will be with him. That she will be thinking of him and wishing that he will keep this heart of his.

But there is a loud smack as the door slams open, and

King Fernando strides in, followed by a slender guard riddled with scars on his face.

Davida lets the book fall to the ground as she does her best to kneel before him. "Your Grace. I didn't expect you."

"Silence. You're the reason my son has been crying all over the palace about the start of his training."

"Father, I—"

The king grabs a vase from the table and throws it against the fireplace. The glass shatters and bounces off the wall. A bit of it nicks Castian's cheek. The boy wipes the blood with the back of his hand, his mouth open and startled.

"When I say I want silence, I mean it." Fernando picks up the book at Davida's feet. Her heart is in her throat as he turns the pages. She knows how this looks. She knows that there is no forgiveness. She knows that these words, these stories, are met with punishment.

"I put my trust in you and this is what you do? Poison my only son's mind?" He tosses the book into the flames and Castian lunges for it.

"No!" But as his hand begins to reach for the corner, the book is swallowed by the fire, and the king's fist comes down across the boy's face. One of the rings on the king's knuckles leaves a neat slash that draws blood down the prince's brow.

Castian's lips tremble as he stands before his father and his father's guard. He holds in the cry as long as he can, but Davida knows his heart and she knows that this boy is filled with more sorrow than he'll ever know what to do with. So she rises and she holds him and whispers into his ear. "You'll be all right, my darling boy."

She can feel the king's rage, like a cold snap against her cheek. He motions to the guard, who grabs Davida by her throat. He pulls out a crude iron weapon. A clamp.

Castian screams and kicks at the soldier, but his father grabs him. Holds the boy by his shoulders. Forces him to watch.

"I warned you to be silent," the king says.

Davida's anguish licks like fire at my hands. I pull away, knocking into a stack of crates. The top one tips over and cracks, spilling dozens of plums, plucked before they could ripen. I get down and pick them up for something to busy my fingers with.

"I'm sorry." I repeat it over and over, both of us shaking. She won't remember that day again, but I fear this is one of the memories that will haunt me forever.

It was the king who did it.

The king ordered her punishment, not the prince. Castian was a boy. Castian, by the looks of it, cared for her, trusted her. How did that boy become the Castian I know now? Why do the stories say the prince had her tongue cut out? I want to wrench out the worry I felt toward him because of this memory. A scared child locked in a library.

Like I was.

And she is not the spy I'm looking for. She's another Moria who was caught in a war we didn't start. She could have left with the others. She could have found her way to a safe house. But she didn't. I shake my head, unable to understand why she'd willingly remain in the palace if not to help the rebels. Some people fight.

Some people hide. Some people help in the only way they can. Now I see Hector's memory differently. Davida wasn't observing Castian during his training to spy. She was there to see his progress, like a mother watching a child grow up.

"You stay for him, don't you?"

She nods and holds my hands in hers. Davida taps the space over my heart. Her eyes water. She still has dozens of good memories of that little boy. I think of the words Nuria spoke after I took her memory. The cold, empty room in her mind. Is that what Davida is feeling now? She pats my cheeks with a gesture I want to remember.

In Hector's memory, he said his favorite quality of Davida was her warmth. Persuári can bring out emotions that exist. Empathy. Kindness. Not just action. What was done to Castian that she would use her power on him?

"I won't tell anyone, I swear it."

Behind us there's a loud clattering and pots and pans fall to the floor. I leap to my feet and position myself in front of Davida. Fear tightens in my belly as I open the storage closet door.

"Judge Alessandro," I say as fear floods my body. Not for me but for Davida.

Alessandro stands in the empty kitchen, an alman stone in his fist. It pulses with a memory of Davida and me. His face is twisted in cruel delight as he brandishes it. Davida tugs at my sleeve, and I try to give her a reassuring look.

"Leo didn't believe me when I told him you've been faking your injury. He wanted proof before we went to Méndez. Imagine needing to prove *my* word against someone like you."

Did Leo tell him where I would be? I think of the moments we've shared, the secrets we keep. No. I have to believe Leo wouldn't. . . . But I can't think of that now. I need to get Davida to safety.

"I don't know what you think you've seen," I say, raising my gloved hand and my exposed bandaged one in the air. "But we are simply sharing a midday meal. Or is there a new order that outlaws that?"

"No more from you!" Alessandro shoves the alman stone in front of my face. His slender body is taut with fear. I've seen carnival hands feed caged wolves this way. I shield my eyes from the brilliant light of memory in the crystal. "Every word you speak is a falsehood. There's nothing wrong with your hand, and now Justice Méndez will see it."

"Who's going to read the stone?" I ask, voice calm despite my screaming thoughts. "There are hundreds of judges. There is one Robári."

"Bestae." He spits at my feet. "You overestimate your worth."

"I only stated something we both know to be true."

"You're right, Robári, that I can't touch you. Not while you have the good justice blinded and bewitched. But"—his cold eyes shift to Davida—"if I recall, some of the ladies have reported jewels missing. Do you know what the punishment is for thieves?"

Their fingers are broken, then healed, then cut off. Davida makes a terrible choking sound. I stand directly in front of her, but I can't shield her from Alessandro for long.

"The torture she'll endure," Alessandro says, and his eyes light up with something more than fear. There's a cruelty there that I hadn't seen before because I dismissed him as a sniveling apprentice. He's far more dangerous than that. As he unsheathes a dagger, I see the part of him that feeds on inflicting pain. "Pity. But I've heard she's no stranger to punishment. I do not believe the king will forgive a second infraction."

No matter what I do, someone is going to fear me. The maids, the courtiers, the judges. I chose to return to the palace. I chose their fear. Davida didn't. She's Moria, living in secret. And I've put her in danger. I've bought myself time until my hand heals in the eyes of Justice Méndez, but what after that? Alessandro will not forget this.

Unless . . .

I get on my knees and hold my hands up in supplication. "Please," I beg the young justice. "Don't hurt her. I have been lying. Arrest me. But let her go."

Davida yanks at my sleeves and shakes her head. I shove her off as the rattle of a manacle clangs. When I look up at Alessandro, his smile is arrogant.

The moment he yanks my hand to clap it in irons, I grab his face with my bare fingers and grind my teeth against the rapid burn of my magics. I drain his memories of the last day. I watch his day unfold. Slinking barefoot into the kitchens with the alman stone, taking one from the vaults, shouting at Nuria, demanding answers from Leo. His mind makes me sick because it leaves me with hate. Hate for myself. Hate for things I don't know. It slithers like pus from a festering sore, and when I let him go, I fall right beside him.

I rest my head on the cool kitchen floor. Pinpricks of light race across my vision. Davida drops down at my side.

"I'm all right," I say, and take the hand she offers to help me stand.

We have a mutual understanding as we look at the unconscious judge at our feet. I survey the kitchen and find a bottle of clear liquor. I unstopper the cork and spill it on his pristine black robes.

Davida raises an eyebrow and signs, *Where do we take him?*

"The only place he won't be able to make excuses," I say.

Together, Davida and I drag him through a side door in the

kitchens and down a service hall that leads to Justice Méndez's office. We prop him on a chaise. Davida removes the almost empty bottle from her apron. She unstoppers it with her teeth, takes a swig, then wedges it in the crook of Alessandro's arm.

When we hear the cathedral bells marking the end of the midday break, we slink out of the office's main doors. The corridor is empty.

"He won't remember," I assure her.

Be careful, she signs.

We walk back to the main tower in silence, where the festival preparations have doubled. We are two servants walking to our next task hand in hand. When Davida stops trembling and we reach the kitchen entrance, she takes my hands in hers and kisses my cheeks. I summon all my strength to swallow the desire to be held, to have something so close to a mother's touch.

"I'm sorry I brought this to you," I whisper. "I'm supposed to protect you."

Davida signs, but I don't quite understand when she says, *Good heart. Protect us all.*

I run back to my room, sweat soaking the underarms of my dress. I'm confident I removed Alessandro's memories of our encounter, but he'll still have his suspicions. Eventually I'll be caught. I can't repeat what I've done today. Davida is not the Magpie, she's a Moria working in the palace. That means the spy is still out there, and I don't feel any closer to finding them.

I stop when there's a pinch at my side. A cold breeze blows against me, and for a brief moment I hear voices coming from the end of the hall.

All the memories I've stolen are taking a toll, playing tricks on me. When I get to the library door, the voices get louder, the ache in my temples returns harder than ever. There's something here. I can feel it. An ache wedged like a knife between my ribs.

I try the library door. It's locked. I fish for the clip in my pocket and the door sighs open with the right turn of my wrist. White rays filter from the windows, illuminating the dust in the air. The room is cold. As cold as Lady Nuria's rooms downstairs, but without the lit fireplace to help. The windows here are not barred like mine. There's no need, I suppose.

As I stand here, I can't breathe. It's like I've stepped into the Gray. The color is vibrant at first and then washes out from the books lining the walls, and the chaise where I sat watching the city, my home in the woods, fall to flames. I stumble to the window and fumble with the latch. I open it and let in the cool air. Down below is the maze of royal gardens. I breathe the scent of freshly cut hedges and filth of the capital that can never truly be masked.

I grip the sill for support. Memories press into the forefront of my mind as if trying to break down a wall. I shut my eyes, but I can't escape the images flashing by.

Trays of cakes and pastries. Roll of a die. Dez asking me, "What are you doing here?" A book burning in this very fireplace.

Why would the prince of Puerto Leones have a book filled with Moria legends in this library? Why was he here? This was my favorite place. Can't I have one thing without Castian staining it with his whole *existence*?

My breath comes in short, fast pants and I let myself fall. I sink my face into my folded knees.

Stop, I think to the Gray. *I need you to stop.*

I wish I could carve out my own thoughts the way I do others'.

I wish I'd never returned here. Every thread I pull unravels something else.

I hear Dez's voice. *Trust me.*

"I do," I whisper to an empty room, to a boy who is dead.

Suddenly, I want to see him. I want to conjure Dez amid the terror of my thoughts. I find him in small memories tucked behind others. The one that I want is the one of the night he rescued me. It is unfinished, wedged in the Gray. Breathing fast, I wade through the dark of my thoughts, like retracing the paths in the dungeons, the halls of the palace.

But I know what else I will find there. Dead eyes gaping back at me. A little girl eating sweets. My own hands, small, covered with the beginnings of the scars and whorls I bear now. I promised Illan once that I would work on unlocking the Gray, but that was a different time. I wasn't alone. I wasn't in a palace full of the Arm of Justice. Dez was still alive. He would have helped me through it, told me that I was strong enough to face a lifetime of stolen pasts. Right now I can't even face one. Shouldn't seeing him be enough for me to try harder?

"I miss you, Dez," I say. "But I can't go there alone."

I'm not going anywhere because tomorrow is the Sun Festival, and I have run out of time.

21

THE QUEEN'S COURTYARD HAS BEEN MADE EXQUISITE FOR HER GARDEN PARTY, decorated like the Second Heaven reserved for those whose truest virtue is love. As the princess of a foreign kingdom, and queen of Puerto Leones, it is clear she does not want to spare any expense for the first celebration of the day. Leo said it is tradition for the queen to host a party for select guests, though everyone seems to have noticed the absence of both the prince and the empress of Luzou.

The young queen sits under a canopy with her handpicked favorite ladies of court, radiant in Dauphinique violet under the afternoon sun, while the king sits on a newly erected throne covered in bright green ivy and flowers. He stares at the crowd, simmering in a mood so foul, not even Justice Méndez, who just returned from Soledad this morning, approaches him.

The Hand of Moria stands directly behind the king on two out of four marble pedestals. I'm surprised to see the new Ventári without Méndez in sight. She's gaunt and seems familiar because I see myself in her and the Persuári beside her. Everything about them is clean, stiff, their eyes so still they don't even seem to blink. It's as if they're almost made hollow but hold just enough memories to perform their duties. I look at the empty pedestals. That's where I'm supposed to stand, after my demonstration. When I become one of them and Justice Méndez unwraps my bandage and fits my hands with manacled gloves that only King Fernando will have the key to. They tell me my power is a curse, but they keep presenting me as a gift.

Fear floods my stomach as I linger behind a hedge. I can't stay in this manicured garden surrounded by the swish of silk gowns and twinkling jewels, mouths stuffed with delicacies and nobles drunk on fizzy cava, swaying to the musicians in the corner.

I turn down a hedge-lined path. The farther I go, the fewer partygoers surround me, so I continue, reveling in my moment of solitude. I press my hands to either side of the leaves that flank me, the gravel crunching beneath my heels.

It feels too familiar. Like I've walked it before, when I know I haven't. It is a sensation that jumps out from my memories. I pick up the heavy layers of my pale pink skirts that Leo chose to match to the queen's court, and follow this feeling. Several times I nearly trip, but with my heart at my throat, I follow the winding turns until I'm at a dead end. A breeze parts a curtain of ivy. Within the hedges is an enclosed garden with overgrown manzanilla and weeds. It looks forgotten compared to the rest of the meticulously trimmed and manicured grounds. That's when I spot something that doesn't belong. A white statue.

Kicking off my heels, I dig my feet into the grass and kneel down. I move the limp green grass and discover the statue is an angel. It isn't one of the kneeling angels that usually ornament sculptures of the Father of Worlds. It's the standing guardian that protects the Moria with the sword in her hand. What is it doing here? Is it by accident? Do they just not know? Or did someone meticulously plan this, hiding their rebellion in plain sight?

I press my hands to the grass in front of the angel's feet. A cord of magics strikes the bare fingertips of my right hand. The scars and whorls come alight. I look from my hand to the angel's. There's a crack beneath the stone that wasn't there before, a soft white glow emitting from the fissures.

Alman stone.

I glance over my shoulder. The music from the garden party is in full swing. Sweet laughter and chatter fill the air. Who knows when I'll be able to come back to this garden, especially after whatever happens at the festival. I grab hold of the statue's hand.

Illan's beard has patches of black in it still. His pale blue eyes are stark against skin burnished bronze by the sun. Red bleeds where the sun kisses the horizon.

"You must be calm, Penelope," the old Ventári says. His hands are slender, reaching for the young queen's shoulders.

There, in the enclosed garden, she sinks to her knees. The heavy embroidered silk of her skirt pools around her like rose petals. Her golden hair has come undone at her temples, escaping the tight braid around her head. She clutches a slender gold diadem in her left hand.

"How can I be calm after what you've asked me to do to my children?"

Illan kneels beside her, his face a rigid mask of honor and duty. "It is far better than what the king will do to them. You know this is the only way we can save both their lives."

She shakes her head. She's small, slender as a wilting flower, but there is still strength behind her grip. She takes Illan's shirt into her fist. "Find another way. It wasn't supposed to be like this."

Illan places a gentle hand over hers. "How? Tell me, Your Highness, because we have tried other ways to stop the crown. Take them both and the king will hunt you forever. If Castian stays, if we give the king a reason to trust him, if he sees himself in his son, Castian will be secured as the next heir. The only heir." He taps her chin, but the young queen won't look up. "It is up to you, Penelope."

She slaps him, her hand a sharp sting on his skin. "You give me an impossible choice."

"I give you a choice to save both your children."

The queen looks away, her face fading like a portrait left out in the sun. Streaks of tears carve rivers down her face.

"Please forgive me for what I am about to do," she whispers to no one and everyone all at once. "Forgive me."

She faces the setting sun, staring until it is gone and her world is dark.

I wrench my hand free as though I've been burned, the sight of a young Illan etched like a brand into my mind.

My skin prickles into gooseflesh, the angel's eyes demanding something from me. Secrecy. I know, beyond everything else, that this is the most dangerous memory I could ever possess. Queen Penelope met with Illan.

And whatever happened to Castian's younger brother, it was clearly not all Castian's own doing. The Whispers had something to do with it. *Illan* had something to do with it. He had wanted—had offered—to help save the boys' lives. Both of them.

Why would he have done such a thing? Why would he have ever wanted to help the last queen?

It makes no sense. Too many thoughts race through my head, too many memories. I have to get out of here.

I grab my shoes and run back out the way I came. At least, I believe I do. The hedges appear to line solid paths but have clever narrow entryways, secret passages that allow you to cut across into other gardens. I could be lost in here for days.

A warm alto voice drifts from the end of this path. I need to see a familiar face.

"Leo!" I cry, turning the corner. He's leaning against a pillar, his face nearly touching someone else I can't see. When he hears me, he snaps in my direction, eyes wide.

"Miss Renata! What are you doing here?"

The other person behind the column slinks away into the shadows. My mind goes to Alessandro, and I back away a few paces.

"My apologies," I say. "Who was that?"

Leo's initial shock fades. "Well, you know me. I always find my own entertainment." He winks, but I'm certain this wasn't a dalliance.

"Did you speak to Judge Alessandro yesterday?" I ask. I don't have any smiles left for him. For anyone.

He stands straight and offers me his hand. "On my life, on the memory of my husband's, I did not tell the judge where to find you.

Nor do I know how he ended up in Justice Méndez's office fully asleep. Even if you did not hold my secrets, Renata, I would think you and I are friends by now."

Friends. The word hurts as much as it brings me joy. I take his hand with my gloved left one, and at least this part feels right.

"Do we have to go back?" I ask.

"Only until the last of the performers. Then we have to prepare for the evening festivities. There's a surprise."

"Is the surprise that we're celebrating the sun at night?"

He laughs and I grip the fabric of his emerald jacket too hard. He brushes my hand with his in that way he has of calming me down.

"You know I don't like surprises, Leo."

"This one I believe you will like." He takes a different path than the one I came here on.

For a moment, I think I'm seeing things. There's a woman the same height and build as Sayida walking past me. Newcomers hurry into one of the many archways that lead to the center gardens to join the party as waiters weave through the crowds with glasses full of cava. I hurry after her, but dozens of bodies cut between us before I spot her again.

I don't think, I just grab the woman's sleeve.

The young woman in the golden dress turns around, black hair twisted in twin knots at the base of her neck. Part of me is so desperate to see my friend that I didn't consider what it would look like, a Robári grabbing another person with my open hand.

"What *are* you doing?" she snaps at me, so very much not Sayida that I don't know how I could have mistaken her for my friend. This woman's large blue eyes stare bewildered at me. She holds a hand up to her lips, as if she's waiting for someone to come and rescue her.

"Lady Armada, may I escort you?" Leo bows to her, but shoots me a look that asks if I've come unhinged.

She spreads a delicate fan open and flaps it about her face, hiding all but the scandalized look in her eyes.

I grab a cava glass off a tray and steer clear of the center garden, where everyone tries to stand as close as they can to the king and queen. I find a shaded spot against a hedge. Though I can still feel the occasional curious stare slink my way from behind fans, it's better than being surrounded.

A group of children next to me is sitting in a circle. At first, I cannot hear the song they're singing to one another. But when I do, my heart sinks through my belly and onto the dirt.

They take turns with each line.

"I dug up a Moria grave to find."

"Two silver eyes to peer in your mind."

"Three golden fingers, illusions I'll cast!"

"One copper heart to persuade senses vast."

"And four platinum veins to lock up the past!"

I turn before they finish the final line, though it's imprinted in my bones. *I dug up a Moria grave!* I've always hated that rhyme, hated how they reduced us to a children's ditty, a joke.

"Renata," Lady Nuria says to my right. I didn't even hear her approach. Can I truly be this far gone that I've let my senses fail? "Where have you been?"

"Leo was showing me the gardens. I hadn't explored them all before."

"Let's dance." Lady Nuria lifts her chin in a fetching way, the sun warming her brown skin and enhancing the creamy mint color of her lavish gown.

"I don't dance," I tell her. I never dance. Even at our Moria bases, when we celebrated the change of seasons, the holy days of Our Lady of Whispers, I didn't dance.

She cackles in a very unladylike way. I can't help but like her.

Even if she has burned the image of the half-naked prince into my mind.

Lady Nuria is already leading me away, past the eyes that watch us behind fans like lynxes in tall grass. I chance a look at the king, but he's got the ear of Nuria's husband, Alessandro.

"Dancing is good for the spirits. I do it quite often in the nude while my husband is away."

I bark an unexpected laugh. "I suppose that would be frowned upon at a holy festival."

She smirks, a secretive glimmer in her eyes. What could this bold, reckless young woman do if she were unfettered? I would like to live to find out.

We go to a sitting area shaded with gauzy sheets. Attendants wearing the crest of the Tresoros family—a mountain studded with stars above it—are at Nuria's beck and call even before her delicate dress hits the velvet bench. She plucks two glasses of cava and offers me one.

"Why are you so kind to me?"

"You've asked me that before." Her dark eyes turn from me and out to the party, where curious stares flick in our direction.

"And you evaded the question. I have done nothing to deserve it."

She sighs, a pretty thing that makes her appear as if she's longing for something. I wonder if it's for Castian. I wonder if taking that one memory has helped ease her heartache or made it worse.

"There is so much wrong in the world," she says. "Sometimes, I feel the only thing I can give is a bit of kindness, even when I can't give hope. I wished I'd get to speak more with you, but my dear husband is always watching."

"You speak like a prisoner." I sip at my glass.

King Fernando has spotted us and is staring as he confides something in Judge Alessandro's ear. My chest tightens with anticipation. But I convince myself that I am safe with Nuria, if only for a moment.

The voice that trills in my mind is Margo's, and it says, *There is no such thing as safe.*

"There is so much the kingdom doesn't know," Nuria continues, dabbing a handkerchief on her forehead. It's the first crack in her armor.

"Like what?"

Her rich brown eyes betray worry. Her smile does not. "The Moria were once trading partners with the kingdom of Tresoros."

Whatever I thought she would say, this was not it. "Trade what?"

"Our metals for information on how you wield them. I know your histories. There is so much that was lost."

"Erased, you mean," I correct.

"A better description." She lowers her voice but pulls me close to her.

An uneasy feeling settles around my gut. "What else was erased?"

"My family is so much to blame for the Fajardo reign. We signed our kingdom away to keep a few mines and our titles, to make sure our descendants would be queens. All I wanted was to marry Castian. I was young and foolish. I gave King Fernando everything. Our platinum mine and a caveful of alman stone."

"That's where the throne came from?" My heart is beating too fast. How can something so precious to the Moria be nothing but a seat of power to the king? Maybe that's all it is meant to be. "But what of the tons of alman stone beneath the palace?"

Her eyes flutter and she settles her gaze on mine. "My dear husband let slip that the justice uses it for more. For the good of the kingdom."

The weapon.

I wish I had Margo or Sayida with me—hells, even Esteban—to tell all this to. I have to get out of here. I can't do this on my own anymore.

She squeezes my arm too hard. "Did you know that there was once a queen of Puerto Leones who was Moria?"

I frown. My ears pop because there's no way I heard her right. "That's not possible. Our royal line was killed during King Jústo's siege of Memoria."

She stops to acknowledge the court vultures that circle her for attention. Her red-lipped smile is striking and deceptive. We are but young women at a garden party discussing things young women usually talk about—the weather, sparkling wine, the pockets in our gowns, secret queens, secret cures. Treason.

"Ah, there's my *darling* husband," she says, holding up her glass as Judge Alessandro makes a beeline for her.

Sweat drips down the side of his forehead. I don't know if the fear in his eyes is because of the king or because he doesn't want to face Lady Nuria.

"Why are you telling me these things?" I ask her.

There's a secret there in her, waiting to sprout. "Because I can't tell anyone else. I don't know what you're planning, but I know you're up to something. And if you kill the king or Castian, you'll expose the hidden Moria in the capital. With the weapon, it will be a slaughter."

I wrap my hand around her wrist, then drop it as Alessandro is upon us.

"We're out of time, Renata," she whispers.

"Lady Nuria," the judge says, adjusting his heavy robes. "King Fernando is ready to speak and present the entertainment before the sunset parade." He turns to me and snatches the glass from my hand. "*You* are to take your place with the Hand of Moria."

He escorts me back across the garden, where the crowd has gathered to listen to the king speak. I stand beside the other two Moria on my own pedestal and try my best to be as still as they are.

"Thank you, honored guests and citizens of Puerto Leones," King Fernando says in that deep, fervent way he has. He takes his wife Queen Josephine's hand into his. "Tonight is our sacred Sun Festival. It marks the occasion when the Lord of Worlds rose from the earth and molded Puerto Leones as an example of paradise. But paradise is not easily kept or won. It demands blood. It demands the sacrifice of every citizen who reaps the treasures of its earth.

"A few months ago, Puerto Leones welcomed Dauphinique into our kingdom with the marital vows between myself and Queen Josephine." He pauses to let the crowd bow their heads to the queen. "Tonight we celebrate this new alliance, as our neighbors to the east have agreed to help Puerto Leones defeat the enemies of the crown. With Dauphinique by our side, Puerto Leones will not only be stronger, but we will become the greatest empire the world has ever seen. To Puerto Leones."

I catch a couple of worried glances when he says "empire." The rest of the court bursts into reverent cheer. Waiters are ready and waiting with ten bottles of cava so large, it requires three people to open each one.

The king turns around suddenly and raises his glass to acknowledge me. I hold his dark stare as long as I can before I bow.

"Please, enjoy the festivities!" The king speaking now is a different man from the one stewing in anger earlier. Even kings wear masks. He settles back into his chair as the band is escorted into the center of the garden.

Four guitarists and a man with a single drum begin to play. A singer whose voice is heavy with tragedy croons a love song that is popular in the coastal cities. As he sings, a woman in a flowing red dress steps forward. She is statuesque with skin like porcelain. Her hair is smoothed down to one side and braided over her shoulder. Her hands hold shells, which add a *clack, clack, clack* to the rhythm of the song. Her eyes are rimmed in shadow and her cheeks are apple red. When she dances, everyone follows the stomp of her black-heeled feet, and the rise of her skirts, which spiral outward to show powerful calves.

At her hip is a fan.

From my place on the podium, I see a brief glint and my breath catches. Though I'm not sure that I'm right. This is too bold, too reckless. I look around the garden, where even the guards are transfixed by her long, supple limbs and graceful arms. The singer falls into a sharp wail, lamenting his broken heart, and the dancer throws the shells into the grass and grabs her fan. When she unfolds it, I know I'm right.

There, concealed between the paper-thin folds, is a flash of slender steel with a delicate rose hilt. Only one person I know owns a hairpin dagger. I *did* see Sayida. Then this dancer must be under an illusion.

She turns to the king, pulling her skirt, distracting everyone from the weapon in her hand. My stomach twists with revulsion.

I have a choice. I could let her kill him. It is what I want most of all. But his death, after the speech he just gave, would ruin everything I came here to do. The weapon would be used before I could get to it. Nuria is right. Lozar was right. I came here for more than my own vengeance.

The guitar strums as fast as my heart. The woman spins, her dress like the bloody red spill of death around her, and when she stops, her arm is raised high.

King Fernando sees the blade too late. Everyone does.

But I didn't. I'm already moving, lunging between the dancer and the king, arm poised to shield my face.

Pain blooms. Her eyes, familiar and blue, are full of hate. Not toward the king who is screaming orders, or the guards who pin her to the ground. The illusion she's created around her holds strong, keeping her blond hair dark and cloaking her in front of all these strangers.

"Take her away!" King Fernando shouts. "Take her! I'll deal with her later."

"Renata!" Leo shouts, running to me from the other side of the garden.

Where did he come from? Justice Méndez is already at my side. The blade is driven right through my forearm.

There is too much confusion, too much blood, too many people touching me and calling my name. Bells ring throughout the entire kingdom and I know I hear people shouting.

But as the medic tends to me, all I can see is the hatred in Margo's eyes as she is dragged thrashing and screaming out of the garden.

22

I'VE FELT WORSE PAIN.

One time, on a mission outside the Memoria Mountains, past the Sedona Canyons, I fell into a nest of ice vipers. I nearly died from their poison. It was Margo who knew a cure. A root that grew in the same desert. Dez spent all night digging for it, and she spent the night keeping my body from freezing as the venom lowered my body temperature.

Then there were the thorn reeds that gave me the scars on my back. A group of young boys from a different unit pulled me out of my tent and onto a raft, where I woke, startled, and fell into the tangle of river thorns. Those boys were sent to a separate safe house across the country, but that's when I started keeping to myself around the Whispers' stronghold.

There was the burn on my right thigh.

The slash on my neck from Esmeraldas.

The poison after that.

Watching Dez die.

"I should've died a long time ago," I say as a guard carries me into the medic's chamber.

"You're not dying, do you hear me?" Leo trots alongside us to keep up. His green eyes never leave my face. There's worry there, and I know that I don't care if he's the spy or just a very good actor or a fabrication of the unraveling threads in my head. He's the only friend I've got within these walls and he's here.

"Was the blade poisoned?" Justice Méndez asks, pushing something off a bed.

They lay me on it. I don't look down because there's blood everywhere. There's always blood everywhere.

A decrepit old medic peers at me, but he doesn't touch my skin. Doesn't get within an arm's distance of me. I can smell the fear bubbling through his pores, and it smells like—aguadulce.

"Move aside," Leo says, frustration overpowering his usual pleasant demeanor. "She had three glasses of cava and she's lost a lot of blood." He holds my arm and sniffs. "If there's poison, it's odorless."

"Bring me the girl!" Méndez shouts at someone.

Leo lowers himself to my face. His warm fingers brush my hair back. "This is going to hurt."

It'll hurt, I told him. *I know*, he said.

Perhaps it was the drink, but when Leo grabs the end of the hairpin dagger, it doesn't hurt. There's a deep numbness stretching from my shoulder to my fingertips. But when I feel hands hold my feet down, my waist, something within me snaps.

"Don't touch me!" I snarl at the guard—Hector—but he doesn't let go.

White-hot pain sizzles inside my flesh, the pain of my latest wound making itself known with a vengeance as Leo makes cuts around the dagger. His beautiful soft words apologize over and over again. Someone holds a weak poultice over my nose to help calm me. Manzanilla and other herbs. But all it does is give me whiplash memories of Esmeraldas. Was it just over two weeks when my life was shaken by the root? Unearthed and splintered. Then the numbness returns, slick wet warmth coating my skin.

I know I've blacked out when I wake to silence.

The splash of cold water.

The rustle of fabric.

Leo is re-dressing my bandage, his shoulders shaking with silent tears.

"Leo," I say.

"Thank the Six Heavens," he says, lowering his forehead to mine. "I'm so sorry, Ren. I'm so sorry we had to do it this way."

I swallow the lump in my throat. But if the blade had been poisoned. If they left it in and it got infected. He acted as quickly as he could even if it hurt.

I want to thank him for tending to me when the cowardly medic would not, but Méndez rushes back in.

"How are you feeling?" Méndez asks, his voice hard despite the tightness of his lips. Is he rattled because I'm alive or because he should've seen the attack?

"I'm well, my justice," I lie.

"You have a hole through one of your extremities," Leo mutters, returning to the bandage. "I do not believe that qualifies as *well.*"

Méndez frowns and snaps, "Now is not the time for your *tone,* Leonardo."

Leo mutters an apology.

My mind is racing. Margo is somewhere in the dungeons, and

if she's here, then that means that the others are, too. I'd wager my life on it. The only question is, how many others are there? Did they see me save the king? Would any of them understand? That I was losing a battle in order to win the war? Sayida flashes through my mind. I *knew* I saw her earlier. I *knew* it, but I blamed it on my traitorous memories. Traitorous. Traitor. Is there anyone who believes me to be anything but?

There's something sour on my tongue that forces me to remain silent.

"Drink this," Leo says, offering a brown glass bottle whose bitter contents remind me of rotting fish. "It's a sedative to numb the pain."

I have to get up. That's the only reason I nod and let him tip the wretched liquid down my throat. Almost instantly, some of the pain subsides.

Méndez turns to the medic who is pressed against the walls. "Did you test for poison, Arsenál?"

"No traces. She's no worse for the wear," Arsenál proclaims. "I am given to understand her kind have a high threshold for pain."

I sneer at him. "Do you want me to show you how much pain I can tolerate?"

"Easy," Leo tells me, careful not to touch me but guiding me back to the bed.

Méndez is wilder than I've ever seen him. His dress clothes are stained with my blood and his eyes have deep shadows. Have they always been there, or did a part of me want to see something else?

"Take Renata to her rooms, and don't come back down until the festival begins."

Leo looks stricken, as if he can't believe the orders. I tug on his hand. Let him know that this is the way it has to be. He lowers his face. "Yes, my justice."

"What of the woman?" I ask carefully.

Méndez tugs on the ends of his jacket. "The *assassin* is in solitary. Every single person within the palace is to be questioned. She has not claimed an affiliation, though I suspect her to be one of the Whispers." He turns his suspicious eyes in my direction, looks at the wound, which is still bleeding through the bandage. "Did you recognize her?"

Her name is Margolina Bellén, and she's an Illusionári of the Whispers' Rebellion. Her mother and father were killed during a raid in a village outside of Citadela Riomar. They were drowned when they refused to reveal where their children were hidden. Margo survived by digging a hole beneath a jetty of rocks along the coast and fed on the crabs that burrowed in alongside her. A week later, half-starved and dehydrated, she was found by the Whispers and given a home.

"No," I say, never wavering from his salt-gray stare. Because I truly hadn't recognized her, not with that illusion that darkened her hair and changed her face. It was the eyes, the weapon, the way I've seen her dance that gave her away in the end.

"You saved the king's life," Méndez tells me. "On behalf of the royal family, the Sun Festival's ball tonight will be dedicated to you. All of Puerto Leones will know what you have done."

Revulsion slams into my gut. I picture myself paraded in front of the kingdom as the example of what Moria should be—servants to the crown. Bodies meant to be sacrificed.

Méndez chuckles nervously. "She's so honored she can't speak. Renata, show your thanks."

"I was doing my duty," I say, finally. Tears sting at my eyes because this is all wrong. I shouldn't have saved the king, and I shouldn't be honored by this. But Nuria was right. Had I not protected the king, it would have caused more bloodshed for innocent Moria.

Méndez seems to relax when I utter the words. "For now, all household staff is to report to my study for questioning, including you two."

"But, my justice," the medic says, "I would *never*—"

Justice Méndez has the kind of stare that could render any man still. "Then you have nothing to fear."

"Yes, my justice." Arsenál bows so low I'm surprised his weight doesn't push him forward.

"Be ready for tonight, Renata. Everyone at the festival will see your power, the power of the king and the justice, and those against us will shake in fear."

"She's lost a lot of blood, my justice," Leo starts to plead. "Lord Las Rosas—"

He dismisses the name with a flick of his hand. "Not him. She will use her powers on the assassin."

Margo. He means fierce, loyal Margo. I can't use my magics on her. I can't. Bile rises and I choke on it.

"My justice," I bleat out. It is a pathetic plea, because I know that between me and the king, he will choose the king. "My arm . . ."

Justice Méndez slams his fist into the wall, his eyes dilated as he opens the door. "No more delays! It is the hands and not the arm you will need. Take her to her rooms to rest. Tonight, you make a Hollow for your kingdom."

23

Leo and I watch the sunset parade of the royal Leonesse families. They make their way down the royal mile in front of the palace. Each family wears decadent traditional clothing showcasing the colors of their family crests to honor their allegiance to the king of Puerto Leones.

The Carolinas in silver and pale blue, and the Jaramillo family with their forest green and navy. There are seventeen of them with direct ties and claims to the throne from before the Fajardo conquest. There's the Sevillas with their red and black. The lord and lady on opposite ends of the open chariot. Lord Sevilla waves enthusiastically and reaches into a bin where he keeps picas, hardly worth anything, but the people rush to his carriage and blow kisses at his handsome face.

"Did they find out who sent the assassins?" I ask as Leo pours the tea.

"She only said she acted alone. The girl's Illusionári glamour has worn away to reveal her true visage. She hasn't said another word despite—"

He's quiet, so I finish for him. "Despite the torture."

I don't say anything, but I let that fuel my anger toward the justice. Toward the king.

Leo opens the door only once to receive the gown I am to wear to the festival tonight. He helps me dress and clean my wound once more. He takes a step away, a rueful smile on his face despite all that's happened.

The Moria mourn in red. We also send our dead into the sea in scarlet robes, so Our Lady of Shadows can spot color from the heavens among the dark waves. Most Leonesse citizens, however, are followers of the Father of Worlds. They mourn in black for their lower realm of the Six Heavens, where only ravens can carry souls in and out. For this very reason, I find it strange that Leo has dressed me in an ink-black dress tapered to my waist with satin panels and whaleboning and a silk skirt embroidered in silver thread and a high collar of raven feathers. Getting out of the bloody clothes has revitalized me. My head is clearer than it's been in days, thanks to the pain tonic.

"The dress was here when I opened the door," Leo says, returning with something red in his hands.

"Who could have sent it?" I ask. "It's too extravagant."

"Everyone will already be looking at you now. Why try to hide?"

Because I don't want everyone looking at me. Not when I have to find a way to get out of here before they force me to turn Margo into a Hollow.

"These are from Justice Méndez," Leo says, presenting me with ruby-red gloves.

"I've never received so many presents," I say, suspicion in my voice.

"It *is* a festival day." Leo's green eyes twinkle as he draws out a tiny key from the inside of his pocket.

Leo unlocks the old glove, then locks on the new ones. The fine red suede comes up to my elbows and they have a black chain mail trim with ruby cuff links that clamp down. Nothing but longer manacles than the ones I had before.

Out on the royal mile, the parade of noble families has come to an end. There's a group of priests from the church of the Lord of Worlds and their followers. At the very end is the royal family's carriage. King Fernando and his young queen, dripping with jewels. Queen Josephine's dress reminds me of clouds drifting by, white against her polished black skin. When she holds her hands out to the crowd, they reach for her lovingly. The king and queen's festival crowns are tall, dotted with the violet crystals of their family's crest.

I inhale through my disappointment. Prince Castian isn't in the carriage with them. Time is running out. My hands are numb with the idea of draining Margo of all her memories, turning her into a shell of the girl who fought beside me in battle, who'd give her life to bring justice to her people.

A troupe of trumpeters follows behind the king and queen to close off the ceremonial parade. The festival that celebrates the Lord of Worlds destroying the Lady of Shadows is far from over. There's a new chorus of trumpets, bells, and singing. The way they wave the purple-and-gold flags of Puerto Leones reminds me of the day Dez was executed. My body buzzes with renewed energy. Purpose.

I take one last look in the mirror before we leave, touching the silver stitching on my gown. There's a snap, like a concentrated crackle of lightning when I touch the dress for too long. It's the elation of having run from the Second Sweep and lived. The heady buzz of a kiss under moonlight. Then I realize. Not silver. *Platinum.* The childish rhyme pops into my head. *Four platinum veins to lock up the past.* My hands buzz as I touch the metal, a metal so rare I dared not dream I would ever have it for my own. It wasn't the tonic that made me feel better—it was the dress.

There's only one person with the means to do this. But why?

The zing of my magics heats up beneath the gloves. Reacting. Fusing. Igniting. My mind is clearer than it's ever been before. The Gray a distant vault that rests.

I am a shadow, I am a drop of ink. Vengeance in the night.

I'm a Robári.

As we enter the ballroom, whispers come from every direction. I want to keep my eyes trained forward, but they're searching the crowd for the prince in the dazzling torchlight. He's my only connection to the weapon—the last person (that I know of) who had possession of the wooden box in Lozar's memory. There's still a chance he could lead me to it. I walk among the lavish gowns, the sparkling glass, fire sconces, the cava that pours like waterfalls.

The palace is not only hosting its royal families and wealthy merchants, but the people from nearby kingdoms. The royals of the kingdom of Dauphinique arrive in their traditional gowns of lace and satin, long dreadlocks piled high atop their heads.

The ballroom is unlike anything I've ever seen. The entire floor is a mosaic of the kingdom's riches. Leo takes my hand and we join the line of people entering the festivities.

The rulers from Empirio Luzou make the next grand entrance. A continent south of the sea to Puerto Leones that makes us look small. Empress Elena and her queen consort are carried on a contraption that is shouldered by six men in golden tunics. The royal women have tawny brown skin and onyx-black hair braided elegantly over their shoulders. Real flowers I've never seen before, a red as rich as rubies, are woven around their necks. The empress wears a crown while her wife's royal status is marked with a heavy necklace of diamond drops.

Everyone around us whispers and gasps at the decadence, speculating about why they missed the garden party. Surely they couldn't have known what Margo was planning, but I catch a suggestion that perhaps the empress may not be here for peace talks.

"Why do you think the king insisted on inviting the empress to this festival?" I ask Leo.

"Empirio Luzou is the wealthiest in the charted world," Leo whispers to me. "But they are the place where the Moria seek refuge. Luzou hasn't stepped foot in Puerto Leones since the siege of the Moria."

Siege, a nice way of saying *slaughter.*

"Lady Nuria bet me ten gold libras they wouldn't show," he adds. "She thought they'd be too ashamed to be here."

I watch the empress and consort being lowered to the ground, where the king and queen of Puerto Leones greet them. The empress and consort wait for the Leonesse to bow, but it is clear that the Fajardos are doing the same. A majordoma comes around and offers the empress and consort drinks, which they accept but do not drink.

I follow King Fernando's gaze to where the Hand of Moria is kept, then to me. My stomach clenches as he raises a glass in my direction. And I know for certain that I am being trotted out like a prize steed. One to demonstrate his power to bring empires to their knees.

I bow, turning just slightly in the direction of the empress. When I stand, I find she was already watching me and hold her stare. Dread for this night sinks talons in my back and remains with me as we keep moving.

Leo escorts me through the ballroom. Dancing is under way, and waiters glide by with trays of amber rum and cava, slices of fried pigskin, and cheeses with raw honeycomb on apple slices. Glass goblets in a rainbow of colors filled with aguadulce and lemon rinds are set on fire, then quickly extinguished before being sipped by thirsty lips.

Through large double doors leading to the gardens I see a band. The singer's voice cuts cleanly through the room. The king and queen move to their thrones once more, accepting each and every citizen and guest that comes to pay them welcome and praise.

When will they bring out Margo? My arm aches, and my heart races. I still have no plan. Do I try to save her and kill us both? Or do I turn her into a Hollow to maintain my place in the palace? Which path would Dez choose?

At every corner and entrance is an armed guard, their swords already drawn. Leo escorts me through the crowd. They part for us and I feel like a dark sea creature breaking through a tall, cold wave. I keep my eyes on King Fernando, on the throne, this one iron and gold instead of the alman stone in the tower. As Leo guides me to Justice Méndez, King Fernando holds his hand up. We stop and go where the king beckons us.

He stands but doesn't take my hand. His deep brown stare slides from my toes to my extravagant dress, the faint scar he gave me on my chest, and finally, to my eyes. My pulse is rapid, and the fresh wound on my forearm concealed by my glove thrums with a constant, dull ache.

At the sight of me between the king and the justice, the ballroom's energy shifts. Dresses rustle as ladies cluster around carved pillars, whispers traded behind flapping fans. Throats clear and conversations come to a halt, instruments hit the wrong notes, and a glass shatters somewhere. All eyes turn to us three.

"Honored guests," King Fernando says. "Today we celebrate our creator of all, the Father of Worlds, his joyous triumph over the treacherous Lady of Shadows and the usurper gods of old. This year we celebrate more than that. This afternoon, there was an attempt on my life by the Whispers during my queen's own celebration."

He stops speaking to let the crowd gasp and speculate among themselves. King Fernando knows how to fan fear.

"You might have noticed the guards. Please, both our neighbors across the seas, understand that this is to protect everyone in this room from those who would try to destroy us. On behalf of my queen and my son, I would like to dedicate the first dance of the Sun Festival to Renata Convida, the Robári of the Hand of Moria who saved my life."

My eyes water with anger at his every word. *Stay calm. Don't move. Don't breathe.* I am petrified as he takes my hand. The heat of his palm radiates through my glove, and my first instinct is to recoil.

He clamps his fingers around mine, too tightly. We've taken two steps toward the center of the dance floor when someone bars our way.

My hands shake, and the air is kicked out of my lungs at the sight of him—wind-tossed golden curls and sparkling war medals on an embroidered blue jacket that matches his eyes: Prince Castian.

At last.

"If I may, Father," he says in a smooth, deep voice accompanied by a charming smile.

There's ire in the king's brow, tightness in his puckered mouth, but he won't dare make a scene, not in front of all these people. He relinquishes his hold on me.

I'm handed over to Prince Castian like a toy it's his turn to play with.

The orchestra kicks up a tune that feels more familiar than it should. I've been waiting for this moment for days, weeks, and now that it's here I shake down to the bone. I'm disoriented. I'm a coward. I can't even look him in the eye.

"You're frightened," the Bloodied Prince says, placing a firm hand around my waist. I clench my teeth and keep my eyes trained over his shoulder, to the red-and-yellow starburst mosaic behind him. My fingers close around his arm, perhaps too hard.

"I'm not frightened," I say, harsh as a winter snap, and I keep a foot of space between us, which makes for awkward dancing.

"When I heard you were here, I knew I had to return."

"You came all this way to see a Robári do tricks for the court?"

"No," he says, so earnestly that I refuse to look at him. I have seen the way he kills, the way he makes people forgive him, the way he lures women in and then wrecks them.

"Then why?" I slip and grab his shoulder for purchase.

He flinches. "Careful."

"You're injured?" There have been no reports of skirmishes or battles. Where did he get wounded so close to his heart?

He sidesteps the question with the easy shuffle of his feet. When he glides his hand high on my back, images spill from the Gray despite my surge in power from the platinum dress.

Clothes strewn over the bed.
  A golden trail of hair over firm muscle.
  Queen Penelope pleading with Illan.
  The Ventári in the solitary cell.
  A wooden box.
  Celeste up in flames.
  Dez, always Dez.

When Castian pulls me closer, the dancers part for us, and I regain control of the Gray. I push the memories back and focus on the polished tiles beneath our feet, so blue it's like we're walking across the Castinian Sea.

"If you aren't scared, why won't you look into my eyes?"

My lips tremble, my nostrils flare, but I say, "Is it not enough that hundreds of eyes are already looking at you as we dance?"

I keep my gaze trained over his shoulder, where I find Justice Méndez watching intently, more intently than the others.

"I'm used to the hundreds of eyes. I am not, however, used to yours."

Something twists in the pit of my stomach, like vipers wrenching themselves into a knot. His breath is cool on my cheek. I shut my eyes and see Dez's severed neck. The blood that pooled over the executioner's block. The blood that sprayed Castian's face, which Davida later cleaned up. Davida, who suffers for this prince. Why? How can he be worth all this pain and destruction?

Castian grips my waist tighter, and I gasp as he tilts me back and pulls me forward in time to the rhythm of the vielles. I squeeze his shoulder harder than I should, and when he rights me, I look straight into his eyes.

The blue is fractured with bits of gold and green in the

candlelight. I find the cuts, faint scars, from Davida's memory. The crescent-moon scar Dez gave him. The divot between his brow is pronounced, like he's trying to place me in a lost memory. But how could he recognize the rebel girl he met, covered in dirt and tears in the forest, in the one I am now, draped in black silk and feathers and platinum, like a promise of death?

"That wasn't so hard, was it?" he says, an infuriating victoriousness tugging his full, peach mouth into a smile.

"I suppose you always get what you want, don't you, Your Highness?" I match his smile with one of my own. *Remember who he is.*

He quietly thinks on this, slowing his steps. We are in the center of the dance floor, but now other couples have joined us, trying to edge closer in attempts to overhear what a prince like him is saying to a monster like me.

"I fight for what I believe in," he says, finally. "And I always fight to win. In that sense, I get what I want."

"Why bother dancing with someone like me when there are scores of ladies waiting for you? Some of them for several weeks."

He grimaces, and I fear I have finally reached the limit of what I can get away with saying. He halts. I stumble, but he rights me with his waiting hand, as if he knew the next step I'd take. He twirls me under his arm, and I feel like a plaything as I spin back into his arms, bracing my red-gloved hands on his chest to keep at least a breath of space between us.

"Have you not been waiting for me for several weeks?" he asks, guiding me back into the song, out of the ballroom, and through the double doors where the feast spills out into the garden. Couples follow, but here the music is louder and the shadows play with silver moonlight. Here he must lean in closer to speak to me, to see me.

Could he know why I've been here all this time? With what I've been able to gather from this dance, he couldn't possibly have the weapon on him.

"I am here for the justice," I answer him. "Justice Méndez."

"And I had hoped you'd come here to kill me." His voice is soft, anguished. The voice of the Castian who broke Nuria's heart. *I can't marry you.* I don't want to feel sympathy for him. I can't.

I harden my heart and remember the words he said to Dez in Riomar. *Do you have a death wish?*

His eyebrows are furrowed. His grip tight. I can feel the calluses on his hands through the silk of my gloves. The most delicate thing about him is the golden circlet that crowns his mane of golden hair. He looks nothing like the simple soldier in the forest who captured Dez. There are different versions of Castian walking around the colorless pit of my memories, and yet none of them are the same boy, least of all the one standing in front of me now.

"You don't remember me, do you?" It's the voice of the prince who wanted to run away before the battle. Nuria's betrothed.

I narrow my eyes. "Are you mocking me, Your Highness?"

"Actually, I'm told I'm not funny at all."

My skin grows hot when I feel the ghost of a tremble against my ribs. Castian's laughter as he gently nipped Nuria in her room. I gasp and pull out of his hold.

The song has slowed to a stop, and Castian uses my movement to spin me. I glide, my skirts flaring around me, the motion so fast my novice feet can't keep up. He's there to catch me. My heart races from the fear of falling, the fear of this trickster boy.

I'm distantly aware of people clapping. Castian resting my hands in his. I refuse to shift under his stare or let him intimidate me. So I stare back, and though we are standing still, we continue a different kind of dance.

"You don't remember me from your time here as a child," he says, evenly. His lips too close to my ear. "You never left the library."

My heart gives a horrible squeeze. There were dozens of Moria children, but we were never allowed to interact with the royal family. I do not recall a little boy with golden curls or eyes of a vast, brutal sea.

I can feel the Gray answer me, dark halls twisting and curving to lead me to a pit of memories I may not return from. Is Castian in there?

"I have no memories of my time here, though of course, I have heard many stories about you throughout the years."

"The stories are all half fiction," he says, arrogant again.

"That also makes them half-truths."

He frowns, but won't let go of my hand, and with everyone staring at us, I cannot pry myself free. The garden is now populated by even more courtiers than the ballroom, their faces a small mob in my peripherals. I glance up to the night, to the tower. From here I can see the lace curtains of my bedroom—Nuria's bedroom.

Castian abruptly releases me, and when I follow his eyes, Justice Méndez weaves through the throng of people to me. He signals the band, and a new song kicks up. People disperse. My muscles relax despite my racing heart.

"My dear Renata," Justice Méndez says, a pained smile on his face. "I do hope you are not causing trouble for our young prince."

"No trouble at all," Castian says, never acknowledging the justice, instead, his eyes trained solely on me.

"If I may," Justice Méndez says to me, "I have to steal the prince away for an urgent matter."

Prince Castian *bows* to me. It is a brief, curt thing, and I can see he didn't mean to do it but he can't take it back. A perplexed

Méndez trails at his heels while I'm left behind in the center of the garden.

A young courtier dances close enough to me that I can smell the sickly-sweet perfume she bathed in. Her hair is in bright blond ringlets coiffed around her long face, which is partially covered by a fluttering purple-and-gold fan. She hisses in my direction, and while she breaks from her partner for a turn, she spits at my feet, her saliva landing on the hem of my skirt.

Everyone around us has seen it. I clench my teeth and straighten my shoulders. I cannot react. I won't.

I turn and walk farther into the center garden, where there are no more torches and the dark can be my shield. I stare at the moon and bask in the silver light. A deep sense of melancholy envelops me, as if all the memories in my head are crying out all at once. The need to be seen. The need to right their wrongs.

Isn't that what I wanted? To make right all my mistakes? But I've only managed to get myself more deeply ensnared in this glittering fortress. And now I'll have to face Margo.

"What do I do?" I ask the sky.

Looking up to the tower windows, I notice something strange. I count the floor levels over and over again. I'm certain my room is the only one with the delicate lace-trimmed drapes. Beside them is a smaller window that appears shuttered from the inside. Beside that is the library on my floor, still with the window I left open. But there isn't supposed to be a room between the library and my apartments. None at all.

I envision the long hallway I take every day and every night. There is only a wall that separates me from the library of my child-hood, the place I keep getting pulled back to. A suspicion digs sharp nails into my chest. I think of Castian claiming he remembers me in that library. Him telling Nuria about his secret hiding places.

My throat tightens as I hear an echo in my head of dice rolling across the floor and a small boy's voice: *What are you doing here?*

When Dez found me that night, he didn't come in through the main door.

There's a hidden room.

I have to get up there. I slink back into the festival to find the shortest way upstairs.

Couples dance in wide circles, colorful ripples moving in time with the music.

Leo is flirting with an attendant, leaning slyly against a pillar while Prince Castian speaks passionately to Justice Méndez in a far-off corner. The justice storms away into the gardens, leaving Castian glowering so fiercely no one comes near him. He's the rude, petulant prince getting served wine from the first courtier's memory I stole.

I am a shadow among their bright jeweled dresses. For a moment, when I look up at the carved pedestals where the Hand of Moria stand, where I would be had this entire Sun Festival not been dedicated to me. My head spins, my stomach aches. The stitches on my forearm itch and pulse. The air itself around me seems to move, as if something is hiding behind a glamour.

I recognize it. Illusionári magics. Margo! *Please, Margo,* I think. *Give me time to find a way to free us both.*

I follow a gaggle of glittering courtiers as they head toward the washrooms, and when they pass an exit, I slip out of the ballroom.

I make my way back up to the tower, hoping everyone at the party is too distracted by the revelry to notice my absence. At the very least I should have a few moments before they realize I'm no longer there. I head straight to the familiar wooden door that has been gnawing on my memories since I've returned. There is no guard in this hallway tonight. The library is unlocked. My eyes get used to the dark after a few quick blinks, but I light a gas lamp on the table. The window is still open, but it is so much colder here, like the cold of Lady Nuria's apartments downstairs. I think of the noises she heard that I thought might be the memories that haunt me, and she believed to be wind. She was right.

There was a draft.

From a hidden room.

When I close my eyes and move my gloved hands along the platinum, the memory of the day I was taken from the palace wants to step forward. The echo of footsteps. The hinge of metals as a boy speaks to me. *What are you doing here?*

I go to the farthest wall of the library, the wall that should be shared with my room, but isn't. There's something in between. There has to be. I frantically pull on the tops of books, ripping them off the shelves and onto the floor until I find the one. I push the shelf panel with all my strength, a rivulet of pain shooting from my wound. There's a trickle of warm blood running down my arm, but I don't care because the door gives, the hinges sighing from disuse.

I hold my breath as dust fills my nose, the staleness of ash and furniture swollen with moisture.

I press my hand to the shuttered window I noticed from the gardens, caked with years of dust. I grab the lamp and frantically search the room. I was drawn here for a reason, to this secret room. I know it's here. The box, the weapon, their "cure." Music drifts up from the festival. They haven't noticed I'm missing. Yet. I turn over the cushions on the moldy furniture, empty the shelves, search behind every hanging painting. There's a faded tapestry of two pirates at the helm of a ship. I remember them from the storybook Castian was reading with Davida. Does this room belong to the prince? A secret place only he knows about, a place to keep things he'd rather leave hidden . . . My heart slams against my chest as I push the cloth to the side, revealing a shelf built into the wall where a child might place their treasures. I raise the lamp in my hand.

There it is. I saw it in my stolen memory of Dez and Castian. A slender wooden box etched with gold designs. How Dez cowered from it, repulsed and afraid.

The hinges squeak as I tip the lid open. It gives so easily that I know something is wrong. My heart stutters when I close my fist around the thing inside.

An infant's dress, the white fabric yellowed with time. Beneath that a round, painted portrait that fits in my palm. The king's soldiers keep ones like this, pictures of their loved ones, usually a lover, in their breast pockets while they fight. This one has two children. One golden-haired and the other one dark. I flip the portrait to find two faded initials. *C & A.*

What *is* this?

The floorboards creak behind me. I spin around and nearly knock over the gas lamp.

Prince Castian stands at the threshold. "I knew you'd find your way back here."

24

THE WEAK GAS LAMP STRAINS TO BURN AGAINST THE DARK OF THE EXPOSED hidden room. I set it on a table and face my Bloodied Prince. Shadows outline his broad shoulders, his gold curls, the medals over his heart.

I'm injured, but so is he. I can still fight.

I throw my weight into my fist and surprise him with a punch. I graze his cheekbone, but it's a miss.

He groans but doesn't step back. He grabs one arm. I swing with my free hand, dragging my nails across his face. It's dirty, but I hear Dez. *It's your life or theirs. Choose the option that brings you back to me.* Except that I won't be coming back to him this time, will I?

Castian shoves me but doesn't try to hit me back. I grab the wooden box and swing it sharply into his side. Whatever he was going to say to me dies on his lips as he clutches his ribs.

"Stop this!" His voice is gruff and loud.

"Where is it?" I've already gone too far. If I stand down now, I won't get the weapon, this curse that brought me back to this place, that lured Dez to his death. I have to best him because the other option is to turn Margo into a Hollow, and if I don't win this fight, there is no doubt I will be sent to the executioner's block. Would Castian behead me himself the way he did to Dez? Would they let me rot in a cell like Lozar? A terrible thought comes to mind—is his corpse still down there?

Castian recovers from my blow, putting distance between us. He unbuttons his beaded and embroidered jacket, his tunic open to the curve between his chest muscles. He tosses the jacket to the side, where it lands on the molded couch.

I undo the clasp that ties my cape around my neck, and it falls to the ground. Pull the corset strings so I can breathe. I try to remember if I saw any weapons, but the room was full of books and old toys. If I could get my hands free from these gloves, I could rip the answers out of him.

Instead, I size him up the way Margo showed me. Think of what I know of him. He's quick on his feet, and he carries his power in his broad arms. When he steps to the right, I step to the left, and just like that, we are dancing again. I channel all the rage I've had to push back as I was paraded before the king and his court and thrust it into my fists.

Castian blocks my jab to the left of his chest. I don't want him to know I'm going to go for his weak spot yet. Bright lights dance in front of my eyes as the tonic that dulled my pain begins to wear off. He grabs hold of my wrists and pulls me to his chest. I kick my legs, knees raising so high that he's forced to use his hands to block, freeing my hands in the process.

I land a punch on his nose, but though he's bleeding, he shakes it off and grabs hold of my shoulders. He shoves me against the tapestry wall. The air rushes out of my chest as he slams me a second time. His belt presses into my stomach, his breath is sweet with wine and warm in my face.

He wants to best me. I can see it in his eyes as he holds my left arm against the wall and digs a thumb into the wound on my right. Slick, hot blood trickles where my stitches rip beneath the glove.

My vision is white with pain, but I grind my teeth and grunt through it. I breathe fast and hard, preparing myself first, then I bash my head into his and take his moment of disorientation to dig my fingers into his chest wound. I can play his game, too.

Castian cries out and drops down to his hands. I grab a fistful of his hair and slam his face against my knee. I yank his head back so he can look at me. *You won't look at me*, he said.

Well, here I am, looking at you now.

"Surrender."

He spits a wad of saliva and blood to the side but doesn't admit defeat.

"The Whispers taught you to fight well," he says, with a chuckle. "Did they ruin your life first? Make you think you were going insane?"

"The Whispers saved me from *your* father." I yank on his hair, but all he does is grunt. I can't listen to him. He's all lies and false smiles. "Where is the weapon?"

And just like that his fist slams into my gut. I let go of him and cradle my stomach. Fall to my knees. *Breathe.* I can't breathe.

"If you'd just listen to me, Nati—" he says, blood spilling into his mouth from his nose.

"What did you call me?" I shout.

My body locks. My throat closes. The memory of my father calling me that name renders me useless. I slam my hands against the stone floor, snapping myself into the here and now. How did he know? How could he possibly know?

I suck in tiny bits of air until I can take a single long gulp. When I press my hands to push myself up I fumble into the gas lamp. I stomp out the flame before it can catch on to anything, then close my fingers around a pointed piece of glass. There's the faintest light coming from the open library. My eyes adjust to the low flame. I breathe through the ache in my body, the dizziness that comes with the rush of adrenaline. I watch the outline of his muscles, the way he staggers for breath.

Castian gives me a wide berth, keeping his back against the wall. His hand rests over his shoulder, where blood seeps through the bandage and shirt.

"We never agreed on weapons," he says. There's still that humor in his voice that lights me up with rage. He pulls out a small dagger concealed in his boot and throws it on the floor.

Since he's discarded his, I should give up mine. That would be the honorable thing to do. If that was in his reach this whole time, why didn't he use it when he had me pressed against the wall? Why didn't he end it?

"Fine," I growl.

I toss the bit of glass aside and charge at him. He blocks each punch, each kick. I go for his injury again, but he anticipates it and traps my arms with his against his torso. I raise my knee and slam it into his groin. It's a lazy shot, but I've always found it to come in handy when I'm out of options. I slap my palm over his ear as hard as I can and he screams. He cups the side of his head, and in this moment of weakness, I strike my hand at his throat. He chokes and stumbles back, coughing through it. He throws a punch that lands on my shoulder.

My body thrums with rage, and even in this low light, I feel it igniting me as if from within. I see the light haloed around me reflected in his eyes. Am I conjuring that?

"You have to listen to me, Nati." He holds his hands up.

"You can't call me that! Stop calling me that!" I punch and he blocks. He tries to pin my arms down again, but I throw myself to the ground and crawl between his legs. I slam my elbow into the back of his knee, and he falls forward.

I can kill him.

In this moment, I know I can.

But death would be too good, too gentle. How soon will the justice, the king, come after me? Isn't that what I wanted to avoid? Does it even matter? Margo would do it. Margo didn't hesitate and now she's locked up and I'm here fighting for the pair of us.

"If you won't tell me where the weapon is," I say, "I will just rip it out."

He turns over on his back, and I pin him down, digging into the wound on his chest.

"Ren—Renata, please." His breath is raspy, blood covering the bottom half of his face. The Bloodied Prince indeed.

I use a piece of glass to rip at the fabric around my top wrist, scraping a bit of skin along the way, but then I can feel air. I tear the rest off with my teeth and free my hand, cold air chilling my sweaty skin.

My power surges through me, lighting up the fissures of scars that wind across my bloodied skin. They burn the orange of fire. A veil of light dances from my skin. I don't have time to marvel at it. I press my finger to his temple.

I don't know what I was expecting. Screams. Begging for mercy. Something.

Prince Castian simply stares at me, his face covered in blood and shadow and moonlight from the single dirty window. His breath comes in quick pants. I recognize the look there. He's daring me.

I let my magics free, push through his memories to grab hold of them and drag them out.

Images flash before my eyes, too quickly to make out places or faces. The rush of wind in my ears and then nothing.

I see *nothing*.

Complete and total darkness, as if there's a wall there I can't breach.

"Impossible," I gasp. Somehow, he's found a way to block my power. *That won't work on me.* He really meant it when he spoke those words in the Forest of Lynxes.

A smile creeps up his face and then he grabs me, and something comes undone. Up is down and down is up. The room spins as he flips me over and grips my wrists.

"What did you do?" I whisper.

He doesn't respond. Damp hair falling over his face. He's weak, barely keeping himself up. I can feel his heart racing to the same rapid beat of my own right through his palms. That shouldn't be. "Surrender, Renata. Please."

Please? The dizzying feeling in my head clears when I hear a scream. Not mine. Not his. We are not alone.

"My prince!"

"No!" Castian shouts. The pressure on me alleviates as he staggers to his feet, stanching the wound at his shoulder. A wound that looks like it was inflicted by my hand.

I realize Leo is at the door, crashing into the room, the attendant he was flirting with beside him. The redheaded man screams and keeps shouting, "My prince!"

They freeze at the sight of us, bloody and ragged on the floor, surrounded by oil and glass and shadows. Leo grabs the attendant by the hand, but the boy wrenches himself free.

"Help!" the attendant shouts, then rushes out of the room before Leo can stop him. "She's killing the prince!"

"Wait!" Castian shouts.

But the young man is running down the corridor crying, "Guards! Guards!"

Leo shuts his eyes and hits the edge of the secret door. He squeezes the bridge of his nose, helplessness making his body slack. "You stupid, stupid girl. She told you not to. . . ."

Castian's eyes change. They're furrowed and dark and angry as the day I saw him in the woods. It's like he's two people in the same body.

"Renata Convida." Castian says my name, his voice like gravel in my wounds. So very different from the whimper of *please* moments ago. He takes off his belt and binds my wrists with it. "You are under arrest for treason and attempted murder of the prince of Puerto Leones."

I don't struggle as Prince Castian leads me down to the dungeons. There are only torches on the wall and the sound of guards far below. I can see his jawline ripple as he clenches his teeth, the vein in his neck pronounced in the firelight that moves across his face.

"It didn't have to be this way," Castian says in the darkness.

"It was only ever going to be this way," I say.

He turns me around, face twisted with rage, distorted by shadow and blood. "I have worked night and day for the betterment of this kingdom. Its people."

"You'll never be more than a killer, Matahermano."

His nostrils flare and his mouth is a taut line.

"You don't want to see what's right in front of you—" he says, but heavy footsteps echo from below.

"Your Highness," a guard says, brandishing a torch as he ascends the steps. "Your father sent me to take the prisoner to her cell."

"As you can see, I am already doing that. Dismissed."

"I cannot obey, Your Highness. The order came from your father. H-he w-wants to see you straightaway."

He doesn't move for what feels like ages, the flicker of fire burning through the torch. Then Prince Castian hands me over to the guard, who tightens the belt around my hands before grabbing the back of my shirt and pushing me along. My hands are numb, and a prickling sensation runs up and down my arm that has nothing to do with magic.

We get down to the cells. The stench of waste and rot hits my nose, making my head spin. The guard nervously twists the cylinder lock, messes up the first time and tries again. Even with my hands bound, he's afraid of me. This time, it feels good to be feared.

Finally, there's a click and the rusty groan of the door opening. He shoves me in. The floor is slick, and I fall on my side.

A soft, dark laugh comes from the corner. I push myself up, try to stand, but only manage to get to my knees.

A girl with matted blond hair and a purple eye swollen shut stands over me. I see past her cuts and welts. One open blue eye. A red dress. Margo.

"Get up, traitor," she says, and spits in my face. "I wasn't aiming for you, but I'm going to finish what I started."

25

"YOU DON'T UNDERSTAND," I SAY, PUSHING MYSELF UP TO MY FEET.

Margo is lighter than me, but she's clawed herself out of more scrapes than I can count. There's a fire burning within her. She needs to let it out. I can see it in the way she paces back and forth, sizing up my legs, the cut in my arm, the belt tying my hands together.

"I'm tired of trying to understand you," Margo says. She lashes out with her fists and pushes me. The floor is so slick I slip and hit my head on the dirty sack in the corner. "You're the reason we're here!"

I crawl to a stand. "You never tried. I've spent years listening to you telling me how worthless and untrustworthy I am." I get in her space, poking at her chest as she slaps my hands away. "But there is nothing you have ever said, nothing you could ever say, that would make me hate myself more than I already do. So yes. This is my fault. And yes, I was part of this, one of them, but I was a child, Margo. I don't want to be forgiven. Everything I've done since Dez saved me from this nightmare, and since I came back, has been to try to fix what I am, what I did. I'm trying to make this curse worthwhile! At least let me tell you what I've discovered."

She steps to me, and I snap back. But she isn't trying to hurt me. Instead, she undoes the belt around my hands. The buckle hits the floor with a heavy thud. Margo resumes her pacing, stopping every time she completes a full circle to grab the bars in the narrow window. There, she sticks her arm through and tries to fiddle with the cylinder lock, trying random codes.

"That's a one in a million," I say.

"But it's still a shot."

"Why did you come here, Margo? Where are the others?"

Margo lets the lock go and settles on the cold floor. She shivers, pressing her hands together and rubbing them for warmth.

"The others are waiting for me outside the capital. After we parted ways with you, we went to the safe house in the town of Galicia until we could come up with a plan."

"Why didn't you return to Ángeles?"

She rolls her eyes, and I flinch, noticing again the bloodied bruise covering her left eye almost completely. "Because after—after what happened, the inspections at the bridges and tollhouses were doubled. We needed to wait, but we were not alone."

"Who was there?"

"Half the Whispers. Mostly scavengers and cooks. After a week they began the night journey back to Ángeles. Esteban wanted to go to keep things in order, but we had to see this through."

"What do you mean, keep things in order?" I ask, though my chest is already tight with what she's going to say.

"Illan is a broken man. You wouldn't recognize him, wasting

away in his bed. It's as if he's lost the will to live. Nothing we say or do snaps him out of it. He mostly drinks broth when he remembers and drinks a fifth of aguardiente until he falls asleep, muttering things we cannot make sense of. He believes we're lost without Dez."

We remain silent, the unspoken thing between us so heavy that I also find my way down to the floor. The cold seeps through my hose, and I kick off my shoes. If we get out of here, they would fetch a good price, even as filthy as they are now.

"Without Dez—it's like everyone has lost all hope. They've only managed to get one ship of refugees to Luzou since that day. No one knows what to do. Where to go. All safe houses are compromised. Many won't even take us in anymore because of the pamphlets the justice released, Dez's picture with a red painted *X* over his face. The leader of the rebellion is dead. They circulated so quickly that Illan found out that way before we could tell him in person."

I try to picture Illan in the forest the night before everything went terribly wrong. The thrill in his old features. How clever he thought he was finding out about the weapon that controlled Moria—used them—destroyed their magics. I imagine picking up that flyer. Seeing the likeness of his son's face covered in what could be blood. The proud boy, the handsome boy who would charm the stars into shining in the middle of the day if he wanted to. The dead boy.

You were born serious, Dez told me, and I don't know why out of all the things he ever said to me, that's the one that keeps repeating in my thoughts when I least expect it.

I stare at my hands, one gloved, the other bare and more scarred than ever. These hands stole the lives of hundreds, including my own parents, but were rendered useless against Castian. How?

"How can they be finished?" I ask. "Illan is the one who sent us on the mission to find Celeste's alman stone. He's the reason we confirmed the weapon's existence in the first place!"

"Black protocol is still in effect across all the Whispers' channels," Margo tells me. "The Moria in hiding will stay hidden. There's nothing we can do. Not while the king and the justice have dispatched troops to all ports. Even if we wanted to sail to Luzou, or take our chances in the frozen Icelands, we can't. Ships are being searched top to bottom. Even the empress's ship. We are being chased to the ends of the world, and now we can't even turn to the sea."

I've never heard her sound so despondent, but I know I have to let her talk through this. I know when I've been the one like this, nothing anyone could say would make me feel better. After a long silence, I work up the nerve to speak.

"I haven't given up, Margo. You haven't either."

"I thought that. When we were in the market," Margo says, "we watched an olive vendor get arrested. All he was doing was resting with his cart on the corner of a street. I watched him beg for his life, but the guards simply rattled off what they usually say. That's what they're doing. Creating panic. It felt the same as the first King's Wrath. I've spent most of my life fighting, but the only time I ever felt that helpless was when my family was killed."

"How did you get into the palace?" I ask.

She looks with steady eyes that unnerve me. "A week ago. One of Illan's informants sent word they needed new entertainment for the festival night."

"You always were the best dancer." Weariness aches deep in my marrow, but I remember how beautiful she looked in her festival dress. Even if she didn't wear her true face. "Did you know the informant?"

"In a way." Margo shakes her head. "It was the Magpie, though they only communicated through messages of where to go and the songs the king preferred."

The Magpie who was supposed to help Dez escape. Someone with access to the prince, to the hidden places of the grounds, the court, the king. She has the freedom to come and go from the palace. *My dear husband let slip* . . . I breathe a sigh of certainty.

"What is it?"

"I've been here for weeks and I've just realized who the Magpie is."

Margo cocks her eyebrow. "Well, they knew you. Asked us to come help you."

"What?" Tears spring to my eyes. She knew all along. The shame of underestimating her hits me.

"Keep the spy's name to yourself. I would not trust myself not to betray it under the right circumstance."

She means torture. But I know that Margo would never reveal the name. Still, I will keep Nuria's secret.

"It was risky, using my magics," Margo continues, picking at a strand of hay in the mud. "But as long as the illusion is on me and not on others, it wouldn't have such a strong effect."

"That was reckless," I tell her. *That was something Dez would do.*

"That was the only thing I *could* do to put an end to this. That man is responsible for thousands of lives. His entire family has destroyed our homes, destroyed everything. Why does he get to live?" She juts an accusatory finger in my face, voice escalating. "Why did you save him?"

"Because anything you did would only befall the Moria tenfold. Even if I was killed immediately after. It would be worse for everyone else. The weapon would have been deployed before

I could find it. We were trained to think of the bigger picture, Margo."

Margo sits back. Shivers again. I wonder just how bad things have become to make her this rash, to act without thinking.

"What landed you down here after being the Moria hero?" she spits petulantly.

"I attacked Prince Castian. After Dez was executed—"

"Murdered," she says.

"After that, a prisoner gave me a memory. The prince was taunting Dez with what was in this box. I believed it was the weapon."

"Did you find it?"

I make a growling sound of frustration. "If I had, I wouldn't be here with you."

I think back to the move that caused me to slip up. I tried to steal Castian's memories. I felt his thoughts slipping into my mind, but then there was nothing. I couldn't break through those walls. How did he do it? I tremble from the cold and the anger of having Castian speak my name. *Nati.* How did he know that name?

"It must have been hard to focus on the weapon while living in the lap of luxury."

I meet her gaze. "Are you *serious*? I ate and I bathed and I smiled at the man who *took me* from my family when I was a child. I bled for the king who killed my parents. Could you have done the same?"

She turns away, but I don't let it drop. "Answer me, Margo!"

"Leave it alone, Renata," she snarls like a wolf.

"You've always hated me. I could never tell if it was because of what I am or because Dez chose me for the unit despite your protest."

She grabs a handful of dirt and throws it at me. "Do you think so little of me that I would hate you because of Dez? Dez was my unit leader. And the bravest of us all. You're *weak*, Renata. Consumed with your past, living in it and rejecting the people around you. That's why I hated you."

I'm breathing fast and hard, and I want to hit her, but her words weigh me down.

"You even managed to hurt *Sayida*, every time you chose to be alone rather than with the rest of us."

"The Whispers had no love for me, which you reminded me of daily," I respond, kneeling forward so she's forced to look at me.

Her voice is hard and jagged. "Illan disciplined every single person who hurt you. He even separated units to make life easier for *you*. I hated watching you act as if the fate of our world was yours alone to bear and the rest of us were simply there to torment you. You had to get the alman stone and *you* had to be the one to find the weapon. Have you even considered that if you trusted us we would have done the same? But *no*. Dez is dead. *You* should have been on that executioner's block. Not Dez. You, Renata."

I want to hit her. Scream at her until I'm blue in the face. Punch the wall because it won't hit me back but it'll still hurt. I want to tell her that I wish it had been me instead of Dez, too, but just then, footsteps echo down the corridor. In this end of the dungeon, the prisoners are not visited and somehow, I've already been here twice in my lifetime.

Just like that, we stop fighting with each other and focus on waiting for the guard to come to the door. We revert to our old unit hand signals because we still have to survive.

Margo presses her finger to her lips and points to the far wall, where I move so we cover the most space. If the guard is alone, we can take him. I want to say that we've been in worse situations, but this is the dungeons of the palace. It's the second-worst place to find yourself. The first is Soledad prison.

The steps drum closer, and through the small rectangular opening on the door, we can make out a hooded figure. I press myself against the wall waiting for the tumbling gears of the cylinder lock that never come. Instead, the rectangular latch on the door swings open and a bundle is pushed through. It hits the floor and the latch is pulled shut, locked, and the cloaked figure moves away down the corridor. I race to the door and grab the bars. There's only one person I can think of who might try to help me.

"Leo?" I call out. The footsteps stop for a moment. I want to say his name once more, but then he keeps going.

"What is it?" Margo asks, touching her foot to the cloth bundle.

I undo the tie and open it up. I've heard of weapons put together by the royal alchemists said to combust, but I doubt that the king would have us killed this way. Not when there's an Illusionári and a Robári missing from his Hand of Moria. The temptation to tame us, add us to his collection, toys for him to control, is far too sweet.

"It's food," I say.

I can hear the growl in Margo's stomach.

I arrange the meal on top of the thick cloth—a loaf of still-warm bread, a small wheel of goat cheese, sliced pieces of dried meat, a bundle of dark purple grapes, and a pot of honey.

"Eat," I tell her. She doesn't move. Her hands are balled in stubborn fists, but we've both known hunger and no matter where this food came from, she can't turn her nose up at it.

I take a couple of grapes for myself and the heel of the bread. I have no appetite, but I need to keep something in my stomach. I remember being on missions together, never knowing when our next meal would come. The taxmen at the tollhouses sometimes robbed us of our food when we passed the checkpoints.

When everything is gone, she tilts the pot of honey, pouring the last few droplets onto her tongue. She shakes the cloth open, but there isn't any more food. Only something metal that falls on the ground.

She holds up a small knife to me with a smile. "Supper and a weapon."

For a moment, I wonder if she means to use it on me. If I were her, I'd be tempted to. I'm no Persuári, but I can *feel* how deeply her anger toward me runs.

She tucks the blade into a hidden pocket on the inside of her dress. "It seems your Magpie has deep influence, Ren."

Even Nuria wouldn't risk coming down here. "No, I think it was my attendant, Leo. He was always kind to me. I wasn't sure if I could trust him because he was in Justice Méndez's service, but I do."

"Perhaps that was his job. To get you to trust him."

"Perhaps." I push myself up. "But then why give us the blade?" The cold has made my legs numb, and so I pace and pace, telling her about my time here, the search for the weapon. The prince must still have it. We can't fight back from this cell.

"Méndez won't be able to stay away for long," I say. I know him. He's going to try to teach me a lesson.

"Méndez," Margo says slowly. "Did he hurt you—before?"

I shake my head. "He has always treated me well. That's how he won me over as a child, and he thinks I am the same now. But I promise, Margo, I'll get you out of here even if I have to leave a wake of Hollows behind us. I swore I wouldn't become a monster. But that's what they want me to be, so I'm going to give them exactly what they're asking for."

"That's all we are to them, isn't it?" Margo asks, and I realize this is the longest we've ever talked without fighting. "Truce?"

It would be nice if we weren't locked up in this cell. "Truce."

After a while, the damp cold weakens me, and we gather on the cot. It has holes and the hay and dirt stuffed inside it is spilling out, but it's better than the floor. I fight sleep, but a moment later, it pulls me in, enveloping me in total darkness.

When I wake, I start to my feet.

"Margo!" I cry out for her, but her reply is muffled by the gag in her mouth. There's the rattle of chains as she puts up a fight.

Someone shoves a dirty rag in my mouth and then covers my face with a black cloth. I gag at the putrid smell of it. I kick and punch, but the guard is too strong. They shove my bare hand into a man's glove and clamp my wrists in irons.

I can feel my heart in my ears, pumping a warning that I can't heed because it's too late. This is how it ends, isn't it? In the dark, always in the dark.

"Sit her there," Justice Méndez says, his voice crisp and cold. "Put the other over there." The guard shoves me into a chair and ties each of my legs around the wooden posts. I rest my chained hands on my lap. My head covering smells like mold and rot. I wonder if someone died while wearing it.

"Shut your mouth," a man's voice shouts. There's a slick wet sound, and Margo lets out a muffled shriek. I've watched Margo undergo worse and never cry out. But now there's a whimper that hits me right in my heart. I shake my head, spitting the rag out.

"Let her go," I say, trying not to choke on the smell. "*I'm* the one who fooled you."

"I'll get to you, Renata." Méndez's voice is right in front of me. Even with my head covered I can smell his cool breath. "But for now, I'll give you the honor of choosing which one of your rebel friends gets to die first."

The sack is lifted off my head. Sweat blurs my vision, and my hair falls over my eyes. My unit comes into focus.

Sayida and Esteban are tied to the wall beside Margo. That's when I realize it wasn't Margo's whimper that I heard. It was Sayida's. Esteban seethes, his mouth biting hard around the cloth gagging his mouth. I let out a cry when I see his injuries. One of his eyes is swollen shut. Blood is crusted on his chin. His dark brown eye looks from me to Justice Méndez, and I see the moment his anger becomes hate.

"It was very clever of you," Méndez says, his stare settling on me. "Injuring yourself to save the king. When you returned, I so wanted to believe you were my Ren, come back to me. I let you wander around the palace to see if you'd expose the spy. But even Illan's informant didn't trust you enough to reveal themselves. You were alone as ever."

He walks up to me and each step rattles my insides. I turn my face to the side and bite down to keep myself from screaming.

"I am disappointed, Ren. We will work it out later. Right now, what I want to know is how you got your little friends into the palace." He grabs my chin, digs his fingers into my jaw.

I spit at him, and he lets go with a slap.

"You could have done great things, Renata. I was a fool to have believed you could return to me whole. You're a broken shell of the girl you once were. You'll never have a home with those who claim to be your people. They'll never trust you."

"You put me in a cage," I manage to say.

"And what did the Whispers do? You told me of their cruelty. We verified it with our Ventári. It seems to me you've only been moving from one prison to the next. At least here you know where you stand. With power. With loyalty."

Castian's voice breaks through my thoughts. *The Whispers taught you to fight well.* He has no place here right now.

"Do not pretend to care for me," I throw back at him.

His salt-gray eyes water, but he blinks it away. His lips pull back to accentuate every word he speaks. "I *protected* you when you lived here. You wanted for nothing. Do you remember how you screamed when they took you away from me? Do you remember how you cried out?"

My memories push against the Gray, color against the void, and I feel a well of tears prickle in my eyes.

A tiny girl lost in the woods was lifted onto a woman's shoulders and taken away. Please don't take me! Please! Papá!

I was that little girl. "I remember."

His features soften. Fingers caress the side of my face. Gray eyes harden like icebergs.

"And yet you chose them. You have cut me deeply, Renata." His calmness evaporates, and I jump from the loud bang as he flips over a small wooden table in rage. "You betrayed me! After everything I've done for you. I gave you a home twice over."

I writhe against my bonds, but the manacles are tight. "You gave a home to a weapon. That's all I ever was to—"

"And what do you think you were to the Whispers?" He chuckles, brushing his disheveled hair away from his eyes. "You were born to be a weapon, Renata. Tell me the Whispers see you as more? Tell me that you've felt at home in whatever hovel they decided to sleep in night after night?"

I catch Margo's blue eyes. Think of her words. That I was the one who rejected their friendship. There's some truth to that. But there's also my truth. I don't want to hurt anyone else. The only home I ever knew was with my parents. And with Dez. That alone is worth fighting for.

"Let them go," I say. "I'll be your weapon, but let them go."

"How noble, but I thought I made myself perfectly clear. I want you to choose. Choose who goes under the knife, Lina!"

Lina? Our predicament is momentarily forgotten in my confusion. All color drains from Méndez's face, and his fists clench as he catches his breath, as if he's seen a ghost. He wrenches his eyes from me and turns to a table against the wall, unfolds a leather roll full of knives and pliers in all shapes and sizes. He picks out a small knife with a serrated edge and a pearl handle. Méndez always loved beautiful things. Deadly things.

"Bring me the girl," he tells a guard. "The other one broke too easily."

Esteban shakes, and I see the effort it takes not to cry. The guard has been so silent in the corner of the room that she's almost become part of it. She clears her throat and asks, "Which one, my justice?"

"The Zaharian with the dark hair. The other one wouldn't last an hour with the way she looks." He polishes the blade, then sets it down. Picks up another, with a curved edge and holds it up, candlelight bounces off of it and around the room.

"Put me on the table," I plead.

"Leave us," Méndez tells the guards.

"But, my justice, they outnumber you," the man says.

"They can't use their cursed magics on me," Méndez says, and I wonder if he has the same defense that Prince Castian does.

When the guards leave, I scan the room for an escape. My hands are in manacles, which are infinitely harder to get out of. If only I had—

A blade.

The moment Méndez turns his attention to Sayida on the wooden slab, I reach to the side of my head and pull at one of the skinny pins that still dig into my scalp. *Thank you, Leo,* I think. I tuck it between my fingertips and angle it into the opening of the lock. I was never as good as Esteban at getting myself out of cuffs. Even now his eyes are wide with frustration, as if he knows he'd be able to do this better. Margo and Esteban struggle harder, shout through their bindings. It is the perfect distraction.

"You'll get your turn," Méndez says, pointing another clean knife at Margo. "You've made a fool and liar out of me in front of my king, Renata. That wretched brat of a prince has been looking for a chance to ruin me, and you may just have given it to him."

I remember Castian lying to his face after dancing with me. Reprimanding Méndez at the ball. Proud men bruise easily. That's a wound I can press.

"Do you know what Prince Castian calls you behind your back? An impotent, ineffective waste nearing the end of his use," I lie.

Méndez snaps his head in my direction, and I sit still. A crooked smile plays on his features. "I know you better than you know yourself, Renata. The prince would never confide in you."

"How are you so sure? He's the one who sought me out. He's the one who wanted to dance with me. You fear getting replaced? Well, you should fear a lot more than that when Castian is done with you."

Justice Méndez drags his finger across the table of weapons at his disposal. He selects a long, slender spike and a small mallet that goes along with it. My heart is in my throat, strangling my breath.

"Use the cure on me!" I plead as a last resort. "I know what it does. Use it on me, and let her go."

"The cure? By the angels, Renata, what do you think I was

doing when I left? The cure has to be better protected than by a weak prince and new draft of soldiers not yet old enough to grow beards. But if you're so eager, I'll make sure you get to see it firsthand."

"What?" My heart sinks. I was never going to find the weapon at the palace. But there is hope. There is always hope. Méndez wouldn't tell me where he went on his trip, but Lady Nuria did. The weapon is in Soledad.

"You're not the only Moria I've broken, Renata. We know how to get through your mountain pass now. Soon, the entire kingdom will be able to witness Memoria fall to its knees."

Margo's and Esteban's heads snap up.

The Whispers are in the mountain. The children, the elders, everyone who is left.

Méndez takes the bind out of Sayida's mouth and pulls it down. "This is for your own good, my child."

"You don't have to do this," Sayida says, and the sadness in her voice brings me such a deep ache I feel my heart coming undone. "There's good inside of you. You weren't always like this."

Use your power, Sayida, I mentally urge. Unless she already is, and there's no scrap of kindness left to draw out and play upon. But there *has* to be. Why else would he have been kind to me? To me . . . but not to other Moria.

Méndez holds the spike over her forearm. The mallet right over its head. "I know you want to think that, but your magics won't work on me."

He slams the mallet on the metal spike, and it drives through Sayida's forearm. Blood splatters across her cheek and on his face. Her scream pierces the deepest recesses of my mind. Sayida, whose smile could convince flowers to bloom. Sayida, whose touch could bring peace to the most troubled soul. The nightingale of the Whispers.

"Stop it! Stop it, please!" I shout. My hands are sweating so much I drop the hairpin. I have to focus. I have to somehow get free before he can hurt her again.

There's a moment of stillness as Méndez selects a second spike. Sayida has her head turned to the side. Her body shakes with sobs, and she tries her best to stay silent. I wish I could take her pain as my own.

"Now, dear," Méndez tells Sayida, and I can't imagine how anyone can be so calm while impaling another. "Who else is in the palace under Illan's order?"

Sayida shakes her head. "We acted alone."

"Are you sure about that?" Méndez readies the second spike on Sayida's other arm, and a single whimper escapes her. "We could save a lot of time if only you'd tell the truth. I want a list of all of Illan's spies and allies. It seems that you, Renata, were not very honest with me when you arrived here. Every safe house you gave me was a dead end. Empty."

"We don't know Illan's spies!" I shout at him. But my thoughts scream, *Nuria Nuria Nuria*, because I want him to stop. "He would never tell us. He'd never endanger them! But it doesn't matter to you, does it? Sayida could shout anyone's name, she'd shout Castian himself to get you to stop!"

The mallet slams down, and this time Sayida's shriek is so loud that it echoes long after she's done. My entire body has turned hot. My power sears across my skin, stronger than it's ever been. I can feel the light running patterns across my flesh as the metal around my hands grows hotter and hotter, fabric dissolving and stripping away. My screams join Sayida's.

I can feel the power burning through my skin and as the pain grows unbearable, I yank my hands apart as hard as I can. The red whorls carve across my flesh. Then I feel the sudden weight of my arms as the metal breaks free.

I freeze in shock. What did I do? I slowly look down at my tattered dress, the platinum still shimmering in the dim light. Bits of cloth and leather stick to my buzzing flesh. This is something new. Something dangerous.

I let the chains fall onto my lap so they don't rattle. I undo the ties around my legs with trembling fingers, but the chains slip and clatter to the stone floor. Méndez's head snaps to me.

"What are you—" He rushes toward me, but he's too late, I'm already free. He swings the mallet at my head, but I duck to the side. I hit the floor, then scramble and pick up the chair to throw at him. He uses the mallet as a weapon but cries out as the wood strikes his shoulder and his weapon slips out of his hands, falling with a resounding thud.

"Guards!" he shouts, but his eyes widen, because we both know the mistake he made in sending them away. Not even the guards like to stick around to hear the screams.

"I'm going to kill you," I tell him. My heart is a mangled, wretched thing and I want to blame him, I do.

"Your magics don't work on me." But even as he says it, it dawns on him that I'm wearing platinum, and there's a spark of doubt in his eyes as he backs away.

I am the thing that *everyone* fears. The creature in the shadows, the warning whispered on lips across the entire court and kingdom.

"You'll never be free, Renata. Not as long as you carry that curse with you."

"I stopped looking for freedom a long time ago," I say, my magics surging to my fingertips. "Do you know what I want now?"

"What?" He looks over his shoulder but there is nothing except a wall. His weapons are out of reach, and he's not a fighter. He never was.

"I want to be the Whisper that silences you," I say, reaching for his throat with my bare hand. My blood rushes to my head in an almost exhilarating way the moment I touch him, but he barrels into me, pushing us to the ground. I struggle to get ahold of him; his skin is slick with sweat and blood. I can't breathe with his knee in my abdomen. I take his hand and fight dirty. I bite so hard I taste blood as it breaks the skin. He cries out and crawls backward like a crab across a sandbar.

I close my hand around his and that rush returns. My power lights up, whorls all the way up my wrist. The heat beneath my skin burns away what's left of the silk.

"My Ren," Méndez whimpers.

A hard breath shudders through me. I want to claw out any weakness I feel toward him. I look at Sayida, and I know what I have to do. He shouts as my bare hand grips his face. My palms tighten around his jaw and I don't let go, my power coursing through my skin, driving its way through his mind, my fingers radiating a stronger light than I've ever seen before. I dig and dig, drawing out his memories one by one. They come to me quickly.

A young man standing in an empty cathedral staring up at the statue of the Father of Worlds.

Méndez fighting in the first war, before the King's Wrath.

Méndez holding the lifeless body of a woman in his arms.

Méndez running in a yard, his hands reaching for a little girl with dark hair. "Lina!" *he shouts. Her eyes dark as night with a laughter that echoes in his heart.*

Méndez weeping before a coffin so small he carried it in his own arms. Lina will never, *he thinks.* Lina will never . . .

Méndez taking the hand of another girl. "Renata," *he calls her.*

Then the memories spill too quickly for me to control, dark edges spilling into the center of my vision until there is gray and then total and complete darkness.

When I let go, I pull myself off Méndez. He lies completely still.

His body is alive. That's how it is at first. A shell of a person. Slowly, he'll fall into a deep sleep and never wake up. His body will starve until his heart gives out.

His salt-gray eyes stare at the ceiling. I shut my own as pinpricks of pain stab in my skull, the aftereffects of taking so many memories all at once. I stare at him for a long time. His eyes blink slowly, mouth slightly ajar.

A fate worse than death. Every memory. Every thought. The ability to make new ones. The name that sent fear into every person in Puerto Leones, Moria and not. Once the leader of the King's Wrath, the Arm of Justice, my captor.

Now a Hollow.

26

None of us look at Méndez, who lies slumped on the chair.

What remains of him.

I did this to him. *Méndez arrives home from the war. He tries to wash blood out of his hands but can't. "Papá!" A little girl calls to him.* I gasp as I break from his memory. The little girl looked like me, but I heard what he called her. *Lina.* Is that why he cared for me the way he did? I want to scream. I want to get his memories out of my head and give them back.

"I need bandages," Margo says frantically. Her shaking fingers are bloody as she wraps them around Sayida's wounds. Esteban stands at the door keeping watch.

"How did they find you out?" I ask him, peeling bits of glove satin from my skin.

Esteban peers out the door, satisfied when he sees a lack of guards. He digs into his pockets for a slender flask and twists it open. "They ambushed us. After Margo was captured, we hid in a tavern cellar. A kitchen servant saw us and called the guards. They thought we were thieves at first, but I was wearing my metals to try to reach other Ventári. We were brought to Méndez and he used his Ventári on us." He laughs at the irony. "On me."

"You should've left without me," Margo grumbles.

The most surprising yet is Sayida, who finds the strength to smile even as she trembles. "And miss this reunion?"

"I'm sorry I wasn't faster," I say, smoothing back her matted hair.

"No time for blame, Ren." Sayida sits up and winces as she cradles her arms against her chest. "Méndez was not lying. They know how to get through the pass and into our base."

"We go to the elders," Margo says at the same time I say, "We go to Soledad."

We stare at each other for a long moment, then Esteban puts his hands up. "First we need to get out of here."

"I need more cloth to make a sling," Margo says. She looks around the room and hesitates at Méndez's Hollow sitting unrestrained, unmoving, unresponsive in a chair. She unties his cravat and bandages it around Sayida's arms. "There. Now what do we do with him?"

"I've never seen a Hollow before," Esteban says, and I don't miss the fear in his voice. He stands in front of Méndez. This man who caused so much pain, this man who took me from my family, who acted like my savior. This man who ruined my life is a living ghost.

"It's almost too good for him, isn't it?" says Esteban.

Who am I to decide that?

"We have to get out of here before the guards come to check on us," Margo says, pillaging Méndez's knives. She decides on a simple dagger with an ivory handle. That one goes in her boot. The smaller one has a diamond shape with a star on the iron hilt. She keeps that one in her hand.

I shut my eyes against the onslaught of the Gray cracking open. There are so many memories crowding my mind that I can't figure out which are mine anymore. But I know that there's something important. Something I should remember. Something about the weapon. The smell of salt air, the roar of crashing waves . . .

"Will you be okay?" Sayida asks me.

"I'm trying to sort out my memories from his. He's seen the weapon."

"Let's get out of here first," Margo says. "Before your mind splits open."

She's right, I need to get myself together long enough to escape. I examine my hands. My skin is red; the grooves of the metal leave bruised ripples on my skin. I remove the torn gloves.

"Keep the rubies. We can bribe the taxmen on the way back to Ángeles," Esteban says.

I guide the Hollow Méndez to his feet. I stare into his stormy eyes. Unfocused. Empty. *Lina will never,* his voice whispers.

"Ren?"

I lift the hood of his robes low over his eyes. "Let's go."

As I watch Méndez walk in front of me, I swear to myself that I will atone for everything. I promise the Lady. For now, I give the Hollow a jostle between the shoulders and he keeps moving.

"It's like steering a wagon," Esteban mutters a few paces back.

Sayida hisses for silence, but even that echoes.

I have to hold Méndez around the arm to help him along. I've never made a Hollow willingly. When I was a child in the palace, I didn't see them afterward. Méndez was careful enough not to let me after the first time. I let out a shaky breath as I guide him.

I tell myself that he's killed hundreds, possibly thousands, in these dungeons. That he would have killed me. Sayida. My friends. Then why does seeing him like this make the vines around my heart twist just a little tighter? Maybe when I take everything from them, they take a little piece of me.

"Ren," Sayida says. "This is a dead end."

As if summoned by the fact that we have nowhere else to go, the sound of someone approaching echoes against the stones.

"There has to be a way out," I say. "I saw it. Dez once came here and—"

"And he never escaped." Margo takes out her stolen knives. "It's too late. We fight our way out."

A figure appears at the bottom of the stairwell. We're stuck. Then I realize who it is. "Margo, don't!"

Leo pulls his hood back, his green eyes catlike in the torchlight. His familiar smile is a welcome sight as he says, "Anywhere but the face."

"*You*," Margo says, lowering her stolen knife. She notices the cape, same as the one we saw earlier. "You brought us the food."

"I did secure—" he begins to say, but stops as I throw my arms around his neck. He stumbles back, caught off guard, though I'm just as surprised as he is. It was an instinctive reaction, one I had been waiting a lifetime to give. He tries to chuckle, like this is just another ordinary day in the palace and we're getting ready for supper or to spend the day with the lavanderas, but it isn't. It will never be again.

"I was worried about you," I whisper.

His hands soften against my back, then we let go. "So was I. The entire palace has gathered its attention on the safety of the prince. The king thinks Méndez is handling you, but that won't last long." His gaze shifts to take in the state of the justice. A question lights up his eyes. I expect him to shrink away from me. I expect disgust. Instead, I see understanding.

"Well, it seems you've been busy," he says. "I had planned to sneak you out the servants' exit, but it would be risky." He takes Méndez by the arm. "Without a justice."

Margo grabs Leo before he can lead Méndez down a corridor.

"While I want to thank you for everything you've done," Margo says, "I don't know if I can trust you."

"I can explain now and let ourselves be caught, or we can walk, but we can't do both," Leo says, glancing over his shoulder.

"I trust him," I say. "We can argue later, Margo."

Leo turns on the heel of his polished boot and leads the way. He grabs a few sets of shackles, rusted and thick, and hands them to each of us. Esteban balks at the idea of being at the complete mercy of Leo, and I understand his concern, but we don't have time to debate. I snap the shackles onto my wrists, trusting Leo with our lives.

Prisoners who are awake shout as we parade before their cells.

"We should free them," I say. Davida's face comes to mind. *Good heart. Protect us all.* "I have Méndez's master key."

"You can choose to save them," Leo says. "But you'll be sacrificing your own freedom."

I hesitate. Then, with shame, I nod and follow Leo away from the other prisoners, vowing to come back, with greater numbers. In time.

When we reach the exit of the dungeon, we're spat out into the courtyard. My back stiffens as I see guards posted along the perimeter, more than I'm used to. With Leo and Méndez in the lead, no one questions us. Though, if anyone looked closely, they'd see the vacant expression in Méndez's eyes and the tight grip that Leo has on his arm as he leads him down the hall.

Instead of heading toward the front gate, Leo loops around to the side, as if going to the gardens in the back. We stop at a thick metal door, so rusted I wonder if it will even open.

"Once you're outside the walls, go down the path for half a mile. It leads to the fish market," he says.

"My trust only extends as far as I can see, and I cannot see beyond this door," Margo remarks.

I open my mouth to defend him. He's had more than enough opportunities to report me, but Leo nods at her, shutting me up, then looks at me.

"I lied to you, Lady Ren. When we met, I told you I was a stage actor, but there was more."

We have to go. I know we do. But I need to hear this from him. "Tell me."

"I'm from Citadela Zahara. I was with the Bandolino Company, traveling the kingdom. My husband was a Persuári. After he was killed I stopped performing and found employ with Lady Nuria. When her marriage to the prince was canceled, I was reassigned to Justice Méndez. I saw an opportunity to get messages for my mistress. Justice Méndez trusted me. I'm no rebel or leader, but I do what I can."

The truth at last. We've danced around it enough times. I'm relieved that through all the confusion of the Gray, my memories, the politics of the palace, my instincts were correct: He was never one of them.

"I'm sorry about what happened to your husband," Sayida says in her gentle way.

"We won't get far once they notice we're gone," I say.

"You will if every guard is busy chasing after the other escaped prisoners." Leo holds out a hand for the master key. The skin-on-skin sensation startles me for a moment when I hand it over, but he doesn't even flinch.

You don't deserve his trust, a voice whispers at me from the bleeding Gray.

"Do you know where the weapon was moved to?" Margo asks in that demanding way of hers.

"No, but maybe Méndez's memories will help." He looks at me questioningly.

I shake my head. There are so many. It would be too hard to sort through them. "No need. I know where to go. It was Lady Nuria who told me."

Lady Nuria who gifted me this dress and told me a story she'd be jailed—maybe executed—for uttering out loud. The traitorous girl from Tresoros, daughter of queens. I bunch up my ruined dress stitched with platinum. I think of her warning to me during the queen's garden party. How she could try to help us and love Castian so much, I still don't understand.

"And we can trust her?" Esteban asks, his voice hoarse, like he's spent hours screaming.

"Yes. Lady Nuria is"—Margo nods sharply in understanding before I need to go on—"a friend."

Leo glances between us all and clears his throat. His features are grave, pleading almost. "Your secrecy is most important to my lady. It is the only way we can keep helping others."

We turn to Margo, who extends her hand to Leo. For a moment, my worlds feel settled, bridged together.

"Which reminds me." He reaches into his jacket and brings out a velvet pouch. "She can't leave the palace without raising suspicions. But here is a parting gift."

"Thank you, Leo. Thank her for me."

"Lady Renata," he says, and pulls me into an embrace. I breathe in his warmth, his laughter. He brought me back to life in a way I never expected anyone to. I owe him a debt and I promise to repay it. "I hope our paths cross again."

"I have faith they will."

"Thank you, Leo," Sayida says, hugging him, even with her injured arms.

"May the Lady shine bright on your path," Esteban says, and Margo shakes Leo's hand.

My feet won't budge because I am not ready to say goodbye to him.

"What will you do with Méndez?" I ask, buying time.

"I'll bring him back to his chambers. Someone will find him there. It should give you a head start."

As we leave the palace walls, I turn around just as he's about to lock the door.

"You're wrong, you know."

"It was bound to happen," he says, "but whatever about?"

"From where I'm standing, you look like a rebel to me."

27

THE FISH MARKET IS RANK WITH DRIED GUTS, AND SCALES GLISTEN ON THE street like winking mica in a mine. The merchants and mongers are just rising, brushing wooden tables down with lye water.

Cool dry air fills my lungs as we keep to the shadows. The day after the festival has left the streets of the capital reeking of wine, piss, and vomit.

At least we are not alone in our bedraggled states—late-night revelers leave cantinas and brothels that have not stopped the celebrations. The cathedral and palace are looming shadows over us all.

"We have to move quickly," Sayida says.

I shake my head. "Not on foot. We won't make it."

"What do you propose?" Margo asks, her head turned toward a rowdy street. Her fingers trace the hilt of her knife.

"Stay here," I tell them, and break into a run out of the market and in the direction of the very place we want to get away from.

With the guards in different levels of disarray, this is the best moment we have. The courtyards at both entrances are filled with coaches and wagons, all left unattended. As a Whisper, I've learned bits of all trades, but the one I've always loved has been spending time with horses.

Or stealing them, rather. I spot two restless stallions with shimmering brown coats attached to a closed carriage. It's modest enough, most likely belonging to a wealthy merchant or lord. When I approach, I see the Tresoros seal on the carriage—three mountain peaks with a sun at the center—and I know this is a stroke of luck. Lady Nuria won't report it stolen—I'm sure she's on our side.

I climb atop the coachman's seat, click my tongue, pull on the reins, and return to my unit.

They hop into the closed carriage and I jerk the reins, clicking my tongue again until the horses trot. I realize that no matter which way we go, we have to take the main road out. But that means retracing our steps from that awful day. The day that set all this in motion—the day I lost Dez.

As our stolen steeds trot out of the gate, I prepare myself for the bloody path that awaits me. King Fernando likes to display his victorious capture of treasonous rebels by lining the street with their severed heads on spikes. I am thankful that I am not up here alone. I am not ready to find Dez among them. Would I even recognize him at this point?

My heart stutters as a merchant and trade wagon passes us in the opposite direction, and the bloody path that was here two weeks ago is gone. It's now replaced by the flags of each provincia and major citadela, which line the road alongside the purple-and-gold flags of Puerto Leones. The carriage door swings open, and because I've slowed down so much, the others jump out and take in the view. Sayida climbs onto the empty seat beside me.

"They're all gone," I whisper as we trot down the empty road.

Sayida nods, cradling her injured arms against her chest. Black ribbons of hair come undone from the braided crown around her head. "For some time now."

"Why?" It's not that I want them there on display. But now all I can think about is what they did with them, the heads, Dez. Where is his final resting place?

"This is the main road. I suppose the king did not want to show our foreign visitors his cruelty. It is one thing to hear about the things our king does. It is another to see them. Now he can deny that he is the monster we call him."

When we get to the end of the road, I stop. Margo and Esteban climb out of the carriage again and the four of us squeeze up on the driver's seat.

"I'm going to kill him," I say. I have tasted blood once more, and now there is no going back.

"He does not deserve to take up space in your heart or mind," Sayida reminds me.

I want to say it doesn't matter, but as my blood rushes through me, I sit back and grip the reins. Esteban keeps an arm around Margo's waist. We're leaving the way we came, only a little worse for wear.

"I support the killing," Margo says. "But first—Leo didn't give you any food in that velvet pouch, did he?"

"I'd almost forgotten," I say. In the rush of getting out of the city, I left it in the cloak pocket. I fish out the small bag and empty the contents onto my palm. Jewelry in three kinds of metals glistens against my skin. Copper. Silver. Gold.

"Not edible," Esteban says, but takes the pure silver cuff etched with pinpricks of lightning.

"These are lovely." Sayida puts on the copper sun pendant. It falls just over her heart. There's a matching chain bracelet and small earrings, but she wants them to go to the elders.

"I suppose you have the whole platinum dress," Esteban tells me.

I laugh, and even that hurts.

Margo cautiously puts on five solid-gold rings; each one fits at a different joint, divided between both hands. She wiggles one hand and creates an illusion at the center of the road ahead of us. A boy we all love looks back at us. He smiles his cocky grin, and when he takes a step toward us, he vanishes.

We take a moment for Dez, but I know that we have to keep going. I have to keep going.

"What's this?" Esteban asks.

A slip of parchment sticks out from the pouch.

"Well? Speak, woman," Margo says.

In delicate handwriting is an address in Sól y Perla, a coastal city near Soledad prison, with heavy port traffic that goes to Luzou. I don't understand what it is at first. But then it dawns on me. An address—26 Calle Tritón.

"The Magpie's safe house," I say. "We need to go there."

"Ren," Margo says slowly, "I know we have to destroy the weapon. But you already tried going at it alone, and you failed. We tried doing this without you and failed. Let's go home, incendiary. We fight together."

This time, the name does not bother me. She's right. I did fail, but for the first time she admits that she failed, too. There are voices in my head that won't let me rest. Méndez. Castian. They tell me that I can't trust the Whispers.

But they're wrong.

"Let's ride," I say.

My stallions break into a gallop, and when we've made it up the sloping hill and past the rows of flags, we hear the distant warning bells singing. We're out of the city, we made it past the most dangerous part, we just need to go a bit farther. My shoulders relax. I'm surprised by our smooth getaway, thinking luck, or Our Lady, has finally smiled down upon us.

My mind is swirling with Méndez's memories. There are moments when he shows a guard kindness by giving him leave to be with his family. Then there are the moments when he enjoys cutting people, watching them bleed. Every time, I end up staring into his daughter's eyes. I can hear him say, *Lina will never. Lina will never.* Over and over again until it syncs with the rhythm of hooves and spinning wheels on the dirt roads.

I think of the soldier who stood in the house in Esmeraldas. He told me I didn't have the eyes of a killer. He was wrong. Wasn't he?

As we ride, plains give way to forest roads, and we do not stop. My hands cramp around the reins and my hips ache. My mind hurts worse, speeding through moment after moment of Méndez walking through halls. Drinking his sorrows, or praying them away. I search and search for a visual of the weapon. There is no doubt in my mind that he used it.

For a flash I see Castian at the Sun Festival. But my vision flickers as the memories shift. Colors bleed into one another.

I see my scar-covered hands being healed by Méndez. Then so much light, I have to close my eyes. Then a terrified, whimpering voice screams, *The pass is on the eastern ridge! The pass is on the eastern ridge!*

That was the weapon. That brightness was blinding. I pull on the reins and shout, "Whoa! Stop!"

"What is it?" Margo asks, sticking her head out of the carriage.

"Do you want the bad or the worse of it?"

Margo and the others pile out. Sayida touches her new pendant for comfort. Esteban holds his stomach and keeps his eyes on the ground.

"Speak, Ren," Margo says.

"I got a glimpse of the cure," I say. I describe it to them, but they're skeptical. "It might be Méndez staring into the sun, or Méndez looking into the throne made of alman stone. But I could feel Méndez's thrill as he shut his eyes against the light. There's a room beneath the palace that is full of the stone. Somehow, they're using alman stone in the weapon."

Esteban crouches down. He rests his hands on the dirt road, then brings his thumb over his torso to make the symbol of the Lady. "Perverting the sacred. Cruel, even for this king."

"What's worse than that?" Margo asks.

"Méndez was telling the truth. He knows about the pass in the mountain range," I say. "I could hear someone yelling it. They were being tortured."

"He couldn't have had time to send someone after us," Esteban says. "Could he?"

"Did you see the traitor?" Margo asks.

The coldness in her voice shocks me. Her golden curls spill over her tense shoulders. I know that somewhere something broke inside her, and I'm not sure if it was with me in the cells or watching Sayida get tortured. I look at where Esteban is nearly doubled over with pain. Fresh blood trickles from a cut near his swollen eye.

"No," I say. "I only heard the voice."

Margo shouts a string of curses as she climbs up to relieve me, and I climb into the carriage with Sayida and Esteban.

We ride, a storm that no one can see coming until it is too late.

We come to a complete halt on the main road that leads to the Memoria Mountains pass. At the border between Puerto Leones and the land given to us by treaty is a city of ruins. Ángeles. Stucco buildings with the roofs torn off, overgrown grass and white weeds that have started to reclaim the land. It is a place of ghosts. Beyond that, in the valley, are the cloisters we call home, safe within the protection of the mountain. The Leonesse forces could never pursue what was left of the Moria army beyond this road and into the mountains because they couldn't find out how to breach the natural fortress. What was once the capital of the small kingdom of Memoria is now crumbled houses and a castle with one wall standing.

We abandon the carriage and split up on two horses to get to the pass. The road is steep and dusty, with narrow footpaths that could mean our death if our horses get scared. The mountains have a way of making you feel turned around. Sprawling gray rock looks the same everywhere. I hold Sayida around the waist the entire time, closing my eyes against the flashes of Méndez's mind.

Castian and the king screaming in the middle of court.
Alessandro knocking over a tray of knives in a gray room.
Myself as a young girl.

When we make it, I could kiss the ground. The San Cristóbal cloisters are nestled at the center of a small valley, fully intact because of its location. Square sandstones with intricate circles, pillars with angels guarding the entrance. The entire western wall is dilapidated, but the rest of the building is fully functional.

Birds flutter from treetops and the wild green grass on the main lawn is absent of the usual groups studying, sparring, or playing the occasional game. We canter through the main archway and stop at a water fountain filled with murky rainwater.

This is the place I called home for the majority of my life, but as I stand here, coming back to what should be my safe haven, I'm suddenly filled with doubt.

The four of us linger a brief moment. I don't know how, but I can sense that we're thinking about Dez. He's a missing limb, a spirit haunting us all.

We unsaddle our horses, and Margo and Esteban lead the way, but I hesitate, immobilized by nerves. Sayida stays by my side, concern clear in her expression.

"The elders aren't going to listen to me," I tell her.

"I will support you," she says. "Swear it."

I squeeze her shoulder gently, thinking back to all the times she tried to provide comfort, and I brushed it away. This is my second chance with the Whispers. I'll do it differently this time, if they allow it.

With a deep breath, I follow the same path Margo and Esteban took. As we walk, I have that sense of remembrance. I am walking in the place I've called home for years but in the skin of another. It is like looking at these walls, the windows, all of it for the first and last time.

We march down an open corridor with chipped gray stone archways. My ears echo with the memory of my first meeting with the king.

We enter through a set of double doors, different from the ones of the throne room at the palace, but I can't shake the irony that I'm once again standing before an entryway, preparing to convince a leader of my worth.

Margo leads us into the council's hall, where they're already gathered. There are only five council members present out of the usual eight. I wonder if the others are dead or simply in hiding. My presence is greeted with cold reservation. I push back my shoulders with false confidence.

Truth be told, there is only one face I'm nervous about seeing. Illan's. My boot steps echo in the halls as the old man watches me approach from the center of the long table. He's in his familiar dark tunic and trousers, gripping his silver fox-head cane with a wrinkled hand. The lines around his eyes are far more pronounced. He is more ravaged by sorrow than by time. I take a deep breath.

"Illan, I've returned from the Palace of Andalucía."

"Back from your rebellion, or your betrayal?"

I flinch at the words. If he knew the whole truth, what I did to Dez by taking his memories in his sleep, would I even be allowed to set foot in this room?

"I went there for revenge and learned many things that I think will be useful to our cause, but the most important thing is a warning. I do not believe we're safe here anymore."

"Why not?" Elder Octavio, with his nearly blind eyes and wrinkled brown face, turns to me.

"Because I have turned Justice Méndez into a Hollow. I have seen his mind. He knows about the passage into the mountains."

There's a rumbling among the elders.

Margo steps forward, and they quiet. "We all heard him say it, and Renata saw it when she took his memories."

"I've seen the weapon. I know where to find it. We need to move out now. This minute."

"And leave the safety of the cloisters?" Octavio asks, incredulously.

Margo clears her throat. "Someone betrayed us. They told the justice about the hidden pass. The king's guard is coming for us."

"But you said Méndez is dead," Illan says, though his voice is distant.

"He's one of hundreds of judges," I say, frustrated. They aren't listening.

"There's a new safe house where we can take refuge. We can't stay here," Margo says.

It's a strange feeling being on the same side of an argument as her, but I am thankful for it.

"Tell us everything," Illan says. "From the beginning."

"There is no time," I say.

"How can you ask us to trust you if we do not know everything you have done?" Filipa asks.

When I glance around, there are rebel Moria gathered all around the walls and on the second floor of the hall, leaning over the wooden banister. Sayida stands close behind me, keeping her promise, but Margo and Esteban flank the rectangular table of the Whispers council. Daylight beams through the circular window facing me, and I realize I am not pleading for a mission. I am pleading my case at my trial.

I explain what happened in the Forest of Lynxes, when Prince Castian captured Dez. I explain about sleeping by the riverbank, how I was trying to calm Dez's sleep. There's a fury of whispers. I've been waiting for that blame. It is Illan who silences it with the beat of his cane on the stone floor. I tell them how I wanted revenge after seeing Dez die. When I describe Lozar's memory, I choke on my words. The elders' surprise shows on their faces. They didn't know Lozar was still alive, but were aware of other Moria in the cells.

I continue with my plot to spy in the palace, to go undercover and find the weapon. Everything I saw in the court. It is like baring my scars to them all, and despite the snarls or disinterested stares of others, this tightened, suffocating weight around my heart begins to come undone.

The elders are infuriatingly still until Illan leans forward, tenting his trembling fingers. "What do you want us to do, Renata?"

"Retain a small unit to find and destroy the weapon and retreat with what is left of the Whispers."

"Retreat?" Octavio asks sharply.

"What do you call what we've been doing?" I ask. "Puerto Leones isn't safe anymore. The king will amass his forces. He'll use the weapon. We won't be able to hide this time if he can detect our magics."

"He'll be weakened by the news of Méndez—"

"Prince Castian will have Méndez *replaced*!" I shout.

"I for one am not satisfied with what you gathered while frolicking around the palace," Filipa says.

"We have to leave," I shout, anger bubbling in my throat. I empty my pockets and set the rubies from the gloves on the table. "These will buy everyone passage to Luzou or the Icelands. Six Heavens, it would buy us a new ship! We have one final safe house. We have one last chance to save this rebellion."

"How are you going to board this ship and also get to the weapon, Renata?" Illan asks me, his eyes unwavering.

"I'm not going to board the ship. I'm staying to finish this. I request a unit to help me. As far as I'm concerned, it's a one-way mission, and I understand if you'd rather stay, but I'm going to finish what Dez started. What you started, Illan."

"I see," he says, his fingers shaking as he sits back into his chair. "We will take what you have told us into consideration. Wait outside for a moment."

"But—"

"Please, Ren," Illan says, and there's a weakness in his voice that tugs deep in my chest. He already looks defeated.

I storm out of the room and head for a place that reminds me of Dez. One of my own memories floods my mind as my feet carry me there. In the small grove behind the cloisters, there's a waterfall that empties out into a basin. This was Dez's favorite place in Ángeles. Illan used to say that his son must have been born part fish because he could spend hours swimming. I run there now because it feels like the only way I can be close to him, and I need him now more than ever.

"They would have listened to you." I speak to his memory and stare at the water for so long that I don't realize I'm not alone until a foot snaps a branch.

"I knew I'd find you here," Illan says. His voice reminds me of someone trying to carry a great, heavy load and running out of breath. "The last time Dez was here I had a fit trying to get him to put his clothes on."

I can't help what I do next, but in the middle of all this sorrow, all this confusion and anger, the image of Illan desperately trying to dress Dez makes me double over in laughter. These are the only muscles I haven't used in a long while, and it hurts to laugh this hard. "He always loved attention."

My laughter stops, my voice caught in my throat.

"I know what you meant to him, and what he meant to you. I saw it and I worried, but Dez was always in control of his own decisions, his own heart."

"I'm so sorry I took him away from you," I say. "I'm going to make this right. Please, you have to make the council listen."

"My dear Renata." I hate the way he says that because Méndez said it the same way. "That's what I came to tell you. The council has agreed to go through with your plan."

A part of me didn't believe that they would ever agree with anything that I had to say. "And the mission?"

"You already have volunteers." He stands, his body so slender it's like he's disappearing before my eyes. "There's something I want to show you before you go."

Tears spring to my eyes. I don't think I can store any more memories. My head is too full. My thoughts unruly.

"Good, because I have questions."

He only takes a few paces toward a willow tree that hangs low near the waterfall. With his cane he taps a polished stone I didn't notice before. It could be just another stone, but there's a name etched into it. *Andrés.*

I have so much I want to say. Why did Illan never tell us he knew Queen Penelope? What would he say if I ask him about the memory I found in the garden? But then my thoughts return to Dez. I want to tell Illan that I loved his son. I want to tell him that I'm going to make him proud. That I owe him my life. This fight isn't over. I'm going to end it.

But I can't say any of that.

Because screams spring from within the cloisters.

We're under attack.

28

"STAY BACK!" I SHOUT AT ILLAN. HE STARTS TO FOLLOW ME, BUT HE CLUTCHES his side and grimaces. He's grown too old for battle, I suddenly realize.

"Hide!" I scream. We have no time for all of my questions, still unasked—how he knew Queen Penelope—how he could tell what Dez meant to me—what other secrets are lying dormant in his past.

I watch as he limps toward the trees for just a moment, before I turn and run into the cloisters, where the purple uniforms of the king's men dot the courtyard. Blood splatters on the stone path ahead of me, bodies cut down without warning. The world has turned upside down. My stomach seizes and I resist the urge to retch.

I have to fight back.

"Ren!" I hear my name called through the fray, but I can't find the direction it's coming from. Then I notice the shadow behind me. I whirl around in time to see a soldier's sword slicing through the air.

Without thinking, I lunge forward, wrapping my bare hands around his throat. My magics rise to the surface as his scream pierces my eardrums. The platinum feels like a wave pushing against me. I don't fight against it, but sink into it. I take just enough to put the soldier in a light sleep. His memories are sharp, clear.

A boy learning how to wield a sword.
A girl waiting for him on the docks.

They slip like silver water through my fingers until I see pitch black, hear the whistles of solitude.

Panting, I steal his sword just as it's about to clatter to the ground and race up the stairs to the council hall.

Even in death Méndez kept his promise. Who did he break?

A soldier appears from behind a pillar. She screams through her fear as our swords clash. My blood runs as hot as lava, and I fight with an anger I've bottled up for nearly a decade. I am so close. I cannot end here.

I ram the sword through her throat. Warm blood sprays across my face and the acrid taste of it finds its way into my mouth. I turn and spit it out on the ground.

I run through the hall and open the double doors to the meeting room.

Fall to my knees.

Three of them are dead, but they took two soldiers with them. I make to move, when a cry catches me off guard.

In the corner of the room is Esteban.

He clutches a bottle of aguadulce and presses it against a wound in his belly. "I'm sorry," he tells me.

"Don't be sorry just yet," I say, pushing back my fear and trying to focus. "You're going to be fine. We need you, you hear me?"

Esteban releases a shuddering cry as I yank the bottle of drink from him. I knock back a swig, then pour it over the gash on his chest. It'll need stitches, but it isn't as deep as I'd feared. I think of the start of our journey. How he told me that there's a lot we don't know about each other. There have been moments when I hated him, but I've never wanted him hurt this way. I say a prayer to Our Lady of Shadows and find the cleanest cloth I can—a swatch of old stained tablecloth—and cut it in strips. After all these weeks being injured, I've nearly perfected the pressure on bandages.

"Stay here. I'll send survivors and a medicura," I say.

He squeezes my hand hard, like he's afraid to let go. "Ren, Ren, it was me."

Seeing him now makes the full memory unfurl. Esteban screaming after they caught him. They separated him from Sayida. Méndez cutting into the tender skin of his eyes and lips. *The other one broke too easily*, he'd said before he started on Sayida.

"I'm sorry," he sobs.

"I know," I tell him, and squeeze his hand in mine.

His good eye blinks away tears. "Why didn't you say anything?"

I shake my head. Because we've already had too much loss. Because no one could have sat under that knife without spilling their deepest and darkest secrets. And if they had no secrets to tell, they would simply make them up. They would say anything to make the pain stop. But I don't tell him any of that. I need him in good spirits.

"Because I need you alive," I say. "And we both know Margo would have kicked your ass."

We laugh and sob together. I have to make him laugh because if I don't give him a reason to keep living, he won't.

"Thank you," he says.

I pry his fingers off mine and race back outside. A group of fledglings are running this way and I guide them inside. "Barricade this door!"

Screams come from down in the courtyard. It'll take too much time to get back to the stairwell, so I hop onto the ledge, take a deep breath, and jump. I grab hold of a tree branch just within my reach. My sword clatters to the ground, but I swing myself down and break my fall into a roll. I misjudged my landing, and I'm face-to-face with a soldier. His dark eyes narrow on me, sword poised to kill.

Blood spews from his open mouth in a final cry as Margo comes up behind him, skewering him in one blow.

I release a hard breath. "Thank you," I say, and take the hand she offers.

Sweat runs down her brow and a bloody gash cuts her cheek-bone open. "Don't thank me. There's too many of them."

"I have an idea," I say. "Where's Sayida?"

"She can't fight. Her arms."

"She doesn't have to."

Margo's eyes light up when she realizes what I mean. For the first time, our thoughts are aligned. Together, we dash across the lawn to the other side of the cloisters. A dozen armed soldiers chase us across the green. There's a small chapel there, and as we get nearer, the doors swing open to let us in and shut quickly behind us.

Sayida, along with dozens of others, stanch their wounds and take inventory of the dead.

"We need to get as many soldiers as we can to stand down. Sayida, gather the Persuári," I say. "We're going to create a diversion."

"There's too many of them."

"Not for long," I say. "Do you still have the metals Lady Nuria gave us? Margo—"

"I know what to do. Yanes, Gregorio, Amina!" Margo rallies her fellow Illusionári. She takes off all the rings on her fingers, except one. Yanes, Grego, and Amina slide them on. For the younger Moria, precious metals are a luxury. I can see them call on their powers, the irises of their eyes sharpening.

With a wicked grin, Margo leads her small group back out to the lawn and whistles between her fingers. The Illusionári spread out. Moving as one, they mirror Margo's body language, pressing their hands against the air until it ripples around them like pebbles breaking the clearest surface water.

Six purple-clad soldiers advance, and Margo's foot trembles with anticipation as she waits for them to close ranks. A deep, thundering cry comes from around us. Four spotted lynxes as big as wolves charge forward with bared teeth and sharp claws digging into the air. Their fur gleams in the sun, and they spring, corralling the rest of the soldiers into the center of the lawn.

My stomach tightens with the aftereffects of their powerful Illusionári magics, but it's working. They're drawing the king's soldiers away from the others.

"Stand down," I say.

Half of them draw their swords.

Sayida and her three Persuári step onto the grass. She shuts her eyes, holds her palms up, and the others follow. This close together, they create a stream of undulating colors. They weave through the air like ribbons, streaming toward the king's soldiers, into their noses, their eyes, their ears. Sayida always tries to draw out the good in people and so those who did not draw their swords fall to their knees. I think of the guard in Esmeraldas, when Dez made him give up his weapon. Some of the soldiers stand down. A few run.

"Stand down!" I shout again at the remaining soldiers.

They don't.

"We fight," Margo says, drawing her short sword. Her unit follows.

We are a fury of metal and bloody fists. Bone ripping through knuckles, the tender skin of lips tearing in half. I shake with the violence that is a living thing inside me. I slip into that rage the way memories slip through my fingers, and as I stand over a fallen soldier, her dark eyes fluttering as my fingers dig into her temples, I know that this anger will be the end of me one day.

It is a cacophony of voices—Méndez, Lozar, Dez—countless others whose names I don't know.

With my heart on my lips, I let go of the soldier.

She blinks, staring around the lawn. She's survived.

But we've won.

We gather the dead soldiers and dead Whispers in the courtyard. The Whispers still living scream in agony. A Moria woman weeps as she carries a young boy in her arms. She lays him down among the others.

"On your word, Commander," a Persuári named Victor addresses Margo.

For a moment, Margo's blue stare falls on me. I see the moment she steels herself, her arms behind her back in the same posture that Dez always took when faced with an impossible task, as if commanding his body to listen to him, to stay still.

"You." She points to the woman I spared. The soldier sways on her knees.

"Tell your king what has happened here. Tell him that we will not fall. Not now, not ever. The Whispers are alive and together— we make a thunderous voice. Do you understand me?"

She nods rapidly, tears streaming down her face when she looks to the three soldiers who refused to surrender. No one speaks of mercy. Not when the numbers are on their side.

Margo turns to the three, who are silent in their bindings. A part of me wants to stop this. We should be better than the crown. But I have witnessed too much pain. Too much death. We did not start this violence, but we will finish it.

"A life for a life," Margo commands. "Your king owes us thousands."

I shut my eyes and hear a series of blades slice across flesh.

When it's over, there is a line of red where the dead soldiers have fallen across the green field.

In the distance, the soldier Margo set free is a purple dot running south, back to the capital to deliver our message.

For a long time, we stand in utter silence. Barely two dozen of us, lingering like ghosts across a field of horror. Not even the wind howls through the mountains.

Then a young girl runs up to me. She tugs at my hand and her cry drives like steel into my core. "Come quick! It's Illan."

Illan lies beside the willow tree where Dez's headstone is marked. He's alive, thank the Mother of All, but there's a dagger driven through his rib cage, his own fingers covered in blood as he tries to stop the bleeding. A young soldier is facedown beside him with a crack on his forehead. A silver fox head split from its cane.

"No." The cry trembles through me as I crouch beside him, pressing my palm over the knife wound in his stomach.

I know I should say more. I owe him my life. I owe him—

"Renata. I must show you this before I go. . . ." Illan takes my hand in his and rests it over a heart that struggles to beat.

I remember his face eight years ago, eyes fierce with rebellion. Hope. He carried me out of the palace himself, and I thrashed and screamed in his arms because I didn't want to go, didn't know he was saving me. He changed my life forever.

"Sayida!" I shout even as I'm already surrounded. "De—" I catch his name on my lips. It feels wrong that he's not here, not by his father's side.

"Please," Illan whispers. His throat makes a gurgling sound. Blood filling his chest, his throat. He guides my bloody hand to his forehead, and when my slick fingers make contact, I know what he wants me to do.

Tears slide down my cheeks, my fingertips glow, as I send a pulse of magic to retrieve the memory he offers.

Queen Penelope is going to change her mind. He can see it in the way she paces the reading room, her golden hair hazy in the sun, like a halo. The hatch under the rug is still open, and dust clings to his hair and clothes.

"Your Majesty," he begins, but she cuts him off.

"No, you do not get to placate me," she says, settling fierce blue eyes on him.

"I only mean to remind you that this is how we end the bloodshed. The king must have a single heir. An heir

he can trust, he can mold. An heir he thinks will carry on his legacy. But you will be there, by the prince's side, keeping his heart full. Our next king must have a full heart."

Queen Penelope takes a deep breath. The daughter of old kings, her bloodline tied to this earth. She lifts her golden circlet and places it on her regal head. "I promised my father we would end this war."

"We will meet by the river at sunset." Illan grabs her hands and climbs back down the hidden stairwell.

"What if the child will not come?" Celeste asks. Disguised in common servant clothes, the spy twists her copper ring, the only sign that she is nervous.

"He will. You've mastered the art of turning emotion into color. No child could resist."

Celeste nods and marches into the wood, where the golden-haired prince sits at the bank of the river. He can't be more than four, but his entire childhood will be gone after today. The prince throws stone after stone while a smaller boy cries beside him.

"Shhh, Mamá is on her way back," the prince says. The second boy tries to crawl away.

"Hello, young one," Celeste says.

Prince Castian looks up from the baby. "Who are you?"

"I am a sorceress." Celeste waves her fingers in the air. She pulls at the boy's feeling of wonder, bright blues and greens swirling all around. "The most powerful in the land."

The prince's eyes widen. "Can you teach me?"

Celeste nods. "But you know what the king's rules about magics are. You must not tell a soul. Do we have an agreement?"

Castian steps forward and holds out his tiny hand. "Wait. I have to watch my brother until my mother returns."

Celeste glances up and sees the queen watching from afar, concealing herself behind thick oak trees, profound grief already etched across her face. "The child will be safe and sound in the basket. Or do you not wish to learn?"

The prince has doubts, but his curiosity wins, and he follows Celeste into the thicket of trees, chasing the colorful ribbons in the air. His small fingers try to grab hold of them, but he can't. She uses that innocence, that wonder, and lulls him into a transfixed state.

It is in that moment that Illan must do his part. He breaks for the second boy and lifts him into his arms. He throws a bundle into the river, then hurries through the forest, this life pressed against his chest.

He pauses for a moment, then looks back to the shore. The queen's cry rings out, true and broken, never to see her second son again. The blankets bob in the rushing waters. Celeste vanishes into the forest. The prince weeps as he watches his mother break apart.

"What have you done?" the queen shouts over and over. The prince would never know she wasn't shouting at him, but at herself.

Illan can't stomach the scene, knowing the pain he's caused, despite the desperate reason. He broke the queen's

heart, took half of it away from her, and carried the miss-
ing piece into the forest, never to look back again.

When I pull away, Illan is no longer breathing. His eyes stare at the sky, mouth slightly ajar with a trickle of blood flowing from each corner.

"Illan," I say. I shake him, my fingers wet with blood and still trembling at the memory he just showed me.

"He's gone, Ren," Sayida whispers beside me.

I know it. And yet, I cannot move. No one can.

I'm momentarily paralyzed by grief, and speechless in my confusion. Prince Castian didn't murder his brother. Illan took him. To what end? I know what this means, but I can't face it. I think of the memory I stole from the garden, the secret rendezvous between Illan and Queen Penelope. Illan said it was to save their lives. From who, the king? Illan said they needed to give the king a reason to trust the prince, someone to mold in his own image. And what better way to mirror such a tyrant than a boy who murdered his own brother.

I'm overcome with disgust, shock, sadness. All I want to do is run as far away as possible, but I'll never be able to outrun what lives inside me. The truths I don't want to face.

I remember the rest of the Whispers now around me. Unaware of what I've become witness to, only focused on the loss of their leader. So I stand, and together, we work silently, building a massive pyre to burn our dead. A few of the older Moria, the ones who have done this time and time again, sing old funeral songs, their voices haunting as they echo in the courtyard. I know these songs, but they are only familiar because they are sung in my memories. I wonder if my mother ever sang them to me.

Night falls by the time we're finished, and Margo comes up beside me, a torch in her hand. She throws it at the grave, and we inhale the oil and smoke.

"We can't linger," I say. "We have to leave as soon as possible."

"I know," Margo answers. "By the light of Our Lady—"

"We carry on."

29

We travel under the cover of dark. Margo and I double back for the carriage and make sure the roads are clear. There is but one elder left, and three dozen Whispers, mostly fledglings too young to fight. Still, we manage to turn a two-day trip into one, and with luck on our side, we arrive at the port town of Sól y Perla near midnight. Here, there is very little presence of the royal guards, and scores of traders swarm in a night market illuminated by large oil lamps, drunken men and women from all over stumbling in and out of cantinas.

While Sayida heads off to do some trading at the harbor, Margo and I scout ahead. The others wait in our stolen carriage. The beach home facing the sea is pitch-black. Not a single light within. The sea breeze is calming here, the boardwalk clear of foot traffic. The house is mostly empty, with just basic furnishings and simple rooms. There's a cellar stocked with bags of rice and jars of salted fish. We might be able to pull this off.

"I'll go get the others," Margo says.

"Hold on." I stand back and wait for her to turn to me. "You were right."

"We don't have time for this, Ren."

"It's only a moment, but it's important. I wanted to tell you that you were right. About the way that I push myself into loneliness. It didn't make sense to me until Méndez said all those things."

"That man should have no place in your heart," she reminds me.

"And yet everything he was is in here." I press my finger to my temple.

Margo sighs. The wind blows the loose strands of her golden hair. "You've gotten through this before. You can do it again."

She leaves me. I inhale the scent of the sea to prepare. I am thankful for the reprieve, as Méndez's memories surround me. When I close my eyes, I see my Robári hands, and Justice Méndez wrapping them in gauze. It was never a father's touch. His gentle hands were moved by the fear of someone who had too much to lose.

One by one, the surviving Whispers file into the abandoned house. Because all the elders but Filipa are dead, she's appointed Margo, Sayida, and a Persuári named Tomás as the highest-ranking members of the Whispers. Everyone has a task—to arrange beds, to make food, to prepare weapons, to be ready to leave as soon as we are able.

Sayida and Tomás haven't returned from their task to trade the rubies for passage on a ship. I shut the door to a washroom and clean my face. Everything hurts in a way I didn't think possible. I strip off my clothes and clean myself, re-dress my wounds. Lady Nuria's lovely gift is ruined, but I salvage as much of the platinum wire and stars as I can. I braid a few strands into two bracelets, then spool the rest and tuck it into a small leather pouch I strap to my belt. When that's done, I braid my hair in a plain plait down my back. What would Leo say if he saw me putting on riding trousers and a rough-spun tunic with holes in it? *At least it's clean?*

I'm scooping more water in my hands, trying to get the muck out from under my nails, when my ears ring, making way for a memory to barrel into me. Méndez's voice is clear as a bell. The slippery memory of him staring at the sea solidifies, ready to be seen.

Justice Méndez reaches the top of the tower, breathing in the salty air as he waits for the guards to open the door. He rushes inside, anxious to test out his new toy.

A frail man, skin the color of ash, rocks back and forth in the corner of the cell. Dull glowing veins stretch down his face, his torso.

"Cebrián, come here," Justice Méndez orders.

The man won't respond. Justice Méndez expected as much. "Bring her in."

Lucia is dragged in, gagged and fighting tooth and nail as they shove her into the cell.

Justice Méndez tries again. "Cebrián, I brought you a gift. She is the first to heal."

Cebrián stops rocking, but doesn't acknowledge the people in the room. Justice Méndez closes the distance to the girl, removing the gag from her mouth.

She shakes in the cold room and asks, "What did you do to me?"

"Use your magics. Look into my mind. If you can tell me what I plan, then I'll let you go."

Lucia eyes the room between each sharp breath. Justice Méndez extends his hand, his thin fingers like a fallen autumn branch. "If you choose not to, you'll remain a prisoner of Soledad until the day you die."

He watches Lucia weigh her options, clearly knowing this is a trick. He keeps his expression neutral, not wanting to scare her off yet.

She grabs his hand and closes her eyes. He feels the probing of her foul magics.

Cebrián's head pops up. Silver eyes and a terrifying smile spreading across his face.

Lucia gasps, jumping back, and drops Méndez's hand. "You can't! You have to let me go!"

He steps back, as do the guards. "A promise is a promise."

Lucia runs to the door, but Cebrián beats her there, his speed and agility inhuman. Before she can utter a scream he is upon her, hands tight around her neck. Her body convulses, color draining by the second. Her skin turns nearly translucent. New veins, pulsing with a faint glow, begin to appear, tracing a path up her arms, her legs. . . .

Justice Méndez is thrilled at the progress.

The door to the cell bursts open. "Stop this."

Justice Méndez turns to face the intruder. Spoiled, wretched prince.

Prince Castian. His eyes are wild. He points a finger at Méndez. "I am ordering you to stop this immediately."

Justice Méndez burns with irritation at the prince,

who remains a constant thorn in his side. Turning slowly, unhurried, he waves a hand at his creation.

"That's enough, Cebrián, you'll drain her dry. Remember, you can't control magic that isn't there. I won't have repeats of the others."

Castian crosses the room to Méndez. Cebrián pulls out a crude weapon hidden in his tunic. He jams the sharp point into the prince's shoulder.

I can't move. Lucia was still alive? How did she recover? Then it hits me. The new Ventári *was* Lucia, and I saw right past her.

"No," I say. I say it over and over again because it can't be.

I step out of the washroom and grab a cloak. Rush through the crowded house and out back to the patio. Here in the port everything smells of the sea and I breathe deep as if I could scrub myself clean from the inside.

A troubling thought digs at the story I've built for myself. Castian stopped the experiment. Castian had a shoulder injury at the ball. The man had stabbed him. That was why Castian had circled Soledad on his map. Why Méndez and Castian had been gone from the palace at the same time. They'd been together. But what is the prince playing at?

The weapon was never in the wooden box Prince Castian had in his secret study and it isn't the alman stone in the vault.

You don't want to see what's right in front of you.

Right in front of me. I look down at my hands. The memory of Méndez healing scarred hands wasn't about me. It was that man— that Cebrián.

Because it is not an object at all.

The weapon is a person.

A Robári like me. It's like a living, breathing alman stone. I think of what he did to Lucia. He drained her power, like a memory, twice. The light that emitted from him was brilliant, a ray of light, a beam of alman stone. Somehow, the justice used alman stone to alter the Robári's magics.

I'm going to be sick.

I take several steps to the fence and cough up my meal and when all that's left is acid and bile, I heave. I go to the well and fumble in the dark to bring up a bucket of water. I drink until my mouth stops feeling so dry. I have to tell Margo and Elder Filipa.

When I take a step back into the house, I know that I can't. If they know that the justice can turn memory thieves into magic thieves, that will only prove that I am as dangerous as they think I am.

You were born to be a weapon, Méndez told me.

I didn't want to hear those words because he was right. That's all I'll ever be to anyone. My parents. Friends and neighbors. Dez.

I look up at the house and the people who are eagerly awaiting a new life. A ship that will help them regroup. I can't take that hope away from them. There is one thing I am good at, better at than stealing memories, better at than hurting the people I love—and that's being alone.

I lift the hood of my cloak and sidestep the house, making my way down the narrow alley that leads back to the boardwalk.

"Where do you think you're going?" Sayida asks, appearing from nowhere like a figure out of the Gray. Her eyes are dark as coal, and the smile leaves her face when she realizes what I'm doing.

"How long have you been there?" I ask.

"Not long. Despite my injuries, I could feel your anguish, Ren. This metal Nuria gave us is strong." Sayida holds out her forearms wrapped in fresh gauze and linen.

"Good. How are you?"

"Better after Filipa's tonic for the pain," she says. "You should know we got the ship. It leaves in two days' time."

I turn to the house. The lights dim enough that they won't cause attention. "Go inside. Tell them."

"Why do you do this, Ren?" She tries to grab my hand, but I don't let her.

"Don't use your power on me."

She winces and rests her hands at her sides. "I'm not! I'm worried about you."

"You don't understand what's happening."

"Then tell me! Ren, I've trusted you with my life. You're the closest thing I have to a sister, and no matter how much I try to be there for you, you push me away."

My eyes sting with salt and anger. "This isn't something that you can understand."

"Let me try."

I shake my head and pull the cloak tighter over my head. "Your powers allow you to feel what others do and to give them comfort. Or push them to action. They don't erase people's lives. They don't take and destroy."

"You're wrong. I could also give them pain," she says. "Don't forget that. We choose what we do with these gifts. That's what we've always been taught. The same way the magicless can kill with their swords and poisons, with their bare hands if they choose to. I have seen you take away trauma from people so they can sleep better at night. Don't you see? You decide who you're going to be. You take someone else's pain into yourself. Even when you're taking, you're leaving something good behind."

"The Hollows outweigh any good I've done. You don't know what I've seen—I tried to put everything in the darkest corners of my mind. But there is no escaping what is in here. I can't dream. I can't conjure Dez's face without dragging another memory along for the ride. There are so many pasts in here that I don't get to have my own. I *shouldn't* get to have my own!"

She walks up to me, and this time I can't fight against her sympathy, her warmth, which I hate and love all at once. She pushes back my cloak, and the sea breeze is cool against the wetness on my face.

"You were a *child,* Ren. You didn't do anything wrong. I blame the damned Whispers. We should have treated you better. We should have been kinder to you." She takes a deep breath to settle her anger. "What are you now?"

"A soldier." The answer is instinctive. Something I feel like I *should* say.

"Yes, but you're more than that. You're not a child anymore. It's time to stop letting the world define who or what you are. You are the girl who has always wanted to prove herself. To best everyone else. To show that she could carry her weight. You are the girl who saved me from a man who would have tortured me for days. You were willing to trade places with me. Why can't you see that girl?"

"Because—" The words are on the tip of my tongue. I see it now. More clearly than I ever have before. I don't know if it's the fresh air, or the magics that Sayida weaves with just her presence. But I see myself. Not as a single person but as hundreds, thousands of fractures, like a mirror with so many cracks spreading from the center that it can't reflect a whole image. "Because I have more stolen memories than ones of my own making. Because I have lived hundreds of stolen lives, and I'm afraid to live my own."

Who *is* Renata Convida?

"I don't know who I am, Sayida. Not truly. It's like who I am is trapped beneath the tragedies that belong to everyone else. There's only one way I'll be free of this."

She rests her hand on my face and in this moment, I am thankful

I didn't get far from this house. "Then maybe, before you can do anything else, you have to let her out."

"What do you mean?"

"I can help you try again." She holds her hand out for me to take.

When I take it, the warmth of her magics trail along my skin, and my own memories begin to flood in, bright and colorful, but the suffocation I usually feel is gone. The fear, the guilt, the darkness, at last, are cracking open, making space for me to breathe. I want to weep with the relief of it.

And so, tentatively, delicately, I wade forward, and the first memory that comes to mind is falling asleep in my father's arms in front of the fireplace.

That's quickly overpowered by the heat of a fire. *All burning villages smell the same.* Leonesse scream as the king's men set fire to houses, trying to smoke out the Moria from their homes and into the streets to be captured. My lungs tighten.

"Focus," Sayida whispers, and sends another push of magics through me.

I close my eyes, but my thoughts are jumbled. I see thousands of strangers. I walk hundreds of paths across the country, across the sea.

"Ren." Her voice is a susurration, a kiss on my temples.

My head aches, as if I'm carving deeply into it, prying open bone to delve into the core of my mind. I remember being six years old, new to the palace. Justice Méndez handing out stellitas like they were gold pesos every time I told him a "story." The stories always came after I stole the memory of captured Moria, prisoners who scared me with their tear-reddened eyes. But I knew, I *knew* that every memory came with a reward. The memory changes, and then I'm in my favorite place in the palace, in that library. There was a couch in front of the tallest window I'd ever seen. Deep in the distance, where I knew my home village was, there was a great fire that consumed every part of it.

Those memories are the things that define me. They made me into who I am.

You were born serious. Dez's face comes to mind. His honey eyes linger on my lips, always. But no, I was not born serious. I was made that way.

The memories unfold faster now. Within the palace there was a long blue hallway. When the justice was too busy and my attendant fell asleep, I wandered around. Large statues decorated halls vaster than any home I'd ever been in. There was a study with a boy in clothes dirty from chores. He was always alone, playing with dice. He'd roll them onto the floor, and then they'd vanish. Then he'd cup his hands over them and make them reappear. It was the simplest magic. It was the first time I was around other Moria children who were not my family. I didn't even know how many kinds of magics we possessed.

After a while, the boy disappeared, like so many of the others. Then one day, the Whispers came and I was gone.

Even now, I can hear the rattle of the dice, like great echoes in my thoughts. A trick of the mind. All of it was a trick, wasn't it? Simple. Easy. Unfair.

I see that girl unwrapping sweets in the library, staring at the fire that killed her parents. I see that girl, and I wish I could hold her and tell her that she couldn't have known. That no one taught her better, that no one was there to protect her.

When I open my eyes, Sayida and I are bathed in a white light. White like that Robári's eyes—the one they made into a weapon to use against us. And I know that no matter what they think I might be capable of, I have to tell everyone what I know about this weapon, about what they've done to Cebrián.

"Thank you," I tell Sayida, looking deeply into her warm dark eyes. "There's something I have to do."

Hand in hand, we go back into the house and call a meeting in the main room. The Whispers gather around me again. Margo and Elder Filipa watch me carefully.

I tell them everything I know. How they experimented on Moria like Lucia and she is likely lost. About the weapon, the Robári, and what the justice has done to him.

"We have to get Cebrián back. I don't know if we can reverse what's been done to him, but at least we can get him away from the new justice, whoever that might be. Take away their precious weapon before they learn how to make more of them. Before he was killed, Illan said there were volunteers for the mission. I'm asking you now to trust me."

Elder Filipa holds a hand up to silence me, and all of my hope that they'd listen evaporates. "You've done well, Renata."

I lean in, because I don't think I've heard her correctly. Filipa never smiles, but her mouth quirks. "Thank you."

"You're the reason why we can keep the Whispers alive. Are you ready to do what comes next?"

Ever since I understood my past and what I was responsible for, I've wanted to figure out a way to fix it. Dez told me that I did belong, and that no one thought of me differently. But he was wrong. This is how I get a clean slate.

"I am," I say.

Filipa looks to Margo, then to me. "Tonight you will lead a group of three to retrieve this poor soul before the king can do any more damage. We have to save him. Amina, Tomás, you will accompany Renata."

"I won't fail you," I say, taking Filipa's hand. Even though she flinches, she does not let go.

Her eyes are cold, and I tell myself that this is because of everything that has happened. Everything we've lost. She narrows her gaze. "Make sure that you don't."

30

THE OTHERS RUMMAGE THROUGH THE HOUSE UNTIL WE FIND CLOTHES THAT make us appear like nobles. I wear a simple tunic dress over trousers and leather boots. Once ready, the four of us take the Tresoros carriage along the rocky path that lines the eastern coast of Sól y Perla.

Margo and I sit on one side of the carriage, Amina and Tomás opposite us. It is strange to be part of a unit again, albeit a group of Whispers I'm not as used to. I draw back the curtain to watch Soledad loom in the distance. It is built in the old Moria style, all pointed arches with large winged beasts perched along the rooftops. It's high up on a hill where a cliff cuts cleanly down to a roiling, restless sea.

"Did you know that the first documented references to angels were in the Song of Our Lady of Shadows?" Amina remarks. As

Elder Octavio's apprentice, she read as many texts as she could on the history of the Moria and Puerto Leones. Whatever hadn't been burned by the king, at least. "About a hundred years ago, King Fernando's grandfather changed them into demons, and turned angels into those fat childlike creatures the justices like to paint on their ceilings."

Margo reaches over me and closes the curtain. "Enough. This is our first mission as a unit. We have to remain calm."

"We are calm," Amina says, tying and retying the knot of her hair. "As calm as we can be rushing into a prison no one has ever escaped."

I tug on my tunic, restless. "Go over the plan once more."

"Tomás will stay with the carriage," Amina says. "While Margo and I clear a path to the south entrance."

"I'll take the north side," I say.

"We meet in the center courtyard. From there, Gabriel said there's a stairwell with a metal sun that marks the door to the high tower where the justices keep maximum-security prisoners."

"Simple enough," Amina says.

Margo shoots her a glare that could petrify. I know Margo, and I can tell she wants to remind the young Illusionári that she hasn't seen the number of hours in the field that we have, hasn't seen first-hand the way even the most straightforward of plans can go terribly awry, but now is not the time, and despite Margo's courage, she's sweating as much as the rest of us.

I won't fail you.

Make sure that you don't.

It's taken a full day's ride to reach Soledad.

I peek out the window. For a prison, there aren't as many guards as I thought there'd be. We are still outnumbered, but we are not ordinary soldiers. We are Moria.

Tomás pulls the carriage to the side of the road, in plain sight behind two others. One of them looks like it must've come from the palace. I wonder if they've replaced Justice Méndez yet. I wonder what they've done with his Hollow.

"I bet you wish you'd stayed behind right about now," Margo tells Amina, whose olive skin has taken on a green pallor as we check our weapons.

Her silence doesn't inspire confidence, but this is our unit, and we have to keep going. We disembark from the carriage and go our separate ways.

Margo grabs my arm when Amina is a few paces ahead of her. "See you on the other side, Ren."

I take her hand and we shake. Dez didn't like to hug or say good-bye, but this feels different. It must weigh on her as it does me.

I scale the side of a wall, my feet searching for the grooves between the bricks. I pull myself up on top of the ledge. There's only one guard on duty here. He has no idea that I'm towering above him until it's too late. I jump, landing on his shoulders and bringing him to the ground with my weight. I immediately dig into his memories, searching for the layout of the prison fortress.

The port of Sól y Perla is bustling in the bright day. Seagulls search the beach for scraps of things to eat. He loves this city. Loves the way that there's always something to look at, unlike his current post in Soledad, where the most exciting thing that greets him is the wailing prisoners. But that's easy enough to ignore when the wind howls louder. Fellow guards posted at the docks wave at him.

It's his only day off this month, and he decides to splurge. He pays ten brass libbies for a batch of fresh

corvina to take home to his wife and son. He swings the
pack of fish over his shoulder and takes a stroll to the docks
to watch the ships set sail.

Superstitious local women in this part of the country
like to come to the dock with baskets full of carnations.
They rip the petals by the fistful and throw them at the
decks of the ships as they pull out into the sea. The riot of
color makes him stop and watch the latest ship. Men and
women with all hands on deck trying to catch the morn-
ing gale that drags the ships out to sea.

I let go of the guard, and he fumbles on the ground, dizzy and disoriented. I replay the memory over and over again. I have ten minutes before the hour rings from the bell tower above. I need to get to the courtyard, but I'm frozen in shock by a detail of the memory that meant nothing to the guard and everything to me.

There, on the deck of that ship catching the morning glare, with carnation petals drifting in the breeze, stood a man I'd know anywhere.

Dez.

Looking just as I left him. Handsome and fierce as ever, with one thing changed. His left ear was missing.

It's impossible.

It must be an old memory, from when he was still alive.

Because I *watched* him die—I saw his head roll and come to a stop right in front of me. I saw the blood drip from Castian's blade. Castian's angry blue eyes as he paraded across the stage. So different from the day he cut into the dance during the Sun Festival. The memory of his murderous hands on me sends angry flashes all over my body.

But still, seeing Dez's face, so recent, in a memory, feels like a dagger to the chest. A fresh wave of grief washes over me. In all this time, I've hardly been able to stop and feel the loss of him. Not truly. Not deeply. The feeling that I will never have him again, never hold him or kiss him or tell him how I feel. My defender, my partner in crime, my best friend.

No, I can't do this. Not yet. Not now.

With the minutes counting down, I shake myself out of my stupor and drag the guard around a corner. I tie him down, then gag him, but continue reliving his footsteps along the port of Sól y Perla, where the rest of the Whispers are now, hopefully escaping to Luzou. I can't stop the questions racing through me. *When was the last time Dez went on a mission that required a ship?* There was an excursion to Dauphinique where he was gone for four months. He'd come back with a scraggly beard, his first real facial hair. He'd tried to kiss me but it looked itchy, so I waited. That was three years ago.

I see the face of the man in the memory over and over. Honey-brown eyes and a full dark beard. It could be anyone. But when he tightened the ropes on the starboard side, I could see him so clearly, see the scars on his bare arms. I know those scars, I've traced my fingers all over them. But Dez looked different in the memory. His ear was missing. How could that be unless it happened recently?

I slap myself. Sayida's magics must be having a lingering effect on me. Altering the things I see. Making me dredge up feelings that I need to control.

I won't fail you.

Make sure that you don't.

The clock marks five minutes to the hour, and I race across the side of the building, guided by moonlight and faint gas lamps. A wail comes from the courtyard of the prison. My heart thunders as I run, and I worry that something has happened to Margo or the others.

Once I make it to the courtyard, I quickly discover it's not a wail or a scream, it's the whistle of the wind. All at once I know why they named this place Soledad. It has a way of making you feel like you're all alone with nothing but an expanse of hills on one side and the cold, dark sea on the other.

I give a quick whistle. Dez used to signal by whistling a sparrow call, and it stuck with us. It made Esteban furious because he couldn't roll his tongue or get his lips to make the softer sound.

Stop it, I tell myself. *Focus. Focus on here and now.*

As I stand alone, I wonder if the scream I heard wasn't the wind at all. I wonder if it was Margo or maybe Amina, who is untested and new to missions like this. At the very least, Tomás is in the carriage, ready to take us away when we've secured the Robári.

When the clock marks the hour, I know something is wrong. They should be here. There's a shrill whistle, sharp like the kind made between fingers, not our familiar sparrow tune. I turn to find the source of the noise, and suddenly I'm not alone.

I'm surrounded by a dozen guards.

Alarm bells go off along with the chime that marks the hour.

And then I see them. Margo and Amina, skulking in the shadows. A door with a metal sun opens, and as they head inside, Margo turns around, staring straight into my eyes. Unflinching.

I won't fail you.

Make sure that you don't.

Filipa never trusted me.

Margo never trusted me.

I didn't realize how much I'd come to feel for Margo until this moment, as the pain of her deception rips me in two.

I don't struggle as the guards drag me into the prison. I understand now how the Whispers truly think of me, and what my role in this mission was all along—the bait in the trap.

31

THE DIMLY LIT ROOM WHERE THEY'VE LOCKED ME UP FACES THE SEA. WHAT once might have been a classroom in the days when this place was a Memoria university is now a bare room with a table of weapons and half a dozen lamps, only one of them on. There's a wardrobe in the corner likely used for storage. Rain pelts the double-paned glass window that rattles in the wind. There is no one else here except for a guard and Judge Alessandro.

"Be sure not to injure her," he says, sniffing. His large eyes are rimmed with dark circles. He takes note of my bracelets. I thank the Lady I hid the pouch with the rest of the metal. "Remove the platinum. All of it. We will need her in prime condition for the presentation tonight. Fetch Prince Castian, won't you?"

I jerk my head up, and cold dread pools in the pit of my stomach. "Castian is here?"

Alessandro crumbles a piece of parchment and throws it at me. "It's *Lord Commander* to you."

"Right away, my justice," the guard says, standing at attention near the door with his sword already drawn.

My justice? Only Méndez carried the title. They must've found his Hollow and already elevated Alessandro. His feet whisper across the stone floor as he paces around me.

"I knew you were not to be trusted. I told Méndez over and over that he should have brought you here straightaway." He shares Justice Méndez's overconfidence. I hope that it will be his destruction, too. "Pity about him. Still, even I could not predict you were foolish enough to enter here by yourself."

They haven't found Margo or Amina. Bitter anger rips through me. For a brief moment, I consider throwing them to the justice, but that feeling ebbs and is replaced with a cruel hurt I haven't felt in a long time. They betrayed me. They left me. And yet, I cannot bring myself to do the same to them.

"You underestimate me," I say. My casual tone seems to bother him. Dez used to do this, and it always worked for him, getting his enemies too enraged to act thoughtfully. "Don't worry, you're not the first."

"Says the bestae who keeps escaping the palace only to be brought right back. This time you will not be given mercy."

Mercy. The word echoes in my head like droplets of water in an empty cell. I stomp on the ache that swells in my throat and force myself to be the person he expects.

My mouth tugs into a grin. "I take it you found the gift I left behind? I would have wrapped Méndez in a pretty Dauphinique lace for King Fernando, but I didn't have enough time."

A muscle jumps in his throat. "I suppose I should thank you, because now here I am, justice to the king."

"Congratulations." I answer his arrogance with a cruel laugh. He leaves the window and marches to face me. There's hesitation in the way he keeps his distance, the way a hard breath shudders through him.

"What's so funny?" he asks.

"Only the things I saw in Méndez's memory about your wife."

His eyelids peel back as he raises his fist. "Silence!"

"Castian was in those memories, but I'm sure you knew that. I wonder how long you'll last as the justice when the prince gets *rid* of you and takes back his queen."

Alessandro's lip curls into a snarl, and he punches me once. Blood spills across my tongue where the inside of my lip has split on my tooth. I spit at the floor but miss his feet.

"You won't be laughing when you're on that table," he says. "You'll be a complete and utter monster. We've already turned one Robári into our own to command. Prince Castian will *reward* me when I present you to him. He is eager to get his hands on the next one. What better gift to give our crown prince than the wretch that tried to kill him?"

I laugh. He doesn't know. No one knows that Castian tried to stop the justice's experiments. No one but Méndez and Cebrián, and now me. My mouth tastes sour at the thought that Castian— the person I hate most—may be my only way out.

"I'm going to drain every last memory out of your skull," I tell him calmly. "When people look at you, they're going to see the *nothing* you already are."

"That'll be difficult to do in chains," he says.

I try to summon my power, but it doesn't surge the same way it did in the dungeons. It is like trying to lift a brick wall with my mind. My whorls light up but sputter, flames in the wind.

Alessandro laughs at my efforts, when there's a sharp, frantic series of knocks on the door. The guard answers it, and there's a commotion out in the hallway. I wonder if Margo and Amina have found the Robári while I've been locked up here. What a fool I was to think that the elder would trust me. I wonder, if I were to become one of those creatures—would they come back for me? To finish me off? Would they even be able to tell the difference between the monster they thought I was and the one Judge Alessandro wants to turn me into?

You decide who you're going to be. Sayida was wrong. Everyone keeps trying to decide for me. At some point, I'm not going to be able to stop them.

I try to listen to what's happening outside the door.

"He's been taken, my justice," a woman's voice says, panicked.

"What do you mean, *taken*? How could the prince have been taken?" Alessandro shouts.

"It appears the prisoner was not acting alone," another guard says.

There's the hard slap of a palm on skin. "Fools. You will be the ones to explain this to the king. I will accept no blame for the poor administration of security by my predecessor!"

There's a rattle as the door to the room slams shut and a cylinder lock twists into place. I pound my fists against the solid wood, when something cold and clammy touches my shoulder.

I whirl around with my fist raised, then stand in shock at the man before me. Where was he hiding?

He holds his hands up to shield his eyes, his skin the color of ash, cracked in places where the flesh is dry. Red welts mark the insides of his elbows. His hair is dark, the only thing that betrays the unnatural aging of his skin. It's as if whatever has accentuated his powers is destroying him from the inside out.

The Robári who steals magics instead of memories.

The weapon.

This is the future that awaits me.

"You." The word slips out, defeated.

"Me," he responds loudly. When he speaks, it is like holding a conch up to your ear.

"You've been here this whole time?" My eyes roam the room. There is a closet with the door swinging from the hinges.

"That new justice does not know my hiding places."

He sits down on the floor, a few feet from the window, and stares at the sea. His stillness makes my skin crawl.

"But I have learned all the hidden doors of this place," he continues. "You will, too."

I go to the window and let myself sink to the floor. No wonder prisoners here go mad. There is no way out. There are the guards on one side and the sea on the other. When I close my eyes, I see Margo staring at me as she shook my hand, the good-bye we usually never said. She knew she was going to betray me.

You're weak, she told me. *That's why I hated you.*

Stupid, stupid, Ren.

Cebrián sits beside me. Even his nearness is icy, like coldness clings to him. Will it cling to me in this same way? I trace the inside of my arms where my veins show beneath my skin. Not as dark as his, not as terrifying as Lucia's.

I hear horses neighing and hooves fading into the distance. They must've dispatched a group of guards to go after the Whispers. The rendezvous point at Nuria's safe house, where all that's left of the rebels will be until tomorrow when the ship leaves. The bell chimes once again, marking an hour since I was caught.

Margo's betrayal hurts, but Sayida is still in that safe house. I think of the fledglings who have no place in the politics and decisions of the council. They don't deserve to be taken. They don't deserve the fate that was dealt me.

I have to get out of here.

"Cebrián, isn't it?" I ask, pushing myself up.

Something about my movement triggers something in the Robári because he looks away from the seascape and at me and says, "Yes, I do believe that is my name."

I rest my hand against the window. There's a storm somewhere out there, the wind whistling through a crack. I shiver.

"Is there a way out?" I ask. "A hidden door?"

"No one gets out, girl." He lowers his voice. "Least of all you and me. They left you here, didn't they? I was left once."

They left you here, Ren. I wanted Filipa's forgiveness the way I wanted Illan's. The way I wanted Margo's. I left people behind, too. But I've never stopped to think about what kind of forgiveness I want for myself.

Why risk my life to try to save them now? They aren't my friends. My family is dead. But that's not right, is it? Dez was my family. Illan. Leo. I promised I'd see him again. Sayida. Oh, Sayida. Did she know what was going to happen? Was she part of fooling me?

"Not everyone," I say out loud. She wouldn't. I refuse to believe that, no matter how naive it makes me.

Sayida is one person. The decision to leave me behind was made by the elder—and Margo. I thought that if I could only get revenge for Dez and destroy the weapon, then—what? What did I think? Deep down, I know that there is nothing I can do now to change the way the Whispers see me.

I've been fighting this weight that clings to my heart my whole life. What if it isn't in my heart at all? What if it's in my mind? Every single memory I've collected is a stone stacking up on top of me, pressing me to death. There have always been too many voices, crammed, and shouting, and trying to claw their way out of my mind. What if I stopped fighting them? What if all of those memories were simply—gone?

I look into the silver eyes in front of me, like liquid alman stone. But when I stare at Cebrián, I see my future. I'm never getting out of here. No one has ever escaped Soledad. But I have another way out.

"Take my magics," I say.

His head snaps up. He watches me like I've crawled from under a rock. A creature he can crush. "Why?"

Because I don't want to become like you. Because if you make me a Hollow, I will never be a weapon again. Because there is nowhere for me to go from here.

I think of Leo's smile and Sayida singing us to sleep. Dez searching for my lips in the dark. Davida signing, *Good heart. Protect us all.* I can't even protect myself, let alone the world. I shut my eyes, and hot tears spill down my cheeks.

"Because I don't want to feel this way anymore."

He twitches, a muscle spasm that shakes him like a hanging skeleton. It passes after a moment, and he's present once again and nods, staring hungrily at me.

I hold out my hand and repress the shiver that courses through me when his clammy skin closes around mine. Pain stabs at my temples and my heart beats wildly. I have seen death in different forms, and I never thought that this is how my story would end. I remember holding Lozar in my arms and feeling his pulse race. Méndez whispering my name in the end. I can't cry out for anyone because the ones I love are gone from me.

So I say nothing and take a deep, steadying breath. The cold Cebrián radiates seems to go right down to his bones. The sting of his power surges up my arm, like sparks of lightning traveling slowly across my skin. I brace for a pain that never comes. Instead, our powers rebound. Cebrián's last memory slams into my consciousness, brighter than any of my own, like looking inside the prisms of an alman stone.

The prince returns in the middle of the night. He's in a foul mood. Cebrián wonders if he is still upset over getting stabbed. But the prince sits in the room and reads the same papers as if he can find new answers for a question he never asked out loud. As Cebrián begins to drift off to sleep, the glint of metal catches his eyes. There is no sound, but the dice roll onto the table. They vanish. When the prince opens his hand, the dice fall out again, perfect sixes. When Cebrián blinks awake, the prince is no longer there.

Cebrián screams. He pushes me back and expels me from his mind painfully. "What did you do to me?"

I gasp, still in the grip of the memory. No. I won't believe it. I can't.

"Get out of my head!" I shout at Cebrián.

The Gray rises all around me, and I sink deeper into the past, trying to recall the boy's face, but there is only shadow. I close my eyes, concentrate, push past the suffocation and delve deeper, further than I've ever gone—into my own past.

The Whispers are setting the capital on fire.

The door opens, and footsteps make their way across the room. There is the hiss of a match igniting, the burn of sulfur, and then his face appears behind smoke.

A young boy.

The one who did the little magic tricks for me. Our secret.

"What are you doing here?" he asked. There's a bruise on his cheek, a deep cut above his brow.

"What happened to you?" I touch his cut with my finger.

"Nothing. It doesn't matter," he says, trying to keep his voice strong. "I'll get you out."

He takes my hand in his and starts to tug.

I pull back. "Where are we going? What's happening?"

He takes a deep breath, that familiar divot between his brows. "The Moria are revolting. It's not safe for you here. Please, Nati. Please, you have to go."

"I don't want to go. There's fire outside. I want to stay here with you."

"Don't cry, Nati. You'll be fine." He takes out a small key from his pocket.

"No!" I withdraw my hand. "Justice Méndez says I'm not supposed to—"

"You can't go out there with Robári gloves," he says.

"I want to stay," I whimper as he unlocks my gloves. "Don't make me leave. I'll help—"

He grips my shoulders. His face becomes blurry until I blink. "You don't belong here. You never did. You don't know what my father is like."

I let him guide me through the dark room with nothing but a candle in his fist and a small blade at his side. He draws back a tapestry, my favorite one of the Pirate Brothers Palacio on their ship. There, a brick is slightly darker than the others, and with the brush of his finger, the bookshelf gives way to a secret hiding place.

A secret room.

I gasp and take a step back.

"Come, Nati. We don't have much time. Don't you trust me?" His face is golden with firelight.

I grip his hand because when I am with him, I feel safe.

"I trust you, Cas."

I brace myself on the windowsill and hold on for balance, because it is as if the floor has dropped from beneath me.

I trust you, Cas.

The phrase repeats, over and over in my head. His name—Castian—on my tongue. Castian as a child. Castian, my friend.

Castian, who saved me that day.

No.

This is wrong. Perverse. This is not my memory. It can't be. I could never have pushed something like that so far down. It isn't possible. He's the Lion's Fury. Matahermano. He's a hundred curses I have yet to speak. The vile, hated killer of Dez.

This can't be true. Something is wrong with my memories.

"You did something," I say, turning to Cebrián's ghoulish face. "*Fix* it."

The little boy from my memory—it was always supposed to be Dez. It was Dez who found me during the raid. Dez who helped me up on the horse and stole me away from the palace. It was Dez. Only Dez.

I pull at my hair. I never let myself think about that night, because I always knew that thoughts of it would tear through me, rip me apart. The night where thousands burned. The night of my own doing. The night Méndez used the secrets I'd scouted for him, from prisoners' memories, to expose the Whispers' camp. The

Whispers' attack against the palace. Countless innocent lives lost. All of it because of me.

But Dez was there outside the palace with Illan, where Castian couldn't follow.

I press my forehead on the floor. My memory must be warped. It fused them together. Where one memory ended, the next one began.

It *must* be.

I think of the way Castian looked at me when we were dancing. I shudder hard, sinking against the wall, barely able to stand. And still the thoughts pummel me. The secret study, why it called to me, tugged at my heart and memories. Castian, calling me by my name when we fought. *Nati.* The name my father used to call me. The name I'd only tell someone I trusted completely, the name I didn't even tell Dez.

Dez, the boy who saved me.

Or was it Castian?

What if both things are true?

The truth has been inside me all this time, buried in the ash of the past, the ash of that most horrible of all nights. Cebrián's memory of Castian. The greatest of all illusions.

Castian is a Moria.

An Illusionári.

"I can *feel* your magics again," the Robári says, his hand reaching for mine. Hunger is heavy in his voice. "I bet it tastes *divine.*"

"No! Don't! I've changed my mind." I scramble back so hard I hit the window. It rattles.

Cebrián charges at me, but I leap to the side. He rams into the windowpanes and cracks the wooden slats in half. He bleeds from a cut on his shoulder, seeping through his tunic. I reach to help him, but he slaps my hand away.

"You did this to me!"

Why does everyone blame me for things I can't control?

Cebrián rips the windowpane from the hinges. Five long metal bars stand between him and the outside world. The sea wind blows in, and he leans toward the breeze, like he's memorizing the feel of rain and wind on his skin. He looks at his hand, suddenly becoming aware of his strength. He grips the iron, his hands white where they press hard. Then he rips the bars apart.

Rain beats onto the floor, and for a moment, Cebrián holds up his hands to cover his face from a flash of lightning. But that doesn't last for long. This time, when Cebrián looks at me again, his eyes are as silver as the bolt. A sinister smile breaks over his features, and in the next moment, he throws himself out of the open window.

"No!" I shout, fearing that he's jumped to his death. I stick my head out the window to see he's landed in a perfect crouch on the narrow cliff's edge. An impossible feat. Whatever they've done to him, he's fast and inhumanly strong, and he runs into the dark, sniffing the air as if he can *smell* magics calling out to him. What if he's going to chase after the Whispers?

I curse as I realize that my only escape is out this window. I know that if I jump, I'm not going to land on the narrow patch of ground that separates the prison from the sea. When I look to either side, I do notice the winged beasts that decorate the sides of the building, like stepping-stones.

Angels, I tell myself, grabbing for the correct word. "They're angels."

I take a couple of deep breaths to give myself courage. One slip, one hard gust of wind, and I'll be carried over the cliff and out to sea.

I grab hold of the first stone creature, swinging my feet out of the window. I grab, then step, grab, then step. There's a moment when the old building betrays me. The stone breaks off under my foot, and I swing outward, a sensation that is as close as I'll ever get to flying. But the next step is solid earth. I crouch down and press my forehead to the sodden ground, breathing in the stability of dirt like air to a strangled man.

I run around the building to the carriages and horses. In this storm, the pampered justice will be staying inside. My fingers are stiff with cold, but I get the ropes undone, and the carriage crashes to the ground. A roll of thunder is my cover as I saddle the stallion and take off into the night, my thoughts reeling.

Prince Castian was the boy who helped me escape the palace.

Prince Castian is a Moria.

Prince Castian—who was captured by the Whispers.

He's one of us.

I kick my stallion. I have to get there before the council executes him, before Margo tortures him beyond recognition. I have more questions than answers, and only he can give them to me.

I pray I get there in time to save him, my greatest enemy.

My oldest friend.

32

I CLAMP DOWN ON CHATTERING TEETH AS I RACE ACROSS THE MUDDY ROAD that leads back to Sól y Perla.

"Please be alive," I whisper to the storm that follows me.

When the ground becomes a wooden boardwalk and the rain tapers to a fine mist, I know that I'm close. This weather does nothing to keep the people of this citadela from being out on the streets. *A little water doesn't bother seafaring folk* is what Dez would have said. My heart stutters in confusion. How could the boy who led me out of the palace be the man who killed Dez? But then—there's the memory I stole from the guard. Dez was standing on a ship. Memories can't be altered. But never in his life had Dez been missing part of his ear. I need answers.

I am afraid that if I stop moving, I will shatter into so many pieces that none of this will matter. Not the Whispers. Not the Robári. Not this never-ending war. Nothing.

I yank the reins and slow to a trot around the back of Duque Aria's house. I swing off the horse and tie it at a post next to an angled wooden structure meant for storing grain. Under the gray cover of dawn, I ascend the back stairs.

My legs tremble with each step. *I remember you.* I want to scratch the sound of his voice from the inside of my ears. I want to shake him until answers fall out of him like ripe fruit from the vine. But first, I have to get inside.

I peer into one of the windows, but the curtain is drawn. My heart thuds rapidly as I step inside and keep to the walls. The commotion coming from the study masks the tread of my boots as I reach the stairs. Margo's voice escalates as Amina tries to explain something to her. I turn to keep following the muddy footprints, but hearing my name makes me stop. The floorboards wheeze under my weight.

"I never agreed to leave her behind," Sayida says. Her voice is calm, but there's an edge to it.

"Renata knew the dangers," Filipa says.

"We can't risk more lives for her," Margo adds.

They conspired together, and it is a small relief Sayida was not part of that decision.

Esteban's voice surprises me the most. "She risked everything to return to us."

There's a strong back-and-forth, Margo the loudest. It sounds like a nest of wasps in my ears.

"Maybe," Margo says, "but we can't know where her loyalty truly lies. Now that we know the Robári are used to make the weapons, everything has changed. These magics are foreign to us.

She'll be sympathetic to that *thing*. That current weapon. Ren was already lost to us."

I think of Margo in the cell with me. *Truce*. I guess that peace is over now.

"Or you just handed the justice a new Robári to torture," Sayida snaps.

"I agree with Margo," Filipa says, and the room quiets at the authority in her voice. "We have the prince. This can be our chance to renegotiate our treaty."

There's dead silence from the study until someone clears their throat.

"What of the Ripper?" Amina asks.

"Is that what you're calling him?" Esteban mutters.

"Cebrían—the Robári—will have to die," Filipa says.

"No!" Sayida shouts along with two others. I recognize Esteban but not the other. "We would be turning into the justices!"

"I'm sorry, Sayida," Margo says, softly.

I've heard enough.

I make for the stairs, hoping I'm not too late. I can't be. They would know the value of Prince Castian, of keeping him alive. And anyway, the prince I've met would have fought back.

Pathetic, a voice tells me, and the voice sounds surprisingly like Dez. *The prince you've met? You're defending him already.*

I push open the first door, but the room is empty, the furniture covered in white linen. I move on to the second room and find a group of the fledgling Moria sleeping. I leave the door as is, so it doesn't creak and wake them. There's only one door left, and I know I have to be prepared for what I see.

Come, Nati. We don't have much time. Don't you trust me? he'd said.

We were just kids. Both so scared. And yet he saved my life that day—he set me free.

A well of strange emotion hits me. Loss for the boy I knew. Anger for the man he became.

As the door swings open, and I step inside, I am faced with both of those feelings.

Castian is bound and gagged in an armchair, his hair matted to his temples with sweat and blood. Still wearing the clothes from the Sun Festival. He makes a guttural sound when he sees me, his eyes darting to his legs. His legs? The boot!

I pull up the hem of his pant leg and feel for the blade sheathed there. He leans back, exposing his throat with relief. He's relieved to see me and that makes all of this so much worse.

"Thank the Lady they were too sleep deprived to search you, eh?" I press the edge of the blade against his throat and stare into Castian's eyes. I see him now. The boy in the study who whispered with me in secret, cupping his hands around the set of dice.

There and then gone.

He says nothing, doesn't even try to scream through his gag. He just watches me. I don't want him to. But I know that if I want answers about Illan and Dez and the weapon, I need to free him.

I cut Castian from the chair with trembling fingers. He rubs his wrists and stares at me with impossibly startled eyes as he rises to his feet. A muscle in his jaw jumps, and I see the moment he searches for the words to thank me but can't.

"You saved me," he says skeptically. "Why?"

"You saved me first, I suppose."

His eyes find me. The furrow returns to his forehead. "You remember?"

"Yes."

"Good. We have to go." Castian grabs his knife back, marches across the room, and opens the window. He's got one foot out, and his hand is extended to me, a lifeline I never thought I'd ever want, or need.

I hesitate, my hatred wrestling with my need to know the truth. He sees it in my face. "Live one more day with me, or stay and die at their hands. Your choice."

"That's not much of a choice," I mutter.

Choose the option that brings you back to me. Could it?

Then I follow him out.

This prince whose friendship made the palace a little less lonely for a Moria girl. The prince whom I've spent half my life hating.

I'm halfway out the window when I hear her whimper my name. I'd recognize her voice anywhere.

"Ren," she says, and I can't help but look back as I continue my escape. What I see I know I'll never forget: Sayida's face as I choose betrayal.

33

We run in the desolate, rainy streets until we lose the trail. Margo is the best tracker, but we have two advantages: It's raining, and there's a surge of patrol guards searching for the Robári and the kidnapped prince.

For now, I follow Castian at a distance. I want him to answer my questions. I want to know how he did all this. *How did I get here?*

Every time I've tried to prove my loyalty to the Whispers, I've failed. To them, I will always be a treacherous Robári. Fine. Let them think that. In my heart, I know who I am. The only thing I don't know is who this person is walking beside me.

"Stop," I say. I yank on the back of Castian's bloodied tunic, and he turns around with an angry ridge on his forehead. How could I not remember? "I can't keep walking behind you like a lost dog. Where are we going?"

"It's only a little bit farther."

"*What* is only a little bit farther?"

He steps closer, his hands on his hips. There's still blood caked along his hairline that he tried to wash away by cupping salt water from the sea. He looks like the picture of the Bloodied Prince I've heard so many stories about. But is he?

"A hidden place," he says.

I am tired of hidden places and jumping out of windows. I am tired of running. I take a deep breath and keep my anger on the surface. "I want a weapon."

The prince hands over his only dagger without a word. He hops off the boardwalk and onto the sand, where the coast becomes rocky, and leads us to tall, dark caves. The citadela is barely visible on the horizon. For the first time the dread of what I have done ebbs into panic. I am alone with Prince Castian. I have chosen him.

When the tide moves out, it reveals a path of shells, broken coral, and stones packed into the rock, leading to the mouth of a cave.

I shouldn't follow him in there. This might be his insidious plan. Recapture me. Make a new magic-stealing Robári. Another weapon. A Ripper. I quickly remind myself I've already lost everything there is to lose and follow him inside.

"Who are you?" I ask the moment we're inside. "You've had half the day to think about something to say, and I swear if it isn't the truth—"

"You'll slit my throat?" His stare dares me.

"Yes." But even I can hear how my voice wavers.

He sighs, and it is so weary that my own abused body does the same. He reaches up above, along the cave wall, and retrieves a dark piece of stone. He takes his knife back from my belt. Before I can protest, he strikes flint and steel until the sparks catch on a torch hooked into a steel loop embedded in the rock. For once, the sudden spring of fire doesn't make me jump. He hands the knife back, and then walks deeper into the cave without waiting for me.

We keep wading into the tunnel in silence, accompanied only by the trickle of water rising at our heels and the snap of the fire in his hand.

When we arrive at the place Castian promised, I breathe a little easier. The cave widens all around. There's a small iridescent pool of water surrounded by sharp rock formations, like we're inside the mouth of a giant shark.

Castian finally comes to a stop at a smooth groove in the cave where there's a cot, weapons, and crates of food. I don't know what's worse, my hunger or my exhaustion.

"Sit," he says. "I'll take the floor."

I don't argue. I pull off the stolen doublet, and even the smallest movement hurts. I sit on the cot with my back against the wall. Castian slides to the floor beside me. This is worse than the Gray. Worse than remembrance, because it isn't like I'm in someone else's life. I am very much here and very much not.

He tosses an apple and a waterskin to me. I drink from it hungrily, and I'm glad he has one for himself because I don't know how I would tear myself away from this.

"Easy, you'll make yourself sick."

"I've spent my entire life on the run," I say, wiping my mouth with the back of my hand. "I know how to drink water."

He shrugs. "Thank you for coming back for me."

"Castian," I say. "Castian. Are you really Castian?"

He brushes his hair away from his face. It makes him look younger. Just a boy trying very hard to be a cruel man.

"I *am* Castian, son of Fernando the Righteous, Prince of Andalucía, commander of the five fleets, *rightful* heir to the kingdom of Puerto Leones." He turns his face to avoid my eye and drinks. "And I'm an Illusionári."

"You remembered me. From when we were kids," I say.

I think of the boy who begged me to leave the palace. That same memory is stomped on by the prince I met in the woods, on the executioner's block before a sea of his own people. I can still feel how the bile rose to my throat as I ran faster and harder than I ever had before across those rooftops.

Too late, I was too late. I breathe short and fast, ball my hands into fists to stop my wretched body from betraying me by trembling.

"Did you kill Dez?" The words nearly choke me.

The beginning of a sad smile quirks at his lips but dies just as quickly. One of his eyes is swollen more than before and ringed with black. It makes it harder to meet his gaze without wanting to feel pity for him.

"This might pain you to hear, as you've wanted nothing more than to murder me ever since we saw each other again, but I've never killed anyone."

I'm either too tired to make sense of his words or he's taking advantage of my exhausted state to get away with a lie. "What?"

"I should say, I've never executed anyone innocent, and that includes Moria."

I shake my head. "No. I saw you. I saw you with my own—"

He hits his head against the wall behind us. "I'm an Illusionári, Nati."

"Don't call me that," I whisper.

"I create illusions. The way Margo created that smoke."

"Your power can't be that strong," I counter, because I can't believe it. I can't. But I have seen it in my newly surfaced memories. The way Méndez's memory of the prince faded into color because he was talking to an illusion of Castian. The way Cebrián saw him make dice vanish and reappear, just like when we were kids.

And yet, it's strange hearing it come from his lips. It is even stranger having to accept that he is telling the truth.

Now he actually smiles, all straight teeth and cunning blue eyes. "What is my crown made out of?"

"Gold." The metal catalyst that strengthens Illusionári. "That was you at the Sun Festival. When I felt sick. And when I was running to get to Dez. I thought it was Margo both times."

He rakes his hair with his fingers. "It was foolish on my part. I needed to follow you, so I created an illusion of me standing in a corner alone. I've done that more times than I should be proud of."

I lean forward, practically crawling to him for an answer. *"Did you kill Dez?"*

"I admit," Castian says as he stands, though I take note of how he cradles his side as he limps to the blue pool of water, "that one was the most challenging illusion I have ever done. Dez was—is— the leader of the Whispers, and the king and the justice needed to feel like they were winning. I had to use a gold-hilt sword as well. It helps if some of it is true. It makes the illusion stronger. I even had to cut off Dez's ear to fool the thousands who were witnessing."

The guard's memory hits me like a brutal, cold wave. Dez standing on the bow of that ship, missing his left ear. Tears spring to my eyes. A hurt I didn't think I was capable of feeling gnaws at my heart, leaving me breathless.

"Dez is alive?"

"Yes."

This single word echoes in the cave. I hear it over and over, and it still doesn't feel true.

Dez is alive.

My elation at this discovery is like the start of a flame—a light stretching across a match. If Dez were alive, why didn't he try to find me? If he is alive, why didn't I feel him? The more questions I ask myself, the more I stomp on that happiness, extinguishing that spark of fire.

I push to my knees. Every step I take to Castian is like walking across jagged glass. He takes off his tunic, hissing as the cloth sticks to his broken, bloody skin. How can he tell me this and then do something so normal as clean his wounds? How can he watch me stagger to him as if he hadn't shattered my world more than once in a single turn of the sun?

My name vanishes from his lips as I punch him. He doesn't expect it but grabs me around the wrist and pulls me into the pool of salt water with him. I wrench myself free. I make the mistake of panicking, attempting to breathe, and getting a mouthful of salt water instead. My feet find purchase on soft white sand, and then I'm breaking the surface and coughing so hard it burns.

The water reaches my waist when I stand and face him. "You've been pretending while your kingdom suffers? You broke my— You broke me."

"I'm sorry," he says, wincing as he touches the cuts on his ribs and shoulder. "I am. You don't understand."

"*Make* me understand."

Water drips down both our faces. In this light, his eyes take on the blue incandescence of the pool. He lowers himself in front of me, his breath warm and sweet like apples gone bad.

"I will explain—if you'll stop trying to attack me."

Salt burns the inner corners of my eyes. I raise my chin. "I should've let Margo kill you."

He winces, from my words or the pain or both, I'm not sure. "You don't mean that."

I've begun to shiver as the water turns cold around us. He's right. I don't mean that. But I wish I did.

"Get out of those clothes or you'll freeze to death," he says, and wades out of the pool and back to his makeshift room.

I hate that he's right. He grabs a deep blue tunic stitched with bright-green embroidery in the shape of ivy and throws it at me. Then he builds a fire while I strip down and put it on. I wrap my arms around my body because the tunic only falls to my thighs. I sit at the edge of the cot and hold my hands out to the fire.

Castian looks up and this time puts more distance between us. "I will continue to answer your questions, Nati. But do not put your hands on me again."

"I will refrain from hitting you if you stop calling me that." I wait for his begrudging nod and continue. "How does your father not know of your power?"

Castian holds his hand up to the crackling fire. He turns it over and over, then makes a fist. "After my mother accused me of drowning my brother, I was relegated to nursemaids. Davida was the only one who knew and cautioned me never to speak of it. I understood why as I got older. That is why she still tends to me and is under my protection."

The memory plays out in my head, colors washed gray, but I see the moment Illan stole the baby from the bassinet. I want to cut out the sympathy that swells in my chest.

"You didn't try to drown him."

"How do you know that?" There's a melancholy to his words I don't want to feel.

"Illan gave me the memory before he died."

Castian quirks an eyebrow. His nostrils flare, like he's breathing deep to restrain his anger. "Did he? So you know that it was his deception that kept me alive and in my father's favor. Well, Celeste and my own mother deserve some credit. Their lie was the foundation of the Matahermano. The boy murderer. Ruthless like his father. My mother tried to tell me before she died, I believe, but I wouldn't go to her sickbed."

I think of the woman tortured by her decision. The portrait in his room. He still loves her, even after what she made him believe.

I think of the wooden box he held before Dez in Lozar's memory. The one Dez recoiled from with such disgust I thought it *had* to contain the weapon. But the box I found in Castian's secret study. The box contained only a portrait of two young boys.

Two brothers.

C & A.

Castian and Andrés.

Andrés? Don't tell anyone.

"You didn't drown your brother," I say slowly. There is something dangerous in these words, as if speaking them aloud will lead to our end. "Because Illan took him. Raised him as his own."

The words scrape my throat.

Dez, my beloved Dez. Illan's son.

Not his son, though. Only raised by him. Kidnapped just like I was.

"Where's Dez? What have you done with him?"

"He boarded a ship to Luzou not long ago."

I shake my head. "He wouldn't have left. He would have come back to the Whispers."

To me.

But I saw it. In the guard's memory, I saw Dez standing at the bow of the ship watching his kingdom fade away.

"Why would he leave?" My mind is reeling with the thought of it, the *hurt* of it.

Castian stares at the dying fire. It must be night outside, because there's a chill permeating the cave I didn't feel before. He finds his knife, the one I retrieved from the Duque's house. He toys with it, like he might use it to carve out a new truth, a new world for us.

"Andrés ran away because he was scared."

Andrés? Don't tell anyone.

"Take that back." I reach for him, but he presses the tip of the blade to my throat.

"Believe me. If I could have made him stay, I would have."

"You don't know him." I hate the cry in my voice and the nearness of him.

We stay like this for a long time, neither of us wanting to back down, but his hand gets tired and I can't look at him anymore. The pressure of the blade falls, and he returns to stoking the flames instead.

I am alive, but I feel defeated. For the first time, I am away from the Whispers, Méndez, the king, but this uncertainty that Castian brings with him is not what I wanted. What do I want? Freedom from my past. A kingdom without bloodshed. Dez.

When Illan took Dez to raise as his own, did he think that same boy would run when he discovered the truth of his birth?

"I don't know my brother, but you do. I need your help." Castian brushes his golden hair back. I don't know how to feel toward him anymore. Friendship and hatred can live side by side in your heart. "There's a way to win this war, and I believe Dez has gone after it."

"What is it?"

"The Knife of Memory."

I scoff. "Dez is a skeptic."

"My brother is many things, apparently. I would like to find out."

There it is again. *Brother.* I still can't quite believe it.

"Whether he wants it or not, Dez is going to need our help. If he sees me, he'll run. But if you're with me—"

"I won't let you use me to get to him."

Castian gives a single nod. "I'm not asking you to do that. Convincing Dez to return to his rightful place in the palace is something I have to do on my own. But if we could find a way to stop the next war and bring peace to Puerto Leones—if we could heal even a fraction of the rift in this world—I'm asking you, Renata, would you help me?"

I stare at the hand that he extends. This prince I've hated for so long. This prince who tells me that Dez is alive. That they're brothers. He remembered me when I wanted to forget.

I was wrong. He didn't give me the answers I wanted, only more questions. I am a different girl from the one he helped escape the palace. Fate has brought us back together in the worst of ways, but here we are.

"We go after Dez and the Knife," I say, lifting my gaze to his face. "At the end of all this, your father dies."

His sea-blue eyes are bright, determined. "As long as I get to be the one to drive a sword through his heart."

I take Castian's hand in mine.

ACKNOWLEDGMENTS

Thirteen gets a bad rap. But because *Incendiary* is my thirteenth published novel, I'm reclaiming it for the lucky ones.

The first people I thank are my family. My grandmother Alejandrina Guerrero. Your last name means *warrior*, and that's what you had to be. Because of you we immigrated to a new country where we didn't speak the language and learned to be new people. This is a book that made me think and rethink identity, borderlines, and who we choose to be. I am this person, this lucky, hopeful, and hopelessly romantic person, because my family allowed me to dream.

To the rest of my family. My incredibly hardworking mother and stepdad. The best brother, Danny Córdova. Caco & Tío Robert. My beautiful cousins Adriana, Ginelle, Adrian, Alan, Denise, Steven, Gastonsito. My aunts and uncles, Roman, Milton, Jackie. The entirety of my Ecuadorian clan. Gracias por todo.

To my wonderful agent, Victoria Marini, and the team at Irene Goodman Literary. To Hyperion for taking a chance on me. I never even let myself dream that I would be part of the Hyperion publishing family, but here we are. Laura Schreiber, who deserves her own Moria power branch. Visionári, maybe? Jody Corbett and Jacqueline Hornberger. The wonderful production team. Marci Senders for the incredible design, Billelis for the gorgeous artwork. Seale Ballenger, Melissa Lee, and Lyssa Hurvitz for being publicity rock stars.

To Glasstown Entertainment for the opportunity, especially Lauren Oliver, Lexa Hillyer, Emily Berge, and Stephen Barbara.

I'm eternally grateful to Kamilla Benko, Rhoda Belleza, and Kat Cho. This book wouldn't be what it is without your magic.

My incredible friends. Adam Silvera for believing that I was the right person for this project. Natalie C. Parker, Tessa Gratton, Justina Ireland, the Goodies, Victoria Schwab, Mark Oshiro for watching me in various stages of my deadline process and not judging me. Well, maybe a little.

Dhonielle Clayton for being a cheerleader, my work wife, and for always saying yes when I go, "Hey, we should have a writing retreat in this random country we've never been to." #DeadlineCityForever.

To the YA book community, online and off, for being voracious readers and uplifting literature.

To Latinxs. That's it. That's the tweet.